Central Library
Cecil Road
Enfield
366 2244

9/12			
16. JUN 90			
-7. OCT. 1985	28. DEC 90		
16. DEC 1985	09. MAR 91		
	02. APR 91		
	20 JUN 91		
26. MAR. 1987	18. JUL 91		
-3. AUG 1987	12. AUG 91		
-9. APR 1988	10. SEP 91		
18. JUL 89			
29. DEC 89			

LONDON BOROUGH OF ENFIELD
LIBRARY SERVICES

This book to be RETURNED on or before the latest date stamped unless a renewal has been obtained by personal call or post, quoting the above number and the date due for return.

The Lively-Minded Women

Books by Betty Jerman

Do Something: Guide to Self Help
Organizations
Home Dressmaking
Know More About Other People

BETTY JERMAN

The Lively-Minded Women

The First Twenty Years of the National Housewives Register

HEINEMANN : LONDON

William Heinemann Ltd
10 Upper Grosvenor Street,
London W1X 9PA
LONDON MELBOURNE TORONTO
JOHANNESBURG AUCKLAND

First published 1981
© National Housewives Register 1981

SBN: 434 37400 8

Filmset by Willmer Brothers Limited
Birkenhead, Merseyside
Printed by
Camelot Press Limited, Southampton

Contents

Prologue — 1

I	How	5
II	Why	15
III	The Founder – Maureen Nicol – Looks Back	24
IV	So What Happens?	33
V	The Register Builders: Brenda Prys Jones 1962–64	37
VI	The Roots	43
VII	The Register Builders: Lesley Taylor 1964–67	56
VIII	The Link	65
IX	The Register Builders: Jane Watt 1967–70	79
X	The Other Link	88
XI	The Register Builders: Anita Brocklesby and Lesley Moreland, 1970–73	94
XII	Profiles	102
XIII	The Trio that Became a Pair	113
XIV	How it got a Constitution	122
XV	The First National Group: 1976–80	129
XVI	Enterprise – Internal	141
XVII	Enterprise – External	150
XVIII	The Men	162
XIX	The Second National Group from mid 1980	172
XX	The Invisible Export	181
XXI	Where Now?	193

Appendices — 206
Bibliography — 229
Index — 231

Illustrations

Between pages 114 and 115

Maureen Nicol, founder and first National Organiser of NHR
Trustees cutting twenty-first birthday cake at 1981 National Conference

Brenda Prys Jones, National Organiser 1962–64
Lesley Taylor (now Shooter), National Organiser 1964–67
Jane Watt, National Organiser 1967–69
Anita Brocklesby and Lesley Moreland, joint National Organisers 1970–73

Josephine Jaffray, Angela Lepper, Pat Williams, National Organisers 1973–76
Marie Price, National Organiser 1976–78, with daughter
Gill Vine, National Organiser 1978–80
Alison Shingler, National Organiser since 1980

Conference at Reading University 1979; chatting over coffee
A typical group meeting
Herne Bay Group participating in local carnival
Member's son, Nick Roberts

Some members of the first National Group, elected in 1976

Members of the National Group in 1978

National Group 1980

The National Conference at Reading University, April 1979

Attendants at first International Conference, Newlands Park College, July 1980

Some gifts presented to NHR in UK by overseas members

Erratum

On page 3 of the photographs, the names of Pat Williams and Josephine Jaffray have been transposed

Dedicated not only to my own,
but to all our lively-minded daughters

Prologue

ARTICLE PUBLISHED on the *Guardian* newspaper's 'Mainly for Women' page on 19 February, 1960: by Betty Jerman and entitled 'Squeezed in like sardines in Suburbia':

'The decision was for a new house, i.e. post-war not pre-war. The vision was architect designed, detached in a large garden. The reality was semi-detached, designed by a speculative builder and a garden smaller than my mother's lawn. The problem is general when the bread-winner works in Central London and a house is wanted within reasonable travelling distance. It is not necessarily a problem of money.

'We could have had our architect-designed house with a large garden at an uncomfortable distance from station and shops.

'The alternative was a house built on someone else's garden. In long-developed areas with good communications land is scarce and people lucky enough to own a large garden with "frontage" can command some very fancy prices.

'I have seen plots that would do nicely for a three-bedroom house. In no time three houses are built on it and occupied. Our house stands in a short road. The owner of a large garden with a lot of frontage easily sold the plots on which three bungalows were built. Beyond these a section of wooded garden was left. From the road it dipped sharply into a valley and then rose as sharply to the back gardens of other houses. It was such difficult land that many builders turned it down but an enterprising firm got to work with mechanical equipment and managed to squeeze in six semi-detached houses. One of the firm admitted it would have been nicer to build four but they only just cleared a profit as it was.

'So we have the advantages of an already settled area with the shops within easy walking distance, a private nursery class round the corner, schools, churches, pubs, doctors, a hospital, and other necessities.

'Our house has more in it than we could have hoped for if we had built it ourselves. The front rather resembles a mews cottage, being made up entirely of garage and front door downstairs and the two large windows of one bedroom and the landing upstairs. Living rooms and the two other bedrooms face south and the whole house is full of light.

'We have full central heating with a boiler in the cellar which also houses indoor fuel bunkers, served through the garage, and leaves plenty of space for indoor drying. There are cupboards everywhere. There is ample floor and wall tiling where needed. The whole house is designed for minimum housework and minimum maintenance. Where then are the flaws?

'First the garden. It is about as private as a field. If we replace our open fences with solid fencing, it would block out the sun and light on half the garden and our trailing plants seem to be taking a long time to supply us with privacy.

'Then the noise. The houses were really crammed into the plot. Our living room is on the attached side. The next door living-room is on the other side of the wall and they have an immensely powerful television set. One evening I asked my husband to turn down our radio; it was not on!

'I was driven to write a note asking if the television could be toned down. The effect was odd. The entire family affected not to see us and the son, about eight, literally stopped dead in his tracks and retreated at speed if he saw me walking along the road. This behaviour stopped after a couple of weeks and now we just put up with the noise.

'On the detached side there is a space which allows easy manoeuvring of two large wheel-barrows, one on their side of the fence (a high and solid one near the house) and one on ours. Their "dining" side is nearest to us and there they keep their radio. They use it for background and sometimes I wonder if Mrs Dale goes on all day. One warm night about eighteen months ago we actually identified the play on the radio, and we heard clearly the eleven o'clock news. Next morning I had a friendly word with the wife (no more notes) but the effect was even more drastic. They have not "seen" us since and we just put up with their noise too.

'Polite notes and polite words have no effect. Neither does shouting. One hot night last summer, around 10.45, the man who sold his garden for development and who still lived in the large house, could stand no longer the bellow of rock 'n' roll coming from the open windows of one of the bungalows. He did not swear but he shouted things like "You selfish lot" at the top of his voice. People heard him streets away; it was the big topic of conversation next day, but not with the occupants of the bungalow. Finally he telephoned them. He has moved. I do not blame him.

'But while foliage will rise in time on our fences and custom tends to deaden one's consciousness of noise, acceptance of the third flaw seems a dreary prospect. Whatever happens to people when they retire to the outer suburbs to raise families? Were they always like this? By comparison the inner suburbs, now with the exception of small fashionable pockets, largely decaying houses or blocks of flats, seem to bubble with vitality.

'The setting is attractive enough with open fields and forest and a few large old houses with sufficient land to lend for local fetes. There is a farm so that our children can see real cows. There are three local stables and while you can still hear schoolgirls pounding out their piano lessons you are more likely to see them clad in jodhpurs and velvet cap on the way to riding lessons.

'The prospect is pleasing, especially if you have only to see it at weekends and evenings, but I have to stay here all day too, and the whole thing falls down on two counts, food and thought. Asking in a local grocers for Patna rice I was told "We only sell rice"; and I hear women order half a pound of "cheese". Maybe the hailed post-war revival in English cooking has been somewhat exaggerated.

'And does no one read? There is no proper bookshop. I can get a well-reviewed book from the public library almost at once. And it is a waste of time starting to discuss some writer's viewpoint on an interesting topic. Unless he or she has appeared on television no one will have heard of them or their ideas. I generalise, of course. There are the odd exceptions. And they tend to be women who regret they were never fully trained and educated for a profession.

'It is not lack of money that causes the stagnation. Some local households have got to the stage of a second car and a private school for the children is the norm. True the argument does not apply that a child can benefit as much from a fine new State school as from a private school since the primary school looks like one of the first ever built, but I am not convinced that sending children to the private schools is entirely based on getting them a better education. This is "keeping up with the Joneses" country.

'No, this example of suburbia is an incredibly dull place to live in and I blame the women. They stay here all day. They set the tone. Many of them look back with regret to the days when they worked in an office. Their work kept them alert. Home and child-minding can have a blunting effect on a woman's mind. But only she can sharpen it. If only once in this suburb I could go to a house where a dinner would be served comparable to one an unmarried girl friend would "throw together" after a day at the office and hear such conversation across the table, then I would think there was hope.

'The fresh air, the comparatively open country make this a good place to bring up children. But I cannot help wondering what effect the mental atmosphere will have on our children.'

I
How

Sir,
Since having my first baby I have been constantly surprised how women seem to go into voluntary exile in the home once they leave their outside work.

Before moving to this district recently we lived in the suburbs of Wolverhampton, and it took me two years to find a *kindred spirit* who was willing to do exchange baby minding during the day.

Indeed most couples rarely left their homes for a night out together, even with offers of baby-sitting. Now I have to start all over again, and here the women seem if anything even more reluctant to prize themselves away from their children for a few hours.

Perhaps *housebound wives with liberal interests and a desire to remain individuals could form a national register, so that whenever one moves one can contact like-minded friends.* There must be many women like myself whose husbands' work necessitates moving house every few years. Or perhaps someone has a better suggestion?

Yours &c., Maureen Nicol, Eastham, Wirral.

This dramatically simple letter, published in the *Guardian* newspaper's 'Mainly for Women' on 26 February 1960, was the proverbial stone flicked into a pool. The outcome was the National Housewives Register which twenty years later, by 1980, had over 21,000 members in the UK meeting in 1,000 neighbourhood groups. The transplanted seed is flourishing in five continents.

The concept is so simple, literally the words I have italicised, that anyone trying to explain it must take for granted that a few words are not enough. Even women soaked in the movement have to struggle to put into readily assimilated words what it is about in order to attract other women who need just this kind of outlet. Over the years, in all kinds of circumstances, women have told me sincerely that NHR 'saved my sanity'. It must have saved the country millions in tranquillisers to damp down the catastrophic effect of mental frustration, getting at the cause, not just the symptoms.

The, to members, legendary letter* was one of three published as a reaction to an article of mine on the page a week before entitled 'Squeezed in like sardines in Suburbia'.

The first letter, in order of presentation, came from Audrey Menhennet of Orpington, Kent, who, after 'ten months aimlessly pushing a perambulator round the area for lack of friends and nowhere to go' decided she had to do something about it herself 'since no one else would bother' and joined a local church young wives' group which had a book study group.

The third was from a Miss R Irlam of Urmston who wrote sympathetically about neighbours' noise levels which she felt should not be endured: 'One or two prosecutions in cases of this kind might have a salutary effect.'

Maureen Nicol's letter was the filling in that sandwich.

I have been dubbed 'midwife' or 'Godmother' to NHR along with Mary Stott, at that time Woman's Editor of the *Guardian*. She had the special gift of reflecting what life was really like for women rather than what it was generally assumed to be. Her 'page' became a kind of club which gave support for a generation of women – many expressed their gratitude during my research on this history. Mary thinks that it will be quite easy for future social historians to see that the late fifties and early sixties were 'a time of most uncomfortable transition for women' but it was not so obvious then. She is certainly not claiming foresight on the effect of an article and a swift reaction to it. 'No one' she commented 'could have predicted the avalanche of letters that descended on Maureen Nicol'.

I have often been asked if I realised what the article would lead to. Absolutely not.

When I left the *Guardian* in 1956, just before the birth of our first child, we lived in a flat in the West End of London. Married to a journalist Leslie Jerman I continued to write as a freelance in my son's sleeping periods, in fact I wrote my first book in that time between the cradle stage and when a child becomes a mobile, mentally demanding personality. I knew no other mothers. Friends who dropped in were still at work. Gourmet-style shops were in short pram-pushing distance.

Then we moved to the house in Buckhurst Hill, in Essex, a

---

* Students of the 'Grauniad' may like to know that I have corrected 'contantly', 'tow years' and 'woben like myself' in the original.

London commuter's suburb. It was not only unknown territory for me but a totally different way of living. Like anyone else I had been spoon-fed at school and at work with company from whom to choose friends.

My kind of women lived there – and no arrogance is intended – the ingredients are always entirely personal. They were propelling pushchairs round the suburban streets as I came to do too after the birth of our daughter. Incidentally, reading the article for the first time while I wrote this history, she pointed out that it appeared the day before her first birthday.

Those women are now life-long friends. But they took time to find, as Maureen Nicol knew too.

Random memories of that time and place. Few married women went out to work. Even those with teenage or grown up families undertook only voluntary work. In the local shopping parade an enterprising woman offered 'continental style' sausages in the corner of a grocer/pet food shop; later the whole became a flourishing delicatessen store. The campaign by the Confederation for the Advancement of State Education (I was a local founder member) to replace the Victorian school with a modern primary, was in the future. We had neither TV, car, nor washing machine, but, being journalists, the telephone ranked with indoor plumbing.

I remember, perambulating to the shops, regularly seeing a mother flapping a duster from an upper window while exhorting her small son 'to play', as he mooned on the pathway between two sections of grass, wearing gloves to keep his hands clean. It was before the benefits of pre-school children socialising with their contemporaries was appreciated, or indeed the importance of the early years in a child's development. The campaign for nursery education for all had yet to form. The 'nursery class' designation in the article was inaccurate; rather a private kindergarten. Playgroups were unknown.

I first met Maureen Nicol in 1978 at the conference, held in Manchester, which celebrated NHR's eighteenth anniversary. I am sure I regarded her as keenly as she did me. In earlier years travelling for both of us had been limited by the care of young children. In the sixties when so many self-help groups were launched by women at home, long-distance contacts were made, and friendships forged, almost entirely by letter or phone, conditions which reverberate through the early years of this history. Then when Maureen handed over the Register to Brenda Prys Jones she dropped determinedly from the national scene, and when the family returned from six years in Uganda still stayed clear of the limelight, only joining her local group as she had said women should be able to do, through a register, all those years ago.

But she had accepted the invitation to the anniversary conference and the chairing of the opening session. Introduced she was greeted by an ovation. Few members, even the long-standing ones, had ever seen her or had the chance to show their appreciation. Composed through this tribute, as though it was not a great deal to do with her personally, she then competently got on with the job of chairing the meeting.

She had one more 'official' function to perform, lighting the candles on a large 'birthday' cake during the tea break. But there were no means of ignition. I handed her a box of matches.

I can imagine any number of Register members flinching at the symbolism of this incident even if it was a totally unrehearsed evocation of what had happened eighteen years before when she read my article and wrote her letter.

But then if I, with no flicker of an idea of the consequences, had set down the frustrations of an ex-career woman while caring for young children, Maureen Nicol had no intention whatsoever of founding a new organisation. Anyone can write a letter to a newspaper in their heads while making the beds or washing up. Some of us actually get it written, posted, and see our suggestions for righting the world's wrongs in print. Luckily it is rare to have your words esteemed and constantly quoted twenty years later as the high principles, to be safeguarded, if the organisation is to remain true to its ideals. Moral: think twice before you join in correspondence columns!

Notice that Maureen Nicol did not offer to start a 'register'. It was just an idea from a fertile mind. The consequences were apparent within days in the letters of women who read into her words the chance for survival. A lesser woman could have replied solicitiously and left it at that.

Instead she took on her own shoulders the responsibility of putting out a helping hand to the desperate women. In one week she got four hundred letters. She was as housebound as they were with two children under three, the chores of a three-bedroom house (no paid help), with no phone and no car. She never even made personal contact with more than a few of the (finally) fifty regional organisers she appointed. Yet, with what must be recognised as an extraordinary level of ability and dedication, and sheer hard work, she set up and, for two and a half years, ran a national organisation.

Fortunately, since Maureen's account of those years (chapter III) neither claims credit nor dwells on what it cost her, Sherry Clarke emerged – by sheer coincidence she is now a secretary in the *Guardian*'s London Office. She must have been the Register's first member.

Twenty years ago she was living on a new housing estate in Eastham, Cheshire. When my article appeared she had only been there a couple of months and the novelty of her first child, only three weeks old, had not yet worn off. Then Maureen's letter was published and she realised the address was just round the corner. 'Maureen seemed just my sort of person so I wrote to her' she recalls. 'She invited me round for coffee'.

'I found this utterly bewildered lady wondering what on earth she'd started. Since her letter had appeared she'd been inundated with letters from women saying what a good idea a National Register was, and why didn't she start one? She had two small children, one a baby and the other a real handful of a toddler, no phone, no typewriter and not much money.

'The housing estate on which we lived was deadly. The reason we were there was because our husbands worked for the Atomic Energy Authority and they were allocated houses on this council estate. We were very unpopular with the neighbours because they'd been on waiting lists for ages.

'I remember we used to sit in Maureen's kitchen surrounded by letters and maps, two babies and a toddler and try to make some order out of the chaos. It was a small kitchen/cum dining room. Two children in one of those rooms and they were full. We were trying to keep the kids out of the letters. We'd work for hours and get little done. It was absolute chaos all the time. Poor Maureen didn't know what hit her.

'People wanted names and addresses. It was impossible to do that on a national scale. We sorted into areas. We'd try to pick out a letter from someone enthusiastic and seemingly organised and Maureen would write appointing them regional organiser, saying "Here are three hundred letters in your area"! I just happened to be the first to turn up. There were two other women quite soon.

'She also received other letters from women in our area and invited them to her house. This little group then began to meet regularly in each other's houses. I don't think it was what she had in mind. It was more an address so you could knock on someone's door and say let's get together. There were plenty of women's groups about but no way of getting to know one like-minded woman.

However that first group was very useful to me and I made a lot of friends in what could well have been a very lean time for me.'

After about eighteen months Sherry Clarke moved. She never joined another group, 'being lucky enough to never be in a position of needing to', though noting the movement's progress with interest.

Thus detached, and unaware of what are now the unwritten but basic tenets of NHR she is able to throw light on the beginnings of some of them.

For instance that only coffee and biscuits are served at meetings. 'That was started by Maureen otherwise you got cookery competitions and "when we're at her house she serves salmon sandwiches so I must". No one was allowed to bake a cake'.

And the 'no domestic trivia' which in members' eyes makes it so different from other women's organisations? 'Maureen started that. We were going to be on higher things. We were not going to be talking about our children. Some of the women liked that, others didn't. Of course we could not vet the women. Some liked listening to a poetry reading. Others thought it the last word in boredom. There were some happy to chatter on about the price of cabbage or getting nappies white. Don't know why they joined. Oh yes, some took the kids off swimming, and I think we went to another group as visitors'.

The shape of NHR was already there in that very first group, a kind of second layer on 'the letter': meeting in each other's homes, not impersonal halls, no competitive refreshments, the mixture of the intellectual and those otherwise inclined, the group's independent choice of activities (albeit with strong leadership) and already offshoots like expeditions and contacting other groups.

There were already, too, the signs of the two central strands, the riches from friendships with 'like-minded' women and the core theme that members would be stretching their minds.

But if outsiders, such as interested and potentially publicising journalists, have a struggle to interpret 'like-minded' what really stumps them is that this army of women is not unitedly campaigning for the many worthy causes their discussions reveal. That was questioned in the mid-sixties by Moira Keenan of *The Sunday Times*, thus helping to harden what was then a half-formed tenet.

In 1980 a *NOW!* magazine reporter, after posing many questions, triumphantly thought she saw light. 'And then when they've had these searching discussions they march in Trafalgar Square say against the cuts in nursery education'. No they do not. Members can and do campaign, fund raise, for any cause that stirs them, *as individuals*, not as members of the NHR. It is NOT a pressure group.

Did this concept also come from Maureen Nicol I asked Sherry Clarke. She thought that funny: 'We didn't know we were an organisation. We were just women having coffee together. We didn't see how it could ever be organised. It could be a flash in the pan and fizzle out pretty quickly. Would women who wrote in the heat of the moment follow it up? One writes in that frame of mind and then forgets it. I suppose really that's how Maureen wrote her original letter and then felt responsible. She suffered rather than gained from it. She just got the hassle and work she could have done without though even in a flap she never looked as though she was in a flap. She would have been happier if someone else had started it and she was just a member I think.'

She became just that when she handed on the job of National Organiser and moved to Birkenhead. For the first time in the Nicols' frequent house-moving there existed 'a register', just as she had envisaged.

She quickly joined the local group, some of whom she had already met. 'It was a really delightfully welcoming feeling to move into a new house and have ready made friends just around the corner. We painted and potted, talked, walked, ran an Oxfam gift shop and became deeply involved in the growing feminist movement, endlessly discussing Betty Friedan's book *The Feminine Mystique*.' After four years they were off again, to Uganda this time.

Back again, after the six years sojourn, there was no seeking of the limelight, no claiming of rights to comment on or influence what she had launched, no state reappearance of the 'Queen of the Cabbages' (a newspaper's title that made her wince) to see what others had been doing with her brainchild. Instead she joined the local group (Warwickshire this time) discovered through the local library and found most members a good deal younger. 'But they are a lively and friendly group and I have again made some real friends. It has been particularly satisfying to see how they have developed the group to fit the needs of current members with absolutely no attempt to girdle or mould them into any national pattern'.

A succession of remarkable women have built on Maureen Nicol's inspired idea. First Brenda Prys Jones, to whom she handed the Register, then Lesley Taylor, followed by Jane Watt, then the partnership of Anita Brocklesby and Lesley Moreland, who were succeeded by the trio of Angela Lepper, Josephine Jaffray and Pat Williams, which later became a partnership.

It was not until 1976 that any form of voting (for a National

Group) was arranged, and then only among members attending the annual conference. The first full membership ballot, by post, for those who were to manage the organisation nationally, did not take place until 1980.

Each National *Group* voted in chose one among themselves as National Organiser; first Marie Price, then Gill Vine, and Alison Shingler in 1980.

Prior to 1976 the National Organisers themselves decided on and appointed their successors!

It was an extraordinary method – sometimes just a question of who volunteered to take over – there was no rush. In retrospect the possibilities for disaster were vast. It has to be understood that there were virtually no checks and balances. The boast of being an unorganised organisation also meant that there was no structure, no channel by which members could formally express views on the conduct of the National Organiser. The register of members was in successive National Organisers' hands, as was generally the only link, the newsletter. Not that, knowing many members, I have any doubts that they would have contrived to get together some form of deposing party if necessary.

It was never necessary. By sheer good luck no one became heady with power, wilfully and autocratically distorting this nebulous phenomena according to her (or their own) personal beliefs.

Instead, then as now, we had women of prodigious energy, immense ability, who fitted the management of a constantly expanding enterprise into their own domestic commitments, physically as well as mentally since there is no 'office'. The work is done in the officers' own homes. (The Moreland household could not fully open its front door and had to go upstairs sideways; Vines seated guests with their backs to the files in the dining-room.)

There is still no salaried staff, neither has there ever been a comfortable financial base, though Treasurer Liz Salthouse (a dietician by training) laid the foundations in the late seventies, nor adequate financial recompense for the officers. Even business meetings between them still depend on the hospitality of other members, not on hotel bills. Commercial executives would back off with disbelief.

Women claim wryly that today they are wife, mother, nanny, cook, char, chauffeur, gardener. They are also the managers of households. Individual women are better at some aspects than others. But when women have had to take on such diverse roles, and in doing so become highly skilled, no one should be excessively

How 13

surprised that the women named here could also take on the management of a national organisation, work needing practical attributes as well as the ability to aid and comfort others. To quote extracts from Josephine and Pat's farewell (the last 'selected' not voted for National Organisers):

> In the early days the biggest strain was being expected by members to act as professionals, when in fact we had had little more relevant experience than they themselves. Eventually we got used to public speaking, but debating from a platform needs years of practice.... It has been a hard and intensive training ground. Whether for good or ill we have broadened our knowledge of human nature, and particularly of women tied to the home who go through all the moods of child-bearing and child-caring ... We have dabbled in the world of charities and other organisations, learned to walk into Fleet Street offices and the BBC without a qualm and become great friends with the local Post Office.

They added: 'On a more personal level we have gained an insight into ourselves and feel confident now to tackle things we would not once have dreamt of.' That sentiment has been echoed by other National Organisers, Local Organisers and many members.

The 'Register Builders' to adopt (National Group member) Jean Stirk's term for the selected, not elected, officers, all safeguarded the movement's concepts. Not a simple matter of making sure everyone was sticking to democratically approved aims and objects. They were not set down in print. What they were protecting was a cluster of customs, many emanating from Maureen Nicol's first group, spreading via the newsletters, and although freely adopted, without corporately expressed agreement. More a condition of 'common-law' than legality. More a case of style than edict, and even today still the unwritten code.

Sixteen years after Maureen's potent letter the first constitution was formally adopted, largely to protect officers and their families from financial liability. Today, as a registered charity, the Declaration of Trust sets out National Group functions, affirms the independence of local groups, but still leaves the code, that has grown through custom and usage, unwritten. That document was signed, 9 April 1980, by the 'Original Trustees': in alphabetical order, myself, Maureen Nicol and Mary Stott.

It applies to the UK, like my story of the growth of NHR, the women who shaped it, the creation of the wider 'umbrella' of management at national level, the controversies, the satisfactions. But just as no one, least of all the founder, foresaw its national spread, so no one perceived that today women are as likely to be hauling up the family's roots in Harrogate and stamping them down in the Middle East as in Buckinghamshire and looking round for the 'like-minded' in a strange country instead of a strange county. So the international scene has its own section in this book.

Allowing for local conditions like having to travel to meetings in convoy in Rhodesia (now Zimbabwe) or the disruptive effect of wandering camels in Dubai, the naturally developed unwritten customs and code are an integral part of the 'invisible export'. 'Like-minded' women across continents also examine a spectrum of mind-stretching topics alongside those who, to quote probably the first member of the NHR, find poetry reading 'the last word in boredom', and, just as in the UK, Local Organisers forget to tell their National Organiser that they are moving house.

Some countries have autonomous Registers (Canada, South Africa, etc) in others there are unlinked scattered groups of expatriates. There is always someone saying 'great idea' and writing to the UK National Organiser to ask 'So how do we start?' The potential for geographical spread is immense. One day the many parts could form an International Register. Meantime those going through the same early stages can find in this history of the UK Register's first twenty years some clear warning signals of where organisational stresses can develop when women take into their own hands the alleviation of a sketchily recognised, even ignored, period of their social history.

II
Why

'BECAUSE WE were probably a unique generation in that we fell into the transition period between the previous ages of full-time housewives and home makers and the future pattern, whatever that eventually settles down to be, I think that, without NHR, a lot of us would have sunk very rapidly with the undiluted strain of the kitchen sink'. That comment, by Wendy Whitehead a member of long standing, puts into a nutshell the reason why Maureen Nicol's suggestion was so ardently seized upon by the original members and since built on. *'Transition period'*; so true.

Equality for women, both of education and opportunities, has a long way to go. We have the beginnings but in the usual manner of taking revolutionary steps without thinking out the full implications. Legalised abortion *followed* by freely available contraceptive advice services is another example, or the legal right to return to your job after giving birth that is not backed up by practical considerations about who is then left holding the baby.

The 1944 Education Act was the watershed; since then girls have increasingly had the chance to acquire academic qualifications along with boys, even if, since generations of custom take a lot of shifting, plenty of mothers denied the chance to reach *their* educational potential now endure mundane jobs, plus the housekeeping chores, to financially back their daughters through further education and training. The little job to 'fill in' between school and marriage is as dated as the debutante season. In fact, today, the clear-eyed, looking beyond the veil and orange blossom and happy-ever-after in this era of two-income families, (and also with the increase of the single parent family) opt for skills that could be marketable even after the interruption of child bearing.

The modern single working woman, given the same educational opportunities as her male contemporaries, can take on jobs which were previously male preserves. She earns a living, controls her own budget, even finances her own establishment before marriage. Above all she has the stimulation not only of the job but of the companionship of others among whom she chooses friends according to personal predilection.

Marriage itself does not change those conditions; the requirement that a woman automatically resigns when she weds is past history.

Motherhood makes the difference. The new woman, overnight, becomes the traditional woman again. It is as if the children of this era, accustomed to running hot water, a wholly heated house, suddenly have to accept pump drawn water, outside lavatories and boiled front, freezing back, from coal fires the only form of house heating.

The twenty-four-hour, seven-days-a-week, invisible tie to the child you have borne has to be experienced to be comprehended. The shock to the system is considerable. No longer can you walk at will and alone out of the front door. And, however co-operative in child caring or sharing chores a husband may be, he still has the right to depart daily into the outside 'working' world.

A woman who opts to stay at home with her children instead of pursuing her career and organising paid care for them (neither an easy decision nor easily arranged) may not speak to another adult through the whole day other than passing the time of day or asking for a pound of mince. Even the friendly exchanges in the corner shop have been replaced by the click-click of the supermarket check-out. It's a child-orientated world which has an effect neatly illustrated by the cartoon of a mother, out to dinner, leaning over to cut up the meat on her neighbour's plate.

It is an isolated world. In the early fifties Young and Wilmot in *Family and Kinship in East London* described the extended family relationships maintained by mothers to support their married daughters which sounds just like a form of mothers' trades unionism.

That network of social contact, which existed elsewhere of course, was disrupted by moving families to better housing conditions in new estates elsewhere. Additionally a more equitable distribution of earned income opportunities has led to aspirations to *own* homes and in more salubrious neighbourhoods than one's parents, thus physically separating mother (and aunts, grandparents, cousins, etc.) and the married child-tied daughter. Husband's job mobility also demands frequent transplanting of the home, nipping off any tendrils of neighbourhood relationships in the process. It takes time to grow new ones as Maureen Nicol knew.

Incidentally the higher standing of housing through increased prosperity has meant that fewer mothers invite another woman into the home if she is inevitably accompanied by a tribe of naturally exuberant little ones. Those who do watch the clock, ready to clear the consequences before Dad's return from work, such as removing the wave-like effect of running small vehicles across the hard-earned wall to wall carpeting.

I will avoid getting bogged down in the argument about women today having it easier than their mothers because of labour-saving devices. Some form of paid domestic help was not so long ago normal even in families with modest incomes compared with today. Somebody at least came in to do 'the hard'. Appliances of various kinds replace that human labour.

But they replace more than that. You cannot talk to a machine, nor will it provide another focus of interest for the little ones, nor care for them while you go to the hairdresser, dentist, ante-natal clinic, or just go and sit in the park and stare, bathing in the brief respite of no piping voice demanding 'Mummy'.

A woman with an alert, exploring, educated mind would no more want to shut it down, to let it lie fallow and atrophy, through inaction, than she would a limb. How is she going to exercise it in these circumstances?

Into all these ingredients of the 'transition period' mix in the downgrading of motherhood, so women and children are treated as inhabiting a second-class world while everyone else gets on with the real business of 'working'. Simultaneously it is ground into mothers that they are the pre-school educators, the influence for success in the school years, the flaw if children default in the academic prizes. 'A woman's place is in the wrong' was one mother's ironic tail-piece to a dissertation on her family life.

Some things are timeless. A young woman in her twenties can expect relatives to be asking when she is getting married. That event will be swiftly followed by: 'When's the baby coming?' and then 'What about another?' What is new is 'surely no more?' followed speedily with 'When are you going back to work?' with its implication that earning money is the only recognisable status.

No wonder the neurotic housewife has joined the mother-in-law in comedians' joke books. Women themselves are pretty muddled about their roles as mothers and as people, wrenching themselves apart about whether to go back to work when the children are old enough – for who can say when that is?

Maureen Nicol's letter has often been praised as being apt in its timing. But what was the climate like (spring 1960) among the *Guardian* women readers who grabbed at the Register idea? Not what was generally assumed.

In 1959 a letter was published from a woman who said regretfully: 'I love both my sons devotedly but I suffer the most excruciating boredom in their company'. It was heresy in the then perceived mother image, but traceably set off the myth of the 'whining graduate' housewife.

In April 1963 Mary Stott wrote that 'fascinated and incredulous' she had watched for four or five years the 'myth taking root' that her page was inundated 'with letters from discontented young mothers wailing that their education was wasted and that their intellects were withering while they are tied to the kitchen sink'. Stung by seeing in print a reference to 'floods of letters from discontented young mothers, usually of better-than-average education which periodically fill the women's pages of newspapers such as the *Guardian* and *Observer*' (which had had a 'Miserable Married Women' series in 1961) she scrutinised four years of files and was prepared to swear that no 'floods' on those lines had been received.

On the contrary the majority of those who wrote in were shocked by the mother who confessed her 'boredom'. I am grateful to Mary Stott for the loan of that file of letters and at her request have passed them on to the Fawcett Library, City of London Polytechnic, Old Castle Street, London, E.1.

There were expressions of pleasure about the company of children, a source of 'constant interest, surprise and amusement, keeping us on our toes, alert and alive', a tart comment that children copy 'incessant, pointless chatter' from mother (following up another published letter). One writer suggested the bored might see a psychiatrist. There were strong overtones of virtue: women choose between marriage and career and should not complain about the flaws afterwards; a defence of toddlers unable to speak up for themselves in print; reports of outside interests largely to do with other children like running a Cub pack, all intermixed with reflections on the maddening, humorous if you can laugh about it (and they could), exhausting child and domestic commitment.

My favourite letter (not all were published) inserted the sharp commonsense of a Yorkshirewoman into the uproar.

The recent correspondence about the boredom of raising one's very young children is like a breath of fresh air in a very stuffy room. How stupid it is to assume that being bored with babies is synonymous with dislike or neglect! But that is the tacit assumption. The thing is, it is a miracle that women can and do simultaneously fill so many roles. Wife and mother are two quite different ones and lucky is she who fills both to the brim, let alone the walking-on parts of cook, kitchenmaid, nurse, valet de chambre and general factotum.

I like to think she was an early Register member.

The letters give a distinct flavour of the attitudes of the late fifties of mothers with 'better than average education'. The seedling of debate on male/female roles had barely raised a leaf above ground.

Mary Stott's article was smartly followed up by a published letter from Maureen's successor as National Organiser, Brenda Prys Jones, quoting Bacon on the 'fruits of friendship', drawing attention to the Register's services in that direction. She affirmed that a woman who describes her problems is not necessarily 'moaning'. In her own large post: 'Not one – sociologists and critics please note – expresses discontent with her family life'. One sociologist was taking note.

Hannah Gavron's seminal book *The Captive Wife*, with 'Conflicts of Housebound Mothers' as the secondary title, was published by Routledge and Kegan Paul in 1966. I read it at the time, delighted that someone at last had set down unemotionally what life was like for the modern woman at home with small children. I read it again in 1979 (it was on my younger son's A level Sociology book list) in a Penguin paperback with rather more cynicism; so little of what she said had been understood.

For her doctorate she surveyed in 1960 to 1961 the changes in society since the nineteen fifties and Young and Willmott's *Family and Kinship in East London* and Mogey's *Family and Neighbourhood*. She used two samples, working and middle-class London housewives, forty-eight in each, all with young children. Thirteen of the middle-class samples were drawn from the 'Housebound Wives' Register' as it was known in early days: 'ones who had felt "housebound" by their children and thus had made an effort to do something about this with varying success'.

The two samples expressed boredom and loneliness. The servantless middle-class wives with young children were found to be leading a life not dissimilar to that of many working-class wives, the advent of gadgets being a mixed blessing since washing machines meant that sheets, previously sent to the laundry, were washed at home and the washing machine does not iron them. That was of course before the widespread introduction of man-made fibres that reduced the need to iron.

Correspondence after Elaine Grande's radio programme (published in *The Observer* 1961) was quoted. The major complaint from lonely housewives was that their role had no importance either to themselves or to the outside world. One found the suggestion that bored mothers can find the interests and intellectual stimulus they lack while knee deep in young children 'arrant nonsense'. Another that men get the best out of life since no one asks them to turn into househusbands when they marry.

A letter in *The Times* (1958) was also quoted: 'If the new lady peers should arrive a little late for the debates it is to be hoped that the noble lords will not fuss. They were probably kept in, waiting for the window-cleaner to finish, or the man to mend the vacuum cleaner or perhaps there were brussels sprouts to prepare for the evening meal.'

(Around twenty years later the chairman of a County Education Committee flurried in on time to meet a delegation of members of the Confederation for the Advancement of State Education, of which I was one, muttering 'that's one supper ready, my husband's', while the Chief Education Officer strolled in, unflustered, his supper having been prepared and served by someone else.)

In Hannah Gavron's sample 75 per cent of the middle-, 68 per cent of the working-class wives wished that they were working. Rather over a quarter of their husbands were opposed to later return to work. By means of education and training over 90 per cent of the middle-class wives had some clearly defined occupation by the time they became mothers and 77 per cent intended to return to the same kind of work when their children were older. The main reason for stopping work in both samples (only 19 per cent of the working-class had had any further education but 29 per cent had acquired some skill while working) was that it was wrong to leave the children. Nearly half had not been out in the evening since their first child was born. Both samples were aware of the conflict over their roles as *mother* and *worker*. Neither saw any great conflict between their roles as *wife* and as *worker*. The majority were on the 'horns of a dilemma', feeling curiously functionless when not working but at the same time sensing their great responsibilities towards the children. Resentment of motherhood as 'a kind of prison' existed.

Hannah Gavron found the system of education, based on male roles, inconsistent with the roles and functions of motherhood as seen by society. It needed to recognise that girl pupils need three stages: school, and further education like boys, then training for re-entry when children are older. Employers too needed to recognise women's multiplicity of roles by offering part-time work, a close relationship between retraining schemes and work opportunities and re-assessment of female capabilities.

Primarily Hannah Gavron saw the need to reintegrate mothers and young children into main-stream society instead of shutting them away in their own homes. She mentioned better facilities like nursery schools, play centres, playgrounds, and making it possible for mothers to lead full lives and take the children everywhere with them by providing places for pushchairs on public transport, making it easier for children to be taken to self-service stores, department stores, art galleries, museums, adult education centres. Then, she concluded, 'life with young children would no longer be so utterly different from life without them and motherhood would cease to be a kind of captivity'.

There have been some improvements noticeable in self-service stores and libraries, but the need to integrate mothers and their children into mainstream society was echoed nearly two decades later by Penelope Leach in *Who Cares*, a Penguin Special.

The Register is a safety valve for women in this lengthy 'transition period'. But why was yet another organisation required? NHR has been described as 'the intellectual W.I.' (Women's Institutes) and one light-hearted proposal in the long-running discussion on the title was 'The Alternative W.I.' When Gill Vine, National Organiser in the late seventies, was making a broadcast on the Register the producer quipped 'If W.I. is jam and Jerusalem I shall think of you as the wine'.

The informality has been vaunted by those who, like the founder, rear back from the 'Madam chairman, minutes of the last meeting' system and take pride in being 'unclubbable'. There are many who resent the recent innovation of an elected National Group, including at least two previous National Organisers who knew the hard way that sheer size was making the Register unmanageable.*

The reasons why are also deducible from a (brief) selection of tributes from members, not only in the U.K.

---

* Some members also join traditional women's groups.

'NHR exists for the intelligent woman, the lively-minded woman, the woman who enjoys conversation, discussion and arguments and who wants to meet others like herself. NHR is the only organisation that caters for her.'

'Before joining NHR I had two titles:— Mike's wife and Donald/Joanna's mother. Now I have another title: Anne – ME!'

'Some of us were in a pretty desperate state before we joined and are very relieved to find that we are not alone in feeling that we need more than home and children.'

'Another move . . . NHR to the rescue again – a lovely, friendly, sympathetic circle of friends.'

'The housebound wife can acquire so many neuroses – lose confidence in herself, become insecure in relationships with other people, lose interest in the wider world, become dependent upon her husband and children as props to disguise the lack of her own personality. You name it – I had it! So a very big thankyou to NHR.'

'NHR fills a need for the peripatetic family whose female member does not wish to join the local church, which used to be the centre of one's life.'

'Surely it is a lifeline for the *mentally* housebound.'

'After a spell in hospital several things helped but chief among them was the fantastic support from the NHR friends . . . How can I ever thank them?'

'When I first joined the group I was a very shy person and would not even have voiced any opinions to a few people, let alone a *roomful* of people as I often do now.'

'One of our members has organised a sick-call service in which anyone can send for help if suddenly taken to hospital or taken ill and sent to bed. We have two lists – one for people who will take children into their own houses – and others who will go to the house to look after the children there; and a special fund to pay taxi fares.'

'It never fails to amaze me how many "butterflies" emerge from their chrysalises' – and then one realises NHR has triumphed again.'

'Several of our group are helping sufferers from agoraphobia to overcome their fears.'

'Our members felt the need for friends of similar interests in a secular organisation which meets in the evenings, as well as the practical help of a baby-sitting rota.'

'I feel personally that it will ensure that my brain doesn't "seize-up" during the years I am away from my profession as a teacher. So much one does in the home seems to be of a trivial nature that the effort one makes towards NHR, i.e. research, preparation of a "speech" and reading, is so refreshing.'

Finally two comments from outsiders.

Daughter, studying A-level Spanish, telling her mother about one of the set books: 'It's about this lively-minded lady who's so bored she spends the whole book plotting how to poison her husband. Mind you it's set in the early part of this century and there was no NHR then!'

And a Health Visitor to a young mother: 'You either want to see a psychiatrist or join NHR'.

III
The founder – Maureen Nicol – looks back

AT SIXTEEN I left technical college with secretarial qualifications, a great love of the theatre and a desire to work in London. I managed to combine all these by getting a job at Nathan's the theatrical costumiers, then in a beautiful old house in Panton Street off the Haymarket. After several exciting years literally rubbing shoulders with stars of stage and screen, as the corridors were very narrow, I left London where I was born, though I had lived most of my life till then in Dartford, Kent, to marry Brian Nicol, an Oxford undergraduate. For nearly four years I worked for Neilsen, an American based firm of market research consultants. The job was interesting and there were many earnest debates on the ethics of advertising. Life in Oxford was enormously enjoyable and I loved it; the place itself, the atmosphere, our friends and the endless discussions. Even being hard-up was a challenge. After graduation we moved back to London for a short while and then on to a village outside Wolverhampton where we bought our first house and soon after had our first baby.

It was an extraordinary experience – from a very outward-looking life full of other people, talk, in-jokes, dashing out for a meal and staying up all hours – the world narrowed down to a small house and a small person who needed my attention all the time and whose idea of communication was limited and loud.

Knowing no one at all I felt cut off and deprived of human contact. Slowly and painfully I sounded out the neighbours and, joy, at last found another woman who felt as I did. We got together for the odd baby-hating sessions, we giggled together and sat for each other. She was interested in the outside world too, in books, theatre, politics. Then came the second baby and a few weeks later another move.

Brian had changed jobs and the new one – Personnel Officer with the U.K. Atomic Energy Authority – entitled us to a council house right on the outer edge of a huge housing estate. The only facility provided for the hundreds of people living on the estate was one public house. No bus service, no shops (though these came later) and no play area for the numerous children. Worse from my point of view was the seemingly friendless nature of the place. All the other families in our road were local people with relatives and long-standing friends living nearby. I needed them but they did not need me.

For the first few months the only person I managed to sustain a conversation with was Brian. There were no women's organisations that I could reach and I always balked at formal type meetings anyway. The 'Madam Chairman, minutes of the last meeting' approach sends me rushing for the door.

I felt myself seizing up mentally and it became difficult even to read a book because there was no one to discuss it with. I did go on reading the *Guardian* though and was very interested in an article by Betty Jerman early in 1960. She expressed the same feelings as mine: 'Suburbia is an incredibly dull place to live in and I blame the women'. Yes, so did I, but what could I do about it? Then I had this foolish-sounding idea. Why not a register of liberal-minded house-bound wives? (That sounded pompous but how else to express that I wanted to get to know other women with leftish leanings, interested in literature, theatre – the world really?) Then, when moving to a new area, all you had to do was to contact the keeper of the register and get a list of other young mothers in the area, also anxious to make new friends and to keep their wits alive.

For the first time in my life I wrote to a newspaper, innocently putting forward this rather impracticable suggestion, not even expecting them to print it. But they did, 26 February 1960, and immediately, and to my surprise, I received several dozen replies.

They all felt the same way, confined at home with young children, usually new to a neighbourhood and desperately missing the warmth, the human contact and the stimulation they had enjoyed at work. Please would I go ahead and organise the Register! I do not know quite who I visualised this 'someone' to be with so much spare time and energy to organise such a register and it was something of a shock to find it was expected to be me.

I thought about it for a few days particularly the drawbacks, including no telephone, no car, no money, no time, and not even a typewriter then. I talked it over with Brian but it was pretty obvious that I would have to go ahead. The best way forward seemed to be another letter to the *Guardian* saying that I was willing to create this register:

'You were kind enough to publish my suggestion concerning the formation of a national register of liberal-minded housebound wives. The object of this would be to enable kindred spirits to contact each other in the deserts of the suburbs. I have received several letters of support, which rather suggests there is some demand for such a register. Perhaps all those interested would write to me with a stamped addressed envelope please, so that I can see whether this idea is worth developing. In any case I shall exchange addresses as far as possible.'

It was printed on 7 March 1960 – then came the avalanche. Within a few days I had several hundred letters. The postman was bewildered (that was before the days when letters bearing my name, followed just by Eastham, Cheshire, got delivered), I was astonished, Brian was apprehensive, but we were launched!

Some of these new letters were very sad and several of the women appeared to be pretty close to breakdown. One striking point emerged. Most were extremely relieved to find that, not only were they not unique and that there were other women with the same unsettled feeling that home and baby were not all-absorbing, but also that the mental deprivation they felt was understood. The letters came from ex-teachers, secretaries, social workers, nurses, doctors, solicitors, air hostesses. One was a civil engineer. There was a sprinkling of commercial artists among the ex-career women.

For the first few weeks after the birth of the register domestic life was shamefully neglected. Fortunately the baby, Sally, was one of the placid sort and I devised various schemes for keeping the monster of energy, Simon, happily occupied. One of these was tearing up all the envelopes.

The first and most urgent task was to spread the workload so I sorted all the letters into counties and picked out the most enthusiastic and constructive letters from six regions and wrote to ask if the writers would take the responsibility for organising their area. The idea was that they would put people in touch within their region and I would keep the central register. While waiting for the response I wrote all the names and addresses I had in a large book. The people I approached all accepted and were all keen to get more members to make the idea of the Register more meaningful. Another letter to the *Guardian* gave the names and addresses of the first six regional officers, North-West, North-East, East Midlands, Home Counties, West Midlands and London. Quite soon after there were two more, for Scotland and the South-West.

I had by now contacted the people living near me. It was great to find three within walking distance as the absence of buses made travelling difficult. (Soon after this Brian and I bought one of the first Minis* on the market and this was a great help.)

We started meeting in each others' homes during the daytime, with all our children, and discussed how best to develop the register. We found that our backgrounds were quite different, our incomes varied and therefore our homes, but that we all had in common the desire to communicate – to keep in touch with life and not to stagnate within our own four walls. We agreed that we must publicise the register, but there was no organisation and certainly no money, so I wrote to *The Observer* and *The Sunday Times* outlining the idea. *The Observer* printed the letter and *The Sunday Times* sent Moira Keenan to interview me.

One of my new-found friends looked after the children while I took her off to lunch and she proved a sympathetic and valuable ally. Her first article invited: 'Housewives, housebound but still longing for stimulating exchange of ideas' to write to *The Sunday Times* for the lists of organisers. 'A snowstorm of letters' resulted, she recorded, nearly a thousand writing in and letters still turning up three months later when her second article 'Progress Report' appeared.

We were quickly topping a membership of two thousand and I was kept busy sending on the letters to the area organisers. I had by then borrowed a typewriter and in June managed to acquire an ancient duplicator on long-term loan from the local Labour Party secretary (longer than he had bargained for – in fact it fell to pieces in the end). This meant I no longer had to write to organisers individually and, on 6 July, I sent out the first newsletter to organisers letting them know what was happening generally.

We were progressing beyond the idea of merely an introductory service and groups were forming, particularly in larger towns. The early ones were in Preston, Chester, Liverpool, Sutton Coldfield, Lytham-St. Anne, and two in Manchester. People wanted to get

---

* Coincidentally the Jermans also bought that automated pram, the Mini, not long after.

together for talks and discussions and found that a group could do very much more stimulating things than just a couple of friends. Where groups formed they were seeking local publicity and several of the organisers were getting letters and articles printed in their own local papers or favourite magazines. It was like a snowball rolling along getting steadily bigger.

The more it grew the more the media became interested and for a while my life became a real nightmare. Nearly all the popular daily and weekly papers picked up the idea and sent reporters for an interview. We had no telephone but that did not stop them turning up on the doorstep at all hours. I really dreaded opening the door to any knock for some weeks and since then have had the utmost sympathy for anyone subjected to the full horror of media exposure. The silliest question was asked by a *Daily Mirror* reporter: 'Will this lead to the break up of the home?' The most insultingly funny headline appeared in the *Daily Express*.*

At this stage we had no proper name as the clumsy 'LIBERAL-MINDED HOUSEBOUND WIVES' REGISTER' that I put on my newsletters just would not do. In the very first newsletter I appealed for ideas. We eventually and temporarily settled for Housebound Wives Register. We still had no membership fee and only asked for stamped addressed envelopes to be sent with enquiries. Later in that summer I managed to meet the London organiser, Margaret Smith, a vital bubbling woman, full of ideas, and just the sort of person I had imagined would join the Register. In London I also met Belle Tutaev currently fighting to get more nursery schools opened. One of the ideas mentioned then developed later into the now flourishing Pre-School Playgroups Association. It would have been very helpful to have been able to meet all the Register organisers but I remained an impecunious mother of two very young children, living in the northern backwoods, so it was just not possible.

In the autumn of 1960 I wrote a script for Woman's Hour about the register and went over to Manchester to do a live broadcast. They decided to do it as an interview and after a perfunctory rehearsal this went out live at 2.00 p.m. I was amazed at the casual nature of the business having imagined stop-watches and strict silence in the studio. The response was reasonably good, although a number of the few hundred writing to me had not heard all the

---

* 'Queen of the Cabbages': the vegetable has turned up many times over the years in articles about NHR.

interview and several thought it was some sort of new lonely-hearts matrimonial club!

I responded to enquiries with a duplicated letter. 'Many women who have had interesting careers before marriage very much miss the intellectually stimulating contacts that they have been used to. They are confined to the house with young children and the situation is often aggravated by the necessity of moving every so often from one part of the country to another. The basic aim of the Register is to put such people in touch with one another. A lot of our present members are graduates and ex-professional women, but let me make it clear that we ask for no special or educational qualification whatsoever. All that is needed is a genuine desire to have someone to converse with about subjects other than the usual domestic trivia'. I explained also how the Register was organised into regions, enclosing a list of organisers, that, where smaller groups existed, the letters would be forwarded to 'sub-organisers for particular towns' and added that: 'In quite a lot of cases, however, our members are few and far between and the regional organisers send out occasional newsletters to keep people in touch'. I went on: 'I hope I have made it clear that we have no lavish organisation – we are all busy mothers of young children doing this on a purely voluntary basis, and that *once you have been given the contacts it is largely up to you to make what you will of them.* It will be the lucky ones who find a ready made group of interesting women, most of you will have to actually make the contacts and arrange your own meetings'. The italics were mine.

At the end of the first year it became clear that the register was indeed developing to fit the needs of members and that, in most cases, individual introductions were not enough. Women needed to get together to get the most out of each other and these groups were necessarily self-organising and self-financing. And that is precisely what was happening. A great groundswell of lively-minded, reasonably educated mothers, torn from families and friends by mobile husbands, were largely solving their feelings of mental stagnation and loneliness by getting together and expanding their own lives.

As numbers grew the original organisers began dividing up their regions and within the first year we had appointed about thirty organisers. As people were moving again they were forming their own groups and I remember one member writing to tell me how she had gone round her new town putting leaflets into prams asking interested mums to turn up for a meeting in her house. About twenty women arrived and another thriving group was on the way.

The early idea of meeting during the day quickly changed. My own group found it virtually impossible to do anything worthwhile while the room was full of children and began to meet in the evenings. During our first year we discussed world government and education for women, we read and discussed the Arnold Wesker trilogy and had speakers from Merseyside Anti-Apartheid movement, the Civil Defence and the Marriage Guidance Council. We painted and visited the John Moore exhibition in Liverpool and of course we baby-sat and helped each other in many ways.

Although I hated the idea of asking for money I found that by the end of 1960 I was becoming seriously out of pocket. I was spending a lot on postage as there was always a sizeable percentage of people writing in after some publicity and not enclosing the stamped addressed envelope requested. Paper and duplicating ink costs were mounting too. I borrowed from the housekeeping money and used the fees I had earned from the broadcasts but it was an increasing strain. I dithered about this problem for some time knowing organisers were facing it too. In my December 1960 newsletter I asked them if they thought it practical to ask for an annual subscription of one shilling (5p). I left it to them to do what they thought best to keep themselves solvent and temporised myself by asking all new members to send a shilling registration fee to their area organiser.

My March 1961 letter to organisers was mostly about money. I had been swamped with letters, 300 after the London organiser's appearance on TV and a quarter without a stamped addressed envelope. I had used up the lists of organisers including 150 copies of the new corrected ones and, after answering twenty letters, thought it better to send them on.

Circulating these facts I reflected 'Unless we can be sure that we are not going to be continually out of pocket I do not see that we can continue', suggesting that I would not take any monies direct but organisers should send me 15 per cent of their annual income, fixing their own fees of course. A month later, with 700 letters in from more publicity, a good third with no s.a.e., putting me well and truly in the red, I told organisers that most of the Home Counties asked 5s (25p) annually but that in other regions nothing at all and that it was a 'good idea' to ask for a registration fee at least for expenses; still adding 'I am not going to lay down any hard and fast rules – most people seem quite happy with this loose organisation – and I leave it to you'.

By September things were more comfortable. I had received

£18.7s.6d in the interim and had spent £12.16s.0d clearing the accumulated debt and paying for that month's newsletter which was mostly devoted to considerations of publicity – where we got results – group activities I had heard about such as play reading, book reviews, visits to exhibitions, theatres, discussions on the bomb, understanding ourselves and our children, capital punishment; plus news of developments in other organisations.

We tottered along like this, managing in a fairly haphazard fashion because of my reluctance to formalise the whole business of finance. In fact it was not until I handed over to the next National Organiser that money was sensibly treated and membership fees put on a proper footing.

We were approached by a number of people for help of one sort or another during that second year. One particularly interesting request came from Enid Hutchinson who was doing research into the possibility of educational broadcasts on radio and television. A number of questionnaires were sent to members and the replies to these gave her the ammunition she needed to press for the development of educational broadcasts. Various consumer and health authorities asked to nominate members for their committees and the Citizens' Advice Bureaux offered training courses for members with older children. A number did go on to become CAB counsellors, including eventually me! There were also requests for Register addresses from commercial firms and these were firmly refused.

There were also requests from our own members too for help with various petitions and some of these were circulated. We did for instance get a number of signatures on a petition organised by the Campaign for Nuclear Disarmament, then surging towards its peak of popular appeal. A small group of us went, with our prams and pushchairs on a day march in Blackpool. I think we felt then that the individual internal power, which we had discovered could be harnessed to solve some problems, might be used to solve everything. We are older, sadder and wiser now.

In a way, though, this use of the Register was worrying and I was aware of the fact that, although I thoroughly approved of it being used for the things I believed in, I would not be so happy about certain other projects. Everyone I believe felt the same way and it gradually became an unwritten law that one could campaign as an individual but not as a representative of the NHR as a body.

After a while I stopped counting numbers and then stopped trying to keep up the central register. There were just too many names involved, something like four to five thousand and as organisers were obtaining their own publicity and recruiting locally it became impracticable for me to keep a note of every individual joining the register. The battered, dog-eared old book containing the names of the original members is sitting on the desk beside me as I think back – a great contrast to the last beautifully printed and produced *Newsletter* next to it.

As we entered the third year tragedy struck. The ancient duplicator did really fall to pieces as something vital fell off and I found it would cost far more than I could pay to repair or replace it. The only answer was to have the newsletter professionally duplicated. At the same time Brian and I were thinking of another move which would mean selling the car for a deposit on a house. All this confirmed my vague feelings that it was time to hand on the job of National Organiser to a new person or persons – a title, by the way, which just happened and became acceptable – like a lot of aspects of the register.

I explained that I wanted to hand over the reins to someone else in my newsletter to organisers March 1962. Adding 'But who?' with a clutch of exclamation marks.

> If one of you is willing to take over the Register as it now stands I should be very pleased, but in any case I would like your comments on the future of the Register.
>
> Do you feel we still need a National Organiser if no one is willing to take over completely, or can we split up without disintegrating? I tend to feel that we need some sort of central clearing-house. Organisers change so frequently that it would be very easy to lose touch, and members moving to new areas might have some difficulty in contacting the groups in their new homes.
>
> If we are to keep some central link we ought to think about how to ensure a *regular* minimal annual income.

The letter concluded:

> Again many thanks for your help and encouragement, and for all the work that so many of you and your members have put into making the Register the bankrupt, disorganised success it is.

Brenda Prys Jones of Croydon agreed to take over.

It was a great release not to have the responsibility nationally and I relished the freedom from guilt. During those two and a half years whatever I was actually doing, work on the register, playing with the children, cleaning the house, or whatever, I felt I should be doing something else!

IV
So what happens?

ONLY BY physically (and mentally of course) attending a meeting is it possible to appreciate the atmosphere, the banter, the level of discussion, the participation and the spirit of camaraderie. Baldly: women gather in the home of one of their number, rarely in a hall or other public place. They sit, often on cushions on the floor if there are not enough chairs, and they talk.

A woman's first remark to a friend is likely to be in the 'How's Johnnie?' category. Her thoughts are still half back in what was happening, being said and done, as she closed her own front door but she is still naturally attuned to another mother's immediate concerns. But once all that has been let out the next remark is likely to be 'Did you see that article on . . .?' And that goes right back to my original wail in 1960 when no one I had yet met in my new neighbourhood was aware of anything outside the suburb except headline news and the lighter entertainment on radio and TV. But it also raises another aspect. Marie Price, later an NO was spurred to join the Register when she started talking back to the radio! She also reflected that a woman caring for a very young child is more likely to fall asleep before a serious TV programme than take it in. Neither media offered participation.

Here then, in someone's home, are gathered women who do read newspapers, books and other publications, watch TV, listen to radio, with all the means of imparting information on philosophies, doctrines, and on social, marital, industrial, international, political, developments and problems. Not always easy with domestic commitments but they know their opinions will not just be silently mulled over on the way to the shops, or formed into those letters to the editor that never get written, let alone posted.

Where else will you find the attention, respect for your formed (and expected to be informed) views than at a Register meeting? Women can be arguing like the furies, without rancour, very much a case of feeling free to disagree, with no polite reticence to avoid upsetting someone else and, still within the same meeting, chat amicably over coffee.

No wonder members (occasionally husbands too) say that the ding-dong of debate is still clamouring in their re-vitalised minds when they should be peacefully asleep.

Invited speakers have been taken aback by the searching questions and informed comment. They may be additionally surprised to learn that some members regard reliance on outside speakers as a form of laziness, a way of avoiding the solid preparation beforehand for a do-it-yourself discussion.

Practical women, not members, will ask how all this getting away from domesticity and stretching your mind can proceed in a normal household among the usual quota of mechanical breakdowns, emotional crises, and physical disasters. I was at a meeting when one of the hostess's young sons, presumed asleep upstairs, called her in distress. Did he get to the bathroom in time? No. Marie Price's group in Abergavenny were in the middle of discussing 'A Woman's Place is in the Home?' in 1975 when member Geraldine (pregnant) was missed, last seen on her way to the loo. 'One hour later having passed screwdrivers, knives, keys, etc. under the door with no success, and attempts at getting the door off its rising hinges having failed, we phoned the Fire Brigade for advice'. [Her written account of this was interrupted when Marie's daughter pushed a button up her nose needing hospital treatment to remove. To continue.] 'The police arrived with walkie-talkies, speedily followed by the fire engine and twelve thigh-booted, jacketed, helmeted firemen pounded up the stairs and on to the landing, informing me in passing that they had a reserve crew of eighteen standing by.' Geraldine released, visitors departed, they returned to the discussion.

Lesley Moreland (National Organiser 1970 to 1973) when a Local Organiser in the mid-sixties, invited two young Mormon missionaries proselytising on her doorstep to address the group. The hostess had one of the early PVC covered (leather-like!) suites. But under the restless limbs of a member's child it emitted a series of vulgar noises. The young men dauntlessly carried on; the women finally lost control in gales of laughter. The same child raided the shopping stacked in a corner at another meeting and ate the cream doughnuts intended for a family's tea and, at yet another, found paint brushes left soaking in turpentine and busily 'painted' a tiled fireplace. That meeting finished with members furiously (physically and emotionally) tile scrubbing.

Activities
'Cake-icers', Lesley Moreland's definitive catch phrase for the domestically inclined, has been adopted by those who fear that the Register's unique tenets can be swamped by the more usually cultivated womens' interests. Some – autonomous, remember – groups have cookery demonstrations! The defenders of the original principles are not saying that an intellectual is not also interested in learning about, for instance, flower arranging, just that it should be sought elsewhere and not within NHR. In a broad spectrum of women, somewhere between the 'cake-icers' and the purists, lie those who resent the Register's implicit downgrading of domesticity. Just to add to the dissension, I cannot forgo including two lists jotted down by Hazel Bell (Newsletter Editor 1976–80) while mulling over the borderline.

Children	Education, psychology, children's books.
Food	Conservation, Third World, economics.
Cooking	Nutrition, hygiene
Health	Drugs, fringe medicine, NHS
Having babies	Home/hospital delivery? Eugenics, cloning, abortion, contraception.

The first list could be headed 'Domestic'. The other?

In 1962 founder Maureen Nicol wrote telling the first few organisers that her local group's activities included reading and discussing books, lectures on modern art, Civil Defence, C.N.D. and a talk by a Marriage Guidance Councillor. She fed back the news that the Glasgow group had heard a Probation Officer and Preston members had not only discussed the death penalty and remedies for the world shortage of food but had amazed local booksellers by buying all available copies of Plato's *Republic* for their discussion on the Ideal State. Bolton members had discussed the Common Market, Leeds the maternity services, Leicester had discussed Apartheid, advertising and women's magazines. Grimsby and Cleethorpes had had speakers on archaeology and the Stock Exchange. She was reporting the activities of a particular body of women. No one then or now is laying down edicts.

But the lengthy 'Ideas for meetings' dated 1977, and a later 'Some topics for discussion' dated 1979 were not dreamed up by some national officer with rose-coloured ambitions about maintaining the Register's high principles. Each listed proven successes with local groups.

Even as a selection they are long so I will stick a pin in. Loneliness in Modern Society. Does the punishment fit the crime? How do you value the Monarchy? Is marriage a dying institution? There is no such thing as rape.... Death – the taboo subject of the Seventies. Take a theme for members to discuss different aspects of, such as literature, poetry, music, climate, customs, language. Seven Deadly Sins – what would be your eighth? Is the National Front a passing phenomenon or a natural reaction to Communism? What shall we do with Granny? What kind of snob are you? Should we expect education, employment and health services as of right? Do you alter your views according to the company or stick to your principles? Add to this fare: choirs; drama groups (I was entertained by the lyrics promoting the NHR for the Carshalton pantomime which had 'Fairy Liquid' as the traditional fairy queen); theatre and concert attendance (more likely when other women demonstrate that family-tied mothers *can* take such breaks); children's parties and expeditions; social gatherings that give commuting husbands a chance to make friends too; participation in sundry charitable causes (though not as NHR); variations of baby-sitting – in the daytime to give mothers a break – an evening out, and even 'exchange' overnight visits that give children experience of another household and its habits.

But, of course, none of this would be happening – or at least not under this particular framework – no one can say what kind of organisation might have emerged elsewhere, at some time, to fill what was an almost entirely unrecognised need – if another woman had not offered to take on the responsibility for the Register from Maureen Nicol. Fortunately Brenda Prys Jones volunteered.

V
The Register Builders:
Brenda Prys Jones
1962–64

BRENDA PRYS JONES recalls her years as National Organiser.

I came down from Oxford during the war, married and got a job (yes – in that order!) as a temporary wartime Inspector in the Ministry of Health. In the years after the war we moved house three times and with my three children (well-spaced or ill-spaced, depending how you look at it) I was certainly in a position in 1960 to welcome the Register.

With my third baby and third location I was so pleased when I saw Maureen Nicol's letter in the *Guardian*: I wrote at once to Maureen offering to help if anything should come of her idea.

Not long afterwards I had a reply giving me the name of someone else who had written from Croydon and who happened to live round the corner. We got together and waited for more to happen. I was in touch with someone in Surrey who was holding a 'county' Register.

At any rate it was not long before we had a group in Croydon meeting in the evenings every fortnight and firmly resolved to eschew the domestic. Most of the members were in a sense lonely people who had joined principally to meet others. Few were in a position to bring friends along. Ages were very varied at first but older members tended to drop out which seemed to me a pity.

When the time came for Maureen to appeal for someone to take over the Register the Croydon group prodded me into volunteering. I pointed out to Maureen that I was no longer a young mother but I felt I had the time to spare and if no one else offered I would cope rather than see this brilliant idea flop. Sometime afterwards Maureen arrived to visit me carrying a suitcase which contained a mass of letters and lists and thirty shillings (£1.50p) – the Register. I admired Maureen tremendously for having got so far in establishing this 'bankrupt success' as she called it.

I felt that the whole thing needed pulling into shape.

I got out a newsletter as soon as possible (June 1962) and had it duplicated at an inexpensive local agency run in a private house, financing that first one myself.

These were my proposals.

Organisation: I shall continue our policy of complete independence and merely mention in newsletters projects that are put to me so that groups can take them up if they wish. Our greatest problem is what to do about our scattered members. Those of you who have charge of them have had a difficult task trying to keep in touch. The following scheme should make things easier:— (1) More groups to be formed, even if small and not meeting regularly. (County Organisers – can you encourage this?); (2) All group leaders to have themselves officially listed at local libraries and/or other information centres. (Use your Group name if you have one, and give our national title as well); (3) Let me have a list of all such groups; (4) County Organisers will then have fewer scattered members. Let me know how many and I will forward enough newsletters to be sent round, with space for a personal note by the County Organiser if she wishes. Perhaps the scattered members could be asked to post the newsletter on to the next one (with comments if desired) and so on back to the County Organiser. We might produce a short duplicated leaflet to help scattered members to get local publicity; (5) Any future publicity will state clearly 'enquire at your local library', or if in difficulty write to ..., (my address at the time).

This should save a lot of writing to and fro but presupposes an efficient newsletter service and finance to cover it. I gather from your replies to the last newsletter that you all want a central organisation and are prepared to pay for it.

Financially, the problem again is what to do about scattered members. As many of you say, it isn't fair to ask them to pay up and receive very little, yet they are the ones who will benefit most from an increase in membership. Let us have a general annual subscription from every member to cover advertising and two newsletters. Groups will receive only two or three letters to pass round or read out, but County Organisers will have more letters provided out of general funds and should keep back a proportion of the subscriptions to cover their heavier costs. I am asking, therefore, for an annual subscription of 5/- (25p) payable each autumn or spring. (If you have the kind of group that pays for speakers or other items of jollity, I assume you will finance that separately.)

I explained that I was willing to deal with all enquiries by post but asked for a volunteer to take charge of advertising and another to handle the newsletter so everything was not run from one place.

I continued:

The Register Builders: Brenda Prys Jones 1962–64

As we are agreed throughout the country that we want the Register to continue, this is perhaps a suitable time – partly for the benefit of new members – to re-state our position, answer criticism and look into the future.

I raised the idea of a 'social ombudswoman' in every town to guide new residents to existing facilities and link together those wanting to do something not available.

There are not enough clubs, especially of the kind for small groups of people to express themselves amongst friends rather than be talked at.

In addition, the assumption that a mother's interest in her home and family enable her necessarily to get on with all other mothers is a false one (no one expects all young, or all middle-aged fathers to share their interests because they are fathers). This, in my opinion, is partly what leads to a lot of unneighbourliness and suspicion that others are 'odd', and unknowable. Probably a married woman needs two kinds of friends – those with whom she shares her interests of homes and children and those with whom she shares her other interests.

Therefore, I feel the Register should not be accused of being exclusive or 'snob' or of catering only for a minority. . . . I cannot see why one should not proclaim that one has some 'different' interests and is seeking others of similar outlook. . . . I hope you will give me your support so that not only shall we all enjoy ourselves but that in future there will be a means of introducing the like-minded.

That newsletter was sent to the organisers on Maureen's list. Some were running active groups such as my own but others were holding lists of isolated would-be members.

Some groups objected to the subscription, but most people paid up. The money began to come in in varying amounts – organisers sending from 1s (5p) to 2.6d. (12½p) per head according to what they could spare. I kept accounts and opened a special bank account. We all owe a lot to those who paid up at that stage of the Register's history. They were not getting that much for their money but, without their financial support, I could not have afforded to go on despatching newsletters and I think the whole thing might have foundered.

I was able to spend some money on our first office equipment, namely a small card index* to keep the list of organisers and groups. It was small enough to send by post to my successor.

By the autumn of that year (1962) I had an answer to my appeal

---

* The Register was simply a card index until 1981 when a benefactor, preferring to remain anonymous, presented a computer.

for help with the newsletter. The Preston 'Delta' group began to produce the prototype of the newsletter as it basically still is. I wrote my bit about organisation, etc. and there were short articles discussing the Register policy, news from groups and a list of useful addresses, e.g. other organisations that members might wish to support.

My section of that autumn's newsletter began blithely: 'The letter box on my front door hasn't been able to stand the strain; it fell off – poor thing! Fortunately I am not similarly overcome'. I then sketched the picture that was emerging. Less total members than were estimated – new organisers in Kent and E. Midlands had discovered many original members who had lost interest or found others – and in some 'regions' or counties division into smaller units. Throughout the country many new groups had formed. There were at least eighty 'organisers' either of large areas or of small scattered groups. I left it to individuals to communicate directly with me or with their regional organisers. All I asked was information on the location of groups since the National Register listed organisers with the number of members each had on her list.

Only two or three regional organisers were still sending out newsletters. I had had requests from newer ones for more newsletters, or some kind of 'letter to new members', or as one put it 'some proof of authority'. I had two duplicated letters, one for enquirers who knew something of the organisation and the other telling of origins and aims. I just filled in the name and address of the nearest local organiser. I offered copies (on payment of subs!) for use in local efforts. That was in effect publicity and, having brought members up to date, I expounded on it since members with successful groups could not see the need for much national effort in that direction but many more welcomed some advertising in the 'quality press'.

> One of the chief advantages of recruiting on a national scale[I wrote] is that it checks divergences which exist. We have never intended to be a network of women's clubs or provide any rigidly organised system of enabling our members to meet, so it is inevitable that there should be differing views as to what to do and who has a 'like mind'. This does not matter – if it does not go too far. If we depend entirely on local publicity I fear that – in time, as we hand over to our successors, the present differences between groups may increase. Thus the Register would lose half its purpose, which is to provide introductions to the like-minded when members move to other parts of the country. Some societies provide a programme: one joins for the sake of the activities and makes

friends incidentally. Other societies draw together members of a certain type and then cater for their interests. We are of the latter kind but our 'certain type' has qualifications somewhat difficult to define, and we leave our members to their own devices once they have met. It is all the more important, therefore, to ensure that our 'certain type' is recruited, or the organisation loses its point.

Reading the pile of correspondence, press cuttings, local newsletters unloaded onto her by me, Jose Newmark, one of the newsletter editors, admitted being frightened by the diversity in the Register. She wrote:

> We vary from the frivolous to the frustrated intellectual; from the highly organised to the point of regimentation, to the disorganised on-the-point-of disintegration. Our individual needs differ – some want only baby-sitters or playmates for their children – others seek intellectual stimulation and want nothing whatever to do with kids in their spare moments. Some want to associate us with various good causes – others believe fiercely that the only worthy cause is their own mental freedom.

I too was frightened by the diversity when I first took over and I sometimes used to wonder whether my weekly Register day was worth the effort. But what stick in my mind most are the heartfelt letters I used to receive from enquirers who had seen the Register mentioned in the press. I spent some of the limited funds on advertising in the national press and there were sometimes articles by journalists (some not quite on the beam).

There were a lot of lonely housebound women about and I had to remind myself that the first purpose of the Register was to put people in touch and that the formation of groups was secondary. But in practice the formation of groups was inevitable. People wanted to meet regularly, someone had to collect subs and distribute news, and above all the existence of a group made local publicity easier.

But my constant appeal whenever I wrote to anyone was to avoid doing what other women's organisations already did. (Laziness on my part, to some extent!) Why should I do all this, I asked myself, if the W.I. or Young Wives, or whoever, are already doing it more efficiently?

The fact that I was approached by organisations hoping for our interest or affiliation was gratifying in that it showed that the Register had well and truly arrived on the scene. I always reported anything of this kind in the newsletter for members' personal use but refused to tie up the Register as a whole.

At about this time I remember meeting Joan Little,* the editor of *Forum* magazine to which we gave publicity. At the same time I met Belle Tutaev, founder of the Pre-School Playgroups Association. She was one of those who thought that the main purpose of the Register should be to organise something to free mothers so that they could do their own thing. But the majority of Register members wanted something for themselves, with child-minding done incidentally. These were the only personal contacts I made. Everything was done by mail.

In the spring 1964 newsletter I appealed for someone to take over as National Organiser. I explained that it was an 'easy-to-run machine' requiring three to four hours work a week, putting aside material for the newsletter, keeping the National Register up to date. 'The new enquiries that come in every week can usually be answered by my duplicated explanatory leaflet. (My small daughter enjoys folding them and sticking on the stamps!)' There were by then 154 organisers. 'I cannot carry on for ever as National Organiser' I wrote. 'Surely you will not let Maureen's brain-child, now such a sturdy growing specimen, fade away?'

Lesley Taylor volunteered. I parcelled up the card index, the Register, and other documents, in fact the 'office' which I had kept in a cardboard grocery box, and posted it to her plus the Register funds. Very simple.

---

* See Enterprise – External.

VI
The Roots

THE REGISTER, a list of names and addresses, is simply the means by which 'like-minded' women find each other. The heart and strength of the organization lies in its membership, the women who have rejected a national hierarchical structure with committees and delegates and only recently have accepted the innovation of an elected group to handle national matters as a way of maintaining the link between autonomous groups.

By 1964 when Brenda Prys Jones successfully handed on responsibility for the Register to Lesley Taylor, the simple framework of NHR was already becoming clear. The County or Regional Organisers were becoming rare. After all they were the practical appointments made by Maureen Nicol to cope with the unforeseen effect of her letter. Isobel Wakeman, moving to a new home with two small daughters in 1960, recalls writing to her 'expecting a long list of addresses' and being slightly disconcerted to receive a note saying 'as I was the only person in Bucks and Berkshire who had sent the requisite shilling' would I like to be the organiser. She thinks, from memory, a few names and addresses of people scattered through the two counties also turned up. She got groups going after publicity in the local press.

Lesley Talbot, mother of four, having just moved from London to Bramhall, Cheshire, and previously round the country without the chance to put down roots, found Maureen's letter 'an eminently practical suggestion'. She was appointed regional organiser for North East Cheshire, with three other names to contact. One was Pamela Ousey. They are close friends still, though separated by distance. I met them at the 1980 international conference recalling with relish how Lesley learned to drive, Pamela navigating by map, as they travelled to far flung and isolated members moving in ever widening circles. The *network* of the many groups they got going was called 'The Cestrian Group', which became affiliated to the National Association of Women's Clubs, contributed to research on toddlers' tantrums by Nottingham University's Elizabeth and John Newson, and supported the early playgroup movement. Lesley wrote monthly newsletters. Her six years as Regional Organiser occasionally strained family life but the most rewarding aspect for her was 'to observe how rapidly our shy and inhibited new members blossomed forth into self-confident and assured women'. She describes the Register as a launching pad, as indeed it was for her. After so much public speaking she qualified professionally in that field and now lectures and examines on spoken English. A surprisingly large number of members could tell similar stories.

Without such pioneers the Register might not have survived. But the days of writing in for your nearest group and being asked to organise a county or two are long past. Occasionally, the idea of Regional Organisers is raised. Noticeably several candidates for national office in the 1980 election, setting down something about themselves and their ideas for voters to make their choices, mentioned the benefits of inserting some form of regional responsibility into the Register structure.

The structure could change in the future but for the most part of twenty years it has simply had a broad base of local groups and a national tip. The absence of a hierarchy lies behind the longstanding boast of being an unorganised organisation. This also means that, since no resolutions are formally framed to pass up through the structure for majority approval by 'delegates' ('delegates' do not exist in NHR), the only expression of opinion emerges in letters to the National Organiser, letters or articles published in the newsletter and stimulating a reaction, or through verbal participation at conferences. Additionally today with a Group rather than one, or two, women at national level (and the finance to cover their fares) there are more officers to get round to local meetings and to absorb the opinions of a broader spectrum of the membership.

The development of NHR depends on individuals rather than on a structure. So often, reading the newsletters over the years—the ever flowing reflective river—I noticed that letters, reports, provocative articles came from women who later became stalwarts, whether reaching national office or not, known to be deeply interested in the whole movement. That is not necessarily true of all members. As guest at a local group at the time when members were being asked, through the national newsletter, to comment on the draft of the first 'constitution' I sought the thoughts of a handful during the informal chat period; they had not noticed their opinions were sought, not having got round to reading their own individual copies.

There are flickerings of change in this general unconcern about how the Register functions nationally; twenty one nominees stood for election to the nine National Group vacancies in 1980. But references to 'HQ' by some, as though an office exists with paid staff present from nine a.m. to five p.m., or alternatively objections by some to 'regimentation', do underline the lack of understanding among members of how the movement works. It's understandable that outsiders are flummoxed.

Qualifications

Qualifications for membership have been redefined through the years, though qualification is too strong a word, it being rather a matter of self-selection considering the kind of programme offered. But there have been constant efforts to present NHR in words which will reach those women to whom it will appeal. Even after twenty years no one would call that an easy proposition.

In the beginning there were Maureen Nicol's: 'housebound wives with liberal interests and a desire to remain individual' quickly complemented by her: 'All that is needed is a genuine desire to have someone to converse with about subjects other than the usual domestic trivia'. In the sixties publicity also leaned towards those 'bringing up small children'.

But by 1969 NO Jane Watt, breezily summing up: 'We are supposed to be an organised collection of women shunning domestic conversation', sought membership reaction to a more formal but still telling presentation. For a period the newsletter contained a short explanatory paragraph: 'The only qualification for membership is a lively and enquiring mind', followed by the information that 'Most members are married, aged between twenty-five and forty and have followed some kind of career before marriage'.

The age group mentioned was taken too literally by some, with objections. Since 1978 the *Newsletter* has contained a short paragraph on how the Register started followed by: 'The aim of NHR is to encourage the formation of groups who wish to participate in stimulating and wide-ranging discussion, creating an opportunity for friendship and other activities. NHR meets the needs of those who want to develop their own range of talents and particularly those with domestic ties during the day. It provides regular opportunities for stimulating conversation between like-minded women.' But no one should regard that as the rigid, unadjustable formula.

Personally I have always fancied the brief legend 'A meeting-point for the lively-minded woman' which has been around since the mid-seventies.

'My Mummy has a lively mind' printed across the front of a child's T-shirt (the NHR now goes in for publicity slogans ironed on to clothes) is guaranteed to get a second look, even in today's jungle of slogans or radical declarations which decorate the T-shirted chests of young adults.

But who determines that qualification? There is no admission test.

When you get down to it, about the only firm qualification is that of being a woman – though there have been occasional male members. You do not have to be married, nor to have children still at home. Even your age is irrelevant, though that aspect is always being raked over. 'Like-minded' or 'lively-minded' is an entirely personal assessment.

Recruiting

Groups are autonomous and jealously guard that state. They organise their own internal management, and may, if they wish, choose titles that give no hint of allegiance. Examples have been 'Cabbage Club', of course, and 'Wives 61' in Essex, 'Topic' in Scotland. Some may be affiliated to the National Association of Women's Clubs, some send representatives to the local Standing Committee of Women's Organisations. That is their affair. So is their support for any cause, just so long as they do not claim to be representing NHR.

With over 1,000 groups in the U.K. and over 21,000 members, an enquirer in the eighties is less likely to hear from the NO that there is no nearby group, and be given a nudge about starting one up with advice offered. But this still happens. The actual Register also contains details of the unattached, called contacts, who could be the embryo for yet another group. Otherwise the one dependable way of attracting new members is still by word of mouth.

Over a decade after relinquishing the organisation of the Register, Maureen Nicol organised a Workers' Educational Association trip to a Birmingham theatre and got talking to a 'very pleasant woman' with whom she had hardly spoken in class. She told Maureen that she had moved to the Midlands only six months before and had met 'a very lively interesting group of women' who had helped her enormously to settle in. After a glowing build-up she enquired if Maureen had 'ever heard of the National Housewives Register'.

Such an intangible concept is not easily and effectively reduced to a few printed words. It is an easier proposition to express your own enthusiasm to someone who is palpably NHR material. After all the 'very pleasant woman' was unaware that she was talking to the founder.

There are those, and they include children, who claim you can pick out a Register member in a crowd; I have done it myself on station platforms when heading for conferences. But the verbal approach to a possible kindred spirit is chancy – as can be read between the lines of Maureen's original letter.

Advertising in the national press was briefly tried in the sixties. But the backbone of publicity has long consisted of getting articles into the local press (and radio), cards pinned in local shops, display of posters, car stickers, and leaflets. One of the logos, known for easy reference as the 'House of Ladies' has female figures entering a house. There was a slight contretemps in the late seventies when members complained all the 'ladies' looked pregnant! That was changed.

Attempts to put over the concept are endless. A 1979-vintage logo has the full title curving underneath, but above, another try at spelling it out as 'New Horizons Revealed'. Well, the initials are the same.

When the national tip was no longer a one-woman job, nurturing new groups was recognised as a specific job in the division of the various tasks, and went first to Lesley Moreland, joint NO 1970–1973, then to Josephine Jaffray 1973–1976. In 1978 the National *Group* hived it off from the NO's responsibilities and appointed a 'New Groups Adviser'. Jean Stirk, the first incumbent ran a 'Dear Jean' agony advice service skilfully guiding new local organisers round the awkward moments that occur as the 'lively-minded' knit (no reference intended to wool and needles) into a group.

Potential founders now get a 'New Groups Pack' which has also been termed a 'Starter Pack', honed from the years of experience. It contains a short history of the movement, an explanation about how most groups function, some copies of newsletters to give the flavour, the addresses of nearby long-standing members who can give valuable personal support, a list of topics for meetings and solid advice on how to get started and keep going, interlaced with the various unwritten codes, like the national movement not being a pressure group and hostesses of meetings serving only coffee and biscuits to avoid competition with elaborate and even more elaborate culinary offerings.

Clinics are one of the places where it is recommended publicity is displayed. That appeals to me. In theory the places where mothers naturally head for to check the progress of their very young children should be the seedbeds of friendship with others in the same boat. It rarely works like that and has nothing to do with the fact that today you pack the children into a car and vanish into the traffic rather than departing slowly behind a pram which is more conducive to conversational overtures.

In the sixties I had anguished letters from women hailing the advent of NHR, since their abortive efforts to raise a spark of adult conversation in other mothers attending clinics had instilled the fear that they were sentenced to years of just child- and home-oriented chatter. There is something about sitting among women and babies, spending unhurried time (after all the next event on the horizon is another meal) on the albeit important matter of your child's welfare, that reduces a woman to cotton-woolliness, a receptacle for advice on the feeding, sleeping, body wastes of young humans. Being addressed indiscriminately as 'mother' from the time when the infant is only a bump, making clothes tighter, and 'mother' means your own parent, adds to this loss of identity. Medical staff of all levels please note.

I relish the thought that today a woman crushed under the effect of this earth-motherhood may glance up, see an NHR poster, and grasp at the radicalism that is inherent in the existence of the Register: that women do not put their minds into cold storage during the child-rearing years.

Publicity material has also been displayed in mothers' natural habitats, libraries, doctors' waiting-rooms, community centres, playgroups, even hairdressers. Health Visitors, Citizens' Advice Bureau staff and playgroup leaders are usually allies. Nowadays, as well as the local paper, details about meetings can be fed into the neighbourhood's free newspapers, where they exist. Saturation is the idea.

But personal contact combined with something on paper is strongly recommended. 'Don't despair if you know no one', the current New Group Pack encourages, 'as it is easier to approach neighbours or strangers at the playgroup and in shops if you are

The Roots

firmly clutching an NHR pamphlet'. That snippet can be traced back to Lesley Moreland. Back in 1968, long before she became a National Organiser, she related in the newsletter her experience in starting a new group. 'First, accost your potential members. As a newcomer to Potters Bar this had to be bare-faced approaching of complete strangers – any likely prospect was fair game. The library and the clinic were fruitful hunting grounds.'

Yet another ploy is to call on a family a few days after the removal vans depart, clutching a pamphlet of course. Jane Watt, NO in the late sixties, knew of an enthusiast LO who popped a leaflet into every neighbouring door which had a pram outside, and of a newsagent persuaded to slip a leaflet into every copy of the quality Sundays, and another who did likewise into delivered copies of the *Guardian*.

An anonymous contributor to a 1969 newsletter gave another view of such strenuous effort. 'In Boston, amid flat fields of cabbages and almost in the Wash, efforts used to attract members in suburbia don't work'. Health Visitors rarely called, posters in all kinds of clinics were unread, the library refused to display permanent information about local societies, – 'NHR information is now available on request, in some secret file under the counter'. Despite that, they nearly quadrupled membership in just over a year. 'The local grape-vine is remarkably efficient and we have just discovered a traders' organisation for welcoming newcomers gives us publicity as a baby-sitting group'. She asked rhetorically, 'Whatever do we do if our non-methods continue to attract new members at the same rate?'

Whatever the location the message seems to be not to be discouraged by small beginnings. 'Don't worry,' soothes the New Group Pack, 'if there are only three or four of you, as it's better to get started with a few keen members and have some definite meetings to mention to further enquirers'. Or, Lesley Moreland again: 'Our first meeting in 1966 was attended by six nervous strangers debating Capital Punishment and as the last one left I ran upstairs and had a good howl, convinced that this group would never be a success'. It had sixty members within two years.

New groups are not expected to pay subs immediately. The total network carries a seedling group for some months through the national financing system before it becomes officially registered. This financial support is of course based on the original principle: that you may easily find the 'like-minded' wherever you may move.

The framework

The Local Organiser is the direct link with the National Organiser and, therefore with the Register itself on which the group will be listed and become traceable to newcomers in a district. Perennially (not only in the UK) National Organisers plaintively ask that, if the LO moves, someone will realise that the Register can be forgotten in the upheaval and take responsibility for passing on the next incumbent's address! Maybe the new residents in the house might be diverted by a packet of newsletters but groups have occasionally been temporarily lost in this way.

The LO is also the channel through which the overall principles are routed, though no one is going to descend disapprovingly from on high; if a group is off the beam it is likely to find another one forming nearby, more NHR, rather than confrontation. Similarly no one is 'struck off' for not paying subscriptions, since no one is excluded on the basis of cost; one of the reasons, with expansion and inflation, why the organisation has been dogged with financial difficulties.

In Maureen Nicol's day Organisers deducted their expenses from the suggested five shillings (25p) subscription which meant that only 1s or 2s (5p or 10p) per member were sent on. A standard *national* sub of 5s (25p) per year per member was introduced in 1970 and had risen to £1 by 1977 – £1.50 in 1980.

There have always been members questioning the payment of a national subscription, unlikely to move and not seeing the benefits of an extensive network, not wishing to attend local get-togethers, or hear about courses, speakers, new services, even read the newsletter.

The national level has the difficult job (not always effective) of putting over that national publicity is needed and a national set up to maintain the standards of the NHR, keep the Register functioning, support new groups and provide advice and information whether or not a particular group or member takes advantage of all that.

Beyond the national contribution for membership, groups decide on their own contributions. They can be five, ten, even fifty pence per meeting. Part will cover the coffee and biscuits served. The rest goes into the group's funds. Researching in the late seventies I learned that for some women with only one income, small children and a mortgage, even such small sums are difficult to justify for a woman's 'interests'.

Most groups are started by one woman, determined not to vegetate in a strange district or a strange country, who taps the

Register for its unattached (not in groups) names and for its expertise. She may find a friend. Together they launch methods of recruitment which, considering the selective appeal, can be a lengthy process. The dynamic initiator generally becomes the first Local Organiser, though this is not a sacred title. For the convenience of a name to be listed on the national Register she might be called Membership Secretary. There can be an Organiser and a Secretary, or joint Organisers, and, as the group grows, someone who runs the book circle, the baby-sitting system or the music group. There may be someone responsible for talking to the press, writing to whoever might come along and give a stimulating talk, or keeping tabs on the finances.

Somebody too has to be aware that walking into a room full of cosily chatting women can deter the most confident, which is why a small-scale gathering over morning coffee is a more sympathetic introduction, and someone, under whatever title, needs to notice whether a member is quietly taking it all in and feeling her feet first or is harbouring resentment because she is not being given a chance to voice her views and is being ignored. A survey by Jane Watt explored why those who could benefit from the Register did not always become members.

Jobs can rotate, as the locations for meetings rotate round members' homes, though not necessarily to every member's home. With unassailable confidence and an explanation such as 'We're open-plan and everyone would join in' or 'my husband would not like it' a contribution can be made in another form. Yet it is one of the imponderables that a member who has attended gatherings where the high level of incomes are evident in the standards of furnishings and spaciousness, could withdraw rather than invite a bunch of women to her, by comparison, more modest home.

The unstructured, unorganised nature of groups, with someone offering to take on a responsibility and fixing on a title for convenience, has long been a key feature, and indeed frequently vaunted as one of the special attractions of the NHR.

When members of the Congleton group, attending a W.E.A. course, conducted a survey in 1966, Worthing group's comment was quoted: 'We would not like to see the informality disappear and for the NHR to get too organised. This would spoil the individuality which makes NHR different from other women's organisations'.

That survey, based on the replies of 160 groups (3,257 members) found one that admitted never planning meetings. Otherwise the figures ranged from just over half planning only one or two meetings ahead to 9.5 per cent planning a year ahead, the latter usually the more formally constituted groups. Similarly 85 per cent considered themselves to be informally organised with possibly only a secretary. The remaining 15 per cent were more formally constituted, with a committee.

The informality allows every member to take part, to contribute in some way to the whole. But it depends on the personality of the Organiser in delegating and sharing, and in stimulating others to apply their minds to new topics for meetings, and their energies to publicising the movement, or organising social and cultural events, instead of passively waiting for it all to be done for them.

Across the gap of twenty years a member of Maureen Nicol's first neighbourhood group still recalls with awe the things she 'had them doing'. In the two decades since, thousands of women have exhibited the same driving energy, persuading, inspiring, and cajoling, their group to stretch just that bit further in their horizons and not just settle for the mediocre, the undemanding.

'It is great fun and very interesting,' a Stourbridge Local Organiser declared in 1980. 'I would recommend every member, in every group, to have a "stint" at being Organiser'. Others through the years have, perhaps unintentionally, waved a carrot by telling of correspondence with and later meeting and hostessing the eminent and famous folk who accept invitations to speak. Audrey Balfour in Rhodesia (later in Register style to become the National Organiser there) entertained UK members in their newsletter with 'A Local Organiser's Nightmare', all about people arriving while she is still in hair rollers, dishes unwashed in the sink, toys round the floor, and how it was in reality, all tidy and organised, except that when the speaker was late the date was checked: wrong date. Rarely, except verbally and privately, do Local Organisers mention husbands refusing to answer the phone in the evenings – 'I know it's for you', or asking: 'You've done your stint; isn't anyone else taking over?'

The informality, everyone being involved in running their own group and not just letting it be done for them, is another part of the unwritten code, though of course it is incorporated into the written advice on how to start a new group. But that ideal is not totally sustained.

By 1980 noticeably more Local Organisers were asking the National Group for advice. Now that might be put down to fewer groups capable of dealing with independence, or LOs less certain about being able to guide members along NHR lines of delegation and sharing responsibility, or simply because, instead of one struggling individual, there are several women at national level who can be tapped for advice.

Similarly there are indications that, unless there is a founder with drive and imagination, new groups with members in the younger age-range will find comfort and support within a committee of members elected through an AGM, though few go in for the paraphernalia of regularly written-up minutes. Some groups favour a constitution and, in the absence of a NHR one, adopt that of another organisation. Though as one member remarked, disapproving of this inclination towards formality, 'At least it lacks bitchiness, vying with each other to get to the top, because there is no ladder or hierarchy to climb'.

The penalty of success

Local groups face a problem that must be envied by other organisations who would count having to hire a larger hall to cater for increasing demand as a sign of achievement. It has to do with the location. Quite simply there is a limit to the number of women who can cram into one living room and still conduct an intelligent and fruitful meeting.

The problem surfaced as early as 1965, swopping experiences on how to cope with popularity. It is discussed to this day, a perennial nut being cracked by someone. Solutions have been: mothers of pre-school children meeting in the evening, those of school-age children in the morning; having several smaller meetings which are good for the shy, or sub-group meetings on rotating dates; splitting into upper and lower age groups (contentious that one); splitting geographically, through choice or by drawing names from a hat, and maintaining contact through a general newsletter; a regular joint meeting in a public hall (or something grander like a conference); or an 'umbrella committee' serving all the offshoots; or social events open to all. Some of these can result in cut-off, except through individual contacts, from the founding group.

No one enjoys splitting a group because of size. Alongside the generous advice in newsletters for those who come after, members have reported how, after two years recovering from the first upheaval, they face the same trauma again.

Of course it is easier to turn inwards, to put a limit on numbers, to become a cosy clique rather than offering mental stimulus for anyone who seeks it – a possibility that appals those who watch out for the health of the NHR – including the founder. Also the size of the membership is no gauge for the condition of a group. Rather the signs are when hostess volunteers fall off because of the cramming problem, when no one is quite sure of who other members are, especially newcomers, so that the personal and welcoming aspect is lost; when publicity is slack because new members cannot be dealt with; when everyone is drawing back from the organising job because it has become formidable, and everyone is turning a blind eye to the impending crisis of sheer numbers.

The first national advisory leaflet on how to handle growth was issued in 1971. The current one (late seventies) emphasises a democratic decision with two meetings, one to talk it out and a second for conclusions after time for thought. Flexibility is emphasised so that members do not feel they have been cast out by their friends, through some geographical or other random form of selection, such as names drawn from a hat, but can continue to attend the first group until they get roots in the new one. Since friendships are the bloodstream of NHR no one calls the splitting of groups an easy option. Various methods of splitting, culled from over the years, are suggested. But the leaflet 'How to cope with Success' recognises that, in rural areas, a big group in a town can be a focal point for isolated members particularly through 'interest' groupings. Members wanting to get out of the house can partake according to their needs: coffee mornings with children, coffee evenings without, book, theatre, music, badminton, swimming, bridge groups, social evenings, lectures, debates. In short a service for the otherwise domestically tied, in the NHR tradition. There are even those who, in all honesty, only want to utilise the baby-sitting facilities.

Maybe the breaking away and the setting up of new groups was in full flood in the seventies. Now the trend tends to setting up an additional group with the help of the existing one, perhaps with a few members switching according to travel/distance, convenience, and with some combined arrangements for a period since splitting has not always been that successful.

Plus ça change

Twenty years on and the contentions, the organisational problems, the views on what NHR is about, still surge to the surface, mirrored in the newsletter. The spring 1980 examples: a consistently expanding group's committee thrashed out a splitting system according to national recommendations, only to have it rejected by the members, who divided successfully when the Organiser went into one room and those who joined her indicated how they would re-form; the gently imposed ban on baby talk in a dwindling group revived it to the stage of increasing membership and having real discussions, not just personal anecdotes. The programme of another included a gourmet evening, with each contributing a dish and, on a different occasion, some members prepared briefs and others formed a jury to attempt to determine the identity of Jack the Ripper. Yet another group, which innocently tried a coffee morning and got swamped with small children, now runs a creche one-morning-a-week where mothers can stay if they choose or take the chance of a break from child caring.

VII
The Register Builders:
Lesley Taylor 1964–67

LESLEY TAYLOR – now reverted to maiden name Shooter – tells the story of her years as National Organiser:

I think I must have been the only applicant when Brenda Prys Jones appealed for a successor because she wrote back: 'I must admit I had been making vague plans for (a) persuading someone (who?) to do it or (b) winding up the whole thing if the worst came to the worst.'

In subsequent letters my offer was accepted and strictly on the understanding that *no way* did I use the Register as a political or religious platform. Points to be continually stressed were that the Register must maintain absolute independence; that the original concept emphasised 'avoidance of cabbagery' rather than the possession of young children, thus membership was open to all who felt *mentally* housebound regardless of age or status; that the Register is a self-help organisation (not a series of women's clubs) existing to provide friendships for intelligent women and a chance to exchange views on anything *but* domestic topics.

Practical tips included how to get free publicity by writing to the press to introduce myself; where best to place paid adverts to bring in regular enquiries; to find a local duplicating agency so that I had a good stock of leaflets ready; give up running the local group; how the newsletter was produced; having a road atlas for reference; and what to do with the money when it arrived. The funds were actually transferred by means of a cheque fastened into the middle of the cash book Brenda sent me.

I was a London University graduate, marrying as soon as I qualified at the end of the fifties. By 1963, having briefly taught science in a small public school, I was living on an estate in a village outside Doncaster where my husband John, an engineer, was working. Life seemed bliss, neat house, new baby (Sean), big

The Register Builders: Lesley Taylor 1964–67

woolly dog to walk. But by the autumn of that year I was beginning to feel the need of something more. Enquiries revealed that an external degree (in Psychology) would take five years. Then I read an advert about the Register and wrote to Brenda.

We got a really good group going in Bawtry and talked about all and everything. One of the original dozen is still my closest friend. It was just what a group should be. I volunteered to run the Register, as I explained to members in the November 1964 newsletter:

> In a fit of enthusiasm, bolstered by a general feeling of uselessness... My offer was motivated by two reasons – a very selfish desire to do something useful in this world and a feeling, shared no doubt by you all, that this organisation is so very worthwhile that it should not be allowed to fold for want of a central organiser.

However, soon after I had volunteered to be the National Organiser – and received the 'office' by post, one card index box and a file of correspondence which Brenda assured me was sorted largely according to the same system presented to her by Maureen Nicol – I became pregnant again and my husband took a job which meant he would be living away from home. With his agreement I moved back to the familiarity of my home town to be near my parents and old friends, which is how the NO's address came to be Bakewell, Derbyshire.

In that same first newsletter, edited by Jose Newmark, I also set out my philosophy:

> I do not intend making any radical changes – unless, of course, they are motivated by you, the members. Some of you are wondering just who is eligible for membership, just how literally 'housebound' should be taken. Personally I feel that the problem is mental rather than physical and that anyone who is enthusiastic and can benefit from the Register should be allowed to join – whether they be literally housebound or returned to full-time employment.

When I took over the Register I was fortunate in having the results of Brenda's survey seeking information and opinions. To summarise: 127 of the 168 questionnaires sent out were returned by August 1964. There were over 3,000 members, 2,277 in groups, 595 'isolated and fringe members' and an estimate of 246 for those not replying, mainly recruited through personal introduction and national publicity, the latter strongly considered to be the only means of reaching those most in need, lonely housebound mothers. Twice yearly newsletters were favoured with the main emphasis on news of groups, followed closely by reports on our progress, and information on 'good causes', etc. Original articles got the smallest proportion of support which was fortunate because they proved very hard to come by.

That survey, reproduced in the same late 1964 newsletter, was accompanied by what was probably the first Register statement of accounts, compiled by Brenda, and covering 1 May 1963 to 1 May 1964.

	£	s.	d.
Income from subscriptions	117	18	3
Expenditure			
Production and despatch of Newsletters	34	4	6
Production of National Register & supplement	4	6	9
Postage	10	10	11
Stationery	3	18	3
Advertising	34	9	0
Production of explanatory leaflets (mainly for new enquirers but also sent on request to organisers for local use)	8	2	6
	95	11	11
Balance	22	6	4

There had been considerable discussion over several newsletters regarding the amount of subscription needed to meet costs at both local and national levels. It had been decided to set this at an overall five shillings a year. Of this sufficient could be retained to cover local essential expenses, the rest to be sent to the National Organiser. This 'rest' was to be *at least* 1s. 6d. a head, which was sufficient to cover the newsletters and basic running expenses. This arrangement – open to constant criticism – relied on close-knit groups with low local expenses 'swelling' National funds so that national advertising and literature could be increased to help less fortunate, more wide-spread groups and isolated members. There were those who objected to this altruistic approach, but surely it reflected the ideals of the Register?

The financial account reveals that the Register was always run on a shoe-string.

I hate handling other people's money and I am very bad at keeping accounts. The first problem I came up against was where to keep the money. I could not get a bank account because I was treasurer, organiser, secretary in one and there was no one to countersign the cheques. The Post Office was not so particular, or far more trusting, depending on how you look at it. In fact the Post Office came to play a large part in my life.

Large bills had to wait while money was withdrawn by a 'Crossed Warrant' and petty cash came out of my purse, being ultimately replenished by cashing stray Postal Orders. It was all somewhat haphazard, as was the arrival of subscriptions, but it worked quite nicely.

The files lived in my kitchen cupboards. The card index, 'The Register', was about 4" × 5" × 18" and contained a card for each group with the name and address of the current local organiser. At the back were the names and addresses of isolated individual enquirers. The aim was for these to gradually move into the front section as they established their own groups in previously untapped areas. There were also one or two County Organisers still in existence, a relic from the beginning. Hertfordshire still functioned as a county unit. Cheshire groups maintained close links – a reflection of the origins of the Register in Manchester suburbia. Their retained enthusiasm for inter-group activities generated the first national conference.

I also inherited a file of correspondence which swelled over the next three years. I kept everything except straightforward enquiries which could be answered with an existing group and in time passed them to my successor. In retrospect I suppose I should also have kept copies of my replies. Never having worked in an office this simply did not occur to me although I believe I did annotate incoming letters to indicate what my response was – but really I just answered everything as I had always answered personal correspondence. There was a standard leaflet outlining the origin, aims, mechanics of the organisation which I sent to enquirers who were lucky enough to live in an area where there was an established group. On top of that I scribbled a 'thank you for enquiring' plus the name of their local organiser. Where there was no established group I used to write a personal letter suggesting that they would perhaps like to start a group locally, with some details on how to do this, plus the names of any previous enquirers from the area. There was also an ever increasing, self-perpetuating, background of continual correspondence with established members, news, views and general chit-chat.

Jose Newmark was editing the newsletter when I took over (3,500 copies duplicated) but immediately had to retire. Sheila Partington wrote in enquiring whether there was a group in her new neighbourhood, mentioned she was a journalist, and found herself being offered the job of editing the newsletter.

The material for the 'job', including practical suggestions on how to cope with it, was dropped off at my door one Sunday tea-time by Jose, a vivacious gliding enthusiast, and was quickly posted off before Sheila had time for second thoughts but it as quickly bounced back again after only one issue as Sheila's circumstances changed. When she had to relinquish the editorship I had no idea who to pressgang into producing the next issue so I was really forced into having a 'bash' myself. It really turned out not to be all that onerous and had the advantage of making me 'stock-take' at least twice a year. In many ways it saved a lot of duplicated energy and allowed the newsletter to truly reflect the current 'pulse' of the organisation as seen through members' own letters.

But for the National Organiser to also edit the newsletter increased the isolation and the dangers inherent in any monopoly. The NO was the sole national figure with absolutely no controlling committee. Fortunately the members were not slow to express their views to me personally and it was these people who were interested enough in the NHR to put pen to paper or hand to phone whose views really determined its slow evolution. But it was this monopoly of power which made me think carefully and decide that three years was long enough for any one person to stay in office.

The newsletter really wrote itself. It was the sole communication between myself and every individual member. Contents followed the lines favoured in Brenda's questionnaire and consisted basically of snippets from members' letters. Original articles simply did not materialise but members' views on a wide diversity of topics were sufficiently controversial to provoke altercations which reverberated through several issues.

To photostat instead of duplicate and staple into an eight page booklet, instead of having separate sheets, was suggested by local printers and tried as an experiment in October 1965. It met with approval; subsequent editions were printed. It was always an exciting moment when the phone rang to tell me I could collect the newsletter, literally off the press, still smelling of printers' ink, often still being stapled. Wrapping and despatching was something else. All that counting out, sticking up, putting in piles of equal numbers, taking a sample to weigh and price so I knew what stamps to buy. The backroom boys at the GPO used to bring out a skip for me as I arrived with bootload after bootload.

The first posters got printed too, both suggested and designed by a member's husband, which I offered at 2½d each. Organisers of new groups got three, free with a supply of leaflets on who we were and what we did.

The Register Builders: Lesley Taylor 1964–67   61

Recruitment and publicity tended to look after itself though talking to journalists was a strange experience (Mary Stott wrote an article in the *Guardian* that did us proud, but a recorded interview for the 'Today' programme was abortive since three major stories broke overnight). I advertised in the quality press at least four times a year, several adverts at a time. These brought in a steady background of enquiries. But far more productive were articles in magazines, usually sparked off by individual members who rarely thought to warn me in advance.

The hairiest time I had coincided with the birth of my daughter on 1 March 1965. Judith Beattie wrote to *The Observer* voicing her intention to set up a Register for mentally frustrated graduate wives. Told of our existence she turned her energies to directly supporting us. My ten days in the local maternity home turned into a marathon. Every afternoon, instead of the prescribed rest, my bed became an office. Hundreds of enquiries poured in, building up to 160 in a single post, and that despite Sheila Partington's volunteering her name and address to *Observer* readers to lighten the load. My parents brought it in. The staff took it out. If the hospital had not been so helpful, and turned a *very* blind eye, I would have been 'drowned'. Can you imagine returning home with a new baby, with a toddler just two, and hundreds and hundreds of letters piled up behind the door?

My 'office' spent many hours in hospital. Sean developed osteomyelitis in the late summer of 1966 and had several spells in hospital over the next three years. When he was in I got up at six a.m., spent about an hour at my parents' who were looking after Siobhan, drove twelve miles to have breakfast with son Sean at eight, stayed until he went to sleep around nine p.m., drove back to my parents' for another hour with Siobhan, and then home to open the day's post and roll into bed. Correspondence went backwards and forwards with me. It also moved around the country, Bawtry to Bakewell, with several months in Redcar and Glasgow as I attempted to accommodate my husband's job changes whilst still maintaining a permanent base – to which I was eventually confined by Sean's illness.

I did not go out and about meeting members. For one thing this did not seem to be expected – no one asked me to – and for another my domestic problems would not have allowed for this, but I did inadvertently meet a fairly wide scattering of members. I began the group in Bawtry and attended Doncaster meetings. I began the group in Bakewell and, during my short spell on Teesside, yet another. Moving to Glasgow I attended meetings there. I also visited groups within easy distance from home, Sheffield, Chesterfield, Buxton, the Cheshire Forum (an annual gathering of Cheshire Register groups).

I think it was as a result of my visit to Buxton that the idea of a national gathering emerged. This was probably the only real legacy I left for 'future generations'. I floated the idea in the spring 1966 newsletter, it met with general approval, so I gave the go-ahead to the North Manchester group who had offered to organise it. I drove to Buxton on the Saturday morning in March 1967 as ignorant of what to expect as the majority of members who attended, naively noteless.

The weekend was a resounding success. Until then the only exchange of ideas had been through the newsletter. For the first time members from all over the country had a chance to meet and talk, and talk, and the *relief* to find out that we really were a homogeneous lot, that groups really were similar in problems, activities and aims, despite the tenuousness of the network which was the essential factor retaining the non-organisational character which we prize. The Register actually did work.

The other thing that emerged with great clarity from that first conference, was, that we were not prepared to be used. Reporting the conference for *The Sunday Times* Moira Keenan focused attention on this aspect. She noted that there was no machinery for gathering opinion and making our voice heard, commented that non-organisation can be 'a weakness as well as a strength', and inferred that, not just the machinery, but the desire to influence matters closely concerning young parents, abortion, drug addiction, under-fives, was missing.

In the account of the conference for the newsletter produced by a member (a custom still retained) the question was posed: 'Should we be a pressure group? Decidedly NOT. We *must* maintain our freedom of outlook and thought and remain uncommitted. There is no bar on individuals or groups campaigning if they so wish but we have neither the machinery nor the *wish* to use our members to pressure in any one direction – and this does *not* reflect lethargy – whatever *The Sunday Times* may hint!' The same newsletter carried an account of a vigorous and successful campaign by the Great Yarmouth Group to improve local children's playgrounds!

One of the appealing features of the NHR is the freedom to embrace all opinions. I did 'stretch' what might have been called the rules if we had had any when I had to make a very quick decision and, after contacting several members by phone, decided to release a copy of the actual Register of local groups to Diane Munday – not so that she could claim our support – but so that she could notify each group directly and rapidly of the need to lobby their MPs immediately if they wished to support the Abortion Law Reform Bill. There was no time to tell everyone via the newsletter; to have sent out a special circular would have looked like a national directive, however carefully couched. No one objected but it did cause me some mental discomfort.

I was always acutely sensible of my duties to members, never more so as my self-allotted three years drew to a close. I was well aware of the hole it would leave in my life but that was no reason to hang on to something which must not be allowed to stagnate, must be given room to grow and evolve beyond one person's ideals. Membership was over five thousand. A survey by the Congleton group, based on 160 groups – approximately half the total number – showed that growth was accelerating; 25 per cent of the answering groups had been formed in 1966.

The Register had been entrusted to me by Brenda – now it was my turn to entrust it to someone else. Despite constant hints in the newsletter there was no rush to volunteer. My friend Deirdre Collins, a Grantham member, told me of Jane Watt and I trusted her judgement. I drove over to see her to explain personally what the job entailed. I met a quiet, gentle, unassuming Scot, with a home permeated by home-made bread and loving warmth. I knew the Register would be safe with her and her family. So one day she came and took it away.

Before handing over I borrowed an adding machine and spent *all* one day frantically trying to balance the books (a little red cash book actually) over the entire three years. When hysteria subsided I had an answer which satisfied me in that it was recurring and 'felt right' and it owed me seven pounds! That was exactly the cost of a set of Victorian kitchen barrels I fancied, so I bought them as a thank-you present to me. I never feel anything but pleasure when I look at them so my sums must have been correct otherwise I am sure I would feel guilt.

The accounts, showing that income from subscriptions had risen to £406 pounds but expenses to £356 pounds, went out on what must have been one of the first circulars (an alternative to the printed newsletter) in August 1967 telling of the handover to Jane and continuing: 'Running NHR helped me to forget domestic cares and gave me stability and awareness of other people's problems when I needed both'.

I continued to attend local meetings and subsequent national conferences in London and Harrogate. The London one I remember because I slept in the room next to the one I had as a student. I had to chair the opening session because the anticipation and journey had proved too much for Jane, and I received a very handsome 'thank you' cheque* about which I knew absolutely nothing. Three weeks later John and I flew to Paris for the weekend. But that was not a magic wand. So I took stock and began to plan for a future alone. In 1969 on my thirtieth birthday I began a degree course in Psychology at Sheffield University.

All contact with the NHR had gone before I went to Sheffield. I returned briefly to teaching but was working in an office when in 1975 the phone rang; it was Lesley Moreland, one of Jane's successors in office, with the shattering news of Jane's death. I had drifted so far away. Perhaps it was this very detachment which allowed me to write her obituary when those who were more able, but had suffered with her, could not. That was my last service to the Register but not its last service to me.

---

* Another custom which has continued through the years.

VIII
The Link

IT MAY SURPRISE some members to hear that there are *two* national channels of communication; the circulars and the *Newsletter*. The first circular seems to have been sent out by National Organiser Lesley Taylor in 1967 and told members of the transfer of that national office to Jane Watt.

Few of the earlier (duplicated then as now) circulars have survived in a movement that did not see itself as an organisation and, therefore, was not archive-minded; they got thrown out when erstwhile Local Organisers moved house. The first 'Archivist' (Margaret Cameron) in the late seventies told me that the records she had managed to assemble – circulars, press cuttings and the like – fitted easily into an ordinary drawer in her home!

It is one of the unexplainable aspects of NHR that not all members see the circulars. A national officer of the late seventies, aware of the time and effort that goes into producing circulars, ruefully described her visit to a local group: 'The Local Organiser announced that a circular had been received from HQ' (which needs interpretation as the National Organiser functioning in her own home) 'but contains nothing of interest for us'. Some LOs do not even inform members of the arrival of the one or two copies of this publication sent out to all groups. Through the years the plaintive request from National Organisers that all members should get a chance to read the circulars has been frequent and ineffective. No one has come up with a solution to this gap in communication.

Yet circulars are rich in information about current events such as national meetings, local ones, conferences, talks, courses, (both NHR and external) on a breadth of subjects and problems.

Apart from providing a constantly supplemented bank of information on a number of interests, problems, contacts, that would find a target among such a body of women, I doubt if any member who does not conscientiously read the circulars can regard herself as conversant with, and therefore equipped to make a valid comment on, the organisation as a whole. The circulars reveal the fabric, which is of course made up of many unexpected threads: the hazard of aggressive phone calls or letters to Local Organisers who display their private numbers and addresses for publicity purposes; the potential members who hit the smug rejecting wall of a group that is 'full'.

At national level too, because that is where the circulars come from, you hear of the structure, changes of personalities, problems financial and organisational, what is going adrift and needs remedying. The signs of national changes in a mushrooming organisation were in the 1972 circulars and, later in that decade, the thinking that led to those who offered or were asked to be National Organisers being replaced by the first voted for National Group, and later yet again, by 1980, the first postal ballot for national officers.

The message: read the circulars sent to your group as well as your own personal copy of the *Newsletter*.

In all honesty the *Newsletter* must be described as the only functioning link between all members. It is their right by payment of membership fees and its cost absorbs a large proportion of that fee – even with economies like precisely planned delivery arrangements such as getting brick-shaped wrapped batches to any meetings and conferences for collection and further distribution by attenders. If the local Post Office brought out a skip for Lesley Taylor in the sixties, the 1971 despatch filled a Post Office van from floor to ceiling. Today the National Organiser has a tight check (in co-operation with the Treasurer) on the receipt of the contemporarily correct fees before the appropriate number go into those wrappings, with the appropriate group address.

As with any other self-help, just-off-the-ground, organisation, Maureen Nicol's first *Newsletters*, which were sent to her appointed 'organisers' were duplicated sheets. Her successor Brenda Prys Jones continued that homely (but never on that account to be under-estimated) production method. Hers were edited by Jose Newmark and Pat Roberts and were available to every 'paid-up' member. She also initiated a pattern, backed by a sixties survey, *still sustained*, of a twice yearly issue led by information from national level but primarily about local experience and containing anything and everything members want to write about, within or without the movement.

I have been fascinated, reading twenty years of *Newsletters*, to note how often a woman concerned enough to write a contribution, either about her own group-forming experience, or on some aspect of the movement, or on life as it affects women, has turned up later as a national officer or strong supporter of the network, e.g. a national conference organiser.

The 1965 issue was the first professionally printed newsletter. National Organiser, Lesley Taylor, was also again the editor.

The autumn 1969 issue (from Jane Watt) did not appear till 1970 as Local Organisers' order forms were late and in spring 1970 she issued only a 'mini-newsletter' because of the avalanche of publicity surrounding the first decade of NHR. But in spring 1971 there was again no issue either, owing to shortage of funds combined with a protracted postal strike. However around that time, with a partnership instead of a single National Organiser doing the lot, Lesley Moreland initiated a new format with a map so the whereabouts and expanding coverage of groups could be traced.

The current format, each with distinctively coloured covers, was initiated in spring 1975 (the map soon replaced by lists) by the then joint NO, Pat Williams. There is even a convenient stiff binder of the correct size today.

Pat took soundings through a questionnaire. Most members were happy with the *Newsletter*, the main complaint being about small print, close-packed pages and dull cover, while still asking for more of everything, an economic problem which Pat tackled with 'landscape', that is longer in width than in height and split into two columns instead of one solid page. Other comments cancelled each other out: 'The group feel we should keep the NL as our own personal mag. rather than have too much outside interest' contrasted with the '*Newsletter* could be more outward looking'. Members thought there were a lot of talented members who could write 'short stimulating pieces' to promote discussion. Typically Pat retorted in print that she was expecting to be inundated with 'short stimulating pieces'. Meantime in the new-style issue she went for controversial contributions. 'Have we done enough, not enough or too much for the African?'; 'One view of Women's Liberation' seen as 'grey-faced, shrill-voiced, bra-burning, banner-toting, pamphleteering and sexually promiscuous cohorts'; and, one of a series of articles that appear from time to time reviewing a specific publication, *She* magazine was summed up as 'the undemanding magazine for the little woman, with handy hints on her cooking, knitting and sewing, pretty views for her kitchen wall, a simpering sense of naughtiness and no danger of strain to the intellect'.

With the emergence of the first National *Group* in 1976 the editing job became one person's responsibility, Hazel Bell, who in fact wrote that review of *She*. Yet another example of the premise that if you raise your head above the crowd you will find yourself doing a whole lot of other jobs. I owe personal thanks to Hazel for the first index of the *Newsletter* without which I would still be groping about muttering to myself that surely I saw a reference to this or that somewhere through the twenty years. She is, coincidentally, editor of *The Indexer*.

Looking back, Hazel goes 'cold' thinking how little she knew, when taking on the job, leaning on friendly printers for the first issues: 'Can you make this more conspicuous please?' rather than 'Use 12 pt bold caps with two-line space underneath'. Her worst moment was when her first NL was nearly ready and at the printers she saw every enormous machine churning out stacks of NLs. 'The responsibility, financial as well as to NHR for content, seemed terrifying. Suppose subs collection mechanism went wrong and we couldn't pay?'. She hardly dared look at the first copy.

She feels no one as inexperienced as she was then should have been entrusted with an enterprise costing so much money as well as so important for NHR. Her 'job specification' as given at the 1980 'Workshop' for potential new National Group members (described in chapter XX) went something like this.

Copy arrives constantly. Read: amend if necessary; give headings; estimate printed length. Write to author, send copy to National Organiser. Decide which section it will go in, list. If revised or abbreviated send author new version. Retype or xerox if not enough copies sent, or not typed, or too revised.

By the copy dates (6 Jan, 6 July) estimate total to hand, chase what is late, consider balance of contents, make final selection and arrangement, mark up for printer (type sizes, headings) amend list of groups on cover.

One week is allowed for correcting galley proofs, sending to major authors, arranging into pages and order, cutting up and pasting the 'mock-up', selecting 'fillers' for spaces left. Only five days are allowed for final checking of page proofs, passing for press and delivery instructions, that is to say the labels from the National Organiser bearing Local Organisers' addresses with the numbers to go into each parcel which are also coded to indicate whether they go by post or other means. Full postal distribution would add an enormous bill so conferences and arranged meetings of Local Organisers are always a distribution point.

Apart from an early one hundred copies to the editor, which she sends out to contributors, book publishers, holders of copyright quoted, statutory bodies, around six thousand copies are still delivered to the editor's home to be fed into this self-help distribution system. All must be recorded and accounted for, and expenses claimed.

A long way from Maureen Nicol running off newsletters on a borrowed and ageing duplicator!

The *Newsletter* reveals NHR. The pattern of the movement's development and of members' concerns are within its pages.

Taken that membership is largely among women with some form of training and careers interrupted by caring for children, it provides a specialised bank of information (for filing for later use, not for discarding) on the return to paid employment, updating, re-thinking, re-training, the openings, the courses and the kind of jobs that can be fitted into school hours.

Not surprisingly, any issues that interlink in any way with the 'to work or not to work' controversy – considering members' domestic responsibilities – stir them to write in. A bristly exchange in 1980 emanated from a Surrey member who castigated members for demeaning other women by employing them to do their housework while they themselves went back to work. It was 'perpetuating the class system' and 'all housewives are now equal'. Under attack, including comparisons of rates and conditions for such work with others that might be open, she retaliated that such women were still being exploited because of their financial conditions and she expected, when she returned to work, that her family would share the domestic workload!

But the sustained agonising circles round what happens to the children who are not old enough for school.

A Stockport mother in 1974, 'getting depressed and restless', wrote about being offered a job as a social worker after an interview which went into how she would cope with childminding and domestic problems. She felt that such an attitude was something which married women will 'have to put up with until we are adequately equipped with good day nurseries and nursery schools, and the climate of public opinion about mothers working has changed'. She set out her expedients: collection from playgroup fell down and the vacancy in a local private day nursery left her bothered about who was actually caring for her son. The saga carried on with a friend minding mostly and her mother partly. A whole group in Chester chose to mull over that contribution and concluded that it was the 'ultimate deterrent' to working, and that seeking employment before making child care arrangements was hardly the way to change 'the climate of public opinion about working mothers'.

To campaign or not to campaign

The plea for campaigning, as a body, for facilities for under-fives regularly turns up. As far back as 1966 a woman, prescribed part-time work as the 'cure' under psychiatric treatment, declared 'we would be better for our children as part-time mums than full-time lunatics'. She pleaded for a nation-wide membership campaign for nursery education.

More recently, in 1979, a Buckinghamshire member, aware the Register is not a pressure group, still wrote that, in the forthcoming International Year of the Child, good pre-school facilities was the 'one single important issue on which we could do something worth-while'. She got two reactions. A Marple member suggested that Register mothers stop moaning about what the authorities should be doing and do something themselves, like starting their own playgroups. She raised the question whether women, who do not need to financially support the family, are not being pressurised to return to full time paid work to provide the luxuries, 'the jam'. The writer considered that: 'if a mother is willing to take her role seriously then her child will not suffer from the lack of pre-school education'. She found the educational cuts on schooling more important than the lack of nursery education.

Another member, from Lancashire, asked how, considering NHR structure, lacking meetings of chosen delegates to vote on resolutions, anyone could determine members' opinions. The means of campaigning for causes, she wrote, lay in other organisations.

In twenty years of *Newsletters* it is possible to trace how what started rather as an undefined feeling, that the Register as such did not campaign, gradually became the unwritten code.

In the sixties National Organiser Lesley Taylor explained that, since a special circular would have looked like a directive, she had released Register addresses to an abortion law campaigning member so that she could approach them directly for support. In the seventies alarmed Local Organisers complained in the *Newsletter* about a national circular suggesting that members should write to their MPs concerning the Dock Work Regulation Bill. They felt this action transgressed the unwritten code that the Register did not voice an opinion.

Pat Williams, part of the responsible though by then retired national partnership which circulated it, replied at length that the circular was internal, not public, and that she was not in the habit of publicising information only on her own political leanings through the Register (as correspondents suggested), that the Register was by then safeguarded against national or local members behaving detrimentally against its objectives. She concluded by asking why individual members were 'so fearful of standing up to be counted' through the normal democratic process.

Not that the question ever really rests. That the Register should back one specially important issue (with nominations like breast cancer as well as the ubiquitous child care) has frequently been raised.

In the early seventies an exchange developed, started by Frances Alexander of High Wycombe, who had been talking to her Women's Institute member mother, on whether there should be an NHR Delegate Conference 'where a corporate voice may evolve'. She imagined the effect on a Secretary of State of massed members' expressed opinions on issues relevant to women. 'If our mums can do it in the WI, can't we in the NHR?' she concluded.

She got more *Newsletter* space to express her personal regret that 'we could not stand up as a body and say we felt that, for instance, smaller classes in primary schools are essential for the better education of our children, or that the overall service given by the gas industry leaves much to be desired'. She took the opportunity to look at NHR as a whole and the need for some democratic say in how the organisation is 'run'. She was horrified to hear that each National Organiser got only £250 per annum, less than £5 a week. For that level of work and responsibility she calculated a salary of £2000 a year in industry. A secretary, if employed, would be paid more than the Organisers. Allying lethargy about the true cost of the organisation with lethargy at local level (poorly attended meetings when members rather than outside speakers provided the stimulating effect) Frances reverted to a national conference in which taking decisions 'might weld us as a group'. She thought that 'it would take us from the realms of being a local natter group and help us to feel part of a movement of intelligent women who are able to give of themselves to their local group, to the national organisation, and to all womankind'. She got little support on her primary theme.

Through the years, in individual members' letters when the question has surfaced yet again, even in reports of full-scale group meetings to discuss whether NHR should be a pressure group, the attitude which emerged after the first national conference of 1967 still prevails. Important issues are examined at meetings, often rousing strong feelings, but the bulk of those expressing their opinions in the *Newsletter* maintain that members who want to effect changes should join other organisations or start their own. Which they frequently do. The *Newsletter* is also a record of members' personal participation in, or commitment to, any number of causes at international, national or district level.

Stuck with the name

The name of the organisation has also been mulled over within the *Newsletter* – maybe surprising outsiders rather than members. 'We really ought to think up a name for this organisation' Maureen Nicol wrote in her first newsletter. 'Would Housebound Wives Register be suitable or not sufficiently enlightening?' She carried on heading her outgoing link in the first few editions with 'Liberal-Minded Housebound Wives Register' though there are still those who always remember it without capitals, as in the original letter.

Legend has it that Maureen herself questioned the more serious connotations of 'housebound'. She cannot recall expressing such an opinion except in correspondence and thinks it was just one of those many things that just 'happened' with the Register. As a gratifying sidelight, women truly housebound by disablement have maintained their lively minds through groups arranging their physical transport to meetings. Adrienne White, severely disabled by a stroke in her thirties, testified in a 1977 *Newsletter*: 'I have a lot to thank NHR for'. She had addressed a group about her previous job for ten minutes 'without running out of breath'.

The second National Organiser, Brenda Prys Jones, started off with National Register of Housewives and carried on as National Housewives Register. The third, Lesley Taylor, even wandered back to Housebound Housewives Register. But once she went into professional printing in 1965 the name steadied. Not that it is not questioned from that day to this. In *her* day a Billericay member found it 'offputting', smacking of regimentation and school. The 1969 national conference, taking a hard look at the organisation, also looked at the name, mostly thinking it 'gave quite an erroneous impression', reported National Organiser and NL Editor Jane Watt. Nothing new emerged in replacement except 'Cabbage Club' though quite a few liked the idea of the 'Cornelian Society' (see chapter XII) like the group in Edinburgh, named after the distinguished and intellectual Roman matron of that name. Jane concluded that National Housewives Register should be retained, since it was known, and to use the initials more.

The well worn and perennial discussion on the name popped up again in 1974 because of two consumer advice groups, the National Housewives Trust and National Housewives Association. Organisers had to admit 'we have no copyright on our name'. A member in Halesowen reacted tartly:

> The question of a name change crops up regularly at each annual conference and, just as regularly, the same old answers are trotted out 'We are well known as we are'. 'Well known?' – by whom one is tempted to ask. Ideally NHR should be so well known that it appeals to potential members before the need for mental stimulation becomes desperate and we have to call ourselves the Society for Neurotic Housebound Reactionaries.

Frances Healey of Winchester took the horns of this long-term dilemma in 1976 as she explained: because of the confusion with other similar names, because 'housewife' emphasised what the Register was getting away from 'not from being a housewife as such but from the price of bacon syndrome', and because 'on top of it all it doesn't even run particularly smoothly off the tongue'.

She started with small reactions but, with the major organisational change, the emergence of the first National Group of which she was a member, declared that 'I think that now – when we have reached a new point in our national organisation – is the time when the UK NHR should make up its mind whether NHR is the right name or a change would be beneficial'. She quoted groups abroad with different names like the National Women's Register in South Africa, Women in Touch in Australia, and asked members whether they minded 'sounding like a list of char-women' and asked if the name reflected 'what we are'.

She listed six suggestions garnered from comments: NHR, National Women's Register, Meeting Point, Minerva, Women in Touch, NKS – Not the Kitchen Sink. A voting slip was provided in the *Newsletter*. She got a good response in Register terms – people appreciating the chance to vote. 1,600 voted, representing 300 groups.

Most, Frances Healey had to report in 1977, could raise little enthusiasm for the choices offered but confessed again to no other ideas. Typical reactions were: Meeting Point, though technically right, sounded too religious, Women in Touch too lesbian, NWR too like a railway, Minerva too blue-stocking. Interestingly Scotland and the East of England gave a majority vote for Meeting Point and that appeared as the close second to National Housewives Register in the South and South East.

So NHR it stayed.*

Editor Hazel Bell took the chance to raise interest in a distinctive title for the *Newsletter* which otherwise 'seems both stodgy and inaccurate'. She put up suggestions like Grapevine, Woman Alive, Symposium, Open Forum. It carries on still without its very own title, just National *Newsletter*.

Age

Yet another issue which inexorably reappears in the *Newsletter* is that of age, the age of members. It needs to be considered in the perspective of the original concept, a break for women at home with young children, rather than the total impact (for some) of the thought that women might wish to keep their minds in trim regardless of their current circumstances.

'We were approached by a welfare worker,' a Banstead member's letter, published in 1965, reported, 'on behalf of two widows who felt they were were too young for the Over Sixty Club and the WI was not cultural enough for their taste. Knowing how a mind of sixty is often as stimulating as one of thirty we have invited them to try us'.

One subject discussed at the 1968 annual conference was reported in the *Newsletter*, for comment:

> A point was raised that older members whose children have grown up must not be asked to leave. So long as a woman is lively-minded she should be welcome. Many older members said that, despite the fact that they had returned to their professions, they still wanted to be members of the Register. They said that it helps people who need extra stimulation and the older women have a special contribution to make.

However, the autumn issue carried a few lines from a Worthing member:

> The idea that we should use the slogan 'For the lively-minded younger woman' was put forward at our meeting recently. In predominantly retired areas like this the assumption inevitably is that the Register is a club for lonely old people.

In 1971 a potential group founder reported: 'We have had two

---

* I heard of a new member in 1978 who reported that to her husband NHR conjured up a picture of militant women pressing for payment for housework and weekends off.

meetings and they have not been very successful, the response being quite poor. It was pointed out that maybe more people would be interested if there wasn't the age barrier in theory of 40 years.' (She was referring to the publicity spiel that most members were 'aged between twenty-five and forty'. That had been dropped by 1973 when another tentative new group reported an enquiry from a grandmother who, welcomed, enthralled them with an account of her part-time job as a social worker.) 'I do feel,' wrote an Earley member, 'that older members keen enough to join often have far more to offer than those at the younger end of the scale', and in the same issue a Hedge End member mentioned that 'our older members say that NHR has greatly widened their knowledge of how the younger generation thinks while I feel the younger ones have gained in understanding by listening to the older ones'. The 'older ones' were in their forties!

In 1974 Hereford members expressed their guilt about not being 'a true NHR group', being part-time teachers and lecturers, though keen to emphasise that they were not 'a clique' excluding new members who might fit the original conception. But such gentleness had a sharp counterpoint in the very same newsletter, from Whitchurch and Pangbourne, who thought 'one should grow through NHR and go on to wider contacts than are possible, geographically, in the Floors and Nappies Stage'. Older members who had survived that stage were castigated as being unable to 'break the umbilical cord' and therefore depressing younger members and preventing free discussion of the 'here and now'. There was the suggestion for an annual party or 'other occasional meeting place for retired members' to retain contact so that the group was not dominated by those 'released from the pressures which sent them in the first place to NHR' or, alternatively, a subscription that covered the first five years 'then out'. A year later a Camberley member 'for more years than I care to remember', and wanting to continue, put up the thought that groups with members 'getting older' and others feeling 'they want to get their teeth into something' might work with their local group of the National Council of Women; possibly NHR, as a whole, even affiliating.

The question simmers on. It was fully faced in an article in 1976 under the title 'Growing Up' from Pat Hicklenton, Daphne Stacy and Jean Stirk. 'At the beginning members of NHR were mainly mothers with babies and young children. Now those people have "grown up" and the members of NHR have children of all ages. Does this mean' they asked that 'NHR no longer fulfils its purpose?

Or has the scope of NHR widened considerably beyond the bounds which it still happily fulfils? Have many Register groups broadened their activities to meet the needs of the increasingly expanding age range and needs of present and potential members?'

They had asked around a dozen groups in different parts of the country what the needs were and how they could be met. Most found that

> it is not only mothers with very young children who need the stimulation of NHR and a means of contact when they move house, but also the single women, women with grown up children, women whose children are away from home, and even women who have jobs. Some people need NHR for human contact with like-minded people when they move to a new area, or because their jobs do not provide sufficient mental stimulation, and some need NHR for the involvement which Register activities offer.

Most of the groups thought the needs were met but foresaw problems, with time, in having such an ever-widening range of members. The authors summarised these as unintentional domination by long-standing members which could lead to imbalance, stagnation, and maybe little attraction for new members. They put up ideas like differing (in times and content) meetings. They asked whether longstanding members wanted to 'grow out of NHR' or continue within a new framework within their local groups, or as a separate meeting – to rouse reaction. There was not that much.

But the subject was aired again in 1977 when two women, having been both overseas and UK members in their time, voiced ambivalent impressions of that year's national conference partly because they thought 'an outsider attending the conference might have felt that it was a slightly superior WI, with a smug middle-class membership who were growing old with NHR'. They found the average age at the conference high, 35–40, and asked: 'Are we growing old with NHR and setting ourselves up as a National Grannies Register? Are we not attracting younger members any more? Do we put younger members off – if so why?' They got a fast answer from a Lothian member on the practicalities of attending a conference when, like one of her group's mothers, twins had to be fed. But a Trowbridge member retorted, why not thirty-five to forty? She was older than when she joined and knew of NHR's original concept but asked:

> Surely we are able to accommodate those who still want a common meeting ground away from the domestic scene. Do you want NHR to remain exactly as it began? Or can we age gracefully, and as an organisation still help the older woman? I think we can – and should.

The spring 1980 *Newsletter* carried an extensive review of 'The Age Range within NHR' by Jean Stirk. She was then Chairman of the National Group and unusually knowledgeable about the Register's past (I owe her a personal debt for generously given advice and help) and the present, gained through extensive contact with members.

She opened with the quote: 'Age ... nor custom stale her infinite variety' and thought that could equally describe NHR members today. 'To be a thinking woman with an enquiring mind is a constant state'. She reviewed opinions, ranging from those who considered 'NHR is essentially a young mothers' world' and that a high proportion of long-standing members could lead to a 'closed-shop' policy, and the reverse, that a high proportion of younger members also leads to insularity and limitations in activities and discussion. She reminded readers that early publicity had been 'merely descriptive of NHR at that time' and how the original publicity about 'while bringing up small children' had long been replaced by 'lively-minded'. ('Just how one determines this criterion is a whole new ball-game' she added as an aside.)

She quoted Mary Stott, in the eighteenth birthday issue *Newsletter* of 1978: 'NHR has a built-in self-renewal factor, because women join at a period of their lives when they have a special need of contact with like-minded women.... NHR does not need "senior citizens".' And, in contrast, the warm testimonies from women with grown-up children, who had even retired before they discovered NHR, complemented by groups' tributes to the value of older members' contributions.

Jean argued that, because Maureen Nicol first proposed the Register when she happened to have two very young children, 'the image of a mother housebound with young children' became welded with that of a woman lacking and needing mental stimulation.

Jean's view was that 'Maureen was stating a more general need for the congenial company of other thinking women interested in a wide range of subjects, something a woman of any age may feel'. In yet another aside she added that Gill Vine, then National Organiser, 'anticipates writing to the *Guardian* in thirty years to say, "There must be many grannies like myself who feel the lack of ...".' But then, as Jean wrote, 'The debate continues'.

Other bodies

Another running debate concerns other womens' groups, largely to do with the differences. So under the riveting title NFWI-NUTG-NHR-BFUW-NCW, the spring 1980 *Newsletter* carried a report by

Anne Grant of a Camberley group's invitation to representatives of other 'wimmen's' organisations to join a discussion meeting. The origins of the National Federation of Women's Institutes and the National Union of Townswomen's Guilds were thought 'most interesting', the first springing from a meeting of women wishing to debate the desirability of extending the vote to women; the latter when a baby's death through its mother's ignorance stimulated local mothers to join together to improve their knowledge of baby care. The newer British Federation of University Women, the article explained, simply provides for women graduates and their needs, and the National Council of Women is concerned for the quality of women's lives.

It quickly emerged in discussion that NHR members saw membership of WI too as 'incompatible'. Did that mean that NHR members were 'guilty of intellectual snobbery'? Both WI and NUTG aim to provide education and opportunities for women to develop their own skills, the meeting heard. 'While crafts and domestic issues are popularly regarded as being their main preoccupation, this is not so'.

The difference, it was finally concluded, lies in the structure, the other four having hierarchy, built upwards from local branches into a large national body with 'rules, regulations and rigidity', particularly NCW, WI and NUTG, which, while wielding power from enormous membership, also 'extracts a price at grass-root level: the price paid is in the ability to change to meet new needs and to continue to attract new members'. Also NHR meets in homes, contributing, questioning, discussing issues, instead of merely attending, listening and going home from large meetings in halls. 'So,' summarised Anne Grant,

> thankfully, we can put aside the idea of intellectual snobbery and conclude that NHR's difference lies not just in excluding domestic issues from our programmes, but in retaining the real power and initiative of the movement within each individual group. It must be the structure that is fulfilling a real need, as I believe we have the fastest-growing membership of any of these women's organisations.

IX
The Register Builders:
Jane Watt: 1967–70

IN THE purple-covered *Newsletter* of spring 1976 the National Organisers Josephine Jaffray and Pat Williams wrote:

> We were deeply shocked to hear of the death of Jane Watt on 11 September 1975. Jane's contribution to the Register as National Organiser from 1967 to 1970 was immense. She faced the problem of a fast increasing membership together with a shortage of funds.

Her predecessor, Lesley Taylor added:

> I was told in the summer that Jane had cancer. It didn't seem real. I wanted to ring her but how does one . . . So I went on holiday, and came home, and got on with my own life. Yesterday I heard that she was dead. The unreal had become reality. I was asked to write a few words for the *Newsletter* but didn't feel qualified to do so. I cannot claim to have known Jane well although we shared the same experience. So I rang the mutual friend who had introduced us and who knew Jane so much better and asked her if she could write something instead. But she could not. Although five months had passed her death was still too near, the loss still too painful, there was still anger that it could have happened. So we talked of other things and gradually of Jane. She was never strong and the voluntary burden of running NHR would sometimes overtax her strength. But she cared. And under this care our organisation spread its wings and took off. It isn't easy for NOs to adjust when they retire. We gain so much from the experience that it's difficult to know what to do with one's new insights. Jane so wanted to become a social worker but her health precluded this. Instead she decided to write a book – about us. Not the string of funny anecdotes one might expect, but more a piece of research designed to help others. In particular she was hoping, perhaps inadvertently, to discover something of why some women find it so difficult to make friends in new surroundings. Much of the work is done. When Robert, her husband, is ready to handle something so very personal, perhaps one of us, who owe her so much, can complete what Jane was not allowed to finish. It is the very least we can do and what she would most want.

Jane's book remains unwritten but it seeded this one; in this manner.

I have long been involved with the Toy Libraries Association of which Lesley Moreland, one of Jane's successors, is the Director. Lesley was devoted to Jane and many times our conversations on NHR scanned the chances of getting the book published, as a memorial to her.

Only the tip of Jane's research appeared in the 1973 *Newsletter*. After 'retirement', working on government social surveys, Jane undertook a sample survey to find out why there was such a gap between those who wrote in and those who actually became members of NHR. The largest number had no group within reasonable (busing) distance, the second were put off by the intellectual image. About a fifth fell into two categories which Jane felt anxious about. One was lacking self-confidence: feeling poor in 'an affluent-seeming group'; feeling not sufficiently educated, with doubts about penetrating the closely-knit group. In the other category came the over-forties who felt 'too old and out of place'.

As the years passed Lesley and I accepted that Jane's research was becoming out of date and gradually our original idea merged into a different one, of telling the story of the Register itself. Put to dynamic Gill Vine, latter-day NO, it became what you hold in your hand.

Not wishing to intrude on her family,* Jane's part in the story is culled from archives and from her friends.

When she took over as NO she admitted in correspondence to me that, from Maureen Nicol's letter, she had pictured a strange woman standing on her doorstep declaring 'I'm like-minded'; not an endearing prospect. I confessed to the same image. In fact when Jane did decide to join she stood on Deirdre Collins' doorstep and afterwards compared notes on their mutual misgivings.

Jane admitted her initial 'cringe of horror' over the 'vision of someone knocking on a neighbour's door and saying "Hello, I'm your intellectual chum"', in an interview published in *The Yorkshire Post* in 1969 headed 'Think Tank for women in the suburbs'.

It was when the Watts lived in Bottesford near Nottingham that Jane Watt finally decided to enrol. 'I had come across more literature on the Register, about how it sharpened interests in things beyond the home, and I decided that I really had to do something because at the time I was

---

*Members of her family who read this chapter before publication added one comment: 'She wasn't very strong physically but was anything but short in determination.'

in a very depressed state. Our youngest baby had been very sick and needed lots of attention, and beyond that I was making no effort to keep abreast of topical things. My husband and I were even finding conversation difficult because I just didn't seem to have anything to say'.

Once she became a member Mrs Watt's interest in the movement burst ahead and two years ago she became its fourth National Organiser, inheriting a membership of about eight thousand people and an average weekly mail of 140 letters. After the slightest piece of publicity, however, the post soars into the hundreds. She remembers with recurrent panic one monumental fortnight when a thousand letters surged through the door. 'When I became National Organiser I simply had no idea of what I was taking on. Answering the correspondents involves a tremendous amount of work and the only way I can get through it is to shut myself away in the bedroom and spread all the files out on the floor'.

On average four evenings of Mrs Watt's week are taken up with such written work. How all the administration fits in so smoothly with home routine seems like a miracle. Even with four children (aged from six to seventeen) and a rumbustious dog called Sammy Footsteps, Mrs Watt still has time to do her own baking and make her daughters' dresses. She claims that she gets things done 'by accident' but she also has a good memory and lots of unobtrusive vigour.*

When Jane took over the 'job' in 1967 her mail must still have been reverberating with reactions to Moira Keenan's catalytic comment in *The Sunday Times* on the first national conference. Coincidentally Moira, another woman deeply concerned with the well-being of the family, was also to die of cancer leaving a young family.

In her first newsletter Jane quoted the controversial paragraphs and in doing so helped to open up for thought, in what was still a rule-less organisation, the primary question of whether it should campaign *nationally* for the many causes which must concern women. Accompanying quoted comments ranged from 'I feel NHR as a whole might be quite influential' to 'Our great value is in being a social group without an axe to grind'.

Another attempt to get members considering guidelines came at the second annual conference, in London, 1968. The Register poster included the words 'women who are housebound bringing up small children'. The gathering deleted 'housebound' but the debate, carried on to this day, divided between those interpreting the original purpose as assisting mothers of young children and those rejecting the argument that older women could join established

---

* Extracts by courtesy of *The Yorkshire Post*.

organisations since they needed the extra stimulation of NHR. Reaching divorced, deserted wives and the absence of coloured members was raised, as again it still is.

What reporting that conference business in the spring 1968 *Newsletter* entailed (plus accounts on what groups were doing, the work of other organisations, the founding of Registers in Canada and Western Australia) was revealed in the autumn *Newsletter*:

> A great sigh of relief can be heard in our house when the last of the eight thousand newsletters are finally bundled and despatched. For days floor space is non-existent: packages line the hall: the sitting-room floor is covered with bundles counted out but not wrapped; in the dining-room are the cardboard boxes (obliging grocer) into which the completed bundles go to be carted along to the post office.... In the midst of all this chaos last time I retired to bed suffering from glandular fever. My thanks to my husband and family for 'clearing the decks'.... A heartfelt thank you too to Rosemary Pritchard, Grantham local organiser, for answering the letters during the weeks I was out of action.

Jane's concern for the well-being of the Register and her influence on its future can best be seen in her spring 1969 *Newsletter*; by which time the Watt family had moved to Doncaster. The third annual conference had been held, in Harrogate, but with only two hundred members attending. Jane, in what was indubitably a seminal *Newsletter*, asked the rest of the membership also to consider and comment on 'domestic' matters, meaning Register, not their households.

From a pre-conference circular on 'The Function of the Register' she had found: 'Most groups felt that the meetings should be primarily non-domestic; most thought that the Register should provide stimulating conversation and contact but many groups seem to be very vague and not at all sure what the Housewives Register is'.

It is a fair assumption that this is why she put together some explanatory words so that the uninitiated could have clues on what the Register was about.

Under the heading 'A meeting point for the lively-minded woman' they read:

> The NHR originated in 1960 from a letter written to the *Guardian* about the feeling of some women that they were stagnating at home, and about the difficulty of making friends in a new district, especially when tied by young children. The only qualification for membership is a lively and enquiring mind though most members are married, between twenty-five and forty, and have followed some career before marriage.

A comparable text, under the same title, still appears in the forefront of today's *Newsletters*; but includes Maureen Nicol's name and excludes reference to married state or age range.

Jane also reproduced a motif, designed by a member's husband; the shape of a house with the linked NHR initials, still a logo today.

The Harrogate conference obviously took time to think about the Register as a whole. The Harrogate group put up ideas such as a condensed leaflet, so that every single prospective member, having one, understood the NHR concept; balance sheets in the *Newsletter* so members could grasp the 'National Financial Burden'. The thought of a constitution was first raised.

Post-Harrogate, at Jane's request, Deirdre Collins (herself anti-constitution) framed a draft constitution to be shot at:)

> No one interested in the aims of NHR and willing to join is to be excluded from any group on grounds of age, marital status or anything else. There should be one session a year at the conference run on formal lines with proposals to be sent to the national organiser long enough before the conference agenda to be drawn up and circulated for discussion by groups. The proposals to be read out at the formal session, seconded, discussed and voted on. Votes to be allocated one to each group of 10 or under and one every 10 members in the group thereafter (e.g. a group of 44 members would have 5 votes). Groups unable to send a delegate to the conference may vote by post if they wish. Some democratic way of electing a new National Organiser – possibly every two years? – to be decided and included in this framework. The group to which the National Organiser belongs must be prepared to back her up and help with the work when necessary.

This seminal *Newsletter* presented a picture ranging from the, then positively revolutionary, proposition of expressing views by voting, to the fact that some members had the vaguest ideas on what the Register was about, and all in an eighteen-page publication which still carried reports on local groups discussing the permissive society, historic and modern Mexico, the Jewish religion, plus members' comments on the *Newsletter* (two groups thought it a waste of money!). It also contained Jane Watt's personal thinking.

From the 'point of view of publicity and an address for would-be members to contact', a National Organiser seemed necessary; but she thought 'the time has come for regional or county organisers'. She favoured counties and asked anyone willing to take on the organisation in her own county to write in. She envisaged the work as:

> Keeping an up-to-date list of local organisers for her county (local organisers change so frequently that the national list is out of date almost as soon as it is printed), dealing with receipts for subs from her area; supplying groups with posters, etc., and helping new groups when necessary. If the groups in her county wished to meet with each other, helping to arrange get-togethers. Answering letters from would-be members when, following some publicity, the NO was swamped.

She added: 'I abhor the idea of NHR turning into an organisation of committee workers but I hope the idea will spread the work load a bit and enable NHR to grow'.

Sketching in how the NO job had been handed down through the years, she explained the 1969 situation briefly:

> answering letters from would-be members – the number of enquiries varies from 2–20 a day rising to 50–100 after any national publicity ... sending posters and leaflets to existing groups; editing and despatching the newsletter (taking from five to six weeks from typing to bundling she explained elsewhere); sending receipts for subs and 'keeping the books'; sending out circulars when necessary; and trying to keep tabs on programmes and group activities to be able to offer suggestions to new groups.

She agreed with Lesley Taylor that three years was long enough for one person to be NO but asked: 'How is the next national organiser to be chosen? I think it must be less haphazard. At the moment I feel that I have no authority to speak for all members'. She appealed: 'Please do discuss this question of how the next national organiser is to be appointed'.

After this indomitable attempt to get members to think about the Register as a whole the next *Newsletter* was *written* in autumn 1969, but not published till 1970. 'I have been loath to have it printed,' explained Jane,

> before all the order forms were returned. Group sizes fluctuate so much that it is not easy to estimate numbers. I had the last newsletter printed before all the order forms were returned and found myself four hundred copies short. To have had four hundred newsletters reprinted would have cost seventy pounds. This was financially impossible.

However, if some groups' interest in the national link was so feeble they could not even get their correct orders in on time, there were others who reacted to the issues she had raised, and reinforced by a post-conference circular, analysed, incidentally, by Anita Brocklesby (one of her successors) and Shirley Howell from Harrogate.

It was an interesting response from which came the first written-down 'rules'.

'The majority of members favour the keeping of the existing NHR structure,' Jane reported:

> A constant theme running through the replies is that informality is the essence of NHR and voting, delegates, etc. would make non-organisation impossible. The autonomy of groups is jealously guarded and some groups mention their inability to think of any decisions to be made which can't be settled by the NO with a circular to each group if necessary. A large number made it clear that they would not feel bound by any decisions taken at a national conference.... Remaining unorganised with such large numbers is recognised as a major difficulty and some groups say regretfully that they feel that, as at a local level, there has to be some internal organisation somewhere if the whole thing is not to fail. The two basic rules to provide a framework which meet with greatest approval are: 1. The annual subscription should be of a fixed amount and sent at a specific time. Local organisers should be aware of their responsibility for this. 2. Organisers should write at least once a year to the NO and keep her informed of changes of organiser.

(The annual subscription to the national register, agreed at Harrogate, was 2s. 6d. – 12½p per person.)

Although groups were mostly in favour of county or regional organisers actual volunteers were too few to make the scheme workable.

The majority of the groups who answered Jane's appeal for comment also saw no reason to alter the system (of which she had strongly expressed her disapproval) whereby the resident NO chose her successor. So she asked for volunteers. There was no rush to head an organisation of nine thousand – a 50 per cent increase in membership during her three years of office. With that sort of growth it is understandable that she told Deirdre Collins that no one person could cope with it by then. Having decided herself on the change from solo to partnership she looked, as was her only option, to those who contributed more than just subscriptions and chose Anita Brocklesby, who had volunteered, and Lesley Moreland, to succeed her.

The important decision and the changeover could only be announced in 'a mini-newsletter', four duplicated sheets instead of the printed sixteen/eighteen-pager, when Jane was swamped by the tremendous publicity built around the 1970 conference, which also marked the first decade.

Jane's concern for the Register nationally did not fade with retirement. Apart from offering an impartial and sympathetic ear to help the new, innovative, partnership knit, her letters to Lesley Moreland in the transition period reveal more than plain statistics of members.

Having been to meetings where only 'three people had any views to express (having done their homework) while the rest sat in a glazed silence', she expanded, 'I have changed a lot in my attitude in the past three years. I used to consider the Register as being very much a minority group, but I have come to realise that it is a valuable bridge for newcomers to an area who are not as intellectual as the original members of the Register would have hoped'.

Jane also illuminated what a no-set-hours, based-on-the-home, job meant. She wrote to Lesley: 'If you are spending forty hours a week regularly on the Register it's time you started shelving, delegating or ditching some of your activities! Over the past year I rarely did anything else – not even attending the local Register meetings – that was with clerical help and a great deal of assistance from the family (and anyone else who happened to be visiting) with the routine letter-answering, beginner's pack making-up, kind of activity. I know that it's very, very easy to spend an enormous amount of time on it – it's like housework – it's always there. You have taken over at the stage I finished and, even though it is now a duo, the work is bound to increase as the Register grows so it's at this stage that you must decide how much time you are willing and able to give. Looking back on it now after a few months away from it I realise I just gave it up in the nick of time – it wasn't doing myself or Robert or the family any good.'

In other letters Jane gave personal details of the effect she could now see the 'job' had had on her family and adjured Lesley: 'If anybody phones you between the hours of 4 p.m. and 7 p.m. tell them that's family time and they'll have to phone back. People have no conscience about phoning at peculiar hours.' (Latter-day NOs echo that.) She concluded what she called an 'outburst' with 'Your health, physical and mental, and the family's well-being comes first. You'll have to sort out the priorities,' and suggested cutting the *Newsletter* size, and its cost, and using the money to pay for some form of help.

Jane's concern for those who held the Register continued even to the next in succession. It was reciprocated. Early in 1975 she wrote from a Newcastle hospital (the family had moved again) thanking Pat Williams and Josephine Jaffray for flowers delivered by a Register member ('It is good to feel that there is someone nearby

The Register Builders: Jane Watt 1967–70

who speaks the same language') who was going to arrange for other members to call. She remembered that, as she had, they faced the daunting prospect of getting an annual conference to consider the hard facts on the management of the Register. 'I hope,' she wrote, 'you have a satisfactory meeting at Crewe and that people are constructively helpful. Surely by now members must realise things can't go on as they are.' But that watershed of a conference was still in the future when the first duo, Anita and Lesley, took over.

X
The Other Link

CERTAIN CITIES REMAIN in the memories of national officers as the locations for a national conference where they anticipated antagonism, like Josephine and Pat facing the members at Crewe, or, maybe less expected but even more distressingly real for the two who took over from Jane Watt, the Birmingham-sited conference.

Yet the warmest recommendation for NHR conferences that I have come across was set down, for the *Newsletter*, by National Organiser (from 1980) Alison Shingler; admittedly before she had faced an AGM from the platform, and even before she chaired a session at the first international conference which speaker Gyles Brandreth concluded by standing on his head on the chairman's table.

Alison wrote;

> I was telling some friends that a national conference, attended on my own, with an overnight stay in the hall of residence, had been more fun than a fortnight in Italy with the family. I'm not sure I convinced them, but it is perfectly true. Everyone is so friendly, and people who are normally morose and wooden at breakfast find themselves talking animatedly to complete strangers over the cornflakes.

The difference between the first national conference, held in Buxton, over a weekend that included 'Mother's Day', in 1967, and the one in Bradford in 1980, was more than that in Bradford the results of the very first national ballot for new officers was announced. Or indeed that the incumbents, the first national *group*, entertained us with a parody of one of their meetings, knocked together the night before, and including a dig at NHR's high principles when the group chairman constantly squashed attempts to exchange cake recipes. This culminated in a chorus line, decked out in NHR emblazoned T-shirts, to the music of 'Three little girls from school are we'. Sample verse: 'Liz is a Scot who kept the books, Rumour has it she sometimes cooks, And gives the VAT man funny looks, A member of the National Group'. Not great poetry but it went down a treat. It was repeated, by request, around two in the morning during a spontaneous, and innovatory for national conferences, sing-song which began with half a dozen in the college common-room. More and more drifted in, some in night-gear. You could tell who had been Girl Guides: they knew the words. Where would you see a scene like that? Grown women, in the pretty dresses that have become traditional to change into for the Saturday evening dinner, leaping up and down for the action parts, nudging each other into yet more inspiration, gratified when they achieved mellifluous precision in a round song (one conducting each section and bringing it in at the right moment) shouting down the member who wanted to sing 'Jerusalem' (which the Women's Institutes sing at their annual Albert Hall gathering) and finally having us all in full voice because it is such a resoundingly satisfying tune.

Some had retired to bed after three sessions, morning, afternoon and evening, of speakers and panels, an annual general meeting, Mayoral reception, entertainment by professionals and amateurs, and the good talk (not a mention of personal mothering problems did I hear) in the refreshment periods which are a welcome break in themselves for women normally personally responsible for the planning, purchase, preparation and clearing up of meals, as well as the location of shirts, socks, or football boots.

But through the corridors, doors were still open as women took the chance to meet old friends again who had been separated by distance. For one long night (I began to wonder if anyone went to bed) they revelled in the freedom of nobody saying 'It's getting late', or having an ear, even when asleep, (it's a knack that comes with motherhood, presumably acquired by 'single' fathers too) for a child's cry in the night, or even, since the age range is wide, waiting for the teenager's key in the front door.

By coincidence I met Sheila Brown from Maidstone, at Bradford, now working as a pharmacist again, albeit part-time. We first met on the train to Buxton for the first national conference in 1967. Like me, she had rarely attended an NHR conference since, and the difference over the years, we mutually concluded, lay in the sophistication, not of the event, but in the confident bearing of women who were not just appendages to husbands at a national gathering, but could contribute their own opinion, either from the platform or from the floor.

I had been invited as a speaker to the Buxton conference (though also reporting the event for *The Observer*) and remember asking 'Why NHR?' and the massed, spontaneous, reply: 'Friendship'. I remember too nipping off to a hairdresser before the conference began, revelling in not having to swivel eyes and attention towards a small child who might be creating havoc among the salon's exotic fitments and sweetly smelling bottles.

Later I saw the long winding queue for the telephone. Many who attended that first conference were away from home alone for the first time since their marriage. Reflex action made them check that the family survived.

There were no queues at Bradford for the phones. In fact one woman leapt in that direction with the cry 'I've forgotten to tell my husband exactly where I am'. More had been financially backed by their local groups and were assiduously note-taking during sessions to channel back more ideas for local debate. I dropped the question of financing the trip at the lunch table (you sit anywhere, talk to whoever is nearby). One woman mentioned that child allowance could be saved up to finance fares and conference fees. Another looked puzzled that the question could be raised and spelled out: 'It's not his income, it's our income, and the cost of a conference is taken as said, if I want to come'. Some had financed themselves, having part-time or full-time jobs. One element remained unchanged, that, extracting today's wider age range, the majority still had to pre-plan for their absence from home, with clean clothes, food and child care arrangements. But the programme content was still as firmly abstract, not tied to women's issues, as when Moira Keenan questioned it in *The Sunday Times* after the very first national conference.

Programmes, culled at random from whoever found themselves drafted to produce a report on the annual event for the *Newsletter*: Southport 1971 'Stress', the 'Modern Family', 'Parliamentary Democracy'; Birmingham 1972, 'Population Growth'; Darlington 1974 'Our Heritage', which encompassed religion, politics, sex; Bristol 1976, 'Population Explosion', 'Food Shortage', 'Resource Scarcity', 'Environmental Deprivation', 'Misuse of Nuclear Capacities'.

Not that NHR itself does not feature. At Manchester in 1978, after we heard about 'World Peace and Fair Shares for All' and 'overkill' in the world arms race, erstwhile National Organiser Pat Williams scratched sensibilities under the title 'Apathy'. She did not see members as MPs but wanted to know why they were not influencing the quality of life as local elected councillors. Then, as so often, there was too little time allowed to explore the challenge to its full potential. A criticism, allied to that of depending too much on the outside world for conference speakers instead of tapping Register talent and opinion, which is constantly voiced, particularly since outside speakers can be wildly adrift in their assessment of the audience's mental capacities and interests, and can waffle on about a few funny events that have occurred in their own particular jobs, instead of presenting the grit for which they were invited. 'We can get such patronisation on the home TV', members mutter. Such comments on conference programmes are often accompanied by compliments about the way the particular local group organises the annual conference, nowadays generally in college premises, including student accommodation. Veteran attenders reckon they are experts on the country's higher education facilities; some student campus housing may be delightfully located for summer but not so practical when it's wet and cold and you still have to traverse windy parkland to reach the lecture hall.

With a National Group to spread the load, a 'Conference Liaison' person was a natural move. Pat Kerr of Harrogate was the first to hold the title, transferred to Antoinette Ferraro of Solihull in mid-1980. In typical Register style this does not mean an officer laying down hard-and-fast rules.

The ten-page leaflet 'Running a Conference' incorporates down-to-earth experience. It's about assessing your aim in deciding to hold a conference, working out who does what (and enough of them), when to hold it (forward planning to book speakers and avoid public holidays), where (asking practical questions like what the quoted charges include). It takes you into a budget, application forms, speakers' charges, briefing and equipment, catering, programme planning, insurance, publicity, with a chronological 'countdown' of when, before the event, all needs to be fixed.

This advice is not only for the group which volunteers to run the annual national conference but for those who still provide a means of linking up through one-day or half-day conferences. A mother finding it difficult to attend a weekend annual conference at the other end of the country might manage a day off in her own region, which is the idea.

From the feedback of a questionnaire, which she asked *day* conference organisers to complete, Pat produced a chart setting out straight facts like numbers organising, numbers attending and what they paid, cost of speakers, expenses from cost of hall to the presentation of flowers – including one cancelled for lack of support

– and a sheet crammed with the pitfalls and hard-learned suggestions of those who had been through the mill.

The Register now has a 'fund' from which money can be borrowed, say for deposits on premises, before booking fees start coming in.

Subjects at day get-togethers have been many and various: 'The Family of Man', 'Stretching your Lively Mind', 'Into Europe', 'The Cost of the Environment', 'The Capacity of Women in the Future', 'Modern Advertising Methods and their Effect on the Public', 'Affluence and Effluents', 'Who Holds the Power'; just to pick at random from the abundance.

Two stand out across the years. In 1972 the Hertford/Ware and Lea Valley groups held a 'Talk-in Walk-About', an open meeting on what to do next once the youngest child starts school, and there is more time. No magical answers were offered, rather speakers on careers for women and on community work, ('Talk-in') and married women with children, who had first hand experience to offer (forty-five in all), answered individual questions (the 'Walk-About') from the 250 who attended, on professions, voluntary work, study and business. There was a lot of printed information displayed too. A Billericay member who attended was so impressed that she got one organised there too, in 1974, with fifty 'counsellors', including a taxi driver and an antiques renovator. Wirral groups also followed up in 1975 and offered forty organisations and individuals representing re-training, further training, employment, voluntary work and a wide range of unusual openings complemented by a tax expert (female), to advise women thinking of returning to work.

More recently, in 1979, High Wycombe organised 'a new sort of conference' entitled 'Get into Action with Communication', which would enable participants to gain insight into techniques used by professionals to help solve complex problems. I was not there but fortuitously Frances Alexander set up a shortened version of the trust games as an 'ice breaker' at the first International Conference in 1980. When you had made eye contact with a stranger (followed by verbal exchange), dropped bodily onto the outstretched arms of two lines of women, sat barefoot and blindfolded on the floor listening to a narrated story and then put out your hand to clutch another's, and followed that by making 'A Machine' (self-consciousness discarded as, linking by touch to the nearest woman, you flapped the other arm and maybe one leg, made puffing noises, or otherwise played trains) there were no strangers. You had communicated. Truly an ice breaker.

Postscript: Comment from a Harrogate member who attended the 1980 national conference, published in the *newsletter*.

The all-time low of the weekend was, for me, the session on Sunday morning, when six speakers were supposed to be speaking on 'living together' in their particular fields of work. With one or two exceptions, the level of information offered would have been an insult to a class of intelligent eleven-year-olds. The speakers assumed that we had no knowledge of what a social worker does, no awareness of the problems of racial minorities, nineteenth century ideas about mental illness, and all avidly read the *News of the World* without ever questioning the truth of what we read. It was a good hour before the steam of fury stopped coming out of my ears!

XI
The Register Builders:
Anita Brocklesby and Lesley Moreland
1970–73

ANITA AND LESLEY are profoundly grateful for the existence of the Register, Lesley to the extent of claiming that her younger daughter owes her life to NHR, that without members round the corner to whom she could pour out her woes, she would have swung the sickly baby by her heels against the wall.

But Anita, after three years in office, became disillusioned, resenting that

> so many groups were being set up as NHR groups which bore no relationship to what I felt NHR was about. I knew of people who had gone to meetings and not been made welcome 'because we're full'. That was a regular problem. Or who had gone and found a group of smug middle-class women whose minds were less than lively. Lesley feels these groups serve a purpose. I feel less charitable because I think of the people who are in the position I was, in a strange town with young children, looking for an NHR group. If they find what Lesley, Jane and I called the cake-icing types, it gives them little and they're stuck. Yet Women's Institute or Townswomen's Guild give much of what that type of group gives – why call themselves NHR?

Lesley felt equally strongly that non-welcoming groups had no justification for their continued claim to be part of NHR. But she could tolerate a wider variation than Anita and always regarded the social support network of NHR as equally important as the intellectual stimulus. 'Human groups are not static and even within three years of office we saw groups go from one extreme to the other, so although not happy about very domestic programmes, it was possible to encourage a more NHR type programme without putting such a group beyond the pale.'

Anita read my article and Maureen Nicol's letter and followed the inauguration of the Register with interest. She married immediately after graduation (Sociology at the London School of Economics), was a mental welfare officer for four years, and a social worker in child guidance for a year before her first son was born. He was two months old when she contacted the just launched Harrogate group, in 1966.

Having seen the broader picture, as an NO, she praises its quality: 'That group was full of professional women with wide interests, most had travelled widely. Altogether they were an intellectually stimulating collection with strongly developed social consciences.' They were involved in the National Association for the Welfare of Children in Hospital, the Save the Children Fund, the Natural Childbirth Trust, Pre-School Playgroups Association, Family Planning Association and OXFAM. She describes it as *really* a group of "lively-minded" women'.

She met Jane Watt, NO, at the 1968 national conference who asked if Harrogate would organise the next. They did, with Anita undertaking much of the organisation, pregnant for the third time with the NHR 'doing for me precisely what was needed'. The day after that conference her husband left to start a new job elsewhere, though the family did not join him for nine months. 'NHR,' recalls Anita, 'again came to my aid'. Jane guided her to Anne Cossey, just returned to Halesowen after starting the Canadian Register, who invited the family to stay while they house-hunted. 'When you consider that my children were three, two and six weeks at the time, that was quite something.' Later the Cossey family, on holiday, lent their house so the Brocklesbys could be near each other. 'All in all', summarises Anita, 'I felt that NHR had given me a considerable share of happiness in my early years of motherhood. I felt I had a debt to pay, which is why I offered my services to Jane as a possible successor'.

Anita–who started another group in Stourbridge, Worcestershire–and Lesley Moreland first met at the 1969 national conference in Harrogate where Jane asked Lesley if the Potters Bar group could organise the next one. If Lesley thought of Anita, 'what a capable and calm person she was to cope with the conference, the pregnancy and knowing that she would soon be moving to the Midlands', Anita, later, had to adjust, as do all who work with Lesley, to her ability to work eighteen to twenty hours a day.

NHR first impinged on Lesley as a student *Guardian* reader in 1960. 'Mother had been a TWG member and I remembered her favourable comments on the social aspects, but reservations about the content and formality.' By 1962 she completed her Diploma in

Political, Economic and Social Studies, got married and left for Nigeria, all within ten days. Back in Britain, in Gorleston-on-Sea in 1964, after losing a baby and still weak from the aftermath of dysentery, Lesley went into a severe post-natal depression after the birth of her first daughter. Enquiries to the incumbent NO, Lesley Taylor, revealed that the nearest group was Norwich where she was 'not capable' of getting herself and baby.

Lesley Moreland recalls: 'One day, out shopping, I saw a young woman outside the Post Office leaning on her pram and crying. I went up to her and asked if I could be of any help. She came back to the flat for coffee and poured out the problem. She was pregnant with her second child and not wanting to be'. Between them they started the Gorleston group which became the driving force behind the opening of the first adventure playground in East Anglia. Lesley's second child was born in the middle of that campaign, but by 1966 the Morelands had moved to Hertfordshire. 'Who is the organiser for Potters Bar?' she wrote to Lesley Taylor. A two-word note came back: 'You are'. Her experiences in setting up a group were vividly reported in *Newsletters*, omitting to mention she was the only member without car or phone.

Potters Bar was a very active group with evening meetings, day-time ones often with children not their own because Mum was in hospital, play afternoons for families, sub-groups (literature and current affairs). No wonder Jane Watt suggested they organise the 1970 national conference! But when Jane, no doubt detecting Lesley's enthusiasm and capacity for work during their sustained consultations before the conference, asked if Lesley had considered becoming NO, Lesley rejected it. Her husband Vic 'thought it would be worth finding out more because once the conference was over I would be bored and hard to live with'.

Jane, by then, had contacted Anita and came back on the phone with the proposal that the job be split into two parts: one person to maintain contact with the established groups, to respond to letters from enquirers and to be Treasurer (which was Anita's preference); the other to help new groups start, handle publicity and edit the *Newsletter*. Lesley's reaction then was, and still is, that 'the jam' was on her side.

They had similar backgrounds – socialist working-class parents though both were inactive politically at the time – NHR commitment, children of similar ages. Once they had sorted out their separate strengths and weaknesses (a rumbustious period with Jane as counsellor; much of the tension caused by worry over finance) they worked well together. By the end of three years they were close friends and still are.

Changeover was affected through a stay at Jane's, who had painstakingly copied out by hand a double set of the Register, index cards with each group's name, organiser, address, and subs. Both were stunned by the amount of work Jane had coped with.

Being geographically separated, contact was by mail, two or three letters a week just to keep the dual Register up to date and meaning tediously copying everything out twice, one to update records, one for the other person, phone calls which got longer and more frequent and, apart from the national conferences, only actually meeting about twice a year in each other's homes amid the domestic round.

They worked out a system. Lesley sent copies of *Newsletter* articles for Anita to see. She also, with the aid of a member's graphic designer husband, devised a smarter *Newsletter* with a map on the back illustrating where there were established groups, new ones and 'contacts'. By the end of their three years, since there are limits to the number of helpful group members who can get into a house to pack *Newsletters* into over six hundred parcels for despatch, the printers took over packaging and despatch.

For their other 'voice', the circular, Lesley drafted and Anita polished and added her contribution and they agreed the final version. Their main disagreement was about money. 'I was the last of the great spenders, wanting the members who had paid the money in to benefit from their subs, whereas Anita was always wanting to save for future problems,' Lesley recalls. 'I was always meaner – I got the money in – she spent it,' admits Anita.

The seriousness of the financial situation hit them as soon as they took over. The rush of enquiries from the publicity surrounding the tenth anniversary had drained the funds. So their first circular set out two succeeding sets of accounts, up to June 1970, to illustrate rising costs. Income from subscriptions was, by then, £866. Funds in hand stood at £256 but, extracting the cost of Jane's 'mini-newsletter' (while she coped with the anniversary onslaught) and *that* circular, left £110 still to be paid and meant there was not enough money to pay for the next (autumn) *Newsletter*.

Lesley, tackling her first *Newsletter* ('I'd never done anything like it before') had to persuade Anita that they ought to commit the money to print it, though they had not got the money at that stage. But they had raised members' annual subscriptions from 2s. 6d to 5s. (12½p to 25p) explaining 'Jane has had a considerable amount of worry about the finances and we both feel that, while we are happy and willing to give our time and energy, we do not want to cope with having constant financial crises to worry about'. They explained how funds were spent, on newsletters, circulars, support for groups, replies to enquirers. 'We hope', they wrote, 'that you will not mind paying just over one penny a week to receive these benefits and to enable us to start off new groups and bring more members into the NHR.'

Some of the letters that came in were hostile, even rude. It was a minority, but quite a shock. Anita phoned Lesley to say she had just swept her stairs down with a hand brush and as each stair was completed she hit it with the back of the brush and yelled 'Bloody Yatton'; that Somerset group having left NHR because of the increase.

Fortunately an informal network of 'ear benders' emerged for each NO (formally called National Secretary – Anita – and Newsletter Editor and PRO – Lesley). Many turn up in this history, even in the National Groups.

Six months later finances were no easier so, with a protracted postal strike also complicating life, no spring *Newsletter* was published in 1971. When the mail was flowing again they joked in a May circular that during the interruption 'the gap was so great that Anita was reduced to doing housework and Lesley to taking on a part-time job!' But the jobs – Lesley's twelve hours a week working with the doubly-incontinent in a local old people's home desperate for staff – and the one Anita took on soon after – two whole days a week as a social worker in Birmingham – were not unconnected with the Register's finances.

'Although all the visible expenses were paid, stationery, stamps; phone calls, etc. doing NHR work was making inroads into our family finances,' Lesley explained. 'I wasn't cooking as much from scratch, dressmaking as much (hooray!) and needed to appear reasonably decent whilst out on "NHR business".'

To make up for the gap the autumn 1971 *Newsletter* crammed so much into its twenty-four pages that the printer recommended each copy be accompanied by a free magnifying glass!

Members' queries, 'What are you doing with our money?', were answered in the October *circular* with a breakdown of the 25p subscription: printing 10p, stationery 6p, postage 5p, telephone 3p, travelling, incidentals, bank and audit fees 1p. There was even a brief summary of what the Organisers did, like writing several thousand individual letters per year *each*, apart from keeping records (while lacking office equipment) and despatching circulars and *Newsletters*. Subs, members were told, had turned up from only two-thirds of the membership, some still sending the old rate, but the NOs were still supporting the full membership, around fifteen thousand. At least a few months later they managed to buy a filing cabinet for Anita (one of the Stourbridge group volunteered to file the piles of letters) and a (reconditioned) duplicator for Lesley, who also had in her small front hall a borrowed six foot desk, a filing cabinet and boxes and boxes of stationery, bulk-bought for economy, duplicating paper, ink, often stored on the stairs so that, apart from coming sideways into the house because the desk impeded the door, the family had to do a 'Mary Poppins' to get upstairs.

That Register-orientated household was also involved when Lesley produced the first little folded, *hand-made* in many colours, leaflet on what the NHR is about for both new groups and established ones (a gap detected by Jane) which is still *printed* today with relevant national contacts. Then they took hours to do and, apart from Potters Bar's working parties, Lesley's two daughters folded 500 for 1s (5p).

Lesley also put together a duplicated leaflet on 'How to Start a Group' though it was always accompanied by a personal letter to give the feeling that someone was genuinely interested. Visits to individual groups by invitation (and getting valuable feedback) was more feasible with two officers, though of course not on today's scale, partly because of lack of money and partly because both had young children and staying away overnight (group meetings being held in the evening) was a major upheaval. But there was an increase in locally organised conferences (Lesley did a first shot at organising a day conference) and they encouraged them and attended most, Anita doing the north, Lesley the south.

By early 1972 they were asking for volunteers to succeed them and asking members to consider whether NHR could continue as for the first twelve years, or whether alternatives should be studied, such as a paid organiser or regular paid clerical help for a voluntary organiser. As usual such thoughts were put into a circular for reaction by mail and raised for verbal discussion at the annual national conference in Birmingham.

'Many good things happened' in those three years, Lesley Moreland reiterates. The Birmingham conference was not one of them. 'A little feminine compassion alongside their lively-mindedness', which the next national officers were to note was missing when they were on a conference platform and which the NO from 1980, Alison Shingler, publicly requested ('Just remember that beneath that prize-heifer rosette the NO wears at conferences there is an ordinary NHR member'), was certainly missing in 1972.

'I have never been so frightened on a public platform, have never encountered such naked hostility before or since,' says Lesley, who has been on many public platforms since that day. 'Lesley and I were subjected to verbal attack – quite an experience that was,' Anita recalls.

Time has dulled the details. They expressed the thought from the platform that their successors would need an honorarium; a sample comment from the floor said, in effect, that the job was little more than would be required from a competent clerk.

Fortunately other members who did have 'compassion' and understood the pressures, extended an opportunity for sustenance and recovery. Eight years later at the 1980 national conference in Bradford, where refreshingly the proposal (passed) to raise the subscription was greeted with 'not enough', accompanied by expressions of disapproval that officers should have the embarrassment of trying to get more funds from members because costs had risen, I heard veterans ('remember Birmingham') marvelling at the change in attitude.

Not that Anita and Lesley's unpleasant experience was reflected in their communications with members. In a *circular* they summarised the ideas put forward: that an NHR group could take over national organisation (attractive, but with problems like husbands' job mobility, thought the Organisers); regional organisers (put up before but volunteers geographically patchy); rented office accommodation with paid/voluntary staff (which the NOs thought would come one day but financially not yet feasible); a paid organiser (which they reported met with hostility since it was felt that someone doing the job on that basis might be doing it for the love of the money rather than the job). They expressed their sympathy with those 'who like to feel that there is a voluntary organiser' but felt knowledge was lacking of what was entailed in terms of the demands made. 'The sheer volume of paper and materials needed to do the job take up a lot of space in a family home. The fact that the work is done from home means that one is never away from it – Lesley's youngest daughter remarked quite recently, "Do you know, you've eaten all your dinner and haven't had to answer the phone".'

They went on to summarise, with gratitude, a possible solution put up post-conference by Sheila Warren of Carshalton Beeches:

two organisers who could take on extra clerical paid help in busy times or in domestic crises, and who would get a lump sum allowance or honorarium of say £250 a year for which they would not account – 'some people may prefer to pay for domestic help in the home, others to send washing to the laundry or to ensure a good holiday for their family to compensate for the inconvenience caused to them'. Such a solution retained the favoured volunteers, but with some financial compensation, so that family finances were not interfered with. However, another aspect was raised (also a pointer to future organisational changes):

> Not many of you will realise that we are personally liable in law for debts we may incur for the NHR. We have no protection whatsoever, although we have unsuccessfully tried to find a way of establishing some without becoming involved in a formal structuring of NHR. Obviously a salaried employee, albeit an NHR member, would have a right to this protection.

A ballot on the honorarium question was conducted by Stockport member Pauline Roberts, and results issued in January 1973. Out of the 550 plus *groups*, those replying provided 2 abstentions with 15 against – on the grounds of a potential increase in subs – or that the sum mentioned (£250 annually) was too high, or preferring realistic expenses to cover hairdos etc so NOs should not be out of pocket; and 286 were in favour, with comments like 'It's long overdue' and 'They're worth more than that', or seeing an honorarium as a safeguard against salaried staff which would spoil NHR's informality. Anita and Lesley each received the £250 honorarium for their last year.

By that time they had decided that the workload needed dividing yet again. Lesley regarded Josephine Jaffray, whom she had advised on setting up a new group in Dumfries, as her natural successor as New Groups Adviser and PRO. Fortunately Josephine accepted. Angela Lepper was recommended by another member and despite her deprecating, what she calls 'backhanded' response, found herself accepted as National Secretary and Treasurer. Pat Williams' name was to hand. When Lesley had domestic problems which could have led to early resignation, Pat had offered her services. As it happened, Lesley was able to complete her stint. Pat became the *Newsletter* editor in the new trio. The changeover was affected, after a get-together at Pat's house, in June 1973.

XII
Profiles

The Cornelians (Edinburgh)

In September of 1960 (the same year as Maureen Nicol's reaction to my article – which just shows that the climate was right) Anne Scott wrote a letter to *The Scotsman* newspaper as a housebound married woman who wished to meet others like herself interested in having discussions on intellectual rather than domestic topics. The response led to a meeting held at an Edinburgh hotel where the Cornelian Society was formed.

Within the first year a constitution was set down, providing for the election of a President, Treasurer, Secretary and Editor of the *Newsletter*, at an AGM, and also a co-ordinating committee nominated from the groups which are named for, and located in, Edinburgh's postal districts. The Cornelian Society is a totally independent organisation and, like NHR, is not a pressure group. The (autonomous) group's activities will be familiar to Register members. The name of the distinguished Roman matron tends to turn up when National Housewives Register, as a title, is discussed.

The Cornelians affiliated to NHR in 1963, paying 5s (25p) a year, receiving therefore one copy of the *Newsletter*, and, surely the main advantage, members were put in touch with a Register group, if one existed, when they moved house. Two representatives of the Cornelians generally attended NHR national conferences and members also attended Scottish-based conferences; they hostessed the one in 1971.

Otherwise the seventies seem to have been a decade when you had to follow the dates and what was going on very closely in order to know whether the Cornelians were in or out of NHR. In 1980 the Cornelians' President, Betty Moffat, told me, in a letter bearing a very near resemblance to the NHR logo – a roof structure cut horizontally with 'Cornelians' – that joining in 1972 she was told that 'we all belonged to NHR and part of the subscription was for NHR, part for the Cornelian Society and part for the local group'.

I will attempt to trace a path through the happenings of the seventies. In 1970 the NHR National Organisers, Anita Brocklesby and Lesley Moreland, after conferring with Jane Watt from whom they had just taken over, wrote a letter to all Scottish Register groups explaining that the Cornelians were receiving all the benefits of Register membership, except newsletters for all, 'without commitment to NHR'. It had been suggested to the Cornelians they should 'now consider being full members'; but they wished to retain their separate identity though continuing the relationship regarding conferences, and offering 'a more realistic payment'. At the Register end it was therefore decided 'that the relationship of each group to the National Organisers must be all or nothing'. So the letter announced with regret that 'the connection in its present form must unfortunately be discontinued'.

After that, what the Cornelians incumbent President called a 'final letter', the pros of being a member of a national organisation, especially if you moved house, were thoroughly discussed by the Cornelians. And the cons. They had a constitution and a businesslike set-up; there seemed little advantage in being taken over, they preferred their own name, and some were indifferent to the debate, not seeing any special advantage in belonging to a national organisation, and only concerned with the activities of their local group.

However, all group members were asked in January 1971 to say 'yes' or 'no' about joining NHR. The result was 121 in favour and 32 against. Despite this favourable vote, indicating the wish to be full members, Cornelian records do not reveal that further subscriptions were paid, apart from 1970 to 1971 when subscriptions were sent, amended to cover six months owing to the increase in NHR subscriptions made at the time.

So far as the Cornelians are concerned they became members in 1971 and officially withdrew in 1973; the debate went on that long.

A *Scotsman* reporter was quite carried away by the disquiet expressed in the Cornelians' 1973 newsletter and compared this 'small defiance of the bureaucratic big guns of the NHR' with that of the 'individual and Westminster, and the individual and Brussels, and so on and so on'.

In fact the essence of the newsletter's reflection of members' opinions was that they were concerned that:

> NHR is functioning as a pressure group within the country: to give just two examples – newspaper articles or interviews in which the secretary

speaks for us all, and the campaigning for Nursery Schools by women in London wearing NHR placards. Whilst this campaign in itself may be very worthwhile, we as individuals within our Society cover a whole range of beliefs and viewpoints, social, moral, religious and political, and most definitely do not wish to be put under one umbrella.... As individuals we are free to act within whatever pressure groups we choose, but not in the name of the Cornelians, or, we would have hoped, the NHR.

The other worry expressed in the newsletter was about paying an honorarium to NHR National Organisers, which was unpopular among Cornelians,

> who feel that providing expenses are paid (which they are) the job should be a voluntary one. The general feeling is that this would be a further step in the institutionalising of the Register. If indeed there is too much work for two individuals, perhaps the answer would be a reorganisation on a regional basis.

The Cornelians' President announced the withdrawal of the Society from the NHR in 1973:

> The NHR dilemma has been resolved by the decision that individual Cornelian groups are free to join the NHR if they wish. They will function as separate NHR groups within Edinburgh. I do hope that this will enable us to co-exist without further trouble.

Two Cornelian groups affiliated.

The question of rejoining NHR was raised again in the committee's meetings and at AGMs. Then, in 1978, an approach was made to the NHR National Organiser to see whether there was a way of solving the problem which would be acceptable to both NHR and Cornelians. It reflected, of course, the feeling of some members who also belonged to NHR. Conversely, to drop the distinguishing name and become completely part of the Register would not be approved by a large proportion of the then 120-strong membership.

So a formula was worked out whereby those who choose become Cornelian/NHR members (23 in 1980), paying not only the 50p Cornelian subscription, which pays for the expenses of general meetings held twice yearly, and any local group subscription, but also the NHR sub for which an individual copy of the national *Newsletter* is the immediate visible benefit.

Bradford

At the 1980 national conference, Olive Steadman, Local Organiser of the Bradford group that made the arrangements, handed me a

Profiles

package with the deprecating comment: 'Any use? Or throw it away'. It contained a much-mended, stiff-covered, exercise book, a diary of a period in the Bradford group's history. Since it did not start till 1969 Olive, by now Head of Modern Languages in a local school, unearthed her personal diaries, and enjoyed checking facts and reminiscing on the phone with Thelma Stewart, another early member; friendships made tend to be lifelong.

Olive, previously a teacher of French, read what she calls the 'frustrated graduate' letters in the *Guardian* in the late fifties and was glad she did not feel like that. But by 1962, living in Bradford and with four children under five, knowing nobody, and mentally linking that correspondence (as others have) with the emergence of the Register, she thought: 'I'd like to meet some of those women – perhaps they wouldn't all be unbearably odd'.

The reply from her letter to the National Organiser, Brenda Prys Jones, told her that she was the Bradford Local Organiser. 'This flummoxed me, as I'd had pleasant thoughts of visiting like-minded women in the area and was astonished to find there weren't any. I can remember standing in the kitchen reading the letter, in dismay, and wondering what to do about it.' She did nothing for a week and then came a letter from another woman who expected a group to exist, Thelma Stewart, two miles away, and she visited, bringing her two little boys while her daughters were at school. The Steadman and Stewart children played while the mothers talked and that went on as a regular weekly arrangement for weeks. The letter from another mother, again expecting an established group, Barbara Haigh, who lived even further away merely widened the circle by one mother, one child.

Deciding that the tiny gathering was hardly satisfactory, an evening meeting was planned, each inviting everyone they could muster. About a dozen turned up at the Steadman house, someone invited back, and they started meeting in each member's home.

'This was interesting,' Olive recalls, 'as we talked about the neighbourhood of each and admired each other's décor and children but after we'd all been everywhere it became less interesting and though one or two of us suggested having a definite topic to discuss, the majority didn't want anything so formal, although the discussions which arose naturally were by no means always trivial. However, we did begin to repeat ourselves and I was not really happy about the situation. It continued, new members being acquired via friends or channeled down after any national publicity. By 1967 the group had problems, being unwilling to welcome new members. Thelma had left the area and returned, and she started a group in Bingley, (near Bradford) to accommodate new enquirers.

In 1968 Thelma was involved in further education in Leeds, and Olive's husband, Ralph, was away from home and her children were ill when the Bradford group called a special meeting, omitting to invite a new member, rather older than most, who had annoyed the majority by her very personal questions. They decided to leave NHR in order to avoid her!

Olive not only missed that 'extraordinary meeting' but also the seceding group's later ones, spending most of her time visiting her children in hospital.

But she was still the Bradford Local Organiser. On 5 February 1969 a letter arrived, from Pauline Martin, explaining that she wished to join NHR, enclosing a cheque for 5s. (25p). 'This galvanised me to action' Olive admits. 'I invited her to coffee'.

Diary of a Group

The diary of Bradford's fresh start, which Olive had so diffidently offered me, opens in February 1969 with a meeting of three members: Olive, Pauline and the lady who caused the secession, to whom the Local Organiser had written. The single decision was to advertise in the local post offices. That attracted Sylvia Ashdown. The March meeting of four decided to advertise in the libraries and clinic and to write 'to ten possibly interested people inviting them to coffee'. The April morning meeting ('Children in playroom') drew six. They decided to hold monthly evening meetings, 'some specific subject for each meeting to be chosen by the hostess', the first to be at Sylvia's, who 'offered to talk about the development of covered marketing and to show a film'.

But before that event a planning meeting was held on 1 May when 'Sylvia agreed to be our secretary'. The 'Suggestion as to how our local register might be run' was led by a motto 'Everyone welcome', which was of course influenced by the secession of the first group. They wanted to make sure any problems were brought into the open. Incidentally the member who caused that break-up attended only a few meetings and then retired saying she felt too old for the group.

The 'suggestions' continued: visitors to be invited to two meetings and then asked to join; three likely sources of prospective members were seen as; enquiries to the National Organiser, replies to adverts, 'friends of our members'. It was also set down that meetings would be held in members' homes in turn, first Tuesdays in the month, subject to be decided by the hostess, and the shape of the evening; from 8 p.m. arrival and ten minutes allowed for chat, before 'Business matters,' such as new members, letters, suggestions, till 8.30 when the hostess introduced the evening's subject followed by discussion.

At 9.45 'refreshments – to be strictly limited to coffee and a snack (*no* knives and forks)'. (I am copying from the record.) Between 10 and 10.15 general conversation was again allowed for but then each member was to be given the opportunity 'to mention anything of interest since last meeting or events in near future, films, plays, books, people, etc.'

These preliminary plans were approved by the three new members not previously present, after all the membership was still only ten, at the May meeting at Sylvia's house on: 'covered markets'. Sylvia still attended the June meeting though taped to the page tersely recording that event is a newspaper cutting announcing the birth of her second daughter six days later.

In 1969 she was present at the July meeting to receive a 'baby shower' at a gathering when local organisers of groups in Halifax, Huddersfield, Harrogate, Bingley (Thelma Stewart) talked about their own local groups and answered questions.

By August Olive was jotting in comments in red ink as a contrast to the usual blue in which she wrote up each meeting of the Bradford group. 'No fixed subject and conversation less interesting' and a month later 'really too early in September . . . More members would have attended AFTER school terms begin'. But they were having a tour of the Central Library, a visit to the theatre with the play's producer coming to talk to them, discussing the Reith Lectures, and they rounded off their first year with a children's party at the Steadman house attended by '23 children, 11 mothers, 3 fathers! Singing games, tea, plays, Father Christmas. Members brought cakes and presents'.

The diary of a group continued: (ornamented with squiggles from Olive's toddler Charlie in April, 1970) logging baby-sitting arrangements, visits to stately homes, a poetry evening, talks or discussions on, among others, 'Parental Responsibility', modern infant teaching, newspapers, attitudes to money, the 'Silent World of the Minority' (the deaf), drugs, 'The New Morality', and a musical evening with a vote on the favourite record, the hostess offering a bottle of wine to the winner. 'But the vote was not decisive so we all shared the wine!' wrote Olive.

Programmes of national conferences are still affixed in the thick exercise book together with mention of local members attending, and press cuttings on NHR including one about Olive, pictured with her five children from three to thirteen years. It was published while she was at an NHR conference, and when she phoned home she heard 'Oh Mum, you look like Lady Antonia Fraser'. She was flattered.

But there was also a financial side. In September 1969 'Decided to have a "shop" to raise funds' was squeezed into the bottom of a page. There were regular mentions, 'shop made 2s. 6d' (12½p) or even £1. The 'shop' started casually when the Steadman daughters, anxious to help, sorted through their books and toys and arranged a little stall of oddments to sell at a group garden party. Since then, when the Bradford group has had refreshments and sits down again for announcements on future programmes, projects, etc., out comes the 'Box' which is filled by members with anything they do not want but others might, magazines, toys, children's clothes, surplus garden produce. "Others" buy at bargain prices but one or two pounds profit at each meeting is normal.

The accounts are set out in the back of the diary. The expenditure was on book tokens, and other 'presents' to speakers such as pot plants, and on postage, say, for inviting other group organisers to meetings, and in early days, like October 1969, the profit from the shop was the same as the two subscriptions received, 10s (50p). But it got better. The dribbling in of subscriptions to National Organisers, in sums amounting to shillings, *and* acknowledged by signed printed receipts, became, by 1978, the flat hand-written statement 'Cheque to Marie £20', meaning to the National Organiser for members' annual subs. By that time national funds were not expended on sending receipts.

But how did the central policy, shaped, after all, by the around half a dozen members who set up the 'reformed' group, work out? 'We decided', Olive explains, 'we'd have, as it were, no talk of Jews or problem children'. That was because the original group had foundered through taking offence at one member's remark about Jews and because one of the newcomers was a refugee from a group which did little but discuss one member's problem child.*

The philosophy hammered out in 1969, then, was that of discussing in advance the possibility of disagreement and deciding

---

* The Bradford group presented four trees to mark the Queen's Silver Wedding, and two more in 1980, after hearing a talk on the Kibbutz – to Israel.

that to disagree was an interesting and valuable thing and that, at any appearance of dissent, they should interfere as carefully as possible. In the fourteen years since, Bradford's LO told me enigmatically, that it has only been necessary twice 'and the two problems have been solved'.

But she does think Bradford functions

> rather differently from most groups in that we have always taken it in turn to plan and hostess a meeting. This has avoided the problem of the Local Organiser having to plan and organise say twenty-four meetings, and also to face criticisms such as 'We've had that' or 'Another boring evening'. No one has ever openly complained of a member's one effort during the year, indeed, if one only has to do one meeting, it's usually a very good one. Another advantage is that we get far more variety this way than one person could reasonably provide.

New members go at the end of the list so they can attend at least twenty-four meetings before their turn comes round.

Bradford maintains a membership of twenty-five to thirty, no dead wood, only those who pay their subscriptions, around a dozen still of the veterans, and the rest moving on after five or six years to be replaced fairly consistently.

Those who move and who are asked to form new groups, or join existing ones, are asked to become the Local Organiser and tend to do so on condition they follow the Bradford practice, that in rotation each member not only provides the location, her own home, but sets up the appropriate theme and launching talk if necessary.

All the original members of the 'reformed' group have taken on some form of employment. Olive Steadman thinks that 'NHR has helped to make them want to. I realise that this has also created new problems – we are in a transitional stage – but I believe more problems have been solved than created. We don't have any "frustrated graduates" these days. Some of our members have actually found new jobs through NHR – one who after a talk by a probation officer some years ago was filled with enthusiasm to be one, now is. A number have taken further degrees after various contacts we have with the Open University.'

She reflected on the roles members play: 'Take me as an example. At home I'm wife and mother, etc., at work employee and teacher, at the boys' schools a parent, at my old school association a rather old girl, at the Trefoil Guild (the Girl Guide old girls) I'm one of the kids, but at NHR I'm just *me* and not really aware that I'm older or younger than anyone else. This I think is what NHR *really* offers, and why I value it so much.'

Olive Steadman probably holds the record as the longest-standing Local Organiser; not that anyone has ever measured it. She regularly offers to resign. 'No one as yet will hear of it,' she reported in 1980. 'It's not that they don't want to do it as that there really isn't that much to do and my address is known so letters don't get lost. All I do is collect the subs, send them in, give out the letters, and take my turn with everyone else at having a meeting.'

Shetlands

Gathering up their possessions and moving on yet again is the inevitable pattern of life for the families of oilmen, a largely unrecorded and unrecognised disruption that goes with the oil and its benefits. Such migrations have dropped NHR members into other countries where they have formed groups. Now North Sea oil has caused the formation of the Register's most northerly group in the UK, in the Shetlands.

The scattered group of islands is only four hundred miles south of the Arctic Circle, on the same latitude as Moscow, but though swept by strong winds, it is fortunately warmed by the North Atlantic Drift. Only one meeting in the first year was cancelled due to snow, which lasted two days.

Although in direct temperature contrast, the group has affinities with those set up in more traditional 'oil' countries, and not only because of the difficulty in getting books to read and discuss.

As often happens the idea was mooted by a woman who had been a member, Dorothy Thomson, in Orkney. She arrived in Brae in 1978 when her husband moved there to work for British Petroleum. She was a nursery teacher and before marriage worked as a hostess on a world cruising line 'for three fantastic years'. The nucleus she gathered around her included Angela Gibbins, who had come from Iran, where her husband worked as a civil engineer and she had taught in a nursery. Angela, a Yorkshirewoman had also been a school meals organiser in London. There was Ruth Kinnear, honours graduate of Trinity, the wife of an instrument inspection engineer with B.P. The fourth founder member was another 'B.P. wife', Pat Moriel, newly from Aberdeen.

In such circumstances potential members are easier to spot than in the urban suburbs. Dorothy's enthusiasm led to a successful meeting in 1979 attended by eighteen women. Ruth, from Northern

Ireland, with qualifications in secondary remedial teaching, led the first discussion which was on 'poverty', the idea coming from a *Sunday Times* article on the high infant mortality rate in Naples, and a later one entitled 'Northern Ireland, What Now?' attended by thirty.

The main idea was to get mothers of young families together, young women most of whom had recently moved to a new and rather strange environment far from their own folk and going through their first experience of what life is like for 'oil families'.

The group is based on Brae and Mossbank, two villages fourteen miles apart, on the largest island, called Mainland, which is about fifty miles long. Transport is by car, the only buses being for school or work, so anyone wanting to participate in any event must be prepared to face a journey. Dorothy Thomson retired from the organising job; there are now two organisers. Angela Smith, immediately from Suffolk, originally from Nottingham, had heard of NHR on 'Woman's Hour' and wrote asking about a group in Shetland. The woman who was recorded then as starting one never got it going, not at all a rare event in Register history. Like her co-organiser, Carol Stevens, Angela lives in Mossbank and both are married to firemen working different shifts. When one is away the other takes over.

Instead of the nine to five, five days a week routine, husbands may have two or three weeks' leave at a time and the families go south to the mainland, which makes for spasmodic attendances. But the group still flourishes. It meets every two or three weeks for a series of debates, discussions, talks. Ambitions to start a book club, run by Ruth, hit a snag when the mobile library calling, three weeks in every four, thought it expensive to get around eight copies of one title if it was not popular and likely to be taken out by the general public. The group was working out a way round that; say four copies to pass round and getting them to the fastest readers first.

Members' husbands are mostly employed by the construction companies involved in building the oil terminal at Sullom Voe, or by the oil companies, or in oil related jobs. Some members are local Shetlanders, but unfortunately few have been keen to join. Members come originally from all over Britain and Ireland, or more lately direct from postings from such places as Alaska, Iran and Jamaica. This diversity adds flavour to the discussions.

No one is complaining about the lack of leisure activities. Members attend evening classes in the local schools and sporting opportunities are readily available. There are two museums, one agricultural and one displaying relics of Shetlands history, crafts, boats.

'We have no art gallery,' Angela Smith told me while fielding the demands of a three-year-old and a five-year-old, and dealing with girls asking for sponsorship for 'a Wellie Throw in aid of our hall funds'. But, she managed to continue, 'shows are put on at the library at different times. Shetland's history is fascinating and you could spend many enjoyable hours researching it. I have been to one or two talks on old Shetland. There is a brass band (my husband plays trombone), orchestra, and, of course, Shetland fiddle groups.' It is just that the NHR provides, as Ruth puts it: 'a much needed intellectual stimulus'.

In 1980 Brae/Mossbank was backing up the 'how to' advice from the National Group to help a contact get a group together in the island's main town, Lerwick. But since that is some twenty-five miles south the distinction of being NHR/UK's most northern group remains intact.

XIII
The Trio That Became A Pair – 1973–76

Josephine Jaffray, Angela Lepper, Pat Williams

Josephine Jaffray likes to think that she used the *Guardian* issue containing Maureen Nicol's original letter as a pillow on a Campaign for Nuclear Disarmament march. She certainly followed the early development of NHR.

'In those days most women gave up work on marriage and I certainly had to give up secretarial work when I married a shepherd and lived in very isolated areas. I kept in mind the existence of NHR for several years, always trying to find out if there was a group within reach. But I was not just looking for NHR. It is highly significant for me that the development of NHR had sown in my mind the realisation that women, on marriage, need not spend their days homemaking, entertaining, and going to the Townswomen's Guild twice a month (which for my mother opened her eyes to a wider world) but that intellectual activities, presumed normal while pursuing formal education, could and should develop as an integral part of daily living.'

Josephine, with two young children, joined her first group while living within reach of Edinburgh. After eighteen months the family moved to Moffat, Dumfriesshire. 'We were five miles, a potholed, five-gated road from the town, but I was determined to make some friends with whom I could exchange ideas of general interest and not just domestic and farming chat'. She contacted NHR, got a 'New Group Pack' from National Organiser Lesley Moreland ('I was later to send out hundreds') and put an advert in the local paper.

The two people who replied directly are still among her friends. Despite the size of the town, population two thousand, they developed a thriving group. 'We have seen each other's children move from nursery school, primary, and now some have left secondary to go on to further education.' Josephine dropped out during her national stint but even now, and working full time, belongs to its book discussion group; the Register group itself now centred on a neighbouring large town.

But about her national stint. She met one of the National incumbents, Lesley Moreland – after 'standing shyly at the periphery of the crowd' – while attending the Scottish conference in Glasgow. She volunteered when they asked for successors.

She remembers clearly the phone call asking her to be one of the three new National Organisers. 'I was in the middle of icing the Christmas cake, having got the children off to bed. The enormity of the task and the responsibility, and the amount of work made my legs turn to jelly. We had a small holding on which I was expected to work, the children were three and four years old, and yet on the phone that evening I accepted it.

'In retrospect I know I was right; the following three or four years were the most memorable since my teenage years and have had an enormous influence on my life since. Naturally there were times when I could have gladly thrown it all up, such as the many times I felt my goodwill and dedication were being abused when members treated me rudely as though I was a distant, insensitive professional (but does anyone deserve such treatment?) and when I was torn, as so often happened, between loyalties to family and to NHR.

'Such divided loyalties were part and parcel of the job which I was usually able to balance, but sometimes they created real conflicts which are still having their repercussions in my family life. My husband was extremely tolerant of my NHR commitment. My children remember those days with a trace of bitterness and with understandable resentment. "Phone, phone, phone" is how my daughter sums it up!

'I literally spent hours on it and of course cheap rate is in the evening when the children look forward to a couple of family hours before bed. They obviously saw it as encroaching uncontrollably, unlike set hours of work, on their lives at a time when Mummy is still the pivot of their universe.

Maureen Nicol, founder and first National Organiser of NHR

The Trustees cutting the twenty-first birthday cake at the 1981 National Conference, Warwick. Left to right, Mary Stott, Betty Jerman, Maureen Nicol

Brenda Prys Jones, National Organiser 1962–64

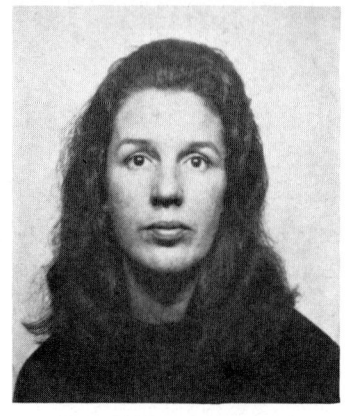

Lesley Taylor (now Shooter), National Organiser 1964–67

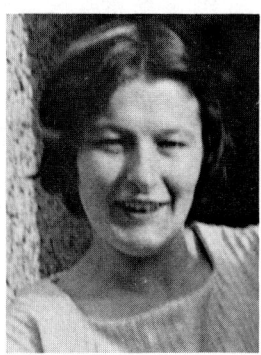

(*left*) Anita Brocklesby and (*right*) Lesley Moreland, joint National Organisers 1970–73

Jane Watt, National Organiser 1967–69

Pat Williams
(1973–76)

Joint National Organisers, 1973–76:
Angela Lepper
(1973–74)

Josephine Jaffray
(1973–76),

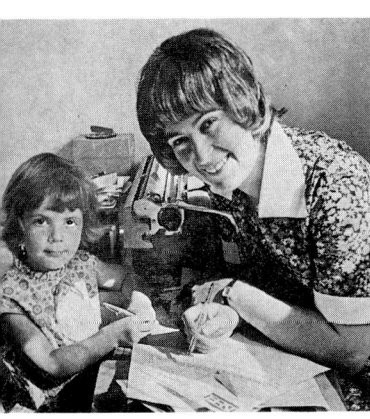

(*left*) Marie Price, National Organiser 1976–78, with her daughter Samantha

(*right*) Gill Vine, National Organiser 1978–80, with '*The* Register'

Alison Shingler became National Organiser in 1980.
('I wondered why there was an empty space in Wiltshire until I realised that it was Stonehenge!')

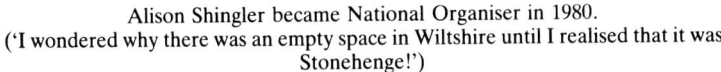

Members at the Reading Conference 1979 enjoying further discussion over coffee

A typical group meeting

The Herne Bay Group taking part in a local carnival

Nick Roberts, son of Jeni Roberts of Vale of Clwyd Group

(*above*) Some members of the first National Group, elected in 1976. Left to right: Hazel Bell, Gill Vine, Liz Salthouse, Joan Harborne, Marie Price, Jane Goodwin, Jean Stirk, Yvonne Bradley, Pauline Webster

(*below*) Members of the National Group in 1978. Standing, left to right: Jean Stirk, Hazel Bell, Val Williams, Margaret Cameron, Jane Goodwin; seated: Pat Kerr, Beryl Bonney, Gill Vine, Liz Salthouse

National Group 1980. Standing, left to right: Val Williams, Sales (Chester), Matilda Popper, Correspondence Magazines (Swansea), Anna Alford, Archivist (High Wycombe), Vivienne Eardley, Overseas Coordinator (Glasgow), Kathy Noble, Minutes Secretary (Leeds), Antoinette Ferraro, Conference Liaison (Solihull); seated: Sue Jones, *Newsletter* Editor (St Albans), Alison Shingler, National Organiser (Bruton), Pat Kerr, New Groups Advisor and Chairman 1980–81 (Harrogate), Liz Williamson, Treasurer (Marple), Vicky Hearn, Chairman, 1981–82 (West Kirkby), Joan Davies, Circulars Compiler (Trowbridge)

The National Conference at Reading University, April 1979

The first International Conference, held at Newlands Park College, July 1980. Front row left to right: Beth Weir (W Australia), Matilda Popper, Rita Cooper (S Africa), Vivienne Eardley, Alison Shingler, Jane Goodwin, Pat Kerr, Suzanne Wyatt (Belgium), Carol Binbrek (Abu Dhabi); Middle Row: Kathy Southgate (S Africa), Lora Killen (Holland), Hilary Welch (Belgium), Helen Formentin (W Australia), Eva Grimley (S Africa), Antoinette Ferraro, Christine Valentine (USA), Betsy Knapp (USA), Lindsay Davidson (Abu Dhabi); Back Row: Dolly Smitka (Canada), Margaret Sanderson (Holland), Rhona Wetzka (S Africa), Cherry Cavill (Canada), Unknown, Sue Marsden (Kuwait)

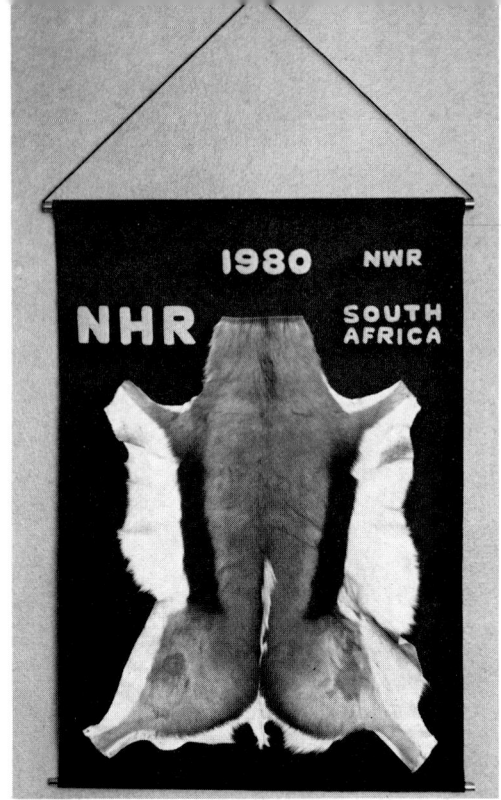

Some gifts presented to NHR in the UK by members in Canada, South Africa, Western Australia and Zimbabwe

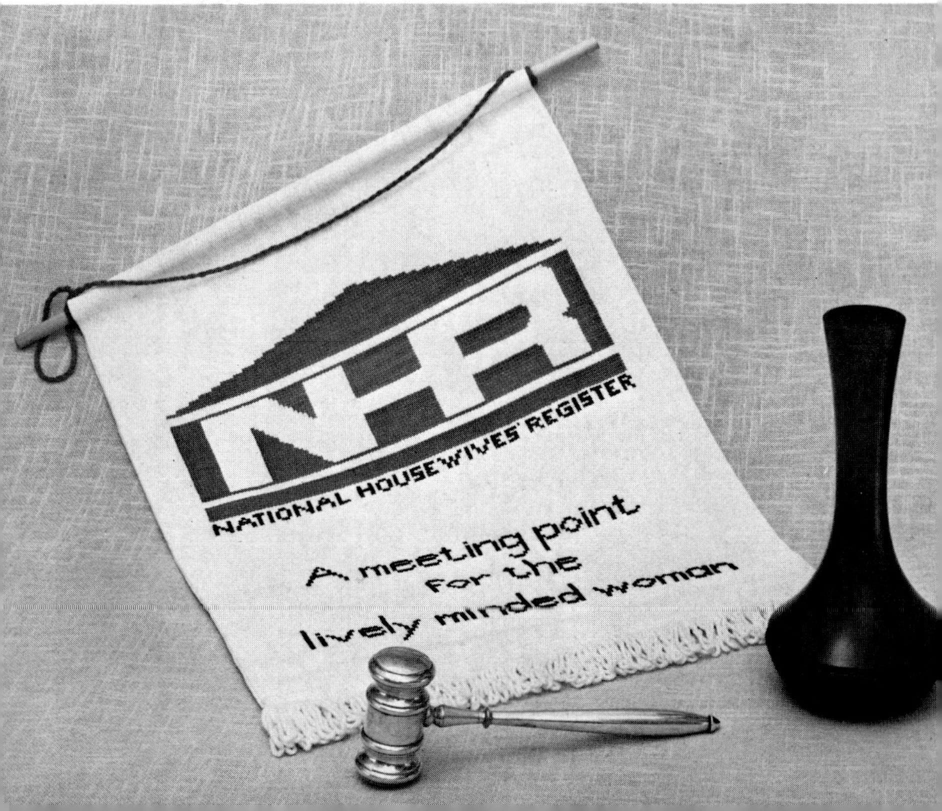

'But there were many positive points. The hours were flexible. So long as I could get away from the phone I was able to be with the children when they needed me, when sick, or unhappy, or to see them in the school concert. I often took them with me when going away on NHR business. They travelled all over the country, staying with friends and relatives while I was at a conference or a meeting, and this broadened their outlook and helped keep up friendships which would otherwise have died.

'Some of the happiest times were when Pat and her family, plus cat, came to camp on our farm. It became quite a regular way of us getting together, good social occasions as well as fitting in work. One of the most memorable periods in our term of office was the Crewe Conference, but such awful memories are superceded by what was happening family-wise that weekend.

'It was Moffat Gala Week, the big event of which was the children's fancy dress. Whilst trying to prepare for the crucial conference both families spent the preceding week feverishly making costumes. The Williams' family spent the weekend at our place and the men ushered the children to the Fancy Dress Competition and must have coped well with the last minute safety pins and creased crepe paper for they all came away with prizes'.

Angela Lepper, B.Sc (Hons) Chemistry, Leeds University, was working as Scientific Librarian/Information Officer for a chemical firm in Harrogate when she first heard of the NHR from a male colleague whose wife was a keen member. In February 1967 the Leppers moved to Bromborough, Wirral, three months before their first child was born and, within days, Angela contacted the Local Organiser of the Bromborough and Eastham group, and joined. It was Maureen Nicol's original group. 'Some of the longer-standing members speaking of her almost with bated breath for the things "she made us do".'

Angela recalls reading the spring *Newsletter* of that year during a sleepless night ten days before her daughter was born and thinking 'But this is me! That's what *I* think. That's what *I* want to do and I realised that here was an organisation through which I could be *myself* and not just "someone's wife or someone's Mum" as I feared for the next few years. I still have this *Newsletter*'. (The emphasis is hers).

When her husband was moved by his firm to London in 1971 Angela wrote to Anita Brocklesby for a list of groups' addresses in the most likely areas. 'Armed with this we househunted. I was determined not to live too far from an NHR group.'

Moving in July, she was devastated to find that the newly formed

Rickmansworth group had no meetings for six weeks during the school holidays. Nevertheless members invited her and her children round and she had made several friends before her first meeting in September. In what she calls 'the unfriendly south', being a northerner, 'NHR was truly a lifeline and provided me with many friends, whereas if I had depended on my neighbours I should still know scarcely anyone after eight years.'

A letter from Anita Brocklesby in autumn 1972, asking if she would consider being National Secretary after her, 'amazed' Angela. Later she discovered that a friend whom she had encouraged to start a group in Essex had suggested her name to the National Organisers with the recommendation of being 'good at writing letters'. After a month's cogitation: 'I wrote the kind of letter which could have been called how not to apply for a job – pointing out the disadvantages from my point of view. That I thought ended the matter. I was dumbfounded when Lesley and Anita accepted my very backhanded offer. Certainly I was attracted by much of the job and knew that my younger child was due to start school about then, so I thought I could fit in the work well at home'.

The third member of the trio, Pat Williams, had various secretarial jobs before marriage. She joined the High Wycombe group in 1969, just after her second daughter Helen was born, in a bad state of depression and having read an article in the *Guardian* and seen a notice in the local library.

'I recovered my humour slowly and took "O" level cookery the following year, vaguely wanting to do an exam subject to see whether I could cope with the discipline after a long gap'. A vocational guidance counsellor advised her to do some 'A' levels. 'NHR was beginning to have the desired effect – others were doing similar things so why not me?' She got two 'A' levels, and having talked to Lesley Moreland at the national conference at Reading 'found ordinary women did have ambition. I was very awed at the National Organiser speaking to me as an equal, and didn't stop talking to all sorts of "equals" all weekend, becoming a conference addict thereafter". She also started fostering children for the local authority.

By 1972 Pat was the literary group organiser for her NHR group, but missed the national conference since it clashed with her first daughter Claire's birthday. Her closest friend in NHR, Frances Alexander, returned to report that Lesley Moreland might have to retire early, suggesting Pat could take over for a year.

Pat recalls the day Lesley and she spent together. 'I was staggered at the amount of work she had to do and the intrusion in her home and family life. I had never really thought about where the circulars and *Newsletter* emanated from. I tried consciously to keep this impression vivid in my mind later on so that I could forgive members their worst transgressions.'

Lesley's domestic problems eased and she carried on. But in November, because of Robin Williams' job, the family moved to Walsall. Pat feels that not only was her name to hand but her offer was strengthened because she was in the Midlands and the other two likely candidates for national office lived in Scotland and London, giving a geographical spread desired by the incumbents.

Pat got a job, temp typing, and gave it up. She mentioned it only because: 'I think I was pretty typical in having to give up a source of income in order to make time for the NHR work. It follows that anyone taking on the burden would have had time to work, even if they had not worked up to that time.'

Josephine, Angela and Pat met for the first time in February 1973, spending a weekend at Pat's house. The retiring pair, Anita and Lesley, explained how the work divided fairly easily into three. Josephine, with the title of New Groups Adviser and PRO would help and support in the development of new groups and seek publicity with the media. Angela with the title of National Secretary and Treasurer would largely do Anita's job, keeping in touch with established groups, financial matters and enquiries, such as from prospective members and those moving, also overseas groups and contacts.

Pat got the duplicator and the typewriter, and hence would be responsible for producing publicity materials as well as the *Newsletter*. An aside from her: 'Equipment is a limiting factor in dividing up a job and will eventually be the reason NHR will have to have a central office and not use someone's home.'

One of their earliest decisions, and economies, was to type letters to members. Josephine had her own typewriter, and use duplicated notes where possible. Pat recalls about the change: 'Some frowned, some approved of that. Until this time letters had been handwritten to indicate the personal nature of the organisation.'

They were introduced to the membership in a circular on takeover in June 1973 which expressed their mutual amazement over the 'bulk of work with which Lesley and Anita have coped and at how conscientiously and indefatigably they have carried out the very menial tasks as well as the more obviously rewarding ones'. They each had £250 a year honorarium.

They were three strangers who had little opportunity for the normal leisurely social discourse which would have helped them get to know each other. They had to work together from a distance; even a phone call (long distance) could only be between two of them. They were three independent-minded women who had jobs of equal status. If there were differences of opinion who was to arbitrate?

Additionally, Josephine and Pat were going through much the same personality clashes during the first year as Anita and Lesley, maybe worse. 'I just did not like her nor she me,' says Josephine bluntly. She continued: 'Over the years a great understanding has grown. We learned to communicate when we opposed each other and solve, and above all understand, our differences. Pat remains one of my closest, staunchest and dearest friends. We have weathered many battles together of a working and personal nature.'

Pat thinks that it took about a year 'to get the measure of each other. This was to become the basis of a lasting friendship and we know Anita and Lesley enjoyed the same experience.' Lesley and Anita were, or course, offering sympathetic ears to their successors. Pat: 'They were really the only ones we could turn to as no one who has not experienced the degree of pressure which is put on to an NO can really appreciate the urgency of settling problems. There is no mental time to cope with extraneous matters.'

Each was having to get the hang of a completely new job. Josephine was encouraging the setting up of new groups, a job that all through was to remain 'closest to my heart'. It was done almost entirely by letter. 'Groups had to stand or fall on their own and above all grow their own identity. I tried to support and not impose. I rejoiced with groups when they made another step forward and I was saddened when, even working together, it had to be admitted we just could not get anything off the ground. Sometimes I despaired when I got letters from women who had to give up because their husbands forbade them from continuing, saying their job was at the kitchen sink, obviously feeling threatened by such subversive activity. I got to know people so well by letter and the highlight was to meet them at a conference or a group meeting.'

'The other main, and the most challenging-part of my job was the PR work. It was difficult, being so far from London, as all contacts were there. In time I went into all the major papers and magazine offices and talked about the NHR, just trying to keep our organisation in mind and get the odd mention, and sometimes major articles. I found this very exciting, extremely interesting and sometimes even terrifying. Television appearances were the worst.'

Pat, who pays compliments to Lesley Moreland for being the first to produce a 'general interest' newsletter, had a hectic summer in her first year producing her first *Newsletter*: 'finding a suitable printer was no small headache'. But between NLs she had very little to do; 'just short sharp panics to get circulars out'.

It soon became clear that the jobs were unbalanced, that the burden fell on Angela even with good support from local groups and two members helping regularly. She was answering letters from enquirers, corresponding with Local Organisers and updating the Register (in triplicate), acknowledging all subscriptions and doing all accounts, and corresponding with overseas groups. As she lived near London a number of PR enquiries were made to her which could not always be deflected to Josephine, since in those days before STD, you could not dial nine numbers and get straight through to Dumfriesshire. She also, like Pat and Josephine, redrafted leaflets; hers was on splitting, and was called 'How to cope with too large a group', and she compiled a document for the use of new Local Organisers.

Christmas, with its extra domestic burdens, was the catalyst for a meeting at Angela's in February 1974. They not only aired the future of the administration, but reached a short-term solution; that Angela should have paid help extending her members' aid, and that the other two should take over the enquiries since they could be easily bundled up and passed over, albeit incurring some delay. But by then Pat was already in the throes of the spring newsletter, and she had a major problem which was no primary source of material from, or contact with, members. She had to rely on Angela fishing out likely letters. Few articles came specially written for publication. That put another burden on Angela.

All three pay tribute to Jane Watt's unstinting counsel during that time, ill though she was.

By Whitsun (May 1974) Angela had to face the fact that the volume of work was not compatible with her family commitments. She wrote to Pat and Josephine regretfully resigning her post, because she was deeply disappointed not to be able to complete the three years she had anticipated.

'My one year proved an interesting, and in many ways, rewarding experience', she told me, 'meeting so many people, if only on paper, phone, or briefly at conferences, and a very few trips to London to meet personnel in other organisations or the media. Ninety-five per cent was sheer hard slog, but I felt it was well worth while since I myself had gained so much from NHR that I wanted to help those who were lonely and needed the lifeline which NHR can provide, and to help those floundering as Local Organiser, a job I had so much enjoyed. The final mark left on me by that year is the deterioration of my handwriting caused by so many letters. I don't type!' Three thousand letters were filed by Angela Wender, a member of her group! Angela Lepper was later to contribute to the Register nationally yet again.

Angela's resignation, says Pat, 'did put the cat among the pigeons'. Josephine recalls it as 'traumatic, surely there could have been some alternative'. They decided against a replacement. 'We had just about got the measure of each other by then and didn't want to risk upsetting the comparative calm,' Pat comments. 'In addition we had no one in mind and reckoned it would be impossible to find someone before the autumn by which time we would have been swamped.' Jo took over the enquiries, and Pat established groups and the files. They decided to use Angela's share of the honorarium to buy (part-time) secretarial help for each; Pat was helped the first year by Rosemary Brown, a Walsall member. They asked for a book-keeper through the Register circular and were grateful when Jeannine Bolingbroke of the Plymouth group volunteered, being paid on a lowly basis. She was, note, not the 'Treasurer'. Such responsibility lay with the two women who both carried the title of National Organiser.

They worked well together, each getting on with the job, trusting each other to interpret this through the philosophy of NHR, not fussing over details. Pat edited the *Newsletter* by and large on her own. Jo wrote most of the circulars when they had agreed on points to cover, and sent them to Pat. Further changes could be made on the phone before she duplicated them. Most communication was by phone.

'Endless hours,' recalls Josephine, 'and I mean that literally. One call could take an hour. In times of stress we phoned at expensive times saying "the members will have to put up with this if they are not going to recognise our voluntary status or improve working conditions".' On one occasion they met in a member's house in Carlisle, the day return being cheaper than four hours on the phone.

'We also wrote a lot to each other. We met at every possible opportunity, I don't suppose ever less than four months apart. The Williams's came to us for holidays. Coincidentally my mother lives in Birmingham. I remember once meeting in Rackhams' store in Birmingham and sitting all morning over a cup of coffee and many papers and notebooks. Certainly I would say it was a full-time job and one from which you never "went home". I don't think it is an overstatement to say we gave up three years of our lives for NHR.'

Pat wonders how her husband survived. 'I became a bit organisationally drunk, each day was planned out, goals were set for deadlines. New problems presented themselves every day, silly things like having to find my way round strange towns. I did little driving before, but now I was driving myself hundreds of miles, visiting groups, travelling regularly by train. I went into a pub alone and bought myself a drink for the first time in my life'.

Both women verged on nervous breakdowns in that middle year in office because they were also forging policy decisions.

XIV
How It Got A Constitution

'TOWARDS THE CHANGE', muses Josephine Jaffray, 'sounds menopausal. For the NHR it was like the onset of puberty, but for us it was like they say the menopause is, hot flushes of embarrassment and anger, not knowing quite where we stood, depression, utter depths, but plenty of laughs and satisfaction too, and the sheer joy when it all was finally and unanimously voted for at Bristol in 1976. We certainly grew with the work, able to give and take more and cope with greater stress as time went on.'

It was Josephine and Pat's role in the history of the movement to introduce its first formal document, but remember they were two women steeped in its adherence to informality.

Jane Watt had seen the danger signs and put up warning signals, querying the method of selecting National Organisers, putting up the cock-shy of Deirdre Collins' 'constitution' – to no effect. Her successors had probed further and aired for the first time the question of national officers' financial vulnerability.

A threesome to carry the national workload – even if it had been sustained – could only have been a tiding-over. Jo and Pat were having to face up, not only to the physical (and emotional) inconvenience to their families, but their personal responsibility for finances which were nearing four figures, and the risk that their own homes would be forfeited if anything went wrong. And that was not an impossibility. Subs for 7,500 members were received in 1973, for 15,000 in 1974 (some even paying at the old rate of 25p). Even by 1975 only 17,000 were paying their dues, though 24,600 printed newsletters, which had to be paid for, were sent out to members.

Josephine 'dropped the bombshell', as someone described it, at the national conference held at Darlington in April 1974, asking 'please be understanding, please think before you speak'. She remembers the stunned silence as members tried to assimilate the hard fact that a movement that had set its face against hierarchy and committees, had got to the stage where some compromise was needed if it was to be held together.

The National Organisers were feeling 'very lonely' and lacking the professional skills they felt were needed. They appealed for volunteers to help them explore feasible alternatives to the prevailing system. The 'Fact Finders' were Yvonne Bradley, Frances Healey, Betty Karplanis, Elsie Kirby, Angela Lepper, Jean Stirk, Pat Thomson, Gill Vine and Anne Watts. Others helped at different stages.

They were to give comfort and confidence to the two NOs who, reaching home after that Darlington conference, and right through to their handing over, got letters which were sometimes aggressive, sometimes destructive, insensitive, hurtful; disagreeing with the proposals. What Jo calls 'daggers through the post'.

The 'Fact Finders', with whom they could share the decision making, also influenced their thinking that some form of supporting group for a National Organiser was essential; women spread around the country who could visit groups, encourage regional get-togethers and do the policy side of the workload.

Jo and Pat had, of course, to carry on with their jobs, (and any item of publicity brought in floods of enquiries) while pouring out information to members on what was happening plus communications to the new team, each of whom assembled a fat file of letters, sometimes barely decipherable after the umpteenth carbon. A 'Round Robin' enabled thoughts and comments to go round by mail in the absence of face to face gatherings.

Questions by post started things off for the 'Fact Finders'. What is the purpose of NHR, who needs it, when, why, where, how can all this be achieved, and, in view of the answers, what do Local Organisers and individual members need from the National Organisers, or an alternative administration? They were examining the organisation fundamentally, and not seeking some temporary and superficial panacea. They turned out to be in general agreement.

While two worked on the constitution side, finding out the obligations and benefits of registering as a charity or limited company, each of the others approached at least two other organisations, mostly those with predominantly female membership, but including the Quakers. They were seeking examples of how organisations are run at *national* level. A lot of other personal and organisational views were sought, including those of past National Organisers and the Founder.

A circular to members in May 1975 distilled the year-long, countrywide, fact seeking and the consultations (which had included presenting ideas to the national conference for discussion back home) and communications to all Local Organisers asking for comments (only eighty replied out of something like seven to eight thousand). The circular reiterated that the national officers had known, when taking over, that the job had become 'too arduous to pass on to a voluntary part-timer', leaving aside the financial responsibility. The Local Organisers who *had* reacted, voiced concern about the loss of local group autonomy and that the gap between NO and LO would widen.

That important circular explained that the idea of Regional Organisers had been discarded because of the fear that a hierarchy could develop and the National Organiser become only approachable through the Regional Officer, thus widening the gap 'and be fragmenting between regions', whereas a supporting group with good geographical spread could strengthen the links as well as helping the NO in decision making.

Suggestions on the future administration of NHR were therefore put forward for the membership to consider.

One National Organiser to be responsible for all correspondence, assisting setting up new groups, advising existing ones, national publicity, public relations, the newsletter, appointing clerical assistants (to be paid a wage) and collecting subscriptions. She would have assistant National Organisers, one to start with, and the spread of the work would be set out. The jobs would be based on the home, or home area, and would be permanent. Clerical assistance would also be available in emergencies such as illness or temporary extreme pressure of work. The 'rate' for the National Organiser, a job similar to that held by the high ranking officers in other organisations, was quoted at £3,000 a year, 'but at first two-thirds of this amount would cover her workload'.

She would be backed by a 'Steering Group' geographically distributed, serving two years, half retiring each year for continuity. Methods of determining who served on such a Group varied from Local Organisers's postal vote on nominees, to a vote at a national. business meeting.

The Steering Group's duties would range from appointing an honorary treasurer, a meetings' minute taker, being a sounding board for membership opinion, safeguarding the constitution, taking decisions of a policy nature, interpreting and keeping up to date 'Guidelines' and, of course, appointing the National Organiser. She would be a member of the Group for six months, or alternatively have done some voluntary work for the Register for the same period.

Jo and Pat explained in the circular:

> On the question of financial liability we were advised that only a constitution or articles of association could provide a measure of protection for the NO.

Three options were therefore open.

> (1) A constitution will give a degree of financial protection for the NO and guidance for the national organisation. We believe if the organisation were a corporate body with its name registered either with the Charity Commission or at Companies House this would enable us to be recognised more easily by outside organisations.

That included being on the list for information disseminated by government offices.

> (2) If we were accepted as having charitable status we could build up reserves without fear of taxation, we could obtain office equipment at reduced prices, and if, at a later date, we wished to have a central office, we would only have to pay half rates. (3) If we became a company limited by guarantee we would have to pay corporation tax.

The circular also explained that everything it had gone into would not need to be written into a constitution the wording of which would vary anyway according to whether charity status was sought or not. It also gave a couple of lines on NHR 'Aims', a definition of a group and a member (those who have paid their annual national subscription), mentioned the need to raise subs and the suggestion of a 'group co-ordinator' who would be listed on the Register.

Altogether a block-buster.

Hazel Bell of Hatfield (later she became *Newsletter* editor) collated the comments of 114 groups, 80 of which turned up by the advertised June deadline, at least 41 more drifting in after it! Her analysis was presented at the very first conference held entirely on NHR itself, at the Crewe College of Education, 19 July 1975.

Hazel reported:

> Most groups reacted with a variety of agreement and reservations on specific points. One had such a diversity of opinions as to be uncountable. Indeed, if 'lively-minded' groups are expected to differ, why should the individual members of any particular group be expected to concur?

At Crewe Pat summarised the main points on which 'almost everyone agreed': retaining group autonomy, NHR never acting as a pressure group, avoiding a hierarchy of national and/or regional committees to retain informality, and safeguarding the essential differences from other organisations. Many groups had asked for Maureen Nicol's views. She felt, as Pat explained, 'decisions should be reached by those who are more closely involved with the present-day running of the organisation'.

Otherwise there was confusion among members about how many National Organisers and assistants were proposed, dislike of a Steering Group as 'hierarchical and expensive', questioning of the rate of pay ('many members seemed prepared to sell their sisters short' Pat noted), concern that the National Organiser should *not* be a career-based woman, but must be a member with a limited term of office. The idea of local groups having a 'co-ordinator' was unpopular (and therefore dropped), the *wording* of NHR aims was still open for refinement and, with many members not happy about charitable status, Pat explained yet again that NOs and their families must have financial protection.

The 123 women (representing 100 groups) attending the conference then divided into groups for discussion under leaders who later presented to the full meeting, first the unanimous views, then the disagreements. There was no voting, though the possibility was raised at one point, as well as that of some regional structure. The proceedings were recorded on tape and later transcribed. Women accustomed to courteous, however passionate, debate proffered a number of interesting suggestions on how the different elements at national level could be handled.

There was an odd 'off court' development. 'The incredible happened, sections of NHR mobilised to fight off', as Pat put it, 'the unwanted changes being foisted upon them by the NOs, without any consultation, and by devious means!'

Earlier in the year Josephine had gone to a small gathering similar to many they were attending at the time. Afterwards Pat was asked for a list of the Local Organisers of groups within a thirty mile radius of one particular group, which she provided. A much larger gathering was arranged just before the Crewe conference, which Pat attended. 'I walked into a hornet's nest. I tried to defuse the situation, because I believed my usual talk and answering questions had not allayed their fears entirely, by promising access for all at the Crewe conference. I had some nasty letters after Crewe saying they had been cheated, that the conference was rigged, etc. They were formidable and wrote to all groups in their area. I replied at length again. I had one more "nasty" letter from an individual around Christmas time – and that was the last I heard.'

Meantime the NOs sent out a lengthy report on the business

conference at Crewe, to all groups. There had been a large measure of agreement on fundamentals; i.e. 'that the National Organisation should do much the same as at present, it should have National Organisers, a steering group and a constitution'. The main points about which there remained doubt were: whether the NO and her Assistant should be equal in status, what form the supportive group should take, how the group should be chosen and how the NO should be chosen.

That same month, September, eight of the women who had been closely involved in the eighteen months of research and consultation met in London to figure out the next step. They were: Hazel Bell, Jeannine Bolingbroke, Frances Healey, Pat Hicklenton, Jean Stirk, Gill Vine, Ann Watts and Pauline Webster. Pat and Jo withdrew in the centre part of the day, as the latter explains 'in case they should feel restricted by our presence; we were very sensitive about *not* imposing our naturally strong views'.

The NOs December circular to Local Organisers was headed in capital letters 'PLEASE ENSURE THAT EVERY MEMBER HAS AN OPPORTUNITY TO READ THIS'. It set out the results of the deliberations.

> It was decided that we should have an honorary NO chosen from the national group to be paid a good honorarium and have a limited term of office. Her job would be to keep in close touch with groups and members and their problems. NHR would employ, on the usual terms, an administrator who would deal with all enquiries from non-members, be responsible for up-dating the register, duplicating, ordering, receiving monies, etc. A staff as necessary would be employed to help both the NO and administrator.
>
> The national group would be elected and have honorary officers, one of whom would be the NO. Some jobs which the NOs do at present could be shared among the national group as circumstances dictate.
>
> We were asked to take legal advice on the question of whether a constitution would provide sufficient protection for the national group or whether it would be necessary to become a limited company. Pat has consulted a solicitor and he has advised us against forming a limited company because he believes this would bring a degree of formality which we do not want ... the solicitor is at present drawing up a draft constitution.

The national group was seen as between five and fifteen and, if there were more nominations than places, the solicitor advised voting at the national conference.

The circular asked for nominations.

Pat was pleased to have got a professional seal of approval. 'The idea was to spell out to the members what the organisation was for and what the national group and National Organiser were supposed to be doing, so that they had a basis for complaint or objection. In addition the members could get rid of a national administration it didn't like and elect a new one. The old system of arm twisting of volunteers seemed inappropriate for such a large organisation with now a considerable turnover of funds, so much in fact that we were now liable for VAT. The financial responsibility was one which scared us most as we knew we could be personally liable for income tax, or more accurately, our husbands, if NHR inadvertently made a profit. We always kept the funds in a building society. In retrospect we were very ignorant and naive in money matters but this was another good reason for putting NHR on a more permanent footing, and being prepared to take, and pay for, professional advice'.

The proposed constitution was sent out just before Christmas 1975. There was little comment. It was presented at the national conference held in Bristol in 1976. Pat 'dreaded a last-minute hitch. There was no hitch. All was sweetness and light.' The document took effect from 1 July 1976.

There were twenty-seven nominations for the four years of office in the new National Group; half had to retire and be replaced after two years. So, with their written personalia, and the formality of proposers, seconders, the very first NHR voting for national officers was undertaken, though only among those who attended the national conference at Bristol.

After their marathon Pat remarks, 'from then on we wound down rapidly'.

Josephine still remembers that first vote. 'It was so sad to see the old ways go but now, hopefully, the informality and consensus of opinion had safety nets in constitution.' In the last stage they had just 'moved on from draft to draft' of the constitution. 'We had given up the idea of charitable status or limited liability. I think we felt we would bear that in mind when wording the constitution but generally just get down something acceptable to NHR and let the next National Organisers fight that one out. And they did!'

XV
The First National Group 1976–80

ONLY THOSE PRESENT at the 1976 national conference held in Bristol could vote and, as the results were announced from the platform, the first National Group emerged, literally, lining up in front of the members. The principle was that half were to retire, and be replaced, after two years and if natural wastage was not effective those with the lowest number of votes would resign.

The fifteen successful candidates were, (in alphabetical order): Hazel Bell, of Hatfield, Herts, graduate, part-time indexer and examiner, ex-teacher. Yvonne Bradley, of Johnstone, a member in Cheshire before she moved to Strathclyde, Scotland. Margaret Cameron, of Arbroath, Tayside, with administrative experience. Elizabeth (Betty) Carrington, of Harrogate, North Yorkshire, with secretarial qualifications. Judith Franklin, of Bromsgrove South, Hereford and Worcestershire, a graduate, teacher. Jane Goodwin, of Ickenham South, Greater London, part-time teacher, and in contact with NHR groups abroad. Joan Harborne, of Grimsby, South Humberside, part-time teacher. Frances Healey, graduate, of Winchester, Hampshire. Patricia Lloyd, of Teignmouth, Devon, pharmacist, working part-time. Marie Price, of Abergavenny, Wales, qualified commercial-subjects teacher with secretarial, administrative, journalistic experience. Elizabeth Salthouse, of Sale, Cheshire, dietitian. Jean Stirk of Ightham, Kent, graduate, an industrial personnel officer, with experience in lecturing in industrial relations. Gill Vine, of Chalfont St. Peter, Buckinghamshire, graduate, who had experience of personnel selection and of public relations. Pauline Webster, of Chesham Bois, Buckinghamshire, Parish Councillor. Lorna Wilson, of Wigton, Cumbria, graduate and teacher.

Many had been founders, or Local Organisers, of their groups, or otherwise hard working members. Four had been among the 'Fact-Finders', five had actually met across a table in London to hammer out a constitution.

At Bristol they assembled, when the conference programme was over, as a roomful of strangers. Somebody said 'What do we do now?' and somebody else said 'I suppose we've got to run NHR'. Judith Franklin remembers: 'The atmosphere was tense and people were reluctant to take any decisions – afraid of being "lumbered" or of seeming "pushy" – I don't know. I suspect there was a lot of unspoken ambition there too! In the ensuing diffidence I found that I'd become co-ordinator for the first meeting of the NG, and that it would take place at my home on 1 May – an entirely optimistic date for the inception of such a new venture! Suddenly the responsibility of keeping NHR running smoothly, efficiently and unofficiously seemed tremendous.'

She circulated a questionnaire seeking the newly-elected officers' views on the role of the National Group, and of the National Organiser and the National Administrator, both being allowed for in the first constitution, plus any other immediate matters, so that she could prepare an agenda. The thoughtful replies provided other information on usable time, interests, skills, such as Hazel Bell and the *Newsletter*, Jane Goodwin and overseas groups, Gill Vine and public relations.

'We were all very cautious at that first meeting,' Judith recalls, 'very aware that we were setting precedents. Nothing like this had ever happened before.' They were in fact starting what is now traditional, meetings in the informal atmosphere of a private house, much like a local group gathering, only with a longer journey, with the local group (Bromsgrove for that very first meeting) rallying round with overnight accommodation and with excellent meals – re-imbursed, of course, by the individuals attending.

The first job at Bromsgrove was to appoint a National Organiser. After discussion on whether there should be one or two it was settled at one, to be the 'general representative', a member of the National Group, and dealing with new groups, the media and receiving an honorarium. Three had indicated interest; Elizabeth Carrington, Marie Price and Lorna Wilson, but the latter had recently given birth and was absent.

Jean Stirk had drawn up briefs for each job. The two candidates present were interviewed by her in front of everyone else, with some additional questions from the others. The Group's vote went to Marie Price.

The functions of the Group Co-ordinator were defined; arranging and chairing NG meetings, and general liaison. It was a title often confused with that of the NO in the early days, and was later changed to Chairman. After Judith the post was held by Pauline Webster and then Jean Stirk.

Joan Harborne offered to be Minutes Secretary and Liz Salthouse let out the quiet remark: 'I don't mind looking after the books'. Without more ado she became Treasurer. Hazel Bell took charge of the *Newsletter*. They decided that claimable expenses should cover travelling, phone, postage, stationery and meals for only the longest journeys.

There was some discussion about the proposed (and, remember, to be *paid*) 'National Administrator' to do the day-to-day work. Later Pat Williams arrived to clarify the assortment of jobs she and Josephine had dealt with.

'How cautious we were,' Judith reflects, 'and so afraid of not getting it right because of having the new constitution, a formal constraint. We circled and sized up one another.'

Marie recalls leaving that meeting with her feelings and thoughts in a turmoil after her election as NO. 'How were fifteen strong personalities such as ours ever going to work in harmony? Was I going to be tied to a committee before making any decision, however large or small?' She was to initiate the 'Round Robins' as a way in which the NG members could comment on problems between meetings, give advice and let her know what was going on in their own areas.

By the second meeting, in Pauline's home in Buckinghamshire a month later, Marie Price was already beginning to settle into an administrative system. Under the constitution they could have appointed a National Administrator, with equal status to the National Organiser. But the Group's talents did not seem to be dividing that way so the idea was dropped. Instead a Public Relations Officer was appointed, to make best use of members' skills. There were three candidates; Lorna Wilson, accompanied by her new baby, Betty Carrington and Gill Vine. They were interviewed singly. Gill: 'I remember feeling very nervous. Hadn't had an interview for years and these were very capable members. Why should I get the job?' She did.

They also decided who should get honoraria and the amounts – set for one year only to see if they had got them right. National Organiser £2,000 (Gill, who held that job later now thinks it 'rather funny' that this was intended to 'cover reasonable personal disturbance'), plus £500 for secretarial help, PRO £1,500 (actually reduced at Gill's insistence to £1,250 to enable Marie to receive more), Treasurer £600, *Newsletter* editor £500, payments to be made quarterly. Margaret Cameron offered to look after the archives. Along with Joan, who made minuted sense out of complicated discussions, she also helped to get more meetings going between local groups.

But this gradual assumption of and greater spread of national responsibility – including explaining why the change was necessary to those members still expressing dissatisfaction – was due for a very nasty jolt.

Liz Salthouse had checked with the retiring book-keeper Jeannine Bolingbroke that no insurance or VAT was involved before offering to be Treasurer. Her knowledge rested on a year's 'Accounting and Business Management' at College, rather as a fill-in on the timetable.

'There was a widely held view,' Liz explains, 'that charities and organisations such as ours would be exempt from VAT'. But when she took over the books someone, she does not today remember who it was, advised her to check. The accountant she consulted sent her straight to Customs and Excise.

The income limit for exemption from VAT was £5,000 a year in 1975. The published incomes had been greater than that for two years!

'We were very lucky with the VAT Inspector who came to sort us out,' records Liz. There were few receipts on which to claim back the little VAT due. 'Anyway the Inspector went through all the records I had and calculated what we owed and what we could re-claim, and came up with the figure of just under £600. We just did not have the money to pay.

'Before the VAT bill arrived we had paid for the autumn newsletter by instalments as we had insufficient money for that initially, and replenished all stationery and publicity materials which were practically zero. We have since ensured that most publicity material and stationery can be used through a change in National Group. We all received the September quarter honoraria

The First National Group: 1976–80

but by December we had no money and had to wait till July the following year for the missing quarter.'

Naturally the dire financial situation was the first topic for consideration at the National Group's third meeting, in November 1976, at Liz's house.

Liz explained that there was a shortage of money because not all groups were paying at the new 75p rate and costs had risen, and whereas subs turned up at all times, the big expenses, like the newsletter printing bill, had to be met all at once.

Then there was the VAT debt. No one liked the thought of a national appeal but it seemed justified. So members were told that £570 VAT was owed for the years 1974 to 1976 and that if the 884 registered groups each sent 50p it would almost be covered. Eventually £468 was received.

Meantime Liz wrote to the Chief Inspector of Taxes begging for time to pay. 'He accepted the payment in two instalments saying it was under "exceptional circumstances" and that "any failure to adhere to this schedule of payments would result in appropriate recovery action being taken in respect of the total amount of the tax debt outstanding". Since then all VAT quarterly payments have been paid within a week of the end of the quarter.

'I am a fairly evenly balanced person but during those six months I started to go grey and my blood pressure rose' Liz added.

No one was looking forward to the 1977 national conference in Edinburgh, particularly Judith Franklin. 'Chairing the Business Session was something I secretly dreaded; I know how vociferous NHR can be and how resistant to imposed change. I also knew we would have to raise the subs from 75p as we'd been through a year of terrible financial crisis which almost had Liz Salthouse imprisoned for non-payment of VAT. We considered 85p or 90p but in committee thought we'd try to get £1 to give ourselves a bit of manoeuvrability. I put it to conference with trepidation and suddenly found myself fighting desperately to keep subs DOWN to £1 – a motion from the floor was in danger of being carried to raise subs to £1.50, doubled at a stroke! I sensed a generous and appreciative response from NHR conference. They were conscious of the problems of the organisation and wanted to help it through its period of uncertainty. The conference, reputedly so hostile to the establishment, had given us wholehearted support when we most needed it.'

The complaints came afterwards from members not present. A few groups 'left' NHR because of the increase.

Marie Price often wonders how she survived the knocks in those early days. The opposition of some members to the constitution and its implications was supplemented by the increase in subscriptions which raised Cain in some quarters. She found it hard not to take criticism personally and had to curb her impetuous nature by waiting twenty-four hours before replying to any particularly nasty letter. Fortunately: 'Surprisingly enough the fifteen "strong personalities" seemed to "gell" remarkably quickly. We rarely agreed unanimously, but this was a healthy sign, and criticism was always constructive. The main thought in all the arguments was always "What is best for NHR?"'

For instance, copies of the national *Newsletter* had always been sent out according to the numbers ordered by groups. Marie and Liz compared subscriptions paid with orders made and found a huge difference. They immediately instituted sending out copies according to the actual subscriptions paid.

After that revealing check Liz counted the membership each year, the criteria being those paying subs. Her figures leave out 'new' groups, usually between eighty to one hundred, who have a period of grace before collecting subs.

	Groups	Members
At 31.12.1976	784	18,955
1977	802	18,993
1978	847	20,008
1979	939	21,222

Another innovation, a budget, was the first thing Marie had requested from the Treasurer. 'The first budget,' Liz describes 'as a question of think of a few numbers, juggle them about and hope'. Later the accuracy of her estimates had her colleagues marvelling. 'We operated at a loss of £850 the first year 1976 to 1977, then swung to "profits" of £4,480 in 1977 to 1978 and £5,397 in 1978 to 1979.' Her endeavours in keeping everyone's spending under control were certainly effective.

'I think I had the reputation of being penny-pinching!' Liz remarks. It was two years before she bought paper clips, re-using ones that turned up in the post, otherwise plain pins from the huge supply in her mother-in-law's work box. She ignored requests for receipts for subscriptions unless accompanied by a stamped addressed envelope, because of the cost. She insisted that the National Group did not use headed notepaper for letters between themselves. Her re-use of envelopes became legendary, even the Post Office complained. (I always know when a letter is from a Group member – quandary, which strip of re-sealing tape to slit open.) Phone calls had to be very early in the morning or during the evening, but cheap rate. Expenses claims were kept to the minimum; no question of claiming for food on a long journey. The newsletter was cut down to thirty-two pages for eighteen months and then allowed to rise again to thirty-six.

During Marie's term of office a lot of work too went into amending the original constitution to allow for a postal ballot for the National Group.

'Pauline Webster', says Marie, 'was a tower of strength on the constitution and its amendments.' It was approved at the 1977 national conference.

The constitution required retirement of a proportion of members after two years. There had also been natural wastage for reasons like pressure of outside work, family commitments, even (Frances Healey) moving to America. The others retiring or resigning were Yvonne Bradley, Betty Carrington, Jane Goodwin (later co-opted back), Joan Harborne, Pauline Webster, Lorna Wilson, Judith Franklin and Pat Lloyd. Since fifteen had been found rather unwieldy, it was decided only five vacancies should be filled. Marie prepared all the necessary paper-work for the postal ballot and waited for the nominations. There were only five, who were of course elected unopposed. It was a bitter disappointment. Surely more members were interested? Two in fact resigned almost immediately.

But the National Group was soon facing another kind of upheaval. Marie was to depart for Saudi Arabia because her husband was changing jobs. Who was to take over as NO? There were no interviews this time. Jean and Gill were the likely candidates. Jean, because of family commitments, felt unable to take it on. Gill discussed it with her husband first: 'I was delighted when Edward said "You'd better do it now or you never will".'

Marie, who had to resign in 1978, feels that one of the greatest benefits NHR has derived from having a National Group is that it lost its insularity. She is convinced that NG members, working hard in their own localities, are strengthening the organisation as a whole by this increase in joint activities.

'I suppose, looking back, this is perhaps the mark I made on NHR overall; it was certainly something I felt strongly about. Autonomy is all very well but isolation is something else.' She also recalls that it was 'lonely at the top' and ponders: 'What an unenviable position it must have been before the days of the National Group.'

Such personal contact with groups, which Marie regards as so important, was certainly shared out. Jean Stirk travelled in fog because the Local Organiser pleaded she try and get through to one particular meeting. Hazel Bell, for some reason, suffered more than most from bad weather. Once she had to get out of her car at a roundabout to wipe snow off the direction board; on arrival at the local meeting she was not even offered a reviving cup of coffee! Gill admits to 'many conflicting thoughts about NHR' while travelling late at night along strange roads.

Marie herself undertook a lot of travelling to keep in touch with groups with problems, which could be either lack of support or the reverse, and how to deal with success. She had problems with secretarial help,* an added strain when on top of routine work the effects of Gill's publicity efforts were felt. A *Woman's Hour* broadcast after the eighteenth anniversary conference brought in one thousand enquiries from potential members in just four days.

I first met Marie soon after she became National Organiser putting her through, gently I trust, her first press interview. When I met her again almost two years later, nervous tension had joined her natural energy and enthusiasm, a toll successive NOs should try to remember when the peculiar fascination of the job starts to dominate their lives.

By the time Gill took over as NO in September 1978 the hiving off of some of that work and, equally desirably, giving specific jobs to other National Group members, had begun. Jean Stirk was dealing with new groups. Of the (as it turned out) only three new members, Beryl Bonney (with much experience of women's organisation in Grimsby) became responsible for sales, key rings and such; Pat Kerr, part-time teacher from Harrogate, was given conferences to deal with; Val Williams, former nurse, Adult Literacy Tutor, and soon to be one of the team of Guides who take visitors round historic Chester, offered to be Minutes Secretary.

The honoraria, juggled about in 1978 to 1979 to NO £2,250, PRO £1,250, Treasurer £750 and Editor (reduced at Hazel's insistence) £250, was shuffled again, in 1979–80. Since Gill was joint NO and PRO she had £2,500, in her final year, Treasurer £950 and Editor £450. The bonus from Gill combining two jobs enabled 'clerical assistance' allowances for the tasks 'shed': New Groups: £400,

---

*One of her helpers did in fact have a brain haemorrhage, also a keen sense of humour remarking that she knew NHR was mind-stretching, had not anticipated it being brain-storming!

The First National Group: 1976–80

Conference Liaison: £100, plus £100 for the Overseas Co-ordinator, for which Jane Goodwin had been co-opted as she had already demonstrated her special talents in that role. Clerical/secretarial aid rose from 50p an hour in 1976 to 1977 to £1.25 in 1979 to 1980. No one is 'employed' by NHR; everyone is considered to be self-employed.

The National Group was down to nine but, explains Gill, 'we worked so well as a team we did not feel the need to co-opt other members to make up our numbers. By early 1979, however, the situation changed. Hazel had serious eye trouble and we realised we would be in great difficulty if she was unable to produce the newsletter. We decided to co-opt Sue Jones, St. Albans, who had considerable experience in the field of editing'. Sue later stood successfully for election in 1980.

They were determined there would be a postal ballot in 1980. Gill encouraged members in circulars and newsletters to take an interest in the election, dropped the thought of standing for national office amongst those who might not themselves have thought of it: a P.S. to a letter to Alison Shingler 'Why not think about standing for the NG?'; asking Antoinette Ferraro the same question after attending a large meeting she had organised in Solihull, as she was so disappointed that there were no West Midlands members at the 1979 national conference at Reading.

At that conference Gill bluntly told members that they would be left with three members of the National Group, and that there would be nine vacancies to fill, since office holders had to resign in accordance with the constitution, having served four years.

They were amazed by the response. People were milling round the platform and the NG was busily taking down names and addresses. Some of course later dropped out.

But the postal ballot, a non-starter two years before, materialised this time. Gill reports: 'My dining room was in complete chaos. It became a direct-mail house for several weeks. There was all the AGM material – minutes, accounts sheets, agenda, personalia details of the twenty-one candidates and voting slips. Voting slips were issued for paid-up members only so every group label had to be marked with its number. Assembling, stapling and stuffing envelopes followed what seemed to be interminable duplicating. Thank goodness we had bought a new duplicator which *did* work automatically. Help was summoned from nearby members and we sat or stood round the table filling the one thousand plus envelopes for groups. When we had finished there were boxes piled high against the walls, each with its own postage rate.

'What would I have done without Marianne Thornton-Vincent, my stalwart "person Friday"? She had worked with me since I took over from Marie and, though not an NHR member, was very devoted to NHR. She came in while I was on holiday; that was a boon, I always dreaded returning because of the mountain of post waiting for me. During that hectic election period she came in evenings and weekends too. I think her husband thought we were quite mad.

'Boxes loaded into the boot, off to the GPO for franking. Help from friendly postman loading them into trolley. Sit and wait for votes. Very slow response at first, then things hotted up. Even our postman asked what was going on. I had previously explained what NHR was about when he questioned me in the street one day. Amazed, he had asked me if I had to answer all the letters.

'Votes were counted daily on large sheets of paper. Members from nearby groups came to help and check the counting. We had promised to let the candidates know the results before the AGM at Bradford on 12 April, 1980. According to the constitution votes must be in seventy-two hours before the AGM. That meant last post on the Wednesday.'

Five and a half thousand voted, representing 25 per cent of the membership.

'Thursday night was spent phoning all the candidates. It was easy telling the successful ones; some were surprised, all were very pleased. The unsuccessful candidates were naturally disappointed. Many had put much time and effort into their mini "campaigns", visiting groups in their own areas and generally engendering an interest in the election. All I could do was to thank them for their efforts and urge them to stand again in 1982. NHR cannot afford to lose keen members like that at National Group level.'

There was another peak at the Bradford conference.

Gill Vine, as a 'Fact-Finder' working on the first constitution had been advised by a Charities Consultant that it was worth proceeding with an application to become a Registered Charity. She raised this in the early days with the National Group and the AGM gave its approval for application in 1977. Many long, complicated, interviews and lengthy correspondence with solicitors followed. Gill had no legal experience, but gradually became familiar with the daunting terminology. She recalls 'the most unnerving interview' of her life; the day she was summoned to the Charity Commission, with the solicitor, to be questioned by the Charity Commissioner handling NHR's application.

'It was almost impossible to supply the answers to the questions he asked. After about half-an-hour I realised that I was making no progress. I also realised that if I did not "turn the tables" then NHR would never be able to re-apply for Charitable status. In desperation I told the Commissioner that he could never appreciate or understand the problems experienced by many of our members because he was a man. It worked. From that moment he was sympathetic; he told us to go away and re-draft our Charitable Deed which would then be considered more favourably.

'The Deed was revised and only two clauses were included this time. The first: The object of the Charity is to provide facilities for the leisure time occupation of female members of the public with the object of improving the conditions of both urban and rural life for them in the interest of social welfare by such means as the Trustees shall from time to time consider appropriate but particularly by education through training and study groups. The second was more nebulous; it dealt with the therapeutic value of NHR for its members and was considered important by the National Group.

'A phone call from our solicitor told me we had been granted Charitable Status, subject to ratification by the Inland Revenue. I announced that to the AGM in 1979. To my utter dismay I was later told that the Inland Revenue would not ratify our Deed. They disputed our claim to have any therapeutic value. It could not end like this. We were advised to obtain unsolicited testimonials from people outside NHR to substantiate our claim. Everywhere we went we asked members to help. The testimonials flowed in, from MPs, GPs, Health Visitors and college lecturers. It was heartening to read what other people thought about NHR and how they valued its work. Whether these testimonials tipped the scales we shall never know. Clause two was dropped from the Deed and it was accepted on the one clause alone.'

Gill admits that 'It was difficult convincing some members as to why we should ask for charitable status. I think some envisaged a flag day and collecting boxes. We had to be *something*. A limited liability company? Surely that was not NHR. Becoming a Registered Charity was the only way of ensuring that NHR would never deviate from its original aims. It could never be used for other purposes while Trustees were there to oversee its activities.

'The National Group had worked hard on the final Deed to ensure that it was what NHR really wanted. The "Rules for the National Group", formerly the constitution, were carefully scrutinised. We, as a Group, had worked together for four years and we were able to review things in the light of our experience. There had been murmurings of "power-seeking" from some members regarding the position of NO. Anyone who has been NO will laugh this off, but, to safeguard the organisation, a rule was included that the appointment should be subject to the approval of the Trustees.'

Gill was determined that she would show the Deed to members at the 1980 AGM before she retired. It was sent out by the solicitors for signature alphabetically so I got it first on Maundy Thursday, and, knowing the Easter postal break was due, I rapidly posted it on hoping that neither Maureen Nicol nor Mary Stott were on holiday. They were not. Gill collected it from the solicitor's office a week later on her way to the railway station en route to Bradford and the AGM.

XVI
Enterprise – Internal

NHR by post

Correspondence magazines are another NHR form of that human essential, the listening ear, giving support for the supporters within a not-related-by-blood extended family. The idea rose and fell in the early years. Matilda Popper participated as a correspondent. She launched the thought again in 1975 and is now Correspondence Magazine Organiser. She was incidentally elected to the National Group in 1980.

Matilda is a veteran Register member. Excerpts from her diary published in the national *Newsletter* in 1978 give a rare contemporary perspective on earlier days.

7 March 1960. Melanie has been crying all afternoon. Can it be wind? The injection she had this morning? Do I pick her up too often? If only I knew someone here to talk to about these worries, and more interesting things too. Perhaps I may yet do so – I've just written to a Mrs Nicol – whose letter appeared in the *Guardian* suggesting a national register of liberal-minded housebound wives. She asked people to write to her so she could see what support she got for the idea, and she would put them in touch with each other. I wrote all about my own situation, telling her my interests to ensure a good match.

30 April 1960. The letter came. There is one other woman in Cambridge who answered that *Guardian* letter. I rushed out to phone her and arranged for her to visit me.

9 May 1960. Mrs B. came, young and shy. We didn't have much to say with me being shy too, but I hope we'll become good friends.

17 May 1960. Went to tea with V.B., met her two dear little children. We got on more easily this time but I told her about yesterday's Plan for Peace meeting and didn't at all like her reaction.

[Mutual visits continued during May, June and July]

1 August 1960. V.B. was here ... we have nothing in common, we disagree fundamentally on everything I hold most sacred. I'm sad that an association begun with such high hopes should end with so profound a feeling of relief.

13 July 1962. Moved to Swansea.

15 August 1962. Wrote to the local organiser of the Housewives Register enclosing 5s.

17 August 1962. The organiser of the Housebound Wives Register in Swansea came. She says there are about half a dozen members, none of them Welsh and pretty spread out. They haven't done anything yet except chat.

11 September 1962. First Housewives Register Meeting. There were six women there and a number of small children. Talk was mainly about Swansea schools of which I know nothing. [Fortnightly meetings continued in this pattern]

7 November 1962. The Housebound Wives meeting was on a new estate at Pennard. Sue invited seven of her neighbours in. One of them said she wouldn't join until she knew more about us. 'You might be Communists for all I know'.

3 April 1963. We decided at Housebound Wives this morning that our meetings were too dull for words and we should have a discussion at each meeting. I am to introduce the first on the Budget.

24 April 1963. After all the work I've put in preparing our first discussion on the Budget not a single Housebound Wife turned up.

[After a number of meetings drew one member or none my last record of this group reads: *4 Sept 1963*. None of the Housebound Wives came this morning]

3 Feb 1966. A letter signed Londoner in the *Evening Post* about a club to be started for people on their own provided the opportunity I've been waiting for to bung in a letter about the Housebound Wives linked to Londoner's.

10 February 1966. Three letters replying to my *Post* letter, one advising me to join the W.I., one almost illiterate and one from Llanelli.

14 Feb. 1966. A letter from the Housebound Wife in Wimbledon who wants to exchange houses with us.

24 February 1966. This was the day for the inauguration of the HBW group* and I was quite excited wondering whether anybody would turn

---

*It may not be clear from a personal diary that the first Swansea group was defunct and Matilda started a brand new one. She has twice been Local Organiser.

up. Five people came. We're planning to meet weekly, Thursdays at 10.30 with a monthly discussion but I see us having difficulty finding a topic to suit everybody, Rhona talked about reading and discussing a book while some of the others want hairdressing demonstrations.

26 May 1975. I'm very pleased that my letter in the NHR newsletter suggesting that, corresponding with other members all over the country through the medium of correspondence magazines would be an additional meeting point, has met with a good enough response to start *Serendipity* today and another magazine to follow.

1 April 1978 (at Manchester national conference). Maureen Nicol chaired the Friends of the Earth meeting. Seeing her in the flesh at last I thought how proud and pleased she must feel to see such a large hall filled with just a fraction of the number of women who are profiting from NHR, the child of her brain. Later it was a fine birthday present for me to be introduced to Maureen Nicol. I was surprised to hear that she hadn't met many of those who answered her letter. Had they all been as feeble as me her baby would have been still-born instead of coming of age in such a healthy state. I hope I've since repaid the debt I owe her by starting in Swansea what have become two thriving groups and linking members all over the UK by means of five correspondence magazines.

Matilda Popper's idea of an additional link between members was first put over in the *Newsletter* for spring 1975:

> The words at the front of the *Newsletter* 'A meeting point for the lively-minded woman' makes me wonder whether NHR members would be interested in another kind of meeting point – a meeting point by letter.
>
> Correspondence magazines exist for just such an exchange of views and news as our groups provide. They work like this. Everybody in a particular magazine writes a letter and sends it to the editor who fastens all letters together inside a cover and sends the resulting magazine to the first person on the rota who reads it and passes it on to the second and so on. What pleasure there is on the mornings when you find on the mat the thick envelope that denotes a magazine! Housework forgotten you sit down and read the replies to that controversial point you raised in your last letter and what somebody has to say about the drawbacks of farming and somebody else on education and a third on the economic situation. You are glad to see that the baby arrived safely, and sympathise over a husband in hospital. Then you pick up all these points and write about them in a long letter, adding a few thoughts on a new topic that has been occupying your mind, and telling of anything interesting that has happened to you. Off goes your letter to the editor and the magazine to the next person on the rota and you wait for the next magazine to come round.
>
> Some people don't like writing letters but, for those who do, a correspondence magazine is ideal. It provides about a dozen letters in reply to one from you. It gives you an interesting means of contacting

others without leaving your home. It brings you new friends all over the country – one gets to know fellow magazine members better through their letters than many of the people one meets face to face. If you are one of those to whom the idea of correspondence magazine membership appeals, please write to me.

She got twenty-five replies initially and, reporting on the solid success of the venture in the national *Newsletter*, issued autumn 1976, took the chance to expand on the attractions, apart from 'the satisfying sound of the fatly filled envelope falling through the letter box'.

> There is opportunity for the kind of stimulating discussion our groups should provide; what is lost in immediate face to face reaction is gained in greater opportunity for reflection and a reasoned reply. There is the chance to unburden oneself of one's worries as well as to share one's joys, to receive a ready fund of sympathy in grief and pleasure in one's good news; advice too perhaps from someone who has weathered similar difficulties. Other useful advice comes regarding books to read, holiday places, best brands of goods to buy, etc. There is the interest engendered by the personal news, and a broadening insight into other people's ways of life: all this, and the satisfaction of knowing that in reply to about ten interesting and amusing letters, one has to write only one letter oneself; a great reward for small endeavour.
>
> For a member of NHR whose nearest group is inaccessible, or who is unable to attend many meetings, the magazine may come to stand for her local group. For most of us, though, the magazine provides a link between groups in different parts of the country. We tell each other how our groups are run and of their activities and discussions; suggest how a literature sub-group might be set up, or what can be done about a group to whom serious discussion is anathema; ask and learn how groups consider and implement ideas, what difficulties arose and how they might be avoided, reporting successes and failures of our own groups. If some idea succeeded with one group and failed with another, it can be enlightening to consider why. The different characters of the groups we belong to come out clearly and add to our feeling of NHR as existing throughout the country and not just in our own localities. The *Newsletter* and national conferences both play a large part in this, but a magazine of our type adds a more personal and perhaps candid impression.

By 1980 there were six correspondence magazines: *Serendipity, Cornucopia, Athena, Catena, Perpetua* and *Kaleidoscope*. Membership averages between ten and twelve members, except the last which is still building up to full size.

Magazines do not diminish in number. Once established they continue indefinitely. Matilda edits the first three named but other members have taken on editorship of the rest. When a magazine is full she asks a member to start another. She has a waiting list of people keen on editing a magazine. With an explanatory letter on how the magazines work she gives an enquirer the name and address of an editor.

With the first two magazines she divided correspondents between the two with only two principles in mind, to ensure widest possible geographical distribution and, since Christian names are used, not to have two people with the same Christian name in the magazine, to avoid confusion. Nowadays she puts new people into the magazine most needing a new member but still retaining geographical spread. Allocating on a more personal basis she considers impossible since introductory letters reveal little; it takes time and confidence, to reveal innermost thoughts and interests.

With such a haphazard method of assembly it is entirely coincidental that *Cornucopia* has a far higher proportion of practising Christians than are present in the population. In various denominations, and ranging from fervent to lukewarm, religious discussion is a constant feature. *Athena* has a lot of politically minded people with highly opposing views, so current events are a staple discussion point. However, no subject is discussed exclusively. There are always a number under debate at the same time. A new venture by *Athena* is a book group within the magazine. Each member can nominate a book to be read by all and each month one of those books is the subject of comment by all.

Like group meetings, the magazines give women a chance to stretch their minds on topics other than the domestic round with women who, by opting for NHR membership, are keen to do the same. But magazine participation also creates an outlet for personal and emotional matters as its contributors get to know each other. A Register member may well pour out deep anxieties, matrimonial upsets, to those with whom she forms close friendships, but that would be in privacy, not with a whole group. But such an outpouring does happen in the magazines, perhaps because face to face meetings are few. For this reason the strictest magazine rule is confidentiality.

Domestic topics are also not in disfavour. News about children is passed on, even recipes. Problems may not be emotional but practical: 'How can I get my small child to stay in bed at night?' Matilda Popper points out:

> With a number of mothers in the magazine who have passed through this stage and come out the other side it would seem silly to make a rule

against domestic topics so tight that all this expertise should be withheld from the sufferer. However such matters form a very small proportion of any magazine's contents. I should look on a preponderance of such items as death to a magazine, but so would everybody else, so it doesn't happen.

Magazine members get together occasionally: *Cornucopia* in 1976, *Serendipity* in 1978 and 1980 and, of course, they seek each other out at national conferences. But the writing is the main thing.

They are a cross-section of NHR, town and country members and only a minority are not attached to a group. By definition they not only enjoy receiving, but also writing letters, and have reasonable fluency in putting ideas on paper. Those who find this is not their scene drop out quite soon. A long-term magazine member who is ill, or under such pressure that she resigns in fairness to the others, can opt to stay on the distribution rota and stay passively in touch until she can resume her place.

Comment from a member of *Cornucopia*, one of the original magazines, in the 1980 *Newsletter*:

> After three years I have met many of these friends in the flesh, and found them just as compatible in real life as they were on paper. A correspondence magazine forges a close bond – after all – in writing to someone twelve times a year one reveals quite a lot of oneself.

House Swaps

With signs of interest among members in a holiday house exchange scheme, Jane Watt, National Organiser, asked for a volunteer to run it in 1968. Anne Crabtree of Colchester offered but there was no rush; thirty-three enquiries in 1970, less than half following them up. Susan Waterhouse of Bedford took over by 1973 and until she emigrated to Canada in 1976 (having appealed for a replacement volunteer) her regular appearances in the newsletter promoting the advantages had the frustrated overtones of one trying to make bricks with very little straw: 'A larger response would in general be very welcome together with a bit more adventurousness in trying the less obvious places.'

Gillian Hill of Harrogate took over and at first made few changes. All enquirers were sent forms to complete: house type, beds (and sizes, types), description of locality, nearby 'tourist attractions', pets left/brought, restrictions, like children allergic to animals, or special requirements like wheelchair access, ages of children (toys to bring or not), and of course where the applicant wanted to go and when. The completed form was then returned together with a supposed-to-be-large stamped addressed envelope and a contribution estimated to cover duplicating costs. Her reproduction 'guesstimates' have not worked out too badly; the biggest profit was about six pounds, the biggest deficit (kindly repaid by the National Group as a grant) was fifteen pounds.

The completed forms were sorted into geographical order with the aid of a geographically-minded husband, trying to spread the numbers evenly and avoiding having one huge 'London Commuter country' area.

Her hand, she says, 'starts to ache' when she thinks of the next part. That was write out the lists from the information supplied. 'In 1976 each entry was split onto two sheets which had to be held side-by-side. Not very satisfactory. So from 1977 onwards the list has been written "sideways" using foolscap or longer paper.' They were then photo-copied by a local printer, photo-copying being more practical than duplicating because of differences such as that between handwriting and typing, and the package assembled: the complete lists plus a general advice and information page, and a 'Dos and Don'ts List' – about maps, keys, milk/paper deliveries cancelled/altered, notes about whereabouts of doctors, hospital, electrician, plumber, how to use equipment, balancing out the larder, telephone, fuel use, taking high chairs, safety gates, rubber sheets for beds if necessary, putting away anything valuable or vulnerable or, in reverse, supervising your youngster's treatment of another child's toys.

The package was then folded up to be placed in the envelope supplied. 'I did not know just how many different sizes and shapes of envelopes existed,' Gillian confesses. 'And if some of the envelopes supplied were "large" I'd be fascinated to know how their senders could fit an address onto one considered "small".'

However all the family would muck in. Then came the grand postage-checking session. Some members put first class, some second; if the list was large the second band of postage was needed. Sometimes the weight of the envelope made all the difference – or the weight of the sticky tape when a re-used envelope had no means of securing. It was then off to the Post Office for lots of low value stamps for "topping up". It did the children's arithmetic a power of good. Then to the sorting office so the lists left Harrogate together. A huge sigh of relief was then heard in the Hill household.'

It is up to members to contact likely 'swaps' direct.

However, despite posting all lists together, by first-class post, they never arrived at the same time. A member receiving her list late was likely to find her first half-dozen choices already booked up.

The biggest change in the organisation of the scheme, made in 1980, was a set 'go-ahead' date and time, 6.30 p.m. 'I rather think some telephone lines still got jammed at 6.31 on the day' Gillian commented. But it seems to have worked, reducing the element of panic, enabling each member to browse through the entire list, allowed to write three days earlier but no arrangements to be made until the specified time on the specified date. 'The mutual trust,' she thinks 'that makes the whole scheme work comes into its own here'.

Then she tackled the time-consuming assembly of the lists with a form having the same format as the finished one. Each member writes her own entry, which may sometimes need clarification or re-writing, but the job is now largely reduced to cutting and sticking. Now also the form sent out is accompanied by a self-adhesive label for the member to complete and return with a contribution. Gillian buys the appropriately sized envelopes ('sheer joy') and the only one value of stamps needed.

She breaks down the contribution of what was, for 1980, £1, in this way: postage of list 23p, envelope 3p, label 2p, photocopying (22 pages) 37p, production of forms and explanations 6p, paper, labels 3p, and spreads the 18p around such eventualities as forms not returned, failure of members to send in a s.a.e. with their first enquiry about joining the scheme, extra lists for latecomers, and such as 'sticky stuff', Sellotape, paper clips, over-estimation of number of forms required, etc.

She summarises the benefits: 'I feel it works because of the common bond of membership of NHR. It gives one the feeling that one's "swapper" will be a person not so very different from oneself. And if they trust you to care for their home, you can trust them in yours'. The Hill family has swapped several times.

'The attractions of the scheme are many and varied. The biggest item is the low cost. Generally no money changes hands (unless in payment for telephone calls, or milk, or whatever) so a holiday costs only the travelling and "outings" – (food costs one has at home anyway). Others are such as washing facilities for mums with nappies to think of, a proper bed for Grandma, the excitement for the children of someone else's toybox (not to be dismissed lightly), care for plants and pets in one's absence.'

In some cases some of these factors have been extreme. The member whose 'comments' included 'Manage part-time smallholding. Swappers required to look after six pigs, five hens, three geese and keep an eye on ten sheep and lambs. No experience needed. Threequarters of an hour's work daily but must be conscientious' got her holiday.

'Those members who live at the seaside can virtually take their pick – there aren't enough of them to go round! We have a preponderance of participants in London and the Home Counties.'

Swaps range from a weekend to a three week summer holiday. In 1980 ninety per cent arranged one or more swaps; five in the year for one member is the highest recorded yet. In 1977 eighty-six took part. That number has now more than doubled, with plenty of response in the UK, but virtually none from abroad.

XVII
Enterprise – External

A Magazine

Women's magazines are an abiding controversy. An example: a Northwich member approached newsagents in 1966 to get a letter about the Register inserted into copies of *She* and *Nova* as 'the liveliest magazines and in our group the most read'. Yet a year later, at the first national conference, *Nova* was roundly condemned from the floor for cashing in on sexual topics purely for sensationalism. That castigation was mulled over during ground-work consultations I was having with *Good Housekeeping* magazine, preceding an article I was to write for them on the Register. It led to the then Editor, Laurie Purden, offering a panel of magazine staff for the next national conference to find out just what this particular group of women *did* want from magazines written primarily for women. Incidentally that second national conference was largely organised by Marina Oliver of the Harrow group, of whom more later.

When Audrey Slaughter founded *Over 21* in 1972 she replied to NO Lesley Moreland's letter about editorial publicity with the offer of free space in the small ads section 'as long as I have the room' and asked for members' views on what 'A modern, intelligent woman's magazine should cover' as well as contributions. *Spare Rib* launched the same year, claiming to be 'the first magazine to approach women as individuals in their own right', also asked for contributions from members and printed an article on NHR.

New Forum, a magazine published in the early sixties, written largely by and for Register members, can fairly claim to have sown the seed for the new-style magazines, as well as influencing the move towards more adult, more relevant to modern life attitudes, of the longer established women's magazines.

It was started by Joan Little in 1962. A graduate, who had worked as a school counsellor for the Inner London Education Authority, she was isolated and lonely for intellectual interests, living in suburbia and caring for two small children. She helped to start one of the earliest Register groups in Harrow, Middlesex, which grew so rapidly it had to keep splitting to form more groups, largely as the result of constant local newspaper publicity, mostly by Joan who had started doing free-lance journalism at twopence, old currency, a line.

She took a journalism course and read the formulae that were supposed to underpin women's magazine journalism. 'In particular the taboo subjects like birth control, sex, etc. fascinated me, since women's home lives seemed so bound to these major topics, yet we were not allowed publicly to discuss them in print! The magazines then printed many articles on the Royal Family, cookery, beauty, child care of a physical nature only, with nothing about cognitive development. It seemed to me women were being artificially tricked into a major stereotype that did not at all fit the women I knew'.

She approached magazines. 'They said they couldn't discuss such things as birth control, women are not ready for it yet. It was so condescending—so "we know what they want".'

New Forum (launched as *Forum* and changed because the title was used elsewhere) was not, and was never meant to be, formally connected to the Register though Joan designed and edited it around the members she had met. 'I wanted to develop a magazine "for the thinking woman" as we advertised it, which would dynamically express the real lives of women. Everyone was very encouraging and offered to write for nothing. I was deluged with articles of quite a high standard after the first issue, also letters.'

The first edition of the quarterly, initially quoted at one shilling, (5p) and immediately raised to eight shillings (40p) a year post free, and raised yet again later, was sold out three days after publicity in the *Guardian* and *Sunday Times*. Even the reprint was sold out in advance. Five hundred postal orders had to be returned.

'I am gloomily certain,' Joan wrote in the second issue's editorial, 'no magazine could fulfil all the expectations which news of our launching seems to have raised.'

On a now curly and elderly copy of *New Forum*, a name above these desperate words caught my eye. Belle Tutaev was listed among the 'Associate Editors'. Belle founded the now nationwide Pre-School Playgroups Association. When a petition to the government for more nursery classes which Belle helped to organise had no effect, she wrote a letter to the *Guardian*, published 1961, saying that if parents wanted playgroups they could, as she and friends had done, organise them themselves. They did just that. The two organisations grew simultaneously with many Register members starting or assisting in the running of playgroups which have alleviated the isolation and claustrophobia of the modern nuclear family.

So how was Belle Tutaev mixed up in a new magazine in 1963? She had helped the NHR Harrow group when it set up a shoppers' creche in the local 'Fine Fare' supermarket. She recalls, 'We all genuinely believed there was the need for a magazine of this type'.

My mind then clicked back to a phone conversation of the time when Belle told me that Joan had more or less vanished from sight under a mountain of letters. After all five thousand turned up. I never knew till now that Belle, knowing personally how an avalanche of letters gums up the normal domestic routine, had gone along to help sift through the letters.

Yet I was still puzzled about Belle's connection with a NHR group. With the triumph of a detective fitting in yet another part of the jigsaw puzzle I learned that Belle had been one of the very early NHR members, joining a group in Marylebone, London. She explained. 'It was a group who used to meet for chats and we then split up and looked at various local matters. The small group I was with looked at pre-school provision. It was from this that the idea of our local playgroup emerged and this in turn led to PPA.' The rest is social history. Belle, long retired from the organisation she founded, has been head of Bristol's largest nursery school since 1968.

There were other names too among those *New Forum* contributors, who wrote about abortion, care of mentally handicapped children, religion, making money while at home, 'mirror' writing now better known as dyslexia, why parents should campaign to improve state education, which strike the chord of memory.

Sonia Willington tore into authoritative attitudes to women in childbirth, having founded the Association for Improvements in the Maternity Services. Her underlying hope was that 'when my daughter grew up conditions should not be so bad'. When we spoke in 1980 her daugher was facing her medical finals. Now National Secretary of the Ecology Party, 'Sally' Willington looked back on AIMS' twenty-one years, concluding that it has won on fathers being present at the birth, lost on home births. I would add that it put the concept of humane treatment of women in maternity wards on the map. Readers can judge how far that penetrated. Sally was not a Register member.

Judith Cook was. She wrote in *New Forum* about 'Voice of Women' the peace group she founded (another letter to the

Guardian in 1961) which aimed 'to make the housebound mother feel she is participating'. Judith joined NHR in very early days and was put in touch with only a couple of other women locally, in Cornwall. But they got themselves involved in all kinds of pressure activities, rather than just being a Register group, primarily over hospital and ante-natal facilities initially. They all had large families. She recalls: 'It did help to feel part of a kind of freemasonry or club when one was so isolated'. Looking back she reflects: 'that getting together with other women under NHR,' brought her out of the home into different kinds of public activity and later catapulted her into the Campaign for Nuclear Disarmament and even into journalism as a profession.

How radically attitudes have changed since the days when an amateur (in status not in presentation) publication was needed to air criticisms of maternity treatment or news of peace groups! But then Claire Rayner (interviewed by Joan for the local paper about her first book, instantly recruited as a speaker for a group meeting) presented *New Forum* with an article no one else would publish. It was called 'Children of Eccentrics' and was about having to conform to suburban mores because otherwise her daughter was distressed. Examples were children jeering because her two-year-old was naked in the sun, having to use 'self-consciously refeened' terms instead of 'good expressive words like pee', being called Mummy. 'How dreadful' she wrote in 1963 'if I have been conditioned into conformity by the time I reach the forties'. Claire, of course, is now an eminent magazine and newspaper columnist, and author, known for her down-to-earth advice on personal and emotional matters.

Looking back over nearly twenty years Joan Little, lecturer, battling with the thesis for a post-graduate degree, toyed for fun with the thought of starting another magazine, though she is less critical of today's magazines. *New Forum* she describes as 'the voice of the educated working class, a new generation of women'. But she, like her potential readers, was still functioning in traditional conditions. Two little heads peeping over the top of the magazines and letters she used to cram into their pushchair to get to the Post Office may be an endearing image. But she says: 'In order to pay for secretarial help I took a part-time teaching job and then the madness of it struck me. I had given up work to devote myself to my family and found myself busier than ever trying to answer letters from despairing housewives. They never enclosed stamps and the postage bill became inordinately expensive. Women rang at six p.m. as my husband came through the door, and I had toddlers round my skirts'. She 'sold' the magazine to Marina Oliver for two pounds, presumably for the subscription list.

Marina had joined the Harrow group in 1961, after her first child was born. When the group was split into three later that year she was one of the Harrow organisers and brought out a newsletter to keep people in touch. The two-page newsletter was a six-page, one hundred copy, effort within a couple of years. She was a 'joint' Organiser for the three groups in 1963 and, again, editing the newsletter in 1965. In 1965 too she launched *Debate*, the successor to *New Forum*.

Debate had articles on how the NHS could be improved, on the problems of being a stepmother, on cheaper and more practical housebuilding techniques, on Humanism, and on the principles involved in nationalisation. While one woman expanded on how education for women benefits not only themselves but the next generation, and another, albeit courteously, condemned mothers for 'shirking' their responsibilities by going out to work, space was given to publicise the 'Register for Qualified Married Women'. That, launched by a teacher, Ann Adam (a graduate who trained as a mature student), was not an employment agency. Its chief aims were:

> to provide a voice for women who are prevented for various reasons from exercising their professional skills in the community, to publicise the obstacles in their way and to urge the introduction of measures which will allow women to return to their work. It is thought that among the main problems are: lack of nursery schools; lack of training and refresher courses at convenient hours and accessible places; lack of part-time vacancies; financial dis-incentives owing to extra expenses incurred; lack of good domestic help.

With almost no capital *Debate* could not be advertised, nor distributed by other than postal subscriptions on which it was totally dependent for income. In spite of a few 'plugs' in *The Times*, *Guardian*, and the NHR newsletter, the subscription list fell. To cut losses it was finally duplicated, and while readers were loyal, too many forgot to renew their subs. When costs were not being covered it was eventually closed. The unexpired subs were sold to a new editor who brought out at least one issue 'for thinking women and their husbands' (Marina gave me a copy) but its subsequent fate is unknown.

Marina, who since 1970 has taught Economics, Politics and Business Studies in sixth form colleges, technical colleges, and

Colleges of Further Education, also has a growing list of published historical romances – possibly escapism from the grim reality of economics and politics.

Law reform

Diane Munday answered Maureen Nicol's original letter in 1960. 'My third child was only a few weeks old and I was feeling isolated and housebound. I was sent the Herts list and we got together and met regularly Countywide and then split into groups. I made friends that have lasted.'

It was also the time that the tragedy of Thalidomide (which Diane had been offered by her doctor) was being recognised. She attended a meeting of the Abortion Law Reform Association: 'A lot of people, like me, became aware for the first time of the prohibitive abortion laws. I was appalled that, had I taken the drug and known of its likely effect, there could have been no possibility of a legal abortion. I spoke to Register groups about it; we were meeting in each other's houses. Those women understood and had mentally faced the agony of Thalidomide too. Many became interested in abortion law reform'. In fact one woman, also with young children, became Membership Secretary of the ALRA and some years later the husband of another member became its Treasurer.

The Abortion Law Reform Association was founded in 1936, its work interrupted by the war. It took on a new lease of life in the early sixties, an effort culminating in the 1967 Abortion Act.

Biochemist and research worker, pre-children, Diane, as Vice Chairman and later General Secretary of ALRA over some fourteen years, became something of an expert and a spokesperson on abortion matters whose name still appears as Public Relations Officer for the British Pregnancy Advisory Service.

'That Register group, containing a lot of intelligent, alert women to shoot down my arguments, provided my early practice ground for debate on the subject.' When her crusading zeal really got going, and she started a personal membership drive for an Association which had 'shrunk into almost nothing', the foundation was the Herts group around half of whom joined it and helped spread the message too. Register groups today, Diane affirms, 'always provide stimulating discussion for speakers'.

HOLS (Help Organise Local Schemes)

In the eighteenth birthday issue of the *National Newsletter*

Wendy Whitehead's article 'NHR Ticket to Freedom' told of her personal appreciation:

> When in the company of our two teenage daughters, who have been described as 'happy, socially mature' and have wide-ranging interests both within the house and beyond – I am bound to apportion much of the credit to the beginnings of NHR.
>
> In 1961, after a weary shopping expedition (more for something to do than to stock the pantry!), and pram-pushing more than a mile each way from our suburban desert, I made strong coffee, resorted to the afternoon TV programme for some mental stimulation – and to my utter amazement got it. For the subject under review was the Register, then in its infancy.
>
> I still have the old Victor Value supermarket check-out ticket with Maureen Nicol's address frantically scribbled on the back; one of my most treasured archives! A ticket not only to liberation but freedom and, in fact, for me personally, possibly a literal life-saver.
>
> With a two-year-old and a new baby, post-natal depression was getting the better of me, and though I had every reason to enjoy life – helpful relatives, friends nearby, church involvement and, thank goodness, an understanding husband – the transition from an exciting job in the City to full-time domesticity was just too much, and I appeared to be sinking fast.
>
> The Register idea was so ingenious that it instantly caught my imagination as having tremendous potential for adaptation locally, and immediately gave me something to live for. I switched off the TV, got out the typewriter – and never looked back.
>
> Duplicated letters were left at the homes of other local housewives who I now realised must, to some extent, be sharing the kind of loneliness and isolation I had grown accustomed to. Each letter was followed by a personal visit which, invariably, resulted in a doorstep invitation to stop for tea or coffee.
>
> That was the beginning of an invigorating five years living in Morden, Surrey, and getting to know hundreds of families. As the local Register grew, so did a toddlers' club, baby-sitting bank and, subsequently, on removal to nearby Stoneleigh, a holiday club for over-fives, and most recently a 'coffee shop' project as a meeting point for all ages, based at the Parish Hall.
>
> I had been brought up in a Christian family, but sadly that was then not sufficient to guarantee my peace of mind. NHR, by its persistent openness and reasonableness, with no senseless taboos, helped me to continue life's quest. After forty-three years of groping and searching, just three months ago, I was led to a deep spiritual experience. Through God's grace all the aching loneliness which kept me busy every second of the day has mercifully gone, and I can at last sit still – relax and be at peace without sneaking off to the biscuit tin or the valium phial!

Without NHR in those crucial 1960s, I might not have survived to tell the tale.

HOLS (Help Organise Local Schemes) was originally begun by a small group of mothers formerly involved in a local Toddlers' Club and Pre-School Playgroup at Stoneleigh, near Epsom, Surrey. Having begun a family holiday club in the same church hall where the former 'toddlers', graduated to day school and could meet up in the school holidays, requests were coming in from other Toddlers' Clubs and Playgroups asking how to start a holiday club in their localities. The requests largely came about following publication of Wendy's booklet 'Toddlers' Clubs' in 1962 (Chester House Publications) and a further booklet 'Holiday Playschemes' to which she contributed (published by the National Council of Social Service 1973).

To save a lot of the individual letter-writing she had experienced after the Toddlers' Club publication appeared, she hit on the idea of the HOLS Correspondence Pack and an exchange of ideas and information emerging from different localities. Initially she produced a nationwide register of HOLS contacts (copying the idea of NHR). The duplicated register was circulated annually on subscription together with a monthly bulletin exchanging news and information. When the charity 'Make Children Happy' started publishing 'It's Childsplay' the HOLS Bulletin, and annual subscription, ceased. HOLS became a free service, each new correspondent being entered on the continuing national register, so the nearest contact is always tappable.

In 1980 the number of correspondents was 520 including those in South Africa, West Indies and Australia – where one correspondent was contemplating launching a similar HOLS in her own country following the chance purchase of Wendy's book *Home for the Holidays* (published by Paul Elek, 1974) from a bookstall on York railway station in Britain in 1979!

'Apart from the original HOLS subscription in the early years, 35p,' Wendy explained,

> the only income has been via magazine and newspaper articles, a book and booklets, plus the very occasional TV interview.
>
> Because I may never have found my way into journalism without the NHR and PPA, it seemed only just that a similar do-it-yourself community-minded scheme such as HOLS should benefit to some small degree when I was so much more, as an individual mother, reaping far greater joys and benefits from the new career which had simply dropped

into my lap at that stage! And, busy as I was with so much writing, it was less laborious (rightly or wrongly) to make this a free service than have to chase up subs and keep accounts when my arithmetic is so abysmal.

The HOLS Correspondence Pack now consists of a leaflet of distilled wisdom about holiday clubs and longer-term holiday schemes more useful to working mothers; the Teenage Chat Shops leaflet giving advice on where, when, stocks, equipment, publicity, 'staffing' (i.e. parents) based on a project tried out in Stoneleigh in 1976; and any free handouts acquired at conferences relevant to play and leisure, such as those organised by Fair Play for Children, the umbrella for all voluntary play schemes, of which HOLS is, of course, a member.

Cancer Control Campaign

NHR does not ally itself to any cause. Yet its members pour out time, energy, talent and understanding to those needing help. This can be supporting a member with agoraphobia, providing transport to a meeting for one physically handicapped, keeping a watching brief in a household where one is in hospital (baby-sitting while an adult visits, a casserole oven-ready for the family). Add exterior efforts (example at random: providing teas for those making prison visits) and, of course, fund-raising for those who, for example, need food or clothes or medicines. So the choice of a specific report to include in this history had to be mine. The information was provided by the Harrogate Branch of the Women's National Cancer Control Campaign.

It was a talk by Betty Westgate, founder of the Mastectomy Association, in March 1974, that set the Harrogate ball rolling at a NHR joint meeting called as a response to the urgings of Janet Harris, who had died three months previously from breast cancer, aged forty-one. Janet, a social worker who had helped found the Harrogate Register group in 1966, knew she had no hope of recovery and set about the practicalities of dying with the courage, dignity, gentle determination and concern for others that had typified her life. She wrote articles about her illness for medical publications, drew up house-keeping hints for her family, replenished their wardrobes, discussed her three children's future education with their teachers – and persuaded her friends to DO something to help other women to talk about and understand more about cancer – even to come through her own experience, perhaps with a better chance of survival.

Enterprise – External

At the March meeting, in Church House, it was standing room only. Betty Westgate had been approached to speak by Ednie Annett and Local Organiser Ann Chaplin, after Ednie had read an article in *The Daily Telegraph*, about Betty, which mentioned the Women's National Cancer Control Campaign.

Following Betty's optimistic and enlightening 'Lumps and Bumps' talk, Penny Craddock and Clare Fitzgibbon (both SRNs), and Judith Wilson, a teacher of German, stayed back to discuss the setting up of some sort of action group. They were joined at later meetings by Ednie and ten other NHR members. There were nurses Judith Dell, Doddy Marlow, Jean Johnston, Sue Stanger-Moore; ex-cardiographer Irene Cheetham and former librarian Joan Fletcher. Elizabeth Crossley, ex-university secretary, agreed to be minute clerk. Ednie, a teacher, undertook visual aids, copy-writer Carole Stead and ex-journalist Janet Barker, publicity, and onetime secretary Shirley Howell the all-important treasurer's job. Penny Craddock, who had had experience of cancer nursing on a radiology ward of Guy's Hospital as a staff nurse, was elected chairman, and Clare Fitzgibbon, previously sister-in-charge of an up-country hospital in Uganda, became secretary. Thus the Harrogate Branch of the Women's National Cancer Control Campaign was formed. Donald Harris, Janet's husband, primed their work as he had that catalystic meeting, with the fees from the articles written shortly before her death.

Penny moved to Hertfordshire after five years, but Doddy and Clare carried on the speaking engagements the three of them had pioneered. They have spoken to womens' groups, schools and colleges, pre-nursing students, women prison staff. They can only guess at the number of women who have gained re-assurance from the talks and the WNCCC film on breast self-examination 'Your Life in Your Hands', for the making of which the Branch contributed five hundred pounds (and seven hundred pounds towards government-sponsored breast screening trials in Huddersfield).

During its existence the Branch has raised over twelve thousand pounds and each year contributes towards the maintenance of one of the WNCCC's five mobile clinics.

The idea is that the unit, which bears a plaque explaining it has been 'adopted' by Harrogate Branch, and to which over seven thousand pounds had been sent by 1980, is used mainly in the North of England. It has carried out industrial screening programmes in many parts of Yorkshire, for which Harrogate members have often acted as receptionists, and in the course of nearly six months in 1975 alone some two thousand women employed in more than fifty factories all over Yorkshire were screened by the unit.

In June 1980 the caravan-clinic was at last welcomed to its home ground and the Branch was able to launch a public programme for on-the-spot cervical smear tests and simple breast examinations, at a cost to it of roughly one thousand pounds. For two weeks the caravan was towed to various sites in the district, to shopping precincts, an Army wives' centre, even outside a pub! The response was overwhelming. The Branch had estimated it could cater for a maximum of 400 women but, as queues formed, the women doctors, nurses and stewards worked overtime to extend the sessions and in fact a total of 739 women were seen, including 170 for breast examinations alone.

A large slice of its money comes from its celebrity Christmas Fairs, 1980 was the fifth. The first, opened by Judith Chalmers (chairman of the WNCCC's Appeals Committee in London), raised over £800 and the 1978 (they are now held every two years) £2,385. Many fund-raising events have been held. Members have welcomed the public to a top-line fashion show, an evening of magic, a sponsored knit, an outdoor punch and pâté luncheon. They have had a waste-paper drive, pottery parties, model railway, patchwork and lace-making demonstrations, and jumble sales.

The fund-raising and social sub-committee organises such events, while the education and publicity sub-committee handles the equally important educational aspects, which include the supplying of leaflets and the showing of films. The Branch has its own films, screen and projector. It also has a screening programmes organiser, Membership Secretary and newsletter.

By late 1980 the Branch had 111 members, including some 15 nurses, and 11 affiliated organisations. An amazing cross-section of talent has been selflessly harnessed to the cause over the years, from the busy GP, herself a mum, who acts as honorary medical adviser, to the former textile buyer and professional embroideress who made the Branch's two superb banners, though a minority today are also NHR members. Moira Davis, who succeeded Penny as chairman, has been a NHR member for eight years. She is also on the London Executive of WNCCC and a member of its Finance Committee. Penny Craddock is now chairman of that Committee and has in addition been asked by London to help set up new groups in various parts of the country. Moira is also on the Yorkshire Regional Cancer Organisation (Information to the Public), while vice-chairman Carole Stead, former NHR Local Organiser in Harrogate, is the Branch's representative on Harrogate District Community Health Council.

XVIII
The Men

HUSBANDS AND THEIR attitudes weave a firm thread through the fabric of the organisation.

In coffee breaks at conferences, and during railway station pauses for connections off the main track, I have heard maddening stories of male arrogance or thoughtlessness. One woman, disgust thick in her voice, told of a husband, passing in the street on his way home, nodding to his wife intentionally sitting at the window during a local meeting. She immediately left to go home and dish up his meal. Equally incensed members told about women unable to attend meetings because husbands are unexpectedly 'late home from work' a euphemism for stopping off at the pub, and giving women no notice to make other baby-sitting arrangements. Several of the potential candidates for nomination to the National Group in 1980 withdrew their names because their husbands did not approve of the expenditure of time and interest outside the home.

Some of the husbands of the Burnham/Taplow group resented the implication that their wives' need for intellectual stimulation was due to husbands' failure to provide this. But that was back in 1965 – surely attitudes have changed?

Back in the mid-sixties too I heard about an evening meeting which, at the very last moment, had to be moved from the Local Organiser's house to another member's who could not get a baby-sitter. During the evening the LO's husband heard a knock on the door. He assumed it was a latecomer. A man stood on the doorstep wanting to check on his wife's whereabouts. He refused to believe that the venue had been changed and launched into accusations about a white slave racket through which his wife had been spirited away. The root cause was presumably the difficult concept that women would wish to gather together to talk to other women.

I met his wife soon after, at another Register meeting, hair and best clothes neatly stiff and out of date, but she had courageously taken what was her first independent step since her marriage and the birth of her only child, by then a teenager, by joining her first woman's group, albeit thinking that it was concerned with domestic matters.

After the brief burst of notoriety surrounding her debut as a Register member, which fellow members thought the joke of the year, she became unobtrusive at meetings, contributing little.

Two years later she had to remind me that we had met before when I arrived at a sophisticated Register party which she had helped to organise. The change was more than clothes and hairstyle. She was alert in expression and manner, confident among the other women.

Her horizons had been extended by the sweep of discussions on social justice, abortion, women's rights, even that institutions like public libraries can be challenged if they do not cater for women readers who have to take along small children when they seek books. No longer was she inevitably and dependably at home, presenting a meal for her husband as he walked in, and sitting knitting while he dozed in front of the television or, on occasion, patronised the pub. She had a job. Her own friends. In time the marriage broke up. Her husband's intuitions were not adrift; he had just got his facts wrong. NHR was only, incidentally, the channel through which she began to develop as an individual in a way that affected her marital relationship. There could have been another form – such as the chance, in what started as a run of the mill job, to stretch, to do that much more. Though, oddly enough, she is still remembered among members as the example among several that I cited in an article entitled 'Second-chance wives leave husbands behind' in the *Observer*, January 1976.

She was one of the few working-class members I have come across – defining working-class as low income with a husband engaged in labouring jobs. Occasionally through the years, members have expressed regret at the low penetration into a section of society where women are equally frustrated by child ties.

But to return to mainstream. The logo of a building with bold interlinked NHR initials, still used today, was designed by the husband of a member back in 1969. Even at that time a woman trying for publicity to get a new group started noticed that, on car stickers, it caught the eyes of more men than women and they passed the word on to their wives.

Husbandly kindness, sympathy, tolerance, or whatever you like to call recognition that a wife/mother is also an individual, is the solid support without which the Register would have foundered long ago.

There are, of course, benefits for the family, some intangible. How can you quantify how many of the bumps and skids of family life are less destructive because a woman, corseted by the demands of house/children/marriage, has a personal outlet which gives her time to be herself? Some are definable. In times of stress such as illness of children or adults a network of 'aunts' provide such practical aid as collecting children from school, looking after them, shopping, producing a meal, all the kind of backing once given by blood relations living nearby, before the modern migration.

There are also benefits for a husband in less fraught circumstances. A commuter may have little contact with his home-ground, his own community. If his wife is making friends, through the Register, with the 'like-minded', then logically he may find friends too among their husbands to be met at Register social gatherings. Occasionally reports of male-based arrangements have appeared in the national *Newsletter*: squash games, car rallies.

There have even been flickers of something more structured though they seem to have faded. In 1966 a Burnham/Slough member found Register meetings so stimulating: 'We cannot sleep when we eventually go home to our long-suffering husbands! They have in their own defence formed a group called the "Homeless Husbands" and meet monthly for conversation and a little liquid refreshment!' She quoted in the Register *Newsletter* from the draft manifesto setting out the original aims, presumably framed by her own spouse:

> The Housebound Wives meet from time to time at each others' homes to discuss matters of serious moment. Children and husbands are the only two subjects that are taboo.... To come to the point. I would suggest that those of us husbands who feel inclined to do so should form ourselves into an organisation 'The Homeless Husbands' or some such name. The object would be to discuss any subject connected with the home, particularly wives and children.

The subject for the first meeting was to be Bottle-Feeding (Alcoholic)!

Whether Glasgow husbands had more profound intentions is unknown, but in 1969, after a successful Register group party, some of them were (according to published records) 'planning a "Housebound husbands'" group, having discovered that they enjoy the chance to meet people from a good cross-section of occupations with widely differing interests but with the common bond of having to baby-sit frequently while their wives are out at some sort of "housewives'" activity'.

The common bond is certainly that of having to baby-sit for evening meetings, which is why wives of servicemen, or others away from home for long periods, have problems getting out, a difficulty which also faces the increasing number of single parents.

But the Register custom of holding meetings in homes can impinge even more closely on men.

One main living room in modern homes is not uncommon and if a member volunteers to hold the meeting then her husband can be deprived of his comfortable chair and perhaps a favourite TV programme.

'What do you do with *your* husbands?' asked a Welsh member in 1972. A question which must ring through the years. She reported, in the *Newsletter* of course:

> Our meetings are held monthly at members' homes and it is amusing to watch the various reactions of the husbands whose homes are being invaded! Some have disappeared before we arrive, some made a very hurried exit into the night not to be seen again that evening – one retreated to the bath only to make a very hasty retreat when a member received an urgent call from nature! Others brave it out in the kitchen or television room, switching the latter up full blast, hopefully lulling themselves into a false sense of security! The husband of the year was the one who gallantly ventured from his hiding place to mend a fuse when our meeting was plunged into darkness.

Being absent host or baby-sitter puts few demands on a husband. It is a different matter for the day or weekend conferences. A mother cannot pack her bags and depart taking it for granted that the children are cared for. Many are unwilling, diffident about asking for 'the favour', feeling guilty for wanting to go off on something that interests them. Allowing for one woman's mutter to me: 'Mine gets his mother in', in the majority of occasions the husband takes over.

A Local Organiser who told me 'My husband doesn't answer the phone in the evenings, says its one of "my women"' did not expand on the undertones of that attitude, but another, whose husband kept asking when 'is someone else taking a turn?' read the writing on the wall.

But at national level marriages must be really strong in give and take. When the first warnings of the avalanche she had unleashed by her *Guardian* letter poured through the Nicol's letterbox, Maureen's spontaneous first thought was to confer with her husband Brian.

Looking back across twenty years Brian Nicol remembers: 'The upsurge of interest following the publication of *The Sunday Times* article certainly made an impact on our lives for a short period. A few incidents come to mind. Being summoned home from work to look after the children, while Maureen was whisked off in a car to the TV studios, got my colleagues wondering what it was all about. I also remember one of the husbands of the regional organisers turning up one day to meet us. He seemed to half suspect that the whole thing was a front for some dubious activity that his wife had got foolishly involved in.

'However my main recollection is the radio broadcast. Maureen had gone to Manchester to be at the *Woman's Hour* studio and I was at home minding the children and, of course, was keyed-up to listen. Simon was playing outside the kitchen where the radio was. Just as the interviewer was launching into her introduction of Maureen, Simon started battering on the door and shouting in his inimitable fashion. The only thing I could do was to quickly snatch up the biscuit box and open the door and thrust it into his hands and close the door again. He was a very surprised small boy.

'However, immediately, another heart stopper; the interviewer asked Maureen the first question. Then there was silence. It may have lasted two seconds at the most before she replied but the awful moments are with me still. Maureen said later that the interviewer had indicated what her first question would be and she had mentally prepared a reply, only to be confronted with a different question in actuality when the interview started.

'Several newspapers seemed to be interested in the story including the *Daily Express* which talked about the stultifying lot of housewives who rapidly became little more than "cabbages". The last word, prominent in the headline, caused rueful comment among Register members. It also gave my colleagues at work and other friends, already somewhat curious and mystified, an excuse for witticisms about the whole affair!

'The really quite short period during which various reporters seemed to be knocking continuously on the door was the nearest we have come before or since to being "in the news". It was an interesting experience but not one that one would want particularly to repeat.

'Apart from the time of hectic activity my direct involvement with the NHR has been minimal. I quite enjoy organising things myself and, if the same thing had happened to me, I could not have resisted making a big "thing" out of it, and would probably have attempted to shape it in its early days much as it has subsequently developed. Maureen has radically different ideas of the laissez-faire variety. She also relinquished quite early any active part in the national scene. I could not have done that! Knowing how different our ideas were, and that it was, in any case, Maureen's "thing" not mine, I rightly, I am sure, in retrospect, forebore to advise or criticise and let her get on with it, giving help only when requested. We adopt the same policy in our everyday lives either explicitly or tacitly when there is a major difference of opinion. We decide who is in charge of a particular activity and he or she makes the decisions and the other does what is requested without too much query about the policy. For example we each choose and organise the family holiday alternate years. It is a formula that seems to work well.

'Maureen has always been low key about the Register. Perhaps ambivalent is a better description. She was always afraid of it getting out of hand and forcing her to do things she did not want to do. On the other hand she has been quite rightly proud of the Register and glad about the help that it has undoubtedly been to people. Despite this she has never talked about it much; has never encouraged me to become interested or talk about it, and seems genuinely diffident about seeing her name mentioned nationally in connection with it. When we were in Uganda it was almost completely forgotten for six years whilst it was going from strength to strength back in England. The revival of interest by the media associated with the coming of age, and the Manchester meeting, again brought Maureen somewhat back into the centre of the stage. Again there was the struggle between pleasure and anxiety. Your request for co-operation with the history has crystalised this antithesis in many ways.'

National level
'I think the husbands and families of National Group members should be "honorary members" of NHR,' declared the first National Group Treasurer, in the late seventies, Liz Salthouse. 'If they were not almost as enthusiastic about the NHR as we are, life would be very difficult'.

Gill Vine, explaining what it means to be the National Organiser (again late seventies), categorically includes the husband as the 'crucial' factor. 'If he will not play ball you cannot do the job'. Friends might be relied on to collect children from school, and get them back to school next day if an evening meeting is across country and means an overnight stay. 'But supposing your son is swimming in the county championships when you are at a conference? If Dad can go that's fine. The same thing with the first football match. It comes back to Dad. You cannot overstress it'. He also has to be forebearing about the mini-office that occupies part of his home.

Like any woman who takes on the NO's job, husbands cannot be aware of the full implications until they actually experience them.

For any member of the National Group the Register will spasmodically impinge even more closely on home life. Expenses do not run to hotel bills. So when one of the regular meetings are held, taking over living room, kitchen, at least, the hospitality of the hostess's home backs it up. Husbands can find themselves setting out camp beds, ferrying overflow guests to nearby members' homes for the night(s), joining the rota for the bathroom. So bouquets are in order.

I remember Ron Salthouse, husband of Liz, who had his home disorganised in just that way on a Friday in 1979 and was still beaming on the Saturday morning when heading a procession of his small daughters bearing piping hot parcels of fish and chips to revive the gathering, in a nearby Community Centre, of the incumbent National Group and the potential nominees for the next one. Or Brian Shingler, sustaining the twelve National Group women through their weekend deliberations (late 1980) with regular distribution of tea/coffee, while caring for a sick calf. And for that matter Ralph Steadman, with two of his sons, delighting the national conference at Bradford with Haydn in a string ensemble. His wife's group organised the event.

Money

Anyone taking an active part in an organisation, cause, or campaign, will be subsidising it 'invisibly', in that no hard figure features in the household budget for phone calls, petrol, stamps and paper, one of the reasons why active participants in causes tend to be those with an income elastic enough to stretch that little bit.

Since Register members, by definition, are mostly women at home – non-earners – the subsidy is male-financed. At local level I would hope that such expenditure is classed with that spent on theatre tickets, golf club fees, children's sport or cultural interests.

The scene changes at national level. Maureen Nicol found that a stamp did not automatically accompany an enquiry. As the 'bankrupt success' she handed over expanded into a national organisation the costs of running it naturally expanded too; a fact not always grasped by members. There are always rumblings about the cost of membership; short-sighted considering the fundamental idea of a 'Register', tappable when you move house. It is still run on a shoe-string.

The men who supported their wives' commitment to the Register at national level were, up to very recently, risking (possibly unaware) more than just the domestic disruption of phone calls and wives' departure to distant cities; in fact they were risking personal financial liability.

Discussing the financial responsibilities and problems with one time National Organiser Pat Williams she interjected: 'You should hear Robin on the cost of NHR.' Naturally I said, 'Yes, please.'

This is what Robin Williams had to say, in retrospect.

'I am rather loath to write about Pat's time as National Organiser from the point of view of the NO's immediate family, as I considered at the time that it was Pat's show entirely and one in which I should not intrude, except in a personally supportive role. Certainly I would not have commented nearer the event, with which I had a second-hand but nevertheless strong love-hate relationship.

'Looking back I suppose I was immensely proud that Pat was doing a job which gave her a certain amount of prestige within a limited sphere, and one which we both thought was providing a very useful function. Against that was the constant pressure of the job, telephone calls at all hours, letters that had to be answered promptly if the NHR was to flourish, printing deadlines for the *Newsletter*, etc., and the thought that any break for more than a day just meant extra work to come home to. This naturally put pressure on the whole family. It was an eternal presence, rather like a loved but over-bearing mother-in-law living in the family home, over-staying her welcome by two or three years.

'I felt that there was an unreasonable lack of support and appreciation from the membership as a whole and, what must be the burden of most small or women's organisations, an incredible meanness about money. This was certainly helped by the attitude of Pat and Josephine who did not want to be open to criticisms for profligacy. But it seemed to me that we (the family) were subsidising the NHR. I cannot say that I really resented all this at the time, or that we ever went short as a result, but I did feel that there were more deserving causes, in financial terms, than a Register of mainly middle-class women. On a philosophical note, I thought it symptomatic of women to want things on the cheap, particularly when it came to other women's labour, and it was one more way of ensuring that women stayed in their chosen place as second-class citizens.

'On the positive side the three years as NO helped Pat and us through a difficult time when a "lively mind" is committed by social pressure to stay at home, and it gave Pat enormous confidence to get out into the world after her stint had finished. This may sound patronising but it is meant more as a comment, looking back objectively on a person who is very close and who changed considerably over the three years. To my mind this change was for the better and I hope was a joint experience.

'The last, and one of the biggest benefits that we got as a family, was the friendship we developed with Josephine and her family. Even at the blackest times there was always the thought that we could ring them – they would understand.

'Summing up: NHR was an experience I wouldn't have missed for worlds, but over the passing of responsibility from this household I have no regrets; the return would be most unwelcome.'

Male View

Husbands are diffident about using the pages of the national *Newsletter* to express their own views. Even reports of role-swapping, husband at home, wife at work, come from wives.

Malcolm Goodwin, husband of Jane, then Overseas Co-ordinator, bravely took the plunge (was he pushed?) in 1979 with 'A Husband's View of NHR'.

> I have learned not to answer the telephone when it rings but to call Jane from the furthest reaches of the house. It is, after all, only someone moving to the middle of the desert who wants to start an NHR group at the nearest oasis: or perhaps someone who can/cannot attend the local group meeting on 'Husbands – Can We Do Without Them?'

He thought:

> There has to be something remarkable about an organisation strung loosely around the world with no policy (except not to discuss babies!) and precious little organisation.... Power remains where it should be, at the grass-roots end of the structure.... Given a lack of centralised control – i.e. bureaucracy, the NHR will continue to perform its mind-touching feats on housebound women until such time as there is true equality – that is – men and women sharing home and business duties according to their individual inclinations. Then, of course, there will be a need for a Register for men. Or, perhaps, just a Register!

Newsletter editor Hazel Bell invited other members' husbands to contribute to a male-view symposium. Well she got one, from Patrick Shanahan. When his wife Lesley joined NHR he had mixed feelings. 'I didn't know anything about the outfit, and it crossed my mind that it might be a society consisting largely of shrieking harpies hell-bent on promoting the dottier aspects of feminism.' His fears were soon laid to rest. 'I was and am extremely impressed with the thought and effort that goes into producing the programme of events, and on occasions, rather put out that we men are banned from the cloisters.' He commented also:

> One lesson which Lesley's membership of NHR has taught me is how wives feel when they are introduced to their husband's friends or more particularly colleagues. I still remember the first time Lesley and I went to, I believe, a barbecue laid on by the West Wickham group. Lesley, of course, knew most of the people whilst I didn't know a soul. The husbands sniffed around each other like wolves around a meal before exchanging gambits.

He reported a by-product: husbands getting together to play squash, 'go drinking', etc.

But, he concluded:

> Without wishing or indeed thinking of being at all patronising – women are on to a good thing with NHR and should guard it with their lives. These opportunities do not appear twice in a lifetime.

XIX
The Second National Group from mid-1980

THE WOMEN OFFERING themselves for election to national office in 1980 were well briefed beforehand, by means which could become traditional. Of the twenty-nine who originally volunteered twenty-one were able to stay the course. They learned something of each other's thoughts on the Register through a 'Round Robin'.

It was Val Williams, an NG incumbent, who suggested that it would be helpful to get the potential nominees together to exchange ideas and to put queries personally instead of by endless letters. The National Group wanted no repeat of 1978 when a member went onto it not realising the work involved and when she did, promptly resigned.

Having checked that fares and hospitality could be borne, Manchester (Sale) was chosen for the venue in November 1979. Potential nominees discovered that physical failings had not deterred national officers from attending first a Group meeting followed the next day by the workshop; though one could not see properly, one could not hear properly, one had a sore throat and could not speak properly and one had a very stiff neck.

Outlines of specific national level jobs had been set down on paper for the benefit of potential newcomers and at Sale those holding the jobs made personal comments. The exercise also provided more insight into the expanding national demands of an organisation that could once, say up to the late sixties, be administered by one person.

National Organiser
Maintains the Register (i.e. card index of Local Organisers); promotes aims and ideals of NHR; encourages development of new groups, presents aims and image of NHR to media and other organisations; co-ordinates work of National Group; deals with

enquiries; advises established groups; visits groups and conferences; has overall responsibility for *Newsletter*; prepares and sends out circulars; keeps stocks of stationery, publicity materials and NHR pamphlets; orders or duplicates; houses office equipment and group files.
TIME: Full-time plus evening and weekend visits; TV appearances, broadcasts and media meetings; telephone calls at any time *of* day; aided by a part-time secretary/clerk/typist.

Public Relations Officer

Develops and maintains contacts with media; presents aims and image of NHR to media and other organisations; advises groups on publicity; handles publicity material. TIME: Variable. Great deal of telephone work and personal appearances.

Gill Vine had the two jobs. She picked from the 'Outline' the point about promoting the aims and ideals of the NHR because 'so many have no clue who we are and why we are there, even some groups unfortunately'. She got enquiries by every post, 'pouring in' after publicity. They were answered by personal or duplicated letters. The answer to 'Where's the nearest group?' could be six or twenty-five miles away. In the latter case she put together another enquiry in the same area, sent *Newsletters*, perhaps met the enquirer and offered help to get a new group going.

But problems also arose in established groups. 'A vociferous member can be putting everyone off. An outsider might sort it out, listen to arguments and, in the nicest possible way, adjudicate'. She thought she had probably been to the largest number of groups of any National Organiser: 'thoroughly enjoyable'. And added: 'Some feel more involved, more part of NHR after a visit. People like to *see* you'.

Of her work, aided by clerical paid help four mornings a week, she mentioned doing the labels for the newsletter distribution, duplicating leaflets, one thousand letters at a time, to new organisers, writing the circulars, stapling them and getting their envelopes labelled, filled and stamped: 'The children help. We slip them pocket money'.

She mentioned the office equipment which was in her own home, three four-drawer full size filing cabinets, a duplicator, an electronic scanner which cuts stencils from any originals (bought cheaply secondhand), a 'beanstalk' of filing baskets, an electric typewriter and a typist's chair.

With intentional emphasis she told her audience that the husband's attitude is the most crucial factor in the job. 'You could not do the job without co-operation of husband and children'. There were murmurs of agreement from the other National Group members.

The National Organiser now has a separate NHR phone. Gill spoke of how 'In mid-supper the phone rings, maybe some poor desperate woman.' She recalled returning from a weekend conference 'late, tired, hungry'. A phone call had been taken by the family. She phoned back on the Monday but later got a letter expressing surprise that she had not returned the call over the weekend. 'They expect you to be available seven days a week'. Gill estimated that future annual growth in membership will be at least five per cent.

Treasurer

Collects money; pays bills; keeps accounts and records; prepares annual and longer term budgets; deals with bank manager, auditor, VAT Inspector, tax inspector, insurance broker. TIME: part-time, mainly steady flow. This 'broad outline' for distribution to nominees was certainly just the bones; a job description Liz Salthouse wrote out for my information covered three pages!

At Sale Liz spoke about cheques coming in without addresses, or unsigned, about new groups forgetting to say they have got going, about checking the records for unpaid subs during 'Dr Who', and returning from holidays to find a front door difficult to open because of delivered accumulated mail. She spoke too, of course, of the dire financial situation when the first National Group took over.

Newsletter Editor

Compiles newsletter material; commissions articles; responsible for copyright and acceptability; deals with printer; deals with technical aspects, e.g. pagination, proof reading; distribution of newsletter. TIME: Heavy commitment several weeks around publication date – otherwise variable.

Hazel Bell described it as 'a professional job' and went into details of the mechanics (see chapter on The Link) including the method of getting the newsletter out to Local Organisers' meetings so members can collect and save postage, which is why a 'Great Pile' of copies are delivered by the printer to the editor's home to await NHR's special method of distribution.

New Groups Advisor

Promotes aims and ideals of the NHR; deals with enquiries; promotes setting up of new groups; advises on setting up of new groups, provides starter pack, contacts, etc.; regular follow-up of new groups; visits; deals with problems and development of new groups; keeps files and index cards – 140 plus groups and 12 overseas. TIME: Average six to seven hours per week on correspondence, plus telephoning at any time, and visits – and increasing. The job also includes keeping the register up to date. TIME: average one hour per week over a year but heavy periods January and September.

Chairman

Helps NO co-ordinate work of National Group; ensures regular communication between National Group members through Round Robin; arranges and notifies NG meetings; chairs NG meetings and AGM at national conference. TIME: variable.

These jobs were Jean Stirk's responsibility. At Sale she spoke about controlling a National Group meeting when everyone 'talks too much' (omitting to explain how firmly and skilfully she got them through the agenda); and about the incredible number of potential new groups who are never heard of again though followed up, and what it costs in money, but still 'an investment'. The contact may have moved, may have been unable to get a group going, or may even have started one and forgot to record that fact! 'Two-thirds of enquirers become established groups and pay subs'. She sent out fourteen to fifteen new group guidance packs a month. She saw the job as encouraging, re-assuring if wanted, and also as needing 'time', which had not been possible in the past when it was just one aspect among the many tackled by the National Organiser.

Overseas Co-ordinator

Promotes and advises on setting up of NHR groups overseas; keeps contact with overseas groups; compiles and circulates overseas newsletter; keeps index of overseas groups. TIME: average three hours per week over a year, but intermittent. Jane Goodwin, who had personally met many far-flung members during family holidays, described the international newsletter she had started as a means by which they could keep in touch with home. A National Organiser, coping with everything else, could not give the overseas side time, and she saw the job as almost 'a mini NO', to whom expatriates could write with their problems. 'Going overseas it's the same system of "where's the nearest NHR group?".'

Conference Liaison

Advises on organisation of conferences; keeps up to date on conference facilities and relevant information; co-ordinates arrangement of conferences; encourages development of local conferences and get-togethers of Local Organisers. TIME: average three hours per week, plus visits and conference attendance.

Pat Kerr talked about the growth of interest in conferences over her two years in the job, more day conferences and attracting members from a wider radius. She was getting feedback of opinion on facilities; visiting universities and hotels for locations, and had learned about certain things to watch out for like 'inadequate loos'.

Archivist

Maintains and develops records of NHR events and activities, national and local documents; classifies and indexes material; supplies copies of archive material. No estimate of time was given.

Margaret Cameron said succinctly: 'When I started I was offered one large envelope.'

Minutes Secretary

Writes and circulates minutes of NG meetings and AGM at national conference; keeps minute books by hand; maintains policy books.

The incumbent, Val Williams, who had bravely taken on that job though lacking technical skills ('The NHR', she told me 'challenges you to do things you didn't think you could do') sees the job as more than the brief circulated outline. She keeps a list of groups in her area, gives them a ring so they know that a National Group member is nearby.

Sales

Maintains stocks of NHR key rings, biros, diaries, and handles sales to members.

Beryl Bonney explained that the purpose was publicity. She had at that time one thousand pens stored in her home.

There was not, I thought, much emphasis on the fact that these committed women also attended NG meetings, national conferences, local conferences, local group meetings; but otherwise the nominees for national office got it from 'the horse's mouth' at the Sale Workshop.

The Second National Group from mid 1980

They each then spoke briefly of themselves and some of their ideas about NHR. What came through strongly was their gratitude for what the Register had done for them personally which they wanted to repay by working on the National Group. All had been active at local level. They offered a broad band of professional skills as well as enthusiasm.

Four months later nine were elected and, with Beryl Bonney having unexpectedly to resign, Vivienne Eardley was co-opted – to gain Scottish representation.

The twelve who were to form the second National Group (Val Williams and Pat Kerr had another two years to serve) were then asked by the first NG to set down the qualities needed today for specific jobs. The important National Group chairman was omitted because, to bridge the two administrations, Pat Kerr already held that post.

The resulting memorandum is a statement in itself of how NHR has changed over twenty years. These pictures emerged of what each job requires.

National Organiser: articulate, writes well, easy manner, good appearance – to put over the image and ideals of NHR. Equable temperament, personality (charisma was mentioned), sense of humour, discreet/diplomatic, perceptive, sensitive, good listener, flexible but firm, able to use initiative, wide experience of NHR. Needing too the ability to delegate, co-ordinate, organise on a large scale, and accept a high degree of responsibility. All this and time, stamina, family support, accommodation (the office equipment).

Public Relations Officer: experience, expertise, plus ability to write well, and to present young image of the NHR. Also articulate, quick thinking, persuasive, able to use initiative, resilient, persistent, with an easy manner, good appearance, and family support for when she needs to travel about.

Newsletter editor: experience, expertise, with good English, good judgement, imagination, being erudite, perceptive, able to use initiative and work at speed in peak periods.

Treasurer: expertise, experience in handling money and budgeting, with integrity, but also methodical, meticulous, numerate, resourceful, able to present accounts so laywomen understand them, able to deal with tax, insurance and similar technicalities, and to be firm in order to extract subscriptions from the laggardly.

New Groups Adviser: wide experience of NHR, articulate; able to write well so as to put over image and aims; diplomatic; encouraging; reassuring; imaginative; of good appearance and easy manner;

flexible, being sensitive to shortcomings of groups yet able to give firm guidance.
Conference Liaison: articulate and able to write well with an easy manner, good appearance, supportive, encouraging, diplomatic, able to co-ordinate, listen, advise and guide, and keep a cool head.
Overseas Co-ordinator: an enthusiastic and able letter writer to maintain the link and put over NHR aims and image, well organised, able to co-ordinate, with overseas knowledge and interest.
Archivist: methodical, meticulous, good at presentation, able to index and enterprising in getting resources and using them.
Sales: methodical, imaginative, numerate, able to use initiative.
Minutes Secretary: shorthand-typing skills, able to concentrate, to precis, with good basic English.

I can imagine the National Organisers of the past (pre-1976) who after all, albeit over a narrower field, took on the jobs listed (excluding chairman and minutes secretary – no group, no minutes – and sales, no products) being entertained, even flattered, to think that they presumably incorporated in their persons many of the qualities now considered desirable.

But I am sure they will also note the emergence of 'appearance'. To quote Jean Stirk's aside in the context of defining 'lively-minded': 'Just how one determines this criterion is a whole new ball-game'.

Expertise, which I interpret as having the technical skills and qualifications required for the job, is also a newcomer. Many a National Organiser of the past has had the (maybe mixed) pleasure of picking up extra skills as she went along.

Having been well briefed on the jobs and seen each other's views on the talents required, the twelve who were to take over as the National Group from mid-1980 met beforehand (at member Liz Williamson's home in Marple, Cheshire) to submit themselves for internal Group vote for the jobs that interested them, i.e. National Organiser, or otherwise Treasurer, NO but otherwise *Newsletter* Editor, and so on, with a vote required only when there were several candidates.

I found it a nail-biting occasion.

The questions put to each separately in turn by Jean Stirk (by invitation, because she is soaked in NHR and its needs and because her pre-child bearing skills were in personnel and fitting the right square into the rightly shaped hole) exposed their strengths and weaknesses to themselves as well as to those who were to vote for them, or not. The 'short-list' (in usual commercial terms) was applying for jobs working out at about one pound an hour, which in some districts would not attract a daily domestic cleaner!

Four women then went through the mill, talking about why they wanted to be the National Organiser, how they would cope with some of the more awkward problems thrown up in the job. Each, it is a point worth making in 1980, mentioned they had space to house the 'office'. Gill Vine, incumbent National Organiser, was present by invitation and gave generously of advice on technicalities. As the only trustee able to be present I was handed the plastic kitchen bowl into which the votes were dropped and had the job of counting the slips of paper and announcing the result.

By a large majority the Group's vote, for National Organiser, went to Alison Shingler, self-confessed 'workaholic' previously not only lecturer in French or shorthand but in French shorthand, who said 'NHR brought my life back into Technicolor again', founder of the Dawlish group, addicted to badminton, hand bell ringing, language lessons, mother of three, and married to a farmer.

We worked our way through the other appointments in much the same manner. I would assure those considering nomination in the future, who might be daunted by the professional method of selection, that the atmosphere, at a meeting of women who had seen this as the fairest way of sorting out who does what, was strong in genuine warmth, friendliness and understanding.

By the method then of exposing abilities, ideas, relevant experience, temperament, potential, and then, where necessary, by voting, the National Group arranged for specific responsibilities, from mid-1980.

Reporting on the new NG in the national newsletter, chairman Pat Kerr wrote:

B.(efore) C(hildren), the 12 members were 6 teachers (2 of these were also involved in banking and secretarial work) 1 secretary, 1 nurse plus GPO switchboard girl, 1 bank teller, 1 administrator, 1 sub-editor and 1 research biochemist. Six now do paid work ranging from 6 to 20 hours per week, in addition to being Domestic Economists and members of the NG! Two hold voluntary work offices. We have a total of 25 children (14 boys, 11 girls) ages ranging from 3½ to 25 years. Our ages range from 31 to 40 plus years, and our interests are as diversified as we are, anything from mountain-climbing to handbell ringing. We mostly joined NHR to find 'like-minded' women to talk with when domesticity got too much for us. The papers we take are: 3 *Telegraphs*, 3 *Observers*, 4 *Guardians*, 2 *Daily Mails*, 1 *Glasgow Herald*, 5 *Sunday Times*, various local papers, *Radio Times*, *Punch* and various comics to keep up with the children.

Some of these women, who were the second wave, taking over from the first expanded national base, new-style NHR at administrative level, may, through personal circumstances, drop out of the national scene, having made their contribution. But others today are keen to serve. The Register has come a long way since its existence depended on one volunteer to take over the singular responsibility of being National Organiser. It could, after all, have disappeared into oblivion.

XX
The Invisible Export

HUSBAND'S JOBS CAN move families thousands rather than just hundreds of miles. The Register concept has travelled with them and taken root, in Australia and Canada in 1968, South Africa in 1969. By 1980, when the first international conference was held at Newland Park College, Buckinghamshire, under the title 'Destiny 2,000' there were nearly two hundred groups in five continents, Africa, Asia, Australia, N. America, Europe.

The idea of an international gathering was first mooted by Julia Strickley of the Canadian Housewives Register. It was brought to fruition, with the aid of a 'Think-tank' of UK members and a grant from the Equal Opportunities Commission, by Jane Goodwin. Jane was the first to hold the title Overseas Co-ordinator and have only that responsibility; previously the encouragement – a New Groups pack and contacts – had been part of the workload of the National Organiser. Jane, a member of the first National Group, had been an expatriate herself. She launched the twice-yearly link, 'Register Worldwide', in 1977, a duplicated publication about what was going on in the UK Register and elsewhere, compiled from correspondence or longer specific contributions from the international membership.

The UK NHR has financed the 'New Group' packs despatched to help set up the international network since the first overseas group got off the ground in the late sixties, and also largely the linking publication. Donations in the late seventies from overseas ranged from £3 to £34. Jane worked out that 'Register Worldwide' expenses over her last months of office in 1980 alone were £160. But then no 'subscriptions' had ever been asked for. That was remedied at the first international conference.

It was timed to take advantage of family 'home leave'; other women paid their own fares. Twenty women managed to attend, coming from Australia, South Africa, Abu Dhabi, Canada, Dubai, Holland, the USA, Kuwait, Belgium. Many of the other 130 attending had been expatriates and could be again when husbands work for multi-national concerns.

The only criticism concerned the high proportion of time given to outside speakers even on such topics as 'Future trends in Adult Education', 'The New Genetics', 'Space Age Technology', but, as three months beforehand, only eight overseas bookings had arrived, it was a brave decision to proceed, throwing open the event to UK members.

The criticism was valid; but after all it was the very first of such get-togethers and there were plenty of meal-times, and late night interchanges. In fact the 'Business session', started in the College hall, was carried on till nearly midnight outdoors on a warm summer evening and UK officers and overseas representatives even met yet again before breakfast to work out details.

The international contingent expressed keenness to pay dues so as to remain part of the network, though it was recognised that the benefit would be clearer to women moving home to a strange country every few years than to the indigenous. Discussion ranged round how to differentiate between a single group in a country and the autonomous national Registers running their own ship (South Africa for one). The first thought of an affiliation fee regardless of membership numbers raised good humoured suggestions that it would be 'cheaper' to be an autonomous Register, and led to the possibility of the scattered European groups joining together to become one. A Middle East Register would be more difficult because of air fares. But it was a fascinating indication of possible future developments.

Ideas were offered on how the job of running the international linkup could be taken off the UK; for instance, rotating among countries the job of Overseas Co-ordinator. Since, foreseeably, no other country can yet take it on, it stays here. Jane Goodwin star-gazed to a time when each country had one, with even a 'world' co-ordinator as well. Meantime even the 'mini-committee' proposed is hardly practical considering distances and resources. Ideally future international conferences would also be hostessed in turn. But there is the hard fact that the UK is where many overseas members return for 'home leave'. An option is to expand some UK annual conferences with an international session.

Suzanne Wyatt from Belgium thought it was time the UK changed its name to the International Women's Register, a title already used by her group; she also asked why the UK and international newsletter could not be amalgamated. Answer, not economically practical.

But the main objective was to make the international side self-supporting. A three-tier system of payments was hammered out, to be taken back to own groups for ratification.

For £10 a year a 'country' to get two copies of each of the twice yearly UK national *Newsletter* and of the 'Register Worldwide'. But no support like new group packs or publicity material.

For the same sum a 'group' to get the same number of both newsletters plus new group packs and advice by correspondence, but no publicity material unless requested and paid for. Neither of these categories have UK voting or nomination for national office rights, but both have access to the Register (advantages for nomadic members) and, of course, close links with the international side.

The third tier pay to £1.50 *per member*, plus £1 postage, each to receive a copy of the *Newsletters*, get support like new group packs, advice through correspondence, and free publicity material if they want it. They however have full voting and nomination rights, like UK resident members, as well as access to the Register and close links with the international set-up.

Not that the first international conference was all outside speakers with 'business' jammed in between. A 'decision-making' session had us sorted into clusters to debate, and report, on different situations to do with women's conflicting loyalties, families, career and educational aspirations. When the group who had debated the case of a husband bounding home to inform his wife that they were off across the world reported you could hear the hiss of breath through teeth! Considerable marital communication and discussion was seen as vital.

Apart from taking their turn at chairing some of the formal talks, members from abroad spoke on the situation of women in countries where some expected to spend the rest of their lives, others with a stay depending on their husband's jobs.

Helen Formentin of Western Australia, who had on her trip met many NHR members in different parts of the UK, painted in the immense space, the small population, the pioneering conditions now changing to suburban comforts; air travel having made all the difference.

Mel Golder told how she fitted in with the Luxembourg practice of teaching your own children in the afternoons. Belgium may offer excellent child care but Hilary Welch spoke not only about educational help at home but about helping children adjust to living in a foreign society. Margaret Sanderson from Holland startled British women who take school dinners for granted by mentioning that there, schools close from 12 to 2 o'clock.

Sue Marsden from Kuwait, where some women are still veiled and secluded, working only in 'invisible' jobs, speculated whether the older women would regret a return to the desert when the oil ran out.

Eve Grimley, still describing South Africa as a super country to live in, recalled the shock of proferring a cheque and being asked to 'take it home for your husband to sign,' and sketched in a system which treats a woman as a minor.

Groupings

An accurate international Register would be difficult to guarantee on any particular date. A group was started in Switzerland, by an expatriate South African member, in 1978, another in Quito, Ecuador by ten Latin American women. One in Oslo, started by a British NHR member, attracted membership between 20 and thirty-five, mainly Englishwomen with Norwegian husbands. One in Hong Kong rose and fell in the late sixties, but a determined expatriate started afresh in 1972, not for the housebound, or housewives, but those in 'need of a change from the social whirl'. The Hong Kong Island NHR was going strong in 1979 with a membership of around seventy. Marie Price, ex UK National Organiser, got one going in Saudi Arabia, (having found three ex-NHR members in situ) with or without children according to the time of day, just as in Wales, and a baby-sitting circle. In Rome, although there was still a hard core of ten in 1980, after five years' existence, no one was taking on the organising job.

'Bright men,' as Hilary Welch, an expatriate in Belgium put it, 'take bright wives along.'

Groups have got going in France, Germany, Botswana, India, Bermuda, New Zealand, to name some. Letters apologising for not keeping in touch so often spell out that the group is still out there – with some surprise that it should be doubted. So in attempting to tell something of the international spread, with a membership which seems as diverse, blue-stocking to 'cake-icers', as in the UK, I am not claiming a definitive record.

Australia
(1) Western Australia. Free-lance journalist Mardy Amos lived in Africa, moved to the UK where she joined the Enfield NHR and, subsequently moving to Perth, started the first Western Australian group in 1968. Another NHR member briefly in Australia (for three years) told me in 1971 about the nearest country group being forty miles from Perth, and the furthest two hundred, linked with a newsletter and exchange visits. Yet there were around two hundred members, and the first national gathering, a 'Forum', that year, attracted seventy.

Helen Formentin reckons there were only about seventeen groups when she became National Organiser (she called it 'only a name') around five years later. Helen took a break of around two years from 'national' active interest. In 1979 she organised a 'Forum' with the approach 'Let it go or get it going' by which time only six groups could be considered enthusiastic. But by 1980 there were 150 members, mostly Australians, under the name 'Women in Touch' and described as 'The Western Australian Division of the NHR' on the publicity leaflet echoing the original Register concepts; paying national subs, although at that stage not getting an internal newsletter. Beth Weir, who was also at the international conference, took over from Helen as NO, the only volunteer – shades of the UK in early days. Helen still provides practical advice, particularly for new groups, and puts her formidable energy at the service of the Register. W. Australia is unusual in meeting on public premises as well as in homes.

(2) The Eastern States. (It helps to look at a map to comprehend the continental distances).

Australian Barbara Lucas found the NHR 'a life-line', living in England (Wolverhampton) for three years with her family. Returning to Australia in 1971, finding 'a great gap' in her life, she soon filled it. Two groups were soon flourishing in Newcastle, NSW, changing organisers annually, with Barbara as co-ordinator between the two.

Barbara, asked why NHR has not spread, sees the reason in the size and lack of communication, each state like a country, even having separate newspapers. But in 1979 a *national* magazine, *The*

Australian Women's Weekly discovered and wrote about the Newcastle groups. Letters flowed in from all over Australia with enquiries for the nearest group or how to start one. 'Without any election', Barbara comments, 'I became the Co-ordinator for the eastern states of Australia. I put a pack together on how to start a group and sent them to all enquirers. The housekeeping took a beating'.

By 1980 there were six groups in New South Wales, (the Lucas family having moved Barbara started another herself), two in Queensland and one in Victoria, with others forming. Membership was around one hundred. Some called themselves 'Women in Touch'; one in Queensland 'Friends Inc.', but they followed the NHR practice, meeting in homes with minimum refreshments, guest speakers, and discussions, programmes compiled by members. Some had baby-sitting arrangements and social get togethers with husbands.

Barbara was trying to get a newsletter going and to introduce subscriptions to finance the cost of keeping in contact and helping new groups to form – 'difficult when I have to foot the bill' she admits – treading the path of the early UK Register-holders. But she affirms how 'many members, including myself, have gained confidence and interest to go on to other things like university and further education'.

Canada

The Canadian Housewives Register was functioning by 1968, set up in Montreal by Christine Read and in Toronto by Anne Cossey, both previously UK NHR members. By 1980 there were twelve groups in and around Toronto (that is within easy driving distance), and one in Victoria (British Columbia) with a handful of 'Members at Large' not belonging to a group.

A constitution sets out the purpose 'to encourage women to stimulate their interest in outside activities and broaden their intellectual horizons'; defines membership 'contributing time and talents', besides paying the required annual fee; explains the structure of the National Executive Board, regional areas and local units called 'groups' (whose members elect their officers) and the duties of those elected to the National Executive.

The National Executive, elected annually with the option of continuing for one more year only, consists of: President, Vice President, Secretary, Treasurer, Publicity Chairperson, Membership Chairperson (who handles registrations, sends out membership cards, keeps a record of all membership, groups, names and addresses of organisers) Member at Large, East and West End representatives (liaison between the Executive and the groups), plus the *Newsletter* Editor who is appointed, and the past President.

An annual dinner is held in Toronto, organised by a different group each year. Twice a year an all-day meeting assists group organisers with their programmes, ironing out any problems, and generally giving feedback and support between Executive and the groups. There is also a one-day annual general meeting and the Executive also organises a conference about every other year.

For the subscription (reduced to just under half for members outside a defined area around Toronto) members get two CHR newsletters a year, plus publicity material and stationery, all designed and produced by the CHR itself, which produces its own advice packs for new groups. Members organise their own group publicity in local newspapers, radio, TV. Groups range in size from five to forty members and in age from twenty-three to eighty.

South Africa

Jacky Harrison, who had started a group in Ipswich, Suffolk took the NHR idea to Johannesburg. Together with two mothers she met in a park she held her first meeting and it grew from there. Publicity in local papers brought enquiries, mostly from immigrants. A letter in a women's magazine brought more from all over the country, and the first group was formed in 1969. Adrienne Rifkin, ex-newspaper reporter, another immigrant, who took over at Jacky's request as National Organiser in 1970, told me at the time about the problems of going out at night (and then advisably in a locked car), the first signs of spreading as members moved house, the discussions about changing the name, there being no housewives in the true sense in South Africa. (The name was later changed to National Womens' Register.)

Altogether South Africa was a fascinating echo of UK experience at national level. Pat van der Linde, another National Organiser oversaw expansion, inspired national conferences on UK lines, with the practical arrangements made by a local group, and with a 'business section' as well as speakers. One hundred and thirty members attended the one in 1978. Journalist Rita Cooper interviewed her about the Register and later took over as NO. By 1979 South African-born Rita, who started regional conferences and a printed newsletter, and who also produced publicity leaflets (entitled 'Lively Lady' in English and Afrikaans) and new group packs, found it all too much responsibility. A constitution now protects national officers, legally and financially, and also provides for an elected committee, so far of three, foreseeably of more, with National Organiser, *Newsletter* Editor and Treasurer. Officers do not get an honorarium.

When the national sub was raised in 1980 there were protests, just as in the UK, but they did manage to buy their first typewriter! In other ways too Treasurer Eve Grimley, who put membership around seven hundred, told me: 'We are the same kind of women with the same problems. South African women don't go back to work because of the tax situation but the educated still need stimulation'. She was referring to white women but specially emphasised that the NWR, like the NHR, is open to all.

Zimbabwe

Ivy Hartmann, on her own with young children in Johannesburg in 1970, while her husband was settling into a new venture in what was then Rhodesia, was 'literally dragged' to what was to be the embryo of the South African Register, by an Australian friend, Pammy O'Connor. Diffident, impressed by those present, she still researched and presented a talk to a meeting, on Women's Lib. She came to relish the 'very rewarding discipline' of the Register which for a woman with no academic schooling opened up 'new avenues for exploration' and 'a million stimuli'.

Re-joining her husband in Rhodesia she also joined the local Women's Institute: 'but it was just not the same. I needed the NHR.'

She founded NHR Rhodesia in late 1971, with encouragement from the UK, the South African Register, her Australian friend, and Audrey Balfour, whom she met at the WI. Audrey, who became PRO sent me copies of the very solid, both in size and content, newsletter which gave a revealing insight into what life was like for women during the governmental changeover. Late 1980 Carole Sargent, nearing retirement as National Organiser, told me how in the farming communities, 'even when it became exceedingly risky to travel... these women met sitting out in the gardens of the respective farms, wearing sidearms, and sometimes with sub-machine guns tucked discreetly under their deckchairs, but despite the hazards, they kept on meeting'.

She was able to report a membership of about two hundred, with fifteen groups including the major centres and a few in more rural areas. NHR Zimbabwe has an annual conference hosted and organised by a group. The annual membership fee is paid to the

PRO who keeps charge of the building society account. Groups then levy a small charge which is paid to the respective Local Organiser. So far there is no constitution. The National Organiser is chosen by the Local Organisers in consultation with their members, and she chooses her own PRO. Terms of office work out at approximately two years, nationally and locally. The *Newsletter* is edited and typed by the NO and the PRO. New group packs are also produced by the national officers.

Carole, and her PRO, Sue Barker, had endeavoured to 'do something constructive about the multi-racial aspect'. She concluded 'the majority of the African women who would be interested in joining an organisation such as our own are either professional women holding down full-time jobs or heavily committed politically'. Eve Grimley of South Africa said much the same.

USA

Christine Valentine was an expatriate between 1978 and 1980. She inspired her neighbour across the street in Hopkinton, Massachusetts, Betsy Knapp, with NHR concepts. They soon recruited twenty to twenty-five members, mostly ex-career women at home taking the chance to explore non-domestic issues at meetings. But in 1979 they were written about in *McCalls* magazine and around two hundred to three hundred enquiries emanated from that nationwide publicity. They sent off material, drawn from UK advice. At the international conference in 1980 Christine and Betsy named four groups in existence from that publicity, which was soon followed up by other forms of media. The Hopkinton group, they explained, was pouring its energies into spreading the Register in the States and fund-raising to pay for postage and duplication of advice, with one of their number holding the title of National Organiser, co-ordinating enquiries and helping new groups form.

Abu Dhabi

Launched by Liz Magee in 1974 it achieved a solid core of twenty at every meeting by 1979; membership was probably double that. Life for Europeans is transient in AD, as in other parts of the Middle East. After only eighteen months Liz found herself 'the only surviving original member'. With a fluctuating population there are frequent changes of Local Organisers. The programme is much like the UK's. As a member commented: 'It's not because we're housebound, nothing to do, but because we're seeking something deeper than the froth and bubble of the giddy life overseas – a cultural desert'.

Dubai

The Register got going in 1978, (founder unrecorded) quickly acquiring twenty-two members. By 1979 membership reached fifty, divided into two groups each, with a Local Organiser. With a mobile population LOs can change half-yearly. Forward planning of programmes is only for half a dozen or so meetings, though these are still in members' homes even when maps might have to be provided to locate them on tracks rather than roads. It was in Dubai that the programme had to be re-arranged when a planned speaker was knocked down by a camel.

Bahrain

Started in 1978 by expatriate Mary Stone who swiftly gathered a membership of twenty-two, largely English but married to a number of other nationalities. Meetings are publicised through Radio Bahrain. Evening travel is difficult, even needing to be in convoy. In a constantly changing membership, departing 'home' or elsewhere across the globe, NHR members turn up. One explained what it means to find an existing group. 'The first few days here didn't seem too promising – a toddler who cried every time he stepped outside the door because of the amazing heat and humidity – a five year old who missed his friends and his bicycle and wandered around the "compound" in the hope of finding some playmates; and me, suffering from "Bahrain tummy" and wondering why we had ever left a cold and wet Porthcawl. (Of course, during this time, my husband was happily getting his teeth into his work having already been in Bahrain for six weeks prior to our coming out to start a two year contract, and so knew everyone at work.)' Her husband spotted the NHR advert about the next meeting in a newspaper and rang for more details. 'I couldn't even phone myself and chat to someone as we live in a new compound and the telephones hadn't been installed'. Within days she was contacted, a coffee meeting arranged, and six months later testified: 'I have made many new and interesting friends, thanks to the existence of NHR both in Britain and in this part of the world'.

Holland

The Leiden group was started in 1976 by two members of NHR, Irene Gawne and Dana Cervenka. Promotion through womens' clubs, word of mouth and advertising in the local supermarket, soon gave it an international flavour, including Dutch women. Its core of nearly forty members, again in a transient community, is closely linked to NHR ideas, even producing a carefully thought out study on just how the international Register should be organised and financed. Two Organisers are elected annually. Members travel from five or six towns to meetings.

Two other groups have been formed in the country, with Hellevoetsluis pondering whether it holds a record by having eleven nationalities among its membership.

Belgium

Suzanne Wyatt, a UK member, fortunate to have a friend from Cheshire days with whom to tackle the sundry problems of family life in a different country conducted in a different language, was 'entertained' when both got a letter from Angela Lepper, National Organiser with overseas groups within her brief, questioning whether a Belgian NHR was viable. Since, for the wives of the foreign community, employment (even among 'professionals', i.e. teachers, solicitors, librarians, nurses) was difficult, the two friends had already considered the attractions of NHR style mental activity. NHR in Belgium was born in 1975. It swiftly achieved twenty members, only fourteen British, mostly among those who move from country to country. Only one speaker was invited during their first eighteen meetings. Research, Suzanne described as high quality: 'especially in view of our lack of that almost indispensable aid to the NHR, an English library with a reference section'. (A theme which runs through many communications from the international contingent). They have debated 'This house believes that the English-speaking population of Brussels lives a colonial life style'. The group is distributed around Brussels. Activities have included Swiss members talking of their country, and the study of French and American literature. When a write up in the English language weekly dubbed them 'intellectual snobs and blue stockings' Suzanne got a phone call from a woman enquiring if she could join though she did not have a degree! In 1977 a sixty to forty vote in favour changed the name to the International Womens' Register.

Luxembourg

Mel Golder went to Luxembourg when Britain joined the EEC. Many of the civil servants of high rank have graduate wives and she found a life of leisure leading to discontent among frustrated wives needing intellectual outlets. Mel was not an NHR member but saw a newsletter on a visit home. She wrote to Jane Goodwin. The nearest groups were in Holland and Belgium. Another letter from Jane inspired action with an advertisement in the British Ladies' Club newsletter inviting the interested to a coffee morning. Five came to draw up a programme, both for day and evening to see which was best. There were fifteen at the third meeting including Hungarian, Dutch and German, English-speaking women. Mel has returned to the UK, but the group was still functioning in 1980 with a membership of twenty and a programme of talks, debates and a book 'morning', reviewing and exchanging copies, since that is the time members seek a break rather than in the evenings.

XXI
Where Now?

NHR HAS GOT through its first twenty years, though who would have bet on such a possibility based purely on a concept, albeit stunning, first put over in a letter. Its survival, to quote several of those who knew of the creaks, groans and stresses, at its administrative centre as the membership grew, seems like 'a miracle'. I echo that. From my bird's-eye view as I wrote this history I have been constantly astounded by the series of cliff-hangers, the possibilities of disaster – Lesley Taylor dealing with shoals of letters in a maternity ward – Jane Watt ill, no money in the kitty for Anita Brocklesby and Lesley Moreland, the VAT debt faced by the first National Group. And, after all, I have been in intermittent touch with the 'clearing house' at the centre over the twenty years!

Will those who have read in these pages how the circumstances of sheer growth have forced changes, reason that continued expansion and the spread of services offered to members could lead to other changes?

The year 1980 could be regarded as the start of a new phase. For sixteen years National Organisers had the sole responsibility of interpreting what members wanted through expressions of opinion by letter or phone, or articles printed in the national *Newsletter*, or voiced at conferences. They also had the sole responsibility of organising the administration as they saw fit, and of choosing their own successors. They gradually became aware that one woman could no longer cope alone, and did something about that too. It was a hit or miss method. Fortunately for the women who have drawn strength, new confidence and friendship from the Register, it was always a hit.

Then came the original constitution. The first National Group, elected from the narrow representation of those attending a national conference, had the task of working out what it was supposed to do, and who did what. The Register, yet again, was blessed with talented women.

At the start of a new decade a National Group took over which was, for the first time, fully representative, if a nation-wide ballot of members can be interpreted that way. Even if only twenty-five per cent bothered to vote that was still an excellent proportion in NHR terms; remember also that twenty-one women were so interested in the Register as a whole rather than parochially that they volunteered for election. A long way from Lesley Taylor as the sole offer!

The second National Group makes an interesting comparison with Brenda Prys Jones in that their role, like hers after Maureen, is to build upon a new foundation, accompanied by much more interest from members.

Maybe it was unfair (considering that I knew that the first National Group had regretted there was not enough time to mutually review NHR as a whole, where it was going, with forward planning on what was needed) to drop into a jammed agenda, at what was after all only their second official meeting, a request for some enlightenment on the thoughts of the National Group who took over in mid-1980.

Alison Shingler was hostess for the meeting. Except for the family piano, which was still in situ, one room in the Shinglers' rambling farmhouse home was given over to NHR as an office. Alison found being National Organiser 'the most fantastic job in the world, even doing a twelve hour day, eight (sic) days a week'. She was answering 460 letters a month even without the kind of media publicity that brings the floods, taking at least two phone enquiries a day, often long distance, (and, I noted during that weekend, often while her meal cooled on the table) which could simply be a request for 'my nearest group' or the outpourings of a desperate and lonely woman.

Pat Kerr, as New Groups Adviser, had dealt with 210 letters over the previous five weeks. The possibility of an expansion of total membership to at least 30,000 was thrown into the discussion. But the trend seems to be towards more groups, maybe smaller in membership numbers, but requiring less travel from home. A group in every community was not foreseen; it would always depend on the local concentration of the 'like-minded'.

There was mention of (and ambition for) more service to groups, and of the increasing number of meetings arranged by NG members to draw together Local Organisers. The latter development, in which ex National Group members (now and to come) are valuable participants, means that the Register could become more closely woven rather than consisting of isolated threads.

Where Now?

There were thoughts about women not being as housebound as in the sixties, having more contacts through playgroups and schools, and indeed adjusting to husband's job mobility. But an enquiry for the 'nearest group' from a young married woman who could not find a job opened up the question of who joins, and the inevitable age controversy. When someone spoke of being 'labelled at sixty as out of touch, dozing off', a comparison was made with the 'second-class' status of young mothers at home. An office was seen as a possibility, though without immediate urgency, and with no fresh ideas of the mechanics considering NHR's special adminstrative structure. The thought of a paid Director is still controversial.

So the debate on the administration rests; after all, it only opens up when circumstances demand. That other element which so often accompanies such debate, regionalisation, was firmly dealt with by the first National Group in a statement circulated at the 1980 AGM. It 'could lead to another level of administration, encourage power seeking and so change the essential informality and spontaneity of the NHR'.

Questions

I still wonder, as no doubt many Register members are also wondering, whether a national organisation can continue to be run from the spare or contrived space in several women's homes. That could preclude an otherwise eminently suitable candidate for the NO job if she could not promise this additional advantage. The extra (or is it still an extra?) facility was noticeably mentioned by each of those aspiring to be National Organiser from 1980.

The first National Group set up a 'property fund'. Would it be feasible to rent an office for four years, NO candidates first finding out if there was one vacant near them? The possibility of a caravan for an office, suggested by an imaginative member, is still remembered. That would need parking space and the tolerance of the family. But an office outside the house would protect the family from the disturbance of a twenty-four hour job.

Today not only the NO needs household space. The *Newsletter* Editor accepts thousands of copies to await distribution at meetings to save postage, whoever has 'sales' responsibilities keeps stocks of pens, diaries, sundry items, and the archives will grow. Other organisations that have grown from one woman's detection of a need have got to the stage of appointing a (paid) Director or someone in a comparable position (Toy Libraries Association,

National Association for the Welfare of Children in Hospital) before or after the paraphernalia of publications, records and equipment, has been gathered under one roof, in an office.

I cannot avoid speculation too whether there will always be women willing to put their hard-won training at the service of NHR, quite apart from the inconvenience to their families. Consider today's ordeal of an interviewing panel as though the vacancies were for high level executive jobs in an industrial or commercial enterprise. But then, to a considerable degree, that is what at least four of the jobs have, or will increasingly become. Add to that an honorarium instead of a competitive salary, which carries more clout, compared with commitment to an organisation, in a family discussion on whether Mum works. At least one member withdrew from the 1980 elections because a job opening was too tempting. But then Alison Shingler turned down the possibility of a paid job preferring to take her chance of being voted onto the National Group! No one I have come across has seen high office in NHR as a career stepping-stone, something useful to put down on a job application form. If they gained a new confidence in their capacities and potential, that was an expected bonus. All volunteered to return something of what the Register had given them so others can benefit.

But there is still the relevant question of how a potential employer would view the merits of a woman applying for a paid job who could say she had been National Organiser, PRO, Treasurer or *Newsletter* Editor of the NHR.

It has not truly been put to the test, though a small club turned down Liz Salthouse (ex-controller of a £20,000 income) because she did not have the paper qualifications to keep their books.

Retirement

As I write members of the first National Group are adjusting to retirement, in more ways than one.

They are going to miss the intense discussions, largely on NHR affairs but many personal. Gill Vine: 'Several NG members experienced crises of various natures over the years and it was very reassuring to be able to discuss them and find the support needed. This, I think, was particularly noticeable in the case of family deaths. It was from conversations like these that lasting friendships developed.

'Policies were often discussed while washing up at NG meetings. We never wasted a minute. Jean and I often shared a bedroom (in a member's or relative's home) and continued discussing NHR. One of us would be about to fall asleep, then the other would suddenly come out with something considered important and so the conversation would start again. The hours of sleep were very short'. Particularly when in these overnight stops in members' homes 'we became part of the family. Children treated us like visiting aunts, looking in to see if we were awake in the morning and bringing their most treasured possessions to be admired.'

After travelling north with the southern-based NG members I quickly grasped the benefits of exploiting the journey to a meeting. The tables were heaped with fat files, documents, notes, letters, passed across the gangway from one to the other – saving postage – much to the amusement and curiosity of other passengers. A lot of the information in this book was garnered on trains. Afterwards long distance train travel, just getting from A to B, is dull by contrast.

The retired members are also adjusting to no longer being at the hub. Not only missing their thrice annually official meetings together, but also the stimulation of finding answers to complex problems both organisational and individual, that came by the post, or over the phone.

The day the furniture van took away 'the office' to deliver to the new NO, (it's not a case of putting it into the post nowadays!) the Vines got their dining-room back again. Gill's daughter Helen went straight to that room when she got home from school and looked in: 'I expect you're feeling sad, Mummy'. As Gill says: 'How right she was.'

Unlike so many of their predecessors, these officers did not come to the end of their terms jaded and thankful to hand over the responsibility. Jane Goodwin is teaching. Hazel Bell still edits the twice yearly journal of The Society of Indexers and would like more editing jobs, having been bitten by that bug while raising the national *Newsletter* to a high standard. Gill Vine is on a magazine's advisory panel which aids self-help in the community schemes, but requires little time in comparison with the demands of the work she has relinquished.

After six months retirement Jean Stirk had not had time to be bored, organising a fund-raising effort for one of her sons' schools, a local pensioners' lunch club, taking a refresher course in French, reviving an earlier hobby of delving into the family's ancestry, and so on.

Liz Salthouse is working voluntarily for the National Trust, and as a result of attending a WEA history course found herself nominated as treasurer-elect for 1981. She also keeps the books for a local Girl Guide section. 'None of these things,' she comments 'seem associated with NHR, but I think it is the self-confidence I have gained during these last four years which has helped me do them because, apart from the guiding, they are all new ventures.'

All ex-officers are, or course, helping local groups if required. Four, Gill, Jean, Hazel and Liz, have been nominated to the Civil Service Department by the NHR, for consideration by government departments when appointments are made to the wide variety of councils, committees, bodies, sometimes referred to as QUANGOS (Quasi-Autonomous Non-Governmental Organisations). *Simple Steps to Public Life*, published by Virago, explains more about such appointments.

So what happened to the other women who held the Register together?

The only woman of whom it can truly be said that the experience of being National Organiser had direct relevance in a full-time job is Lesley Moreland. With only the break of a weekend, after ceasing to be joint NO in 1973, she started full-time work as the first Director of the Toy Libraries Association. Addressing an audience (a skill she has honed), advising, encouraging, sympathising, throwing in fresh approaches to local groups (but running toy libraries), pouring out ideas and news in what look much like NHR-style circulars. The TLA has benefited from her stint in NHR and no NHR member, Lesley is sure, would begrudge the TLA reaping this harvest.

But Josephine Jaffray, in her self-confessed aim of 'emulating Lesley' has not done too badly, though it took longer.

'You may have led a national organisation,' she told me, 'but you have to come down to earth. I had experience and know-how and no qualifications to match the kind of job that would suit me.' Her 'paper' qualifications were secretarial. She had ambitions for a degree and, on retirement from being NO, took the Open University's humanities and social science foundation courses but found she could not continue once she had a full-time job. It was for setting up fund-raising groups, and her experience in setting up NHR groups helped her to get it, but after eighteen months she withdrew: 'They needed a sales director'. There was a period as a hotel receptionist and plenty of applications for jobs to which she could offer experience but no recognisable documented qualifications.

Where Now?

It took nearly four years and, while not as 'high-powered, or national, as Lesley's, my experience in NHR told'. She runs the administrative side of a team of two, in a community resource centre which gives advice, encouragement, information, resources as mundane but as useful as a duplicator, to local organisations who are helping the homeless, the disabled, or mothers whose marital conditions have got beyond bearing and who need a refuge. Encouraging 'new groups' in fact, but in a different context.

Otherwise holding the fort at the centre has led rather to a greater confidence, a greater belief in ex-Organisers' own capacities.

Founder Maureen Nicol, 'elated to do reasonably well' in the O and A levels which she took while a member of the local group in Birkenhead, became University Housing Officer when the family moved to Uganda – when Idi Amin was Chancellor. Back in the UK, by 1977 she was doing an extra-mural course with Birmingham University in Social Psychology and a WEA class on Russian literature, as well as clearing, restoring and walking footpaths around Kenilworth; and by 1980 (when I was pestering her for recollections of early NHR years) actively involved in local politics, tackling a course in French, chairman of the local WEA branch, and swotting for a Certificate in Employment and Welfare Law (achieved) which she felt would be a help in her Citizens' Advice Bureau work (unpaid).

The latter attracted her 'because one can really be of use to people without patronising them and largely with the aid of the good humour and good sense gained, I feel, by being the first National Organiser of NHR'.

Her successor, Brenda Prys Jones, noticed that she had been moved to take the initiative in gathering together people she met at adult education classes (fine art, architecture, literature) and added that she thinks, 'a kind of "Register spirit" prevails among my circle of friends of my own age group, most of whom are interested to hear of the Register and have told me that they only wish it had existed not twenty years ago but as far back as thirty years and more'. Brenda also works voluntarily for the Citizens Advice Bureau.

Lesley Taylor considers that she 'took stock and began to plan for the future alone from the springboard of confidence and a new self-awareness gained from those three years in office'. She undertook a degree in psychology, became Lesley Thom, thinks that the 'awareness' that the NHR job gave her helped through yet another marriage break-up. Becoming an Education Welfare Officer was 'the chance to combine my desire to go on helping others with my teaching experience ... and once more I have a job which puts my own problems well and truly into perspective. If nothing else I have a wealth of experience to draw on.'

After the second divorce she reverted to her maiden name, Lesley Shooter, 'not because I am a women's libber, not because in doing so I hope to recapture the naivety of my teens, but because through the Register I came to believe that – to quote the first conference and Mary Stott – above all else women must retain their identities'.

Anita Brocklesby, already doing two days a week as a social worker while joint National Organiser with Lesley Moreland, discovered post-NHR how the scene had changed, and undertook a professional social work course at Keele University. After another family move and a year as an adoptions officer she is getting 'real job satisfaction,' managing a centre concerned with rehabilitative work with the mentally ill. Her achievements at work, she thinks, 'have given me the confidence I totally lacked before – NHR, for some reason, didn't give me it'.

Angela Lepper (after a year in the trio with Pat Williams and Josephine Jaffray) went on to be a school library assistant for a year and then on to the part-time school librarian's job at a comprehensive which she 'greatly enjoys'. Add voluntary work in the library of her children's primary school, committee membership in the local section of the Federation of Children's Book Groups, attendance at a variety of courses including an extra mural diploma in English Literature, and you get a very busy woman.

Erecting no line between national office and local membership she affirms that for her NHR has provided friends, return of self-confidence (such as speaking to a school audience of six hundred from which she might have otherwise shied away) and made her study lots of topics 'I would never otherwise have done'.

Pat Williams threw herself into local community activities and then read Law at Birmingham University, graduating in 1979. Her aim is to become a solicitor.

Marie Price, the first 'elected' National Organiser, whose term of office was disrupted by the family departure to the Middle East, is back in the UK and in late 1980 was working in a two-women public relations outfit, and for two days a week for a solicitor, while teaching music at home and being a supply teacher for an evening school.

There is no 'pre-retirement' course for the women outsiders tend to call the 'Director' – a title nearer to general practice and encompassing the responsibilities held, than NHR's traditional

'National Organiser' – yet, as the structure becomes more sophisticated, 'redundancy' will become a harder jolt for the national officers.

Uncertainties

The assumption that girls are educated as well as boys is getting more firmly rooted. In the families of women who achieved further education through the 1944 Education Act it should not seem strange that daughters, like sons, will go on to university education, if so inclined. A mother who is a graduate will take it for granted that her daughter(s) will have the same chance. And since, unlike the thirties when the hard choice could have been between a career and a family, there will be a very much larger proportion of our daughters finding, with motherhood, that being parent/domestic leaves a part of themselves unused, like an athlete suddenly going into a sedentary job.

Fortunately there will also be a second generation NHR; daughters of members who know there is a way of keeping their minds in trim, sons of members who can guide their wives to 'the nearest group'.

But alongside the hopeful signs of improved female educational opportunities there are uncertainties at the start of the eighties which will impinge. Greater technical advances through, for instance, the microchip have already promoted thoughts of shorter hours, more leisure time. Applied to fathers this means shorter periods of disappearance, longer periods at home and therefore partaking in the family round; more father presence in what has been the mother's domain.

Technical innovations too (i.e. word-processors) threaten what are still women's staple jobs, shorthand/typing, secretarial; jobs, like teaching (also menaced by cutbacks in educational budgets) that can be fitted among family responsibilities but which do not allow for the climb up the career ladder.

If these conditions are not fluid enough to raise speculation on how life will change, we have also, at the start of the eighties, increasing unemployment which can re-arrange the esteem and mental health within a household if it affects the father, with consequent stress on the mother.

Already, as I write in the first year of the new decade, there are those who see one solution to male unemployment as sending women 'back to the kitchen'.

NHR's long running controversy about to work or not to work

could become academic. Fewer women may find jobs, whatever their qualifications. More could have time to spare whether the children are still at school or have even left home.

The Register might face a renewal of membership from those who have dropped out, having resumed a paid occupation with its concomitant interests, now lost again as in those first years of motherhood. Local groups could be arranging more daytime meetings for reasons other than that the younger children have to be brought along. However, as no one can prophecy the swings of economics or of society, this must all remain open for debate.

Some things remain constant

Around twenty years after Hannah Gavron interviewed early NHR members for *The Captive Wife*, four latter-day members were interviewed for Suzanne Lowry's *The Guilt Cage*. Note the confinement simile in the title.*

A member, reviewing the book for the national *Newsletter*, thought 'they come over as cosy, middle-class, slightly scatty, vaguely intellectual; but very aware, very interested, very involved'. She still thought that the book would give members talking points for meetings 'for the next year or so'.

The message, as with Gavron twenty years before, was still that mothers and children are not part of mainstream society. Erin Pizzey (who put battered wives into a nation's vocabulary and understanding) was quoted:

> Until the government, and men in general, realise that children are the gold of our future, no status will be given to women staying at home to look after the children.... If women are going to use themselves and their talents and their abilities, they have got to be permitted to have children and have them visible.

Suzanne herself, after listening to women talking about themselves, suggested that 'the word "housewife" be struck from the record', it no longer being a 'a proper job description', and 'children are not a good enough excuse for dumping it all onto one partner'. Well, that makes an interesting aside to the running discussion on the Register's title!

Suzanne Lowry, erstwhile Woman's Editor of the *Guardian* was then Editor of the *Observer*'s 'Living' Section. Her book, subtitled 'Housewives and a decade of liberation' was not, she wrote,

---

*(Published by Elm Tree Books).

intended to be a history of the women's movement of the seventies, rather 'to trace the outer ripples of the movement's influence'.

The question never having been put to the vote I can only make an assumption, but it seems safe to say that the Register would not describe itself as part of the women's movement, being more broadly based.

Maureen Nicol, in her letter which inspired the Register, hit on the conditions of mothers in intellectually empty, suburban deserts, before Betty Friedan's *The Feminine Mystique*, exposing the same frustrations, hit these shores as the catalyst for the second wave of campaigning for rights for women, counting voting rights as the first battle.

Maureen's influence is less known, lateral rather than inspiring direct confrontation, but otherwise, surely, can be judged as equally far-reaching in its effect. The NHR is hardly likely to arouse antagonism but it does raise puzzlement and incomprehension, that women, like men, want to be part of the normal adult world outside the home. As the Gavron and Lowry books show, society's concern for that aspect of women's lives is infinitesimal; if women want improvements it is a DIY job such as through the NHR.

Since an article I wrote for the *Guardian* set off that extraordinary train of events it seems appropriate to conclude with another published on the same page 16 February 1966. Much of it is still relevant today after the passage of time. Again it was partly personal, recording those who were for me, in Maureen Nicol's words 'kindred spirits'. It was entitled 'The sultanas of suburbia'.

> Five years ago I wrote about my first experience of suburban life. I wondered what happened to people when they exiled themselves to suburbia to raise a family. I found few who read anything, few who showed inspiration in their food, and, summarising that this 'is an incredibly dull place to live in' I blamed the women. Mrs Maureen Nicol, who had moved into different suburbs several times and seen the 'voluntary exile' women accept, wrote suggesting that a register of women was needed so those wanting to 'remain individuals' could get in touch. The reaction was astonishing and the Housewives' Register was born.
>
> I wrote as a newcomer. Now, having moved away from that suburb, I can see I was half right and half wrong. I know a lot more now about the place and its inhabitants. It is a part of my life, certainly a major influence on my children's lives. The children they played with they first saw in their prams. The mothers and the many other older people who seemed so strange and different at first gave me help and kindness, providing a secure background I could always depend on in a crisis.

I know now, too, more of the whys and wherefores. Many of the women who gave me greatest support in a campaign to get a decent local school sent their sons to private schools to give them a better chance in the rat race. I know what producing four meals a day, seven days a week, can do to your inspiration in the kitchen and that, after carting your children some distance to a dress shop, looking at clothes with one eye and keeping the other on your children, you are lucky if you buy something that fits let alone enhances you. I know, too, that housework, shopping and the constant company of children can blunt your mind.

Many women are learning to drive but most are still not liberated in this way, which can at least reduce the problem of waiting for buses or running to the station when they do get time off. I admire several women. One streaks to London and a first-class jazz concert. Another belongs to a choir and in a long black skirt, which always gets ironed at 1 a.m. the night before, has sung in churches and halls for miles around. A third visits art galleries for her sanity.

Mrs Nicol suggested an outlet for a few, the 'like-minded'. If we are going on living in small family units, and this does seem to me the crux of the problem, then the solution needs to be a much wider one. Too few women are educated to their full potential, academic or otherwise. This may improve slowly. But to what point unless we rethink our approach to the home and family? Whether a woman who takes a job outside the home turns her children into juvenile delinquents has been argued to the point of boredom. I have heard no one argue that a woman is not supposed to be a char but a wife and mother. Husbands can take a fair amount of blame for this. A woman's place is still in the home.

Yet houses are rarely designed with children in mind. Women try, like Canute, to hold back the tide of children's equipment and activities with little assistance from architects or industry, or recognition by husbands that the running of a house should be financed as efficiently as the running of a factory. I doubt if washing machines would have become standard if women had not gone out to work to pay for them.

I came to regard suburban life as a heavy rice pudding with a few well-met sultanas here and there. Women have an immense capacity. Most of it is unused. Enough women with the confidence to chair a meeting, sit on a committee, organise action and we should not be moaning about bad schools, poor maternity services, too few nursery schools.

We should be battling for our daughters' education if we want marriage to be a partnership. We should learn to distinguish between a home and a house that looks as though a staff of servants maintain it. But mostly we can break down the tiny family units by helping each other to get out of the house to develop new or old interests simply by taking over each other's children now and again.

That NHR will continue to be needed – as a safety valve for the emotional pressures of family life – a resource where a woman has the chance to be an individual, herself, as well as the one ('John's wife, Jonathan's, Jane's mum') who listens, absorbs, tries to find an answer to what may be a major or minor problem – is transparently clear. It is one of the few supports for the supporters, and should be cherished and protected as such.

But its unique role lies in providing mental stimulus to those women who, increasingly, suffer from missing that vital element in their lives.

Appendix I

NHR Constitution and Rules 1976
1. The name of the Society is National Housewives Register.
2. The object for which the Society is established is to encourage formation of and to keep a register of groups which aim to encourage participation in stimulating and wide-ranging discussion, thus creating an opportunity for friendship and other activities, and to this end to own property through trustees, to engage such paid officers and staff as shall from time to time be considered requisite (and in particular an Administrator) and to publish whenever practicable a newsletter devoted to the activities of the Society. The Society shall not engage in any trade or business or in any transactions with a view to the pecuniary gain of its members. No member shall have personal claim on any property of the Society or make any profit out of membership.
3. In the event of the Society being disbanded its surplus assets shall be donated to such other women's organisation or organisations as may be chosen at the discretion of the Trustees. The Trustees shall take full consideration of the views of the National Group before exercising such discretion.
4. Membership of the Society is open to any person who is accepted as a member of a recognised local group.
5. A recognised local group is a group of five or more persons who meet together for the objects of the Society at least six times a year which is admitted to the register of the Society by the National Group. Each group shall have its own rules for its internal management but each local group shall have a local organiser who shall be appointed in such manner as that group shall think fit.
6. Every member shall pay to the Society an annual subscription of a sum to be fixed each year by the National Group.
7. Every member who at the end of a period of 24 weeks from its being demanded by the organiser of the local group of which that person is a member shall not have paid the annual subscription shall immediately cease to be a member of the Society.
8. The affairs of the Society shall be managed by a National Group which shall have not more than fifteen nor fewer than five members.
9. A quorum of the National Group shall consist of one half of the members for the time being or if there be an odd number of members, a majority of such members.

Appendix I

10. The National Group shall meet at least three times a year one of which meetings shall be at the same time and place as the Annual General Meeting of the Society.
11. Nominations for membership of National Group shall be sent to the Administrator at any time not being less than eight weeks prior to an Annual General Meeting at which elections are to be held. Persons nominated must be Members of the Society. Nominations must be made either by local groups or by individual members with the consent of the nominee. The nomination must be seconded. A nomination by an individual member must be seconded by a group, being a group other than that of which the proposer is a member. A nomination by a group may not be seconded by an individual member of that group. No group or individual member may be concerned either as proposer or seconder in more than one nomination. For these purposes groups shall act through their local organisers.
12. The members of the National Group shall be elected by the members at the Annual General Meeting of the Society who shall choose from amongst persons nominated any number up to the permitted maximum. The first Annual General Meeting shall be that held in 1976 and if it shall have been held before the coming into force of these rules the members of the National Group who have been recognised as such at that meeting shall be deemed to have been elected in accordance with these rules. Members elected at the first Annual General Meeting shall serve for four years in the first instance save that one half of such members or if there be an odd number of members the minority of them shall serve for a term of two years in the first instance. Which members are to so retire shall be decided by agreement, and failing agreement shall be those members who received fewest votes on election to the national group. All members subsequently elected shall serve for a term of four years. At every second Annual General Meeting after the first election shall be held to fill any vacancies that there may be in the membership of the National Group by reason of death or retirement or because the number of members thereof does not reach the permitted maximum. Any vacancy by reason of death or retirement may be filled between Meetings at which elections are held by co-option by the members of the National Group but any members so co-opted must retire at the next Annual General Meeting at which elections are held. No person may stand for election to the National Group at the Annual General Meeting at which such person retires for the first time nor be eligible for co-option during the two years next following. A person retiring may stand for election at any subsequent Annual General Meeting at which elections are held.
13. The members of the National Group shall elect one of their number to be co-ordinator of the Group and to take the chair at meetings of the Group. The National Group may assign to its other members specific functions and shall assign the following functions: National Organiser, Secretary and Treasurer.

(a) If there is no member of the Group willing or able to be National Organiser the members of the National Group may co-opt another member of the Society to be National Organiser and member of the group notwithstanding that there are already 15 members thereof. Such member shall retire at the next Annual General Meeting at which elections are held and notwithstanding the prohibition in Rule 12 of a member being elected during the two years following retirement for the first time shall be eligible for immediate election for a further term of four years if that member is retiring for the first time.

(b) The National Group may upon the retirement of any member thereof under any provision of these rules co-opt that member to serve for a further term of two years to fulfil the function of National Organiser, Secretary or Treasurer and the prohibition in Rule 12 of a member being co-opted during the two years following retirement for the first time shall not apply to such member. Provided always that there shall not at any time be more than one member of the National Group co-opted under this sub rule 13(b) and provided further that this sub rule 13(b) may only be applied once in the case of any particular person.

(c) Notwithstanding the provisions of Rule 13(a) and (b) no person shall be co-opted who has already served on the National Group for a total of six years.

14 The power of the Society to employ staff shall be exercised by the National Group.

15 The Secretary shall keep minutes for all meetings of the National Group and of the Society.

16 The National Group shall appoint annually a qualified Accountant of the Society who shall have access at all reasonable times to the accounts of the Society and shall verify and sign the annual statement of the a/cs. of the Society.

17 The Treasurer and the National Organiser shall keep proper books of the accounts of the financial transactions of the society and the Treasurer shall cause a statement thereof signed by the Accountant to be published by the Society. Unless and until otherwise resolved by the Nat. Group the financial year of the Society shall end on 30th June in each year.

18 The National Organiser shall open a bank account in the name of the Society and all cheques drawn thereon shall be signed by the National Organiser or by the Administrator and shall be counter-signed by the Treasurer or by such other member of the National Group as the Group may from time to time appoint.

19 The Treasurer shall invest in the names of Trustees such part of the Society's funds and in such manner as the National Group shall direct in accordance with the provisions of the Trustee Investments Act 1961

Appendix I

and shall from time to time realise or dispose of such investments in accordance with the National Group's directions.

20 There shall not be less than two nor more than four Trustees of the Society. The first Trustees shall be appointed by the National Group and the funds and property of the Society (other than cash under the control of the National Organiser or Treasurer) shall be vested in them to be dealt with by them as the National Group shall from time to time direct. The Trustees shall hold office until death or resignation or until removed from office by a resolution of the National Group. If by reason of any such death, resignation or removal it shall appear necessary to the National Group that a new Trustee or Trustees be appointed or if the National Group shall deem it expedient to appoint an additional Trustee or additional Trustees, the National Group shall by a Resolution nominate the person or persons to be appointed the new Trustee or Trustees subject always to the limits hereinbefore provided.

21 The Society shall hold each year an annual conference at a time and place to be decided by the National Group but at all events before 1st July in each calendar year. At least one session of such conference shall be the Annual General Meeting of the Society.

22 If the National Group shall fail to convene a conference as aforesaid then a conference shall be convened by the National Organiser on being required to do so by recognised local groups acting through their local organisers and together being no fewer than one-twentieth in number of the recognised local groups.

23 The National Group may and the National Organiser on such requisition as is mentioned in Rule 22 shall convene other General Meetings of the Society to be called Extraordinary General Meetings.

24 At least 28 days' notice of each General Meeting shall be given by post to the local organiser of each recognised local group and in the case of an Extraordinary General Meeting by one advertisement in the Guardian newspaper. Accidental omission to give notice to a local organiser shall not invalidate the summoning of a General Meeting.

25 All members of the Society shall be entitled to attend and speak at General Meetings of the Society and each member present shall have one vote on a poll.

26 All resolutions for discussion at a General Meeting must be submitted to the National Organiser at least 72 hours prior to the meeting.

27 The Annual General Meeting shall consider the payment of an honorarium to the National Organiser and if thought fit to each of the other members of the National Group delegated to perform special duties.

28 The quorum at a General Meeting shall be any number of members being some members of at least one tenth of the total number of recognised local groups for the time being together with such number

of members of the National Group as for the time being constitute a quorom thereof.

29 All resolutions at General Meetings must be approved by a majority being no fewer than three fourths of the number of members present and voting.

30 The chair shall be taken at the Annual General Meeting by such person as the National Group may decide. In the absence of such decision the Co-ordinator of the National Group shall take the chair or if the Co-ordinator be unable or unwilling to do so a person elected for that purpose by the members of the Society.

31 Amendments to these rules may be proposed at any time, but the full text of any such amendments must be given to the National Organiser at least eight weeks before the date of a General Meeting if the amendment is to be considered at that meeting. The National Organiser shall include the text of the proposed amendments in the notice convening the General Meeting next to be held after receipt thereof and the proposals shall be considered at that Meeting.

32 The Society may be dissolved at any time by a resolution of a General Meeting. A resolution to dissolve the Society shall be deemed to be an amendment to these rules and the foregoing rule shall apply thereto.

33 The Society shall indemnify the members of the National Group for all liabilities lawfully incurred by them as such members while engaged upon the business of the Society.

NHR Constitution and Rules (Revised) May 1977

1 The name of the Society is National Housewives Register.

2 The object for which the Society is established is to encourage formation of and to keep a register of groups wishing to participate in stimulating and wide-ranging discussion creating opportunity for friendship and other activities, and to this end to own property through trustees, to engage such paid officers and staff as shall from time to time be considered requisite and to publish whenever practicable a newsletter devoted to the activities of the Society. The Society shall not engage in any trade or business or in any transactions with a view to the pecuniary gain of its members. No member shall have personal claim on any property of the Society or make any profit out of membership.

3 In the event of the Society being disbanded its surplus assets shall be donated to such other women's organisation or organisations as may be chosen at the discretion of the Trustees. The Trustees shall take full consideration of the views of the National Group before exercising such discretion.

4 Membership of the Society is open to any person who is accepted as a member of a recognised local group.

5 A recognised local group is a group of five or more persons who meet together for the objects of the Society at least six times a year which is

Appendix I

admitted to the register of the Society by the National Group. Each group shall have its own rules for its internal management but each local group shall have a local organiser who shall be appointed in such manner as that group shall think fit.

6   Each member shall pay to the Society an annual subscription of a sum to be recommended each year by the National Group and approved by the AGM.

7   Every member who at the end of a period of 24 weeks from its being demanded by the organiser of the local group of which that person is a member shall not have paid the annual subscription shall immediately cease to be a member of the Society.

8   The affairs of the Society shall be managed by a National Group which (except in the circumstances mentioned in Rule 14 hereof) shall have not more than 15 nor fewer than 5 members.

9   The members of the National Group shall be elected by Postal Ballot at elections to be held every two years. The postal votes so cast shall be counted and the result of the election announced at the Annual General Meeting.

10 A quorum of the National Group shall consist of one half of the members for the time being or if there be an odd number of members, a majority of such members.

11 The National Group shall meet at least three times a year one of which meetings shall be at the same time and place as the Annual General Meeting of the Society.

12 Nominations for membership of the National Group shall be sent to the National Organiser not more than fourteen weeks or less than ten weeks prior to an AGM in the year in which elections are to be held, and the National Organiser shall, not less than eight weeks prior to the next following AGM, send details of the names of persons nominated for membership of the National Group to all local groups. Each member of a recognised local group will then have the right to vote by post by indicating from amongst the persons nominated any number of such persons to serve on the National Group up to the permitted maximum. No such postal vote shall be valid unless received by the National Organiser 72 hours* preceding the date of the AGM. Persons nominated must be members of the Society. Nominations for the National Group must be made either by local groups or by individual members with the consent of the nominee. The nomination must be seconded. A nomination by an individual member must be seconded by a group, being a group other than that of which the proposer is a member. A nomination by a group may not be seconded by an

---

*The May 1977 Constitution read:
No such postal vote shall be valid unless received by the National Organiser *by 6 pm on the day immediately* preceding the date of the AGM.
At the AGM in April 1979, this was amended to: *72 hours* preceding ...

individual member of that group. No group or individual member may be concerned either as proposer or seconder in more than one nomination. For these purposes groups shall act through their local organisers.

13 The first AGM shall be that held in 1976 and if it shall have been held before the coming into force of these rules the members of the National Group who have been recognised as such at that meeting shall be deemed to have been elected in accordance with these rules. Members elected at the first Annual General Meeting shall serve for four years in the first instance save that one half of such members or if there be an odd number of members the minority of them shall serve for a term of two years in the first instance. Which members are to so retire shall be decided by agreement, and failing agreement shall be those members who received fewest votes on election to the National Group. All members subsequently elected to the National Group shall serve for a term of four years. Any vacancy by reason of death or retirement may be filled between elections by co-option by the members of the National Group, but any members so co-opted must retire immediately prior to the announcement of the result of the next election of members of the National Group. No elected member of the National Group may stand for re-election on retirement from that group nor be eligible for co-option during the next two years following retirement except under the circumstances described in Rule 14 hereof. A person so retiring may stand for subsequent elections.

14 The members of the National Group shall elect one of their number to be co-ordinator of the Group and to take the chair at meetings of the Group. The National Group may assign to its other members specific functions and shall assign the following functions: National Organiser, Secretary, Treasurer and Public Relations Officer if appropriate.

(a) If there is no member of the National Group willing or able to be National Organiser the members of the National Group may co-opt another member of the Society to be National Organiser and member of the Group. Under these circumstances the maximum number of members of the National Group will be 16. Such a member so co-opted shall retire immediately prior to the next election of members of the National Group. However, notwithstanding the prohibition in Rule 14 the National Organiser so retiring may be eligible for re-election for a period of office not to exceed a further four years.

(b) The National Group may upon the retirement of any member thereof under any provision of these rules co-opt that member to serve for a further term of two years to fulfil the function of National Organiser, Treasurer and PRO if appropriate and the prohibition in Rule 13 of a member being co-opted during the two years following retirement for the first time shall not apply to such member. Provided always that there shall not at any time be more

Appendix I 213

than one member of the National Group co-opted under this sub rule 14(b) and provided further that this sub rule 14(b) may only be applied once in the case of any particular person.
(c) Notwithstanding the provisions of Rule 14(a) and (b) no person shall be co-opted who has already served on the National Group for a total of six years.
15 The power of the Society to employ staff shall be exercised by the National Group.
16 The Secretary shall keep minutes of all meetings of the National Group and of the Society.
17 An auditor or auditors who may be members of the Society shall be appointed at the AGM in each year. The National Group shall, in the event of any auditor or auditors being unwilling or unable to act, appoint another member or other members to replace them.
18 The Treasurer and the National Organiser shall keep proper accounts of the financial transactions of the Society and the Treasurer shall cause a properly audited copy of such accounts to be published and approved by the AGM. The financial year of the Society shall end on 30th June each year.
19 The National Organiser shall open a bank account in the name of the Society. All cheques drawn thereon shall be signed by any two authorised signatories, one of which must be either the National Organiser or the Treasurer.
20 The Treasurer shall invest in the names of Trustees such part of the Society's funds and in such manner as the National Group shall direct in accordance with the provisions of the Trustee Investments Act 1961 and shall from time to time realise or dispose of such investments in accordance with the National Group's directions.
21 There shall not be less than two nor more than four Trustees of the Society. The first Trustees shall be appointed by the National Group and the funds and property of the Society (other than cash under the control of the National Organiser or Treasurer) shall be vested in them to be dealt with by them as the National Group shall from time to time direct. The Trustees shall hold office until death or resignation or until removed from office by a resolution of the National Group. If by reason of any such death, resignation or removal it shall appear necessary to the National Group that a new Trustee or Trustees be appointed or if the National Group shall deem it expedient to appoint an additional Trustee or additional Trustees the National Group shall by a resolution nominate the person or persons to be appointed the new Trustee or Trustees subject always to the limits hereinbefore provided.
22 The Society shall hold each year an Annual General Meeting at a time and place to be decided by the National Group but at all events before 1st July in each calendar year, and when appropriate at the National Conference.

23 The National Group may and the National Organiser shall within 28 days of being required to do so by recognised local groups acting through their local organisers and together being no fewer than one-twentieth in number of the recognised local groups convene a General Meeting of the Society to be called an Extraordinary General Meeting, and shall within 28 days if similarly required to do so convene an Annual General Meeting if no such Annual General Meeting has been convened in accordance with Rule 23 hereof.

24 At least 28 days notice of each General Meeting shall be given by post to the local organiser of each recognised local group and in the case of an Extraordinary General Meeting by one advertisement in the Guardian Newspaper. Accidental omission to give notice to a local organiser shall not invalidate the summoning of a General Meeting.

25 All members of the Society shall be entitled to attend and speak at General Meetings of the Society and each member present shall have one vote on a poll.

26 All resolutions for discussion at a General Meeting must be submitted to the National Organiser at least 72 hours prior to the meeting.

27 The Annual General Meeting shall have power to approve the payment of an honorarium to the National Organiser and if thought fit to each of the other members of the National Group delegated to perform special duties for the year following the AGM.

28 The quorum at a General Meeting shall be any number of members being some members of at least one tenth in number of the total number of recognised local groups for the time being together with such number of members of the National Group as for the time being constitute a quorum thereof.

29 All resolutions at General Meetings must be approved by a majority being no fewer than three fourths of the number of members present and voting.

30 The chair shall be taken at the AGM by such person as the National Group may decide. In the absence of such decision the Co-ordinator of the National Group shall take the chair or if the co-ordinator be unable or unwilling to do so a person elected for that purpose by the members of the Society.

31 Amendments to these rules may be proposed at any time, but the full text of any such amendments must be given to the National Organiser at least eight weeks before the date of a General Meeting if the amendment is to be considered at that Meeting. The National Organiser shall include the text of the proposed amendments in the notice convening the General Meeting next to be held after receipt thereof and the proposals shall be considered at that meeting.

32 The Society may be dissolved at any time by a resolution of a General Meeting. A resolution to dissolve the Society shall be deemed to be an amendment to these rules and the foregoing rule shall apply thereto.

33 The Society shall indemnify the members of the National Group for all

Appendix I

liabilities lawfully incurred by them as such members while engaged upon the business of the Society.

Charity Deed 9 April 1980
THIS DECLARATION OF TRUST is made the ninth day of April One thousand nine hundred and Eighty by BETTY CLAIR JERMAN of Rushbrooke Coppice Row Theydon Bois Essex EDITH MAUREEN NICOL of 69, John O'Gaunt Road Kenilworth Warwickshire and CHARLOTTE MARY STOTT of Flat 4 11, Morden Road Blackheath London SE3 (hereinafter called 'the Original Trustees')
WHEREAS the Original Trustees have received from certain persons the sum of Five Pounds to be held for the objects of the National Housewives Register as hereinafter defined and declared upon the trusts declared by this Deed and it is anticipated that further money and property may from time to time be transferred to the Trustees as hereinafter defined by way of addition to the said sum or otherwise upon the trusts of this Deed NOW THIS DEED WITNESSETH as follows:—
1. THE Charity hereby constituted shall be called 'the National Housewives Register'
2. IN this Deed the following terms where the context admits have the following meanings:—
(a) 'the National Housewives Register' and 'the Charity' means the Charitable Trust established by this Deed
(b) 'the Trustees' means the Original Trustees or other the trustees or trustee for the time being hereof
(c) 'the Trust Fund' means:—
(i) the said sum of Five pounds
(ii) all monies investments and property paid or transferred to and accepted by the Trustees as additions to the Trust Fund
(iii) the investments and property from time to time representing such investments and additions or any part or parts thereof together with all income thereof
(d) 'the National Group' means the group of members of the Charity who shall be elected by the members of the Charity to act as the National Group in accordance with the rules of the National Group for the time being as set out in the schedule hereto
(e) 'A member of the Charity' and 'a Recognised Local Group' have the meanings ascribed to them in the said rules
3. THE object of the Charity is to provide facilities for the leisure time occupation of female members of the public with the object of improving the conditions of both urban and rural life for them in the interest of social welfare by such means as the Trustees shall from time to time consider appropriate but particularly by education through lectures training and study groups
4. THE Trustees shall hold the capital and income of the Trust Fund upon

trust to apply the same at such time or times as they may in their absolute discretion think fit for the object of the Charity

5. (a) THE Trustees of the Charity from time to time shall be not less than two nor more than four in number

(b) The power of appointing new Trustees shall be vested in the National Group and if and whenever the number of Trustees shall be less than two then one or more new Trustees shall forthwith be appointed so as to bring the number of Trustees up to a minimum of two

(c) The Trustees for the time being shall have power by a resolution passed by all the Trustees for the time being except one to remove any trustee provided that there shall be at least three trustees at the time

(d) Every new Trustee shall before acting in the trusts hereof sign in the Minute Book for which provision is hereinafter made a declaration of acceptance and of willingness to act in the trusts hereof

6. MONEY to be invested under the trusts hereof may be applied or invested in the purchase of or at interest upon the security of such shares stocks funds securities land buildings chattels or other investments or property of whatsoever nature as the Trustees shall in their absolute discretion think fit to the intent that the Trustees shall have the same powers in all respects as if they were absolute owners beneficially entitled

7. THE Trustees shall have power from time to time to make such regulations as they shall think fit for the conduct of their meetings and the proceedings thereat and to amend or revoke such regulations or to make additional regulations and for the conduct of their business including the summoning of meetings the deposit of money at a Bank and the custody of documents PROVIDED THAT

(a) The Charity shall hold an Annual General Meeting and may hold other meetings at such times and in such places as they shall from time to time decide

(b) There shall be a quorum when two Trustees are present at any meeting

(c) The Trustees shall at each of their meetings appoint one of their number to be chairman and as such he shall have a second or casting vote

(d) Every matter unless otherwise unanimously agreed be determined by three quarters of the votes of the Trustees present and voting on the question

(e) Any Resolution of the Trustees may be rescinded or varied from time to time by the Trustees

(f) The Trustees shall provide and keep a Minute Book in which shall be entered the proceedings of the Trustees and which shall be signed by the Chairman at the conclusion of each meeting or at some future meeting if the minutes shall have been duly confirmed

(g) The Treasurer shall be appointed by the National Group subject to the approval of the Trustees

8. THE Trustees shall provide books of account in which shall be kept all proper accounts of all money received and paid respectively by or on behalf

Appendix I

of the Trustees for the purposes of this Deed and shall arrange for the accounts to be audited annually

9. THE Trustees shall not be bound in any case to act personally but shall be at full liberty to employ any agent and in particular any Member of the National Group or any local group of the Charity to transact all or any business of whatever nature required to be done in pursuance of the trusts herein contained and declared including the manner and making of payments and the general receipt or payment of money and the Trustees shall be entitled to be allowed and paid all charges and expenses so incurred and shall not be responsible for the defaults of any such agent Member or Group or any loss occasioned by such employment

10. IN furtherance of the object of the Charity but not otherwise the Trustees shall have the following powers exercisable from time to time as the Trustees may think fit

(a) Power to purchase take on lease receive as a gift or otherwise acquire any land buildings real or personal property and rights or privileges and to erect alter reconstruct and maintain its buildings and to deal with and dispose of its property of whatever kind in such a manner as they think fit and to insure any property belonging to the Charity in the full value thereof against any risks that they shall deem it property to insure

(b) Power to collect and receive donations legacies and gifts (whether periodical or otherwise) as they think fit

(c) Power to issue appeals for donations and periodical reports of the Trustees

(d) Power to decide to what extent and for what purpose or purposes monies are to be applied under this Deed and in whatsoever matter the same are to be applied whether by way of outright grant or long or short term loans secured or unsecured at any or nil interest subject in any event to any or no conditions

(e) Power to employ and pay such staff as may be required for fulfilling the object of the Charity and to provide or make provision for all reasonable and necessary pensions and superannuation for or on behalf of the said staff and their spouses or other dependants

(f) Power to open and maintain such banking account or accounts as the Trustees think fit into such of which as may be appropriate shall be paid forthwith all sums of cash for the time being belonging to the Charity and cheques shall be signed by such person or persons as the Trustees shall from time to time authorise

(g) Power to change or vary any investments for the time being forming part of the Trust Fund for others hereby or by law authorised

(h) Power to defray out of the capital or income of the Trust Fund the expenses of administering the Charity and in particular of having its accounts audited as hereinbefore provided

(i) Power to sell lease demise loan mortgage charge licence and generally manage and deal with any land of any tenure which or the proceeds of sale of which may at any time form part of the Trust Fund as if the Trustees were beneficial owners absolutely entitled

(j) Power to borrow money on such reasonable terms and as to interest repayment and otherwise as they may think fit and whether upon the security of the whole or any part or parts of the Trust Fund or upon personal security only and to use such monies so borrowed in purchasing or subscribing for investments or property duly held as part of the Trust Fund or otherwise for any purpose for which capital monies forming part of the Trust Fund may be used

(k) Power to make investments in the names of two or some only of the Trustees or in the name of any body corporate as nominee for the Trustees whenever it is convenient to do so

(l) Power to establish support and aid in the establishment and support of any charitable associations or institutions

(m) Power to act by a 75% majority of Trustees in connection with all matters relating to the Charity and thereby to bind any minority of Trustees

(n) Power to do such other lawful things as shall further the purposes of the Charity

11. EVERY discretion or power hereby conferred on the Trustees shall be an absolute and uncontrolled discretion or power and no Trustee shall be held liable for any loss or damage accruing as a result of his concurring or refusing or failing to concur in any exercise of any such discretion or power

12. IN the professed execution of the trusts and powers hereof no Trustee being an individual shall be liable for any loss to the Trust Fund arising by reason of any improper investment made in good faith (so long as he shall have sought professional advice before making such investment) or for the negligence or fraud of any agent employed by him or by any other Trustee hereof although the employment of such agent was not strictly necessary or expedient or by reason of any mistake or omission made in good faith by any Trustee hereof or by reason of any other matter or thing except wilful and individual fraud or wrong-doing on the part of the Trustee who is sought to be made so liable

13. NO Trustee of the Charity shall be appointed to any salaried office of the Charity or any office of the Charity paid by fees and no remuneration or other benefit in money or moneys worth shall be given by the Charity to any Trustee hereof except and provided that:

(a) any Trustee for the time being here of being a Solicitor Accountant or other person engaged in any profession shall be entitled to charge and be paid all usual professional or other charges for work done by him or his firm in relation to the execution of the trusts hereof

(b) any Trustee may be repaid reasonable and proper out of pocket expenses incurred when acting in the trusts hereof and interest at a reasonable and proper rate for the money lent or reasonable and proper rent for premises demised or let by such person to the Charity

14. THE Trustees may by resolution in writing dissolve the Charity with the approval of the Charity Commissioners and after discharging all

Appendix I

liabilities and paying the cost of winding up the balance of the Trust Fund shall be applied for such charitable purposes as the Trustees shall in their discretion think fit

The Schedule: NHR Rules for the National Group
1. A Member of the National Housewives Register ('the Charity') is a person who has paid the Annual Subscription to and has been accepted as a Member of a Recognised Local Group (as hereinafter defined) of the Charity PROVIDED THAT any Member who has not paid the Annual Subscription within twenty four weeks from its being demanded shall cease to be a Member.
2. A Recognised Local Group is a group of five or more Members who meet together for the object of the Charity as defined in Clause 3 of the Trust Deed at least six times a year and which is admitted to the Register of the Charity by the National Group. Each Recognised Local Group shall have its own arrangements for its internal management but shall have a Local Organiser who shall be appointed in such manner as it shall think fit.
3. (a) The Local Organiser is responsible for co-ordinating the activities of her Recognised Local Group
   (b) The National Organiser is responsible to the Trustees and to the National Group for maintaining the register of groups and promoting the aims of the Charity.
4. The Annual Subscription is such sum as shall from time to time have been recommended by the National Group for this purpose and approved by the Trustees and by the members of the Annual General Meeting.
5. The National Group shall be elected by votes cast by the Members of the Charity. A postal ballot shall be held every two years prior to the Annual General Meeting. The National Group shall be of not more than 15 nor less than 5 Members and shall meet at least three times a year one of which Meetings shall be within 48 hours of the Annual General Meeting. A quorum of the National Group shall consist of one half of the Members thereof for the time being or if there be an odd number of Members the majority of such members.
6. Nominations for membership of the National Group shall be sent to the National Organiser not more than fourteen weeks or less than ten weeks prior to an AGM in the year in which elections are to be held, and the National Organiser shall, not less than eight weeks prior to the next following AGM, send details of the names of persons nominated for membership of the National Group to all Recognised Local Groups. Each member of a Recognised Local Group will then have the right to vote by post by indicating from amongst the persons nominated any number of such persons to serve to the National Group up to the stipulated maximum number of vacancies. No such postal vote shall be valid unless received by the National Organiser 72 hours preceding the date of the AGM. Persons nominated must be Members of the Charity. Nominations for the National Group must be made either by local groups or by individual members with

the consent of the nominee. The nomination must be seconded. A nomination by an individual member must be seconded by a Recognised Local Group, being a group other than that of which the proposer is a member. A nomination by a group may not be seconded by an individual member of that group. No group or individual member may be concerned either as proposer or seconder in more than one nomination. For these purposes groups shall act through their local organisers.

7. The first AGM shall be that held in 1980 and Members elected at the first Annual General Meeting shall serve for four years save that those members elected in 1978 to the National Group of the previous organisation called National Housewives Register shall retire in 1982. All members subsequently elected to the National Group shall serve for a term of four years. Any vacancy by reason of death or retirement may be filled between elections by co-option by the members of the National Group, but any members so co-opted must retire immediately prior to the announcement of the result of the next election of members of the National Group. No elected member of the National Group may stand for re-election on retirement from that group nor be eligible for co-option during the next two years following retirement except under the circumstances described in the next Rule hereof. A person so retiring may stand for subsequent elections.

8. The members of the National Group shall elect one of their number to be their chairman. The National Group may assign to the other members specific functions and shall assign the following functions:

(i) National Organiser subject to the approval of the Trustees

(ii) Minutes Secretary and Newsletter Editor, and Public Relations Officer if appropriate.

(a) If there is no member of the National Group willing or able to be National Organiser the members of the National Group may co-opt another member of the Charity to be National Organiser and member of the National Group. Under these circumstances the maximum number of members of the National Group will be 16. Such a member so co-opted shall retire immediately prior to the next election of members of the National Group. However, notwithstanding the prohibition in Rule 7 The National Organiser so retiring may be eligible for re-election for a period of office not to exceed a further four years.

(b) The National Group may upon the retirement of any member thereof under any provision of these rules co-opt that member to serve for a further term of two years to fulfil the specific office previously held. The prohibition in Rule 7 of a member being co-opted during the two years following retirement for the first time shall not apply to such members, provided always that there shall not at any time be more than one member of the National Group co-opted under sub rule 8(b) and provided further that this sub rule 8(b) may only be applied once in the case of any particular person.

(c) Notwithstanding the provisions of Rule 8(a) and (b) no person shall be co-opted who has already served on the National Group for a total of six years.

Appendix I

9. The Minutes Secretary shall take Minutes of all Meetings of the National Group and Annual General Meetings.
10. The financial year of the Charity shall end on 30th June each year.
11. The National Group may and the National Organiser shall within 28 days of being required to do so by Recognised Local Groups acting through their local organisers and together being no fewer than one-twentieth in number of the Recognised Local Groups convene a General Meeting of the Charity to be called an Extraordinary General Meeting, and shall within 28 days if similarly required to do so convene an Annual General Meeting if no such Annual General Meeting has been convened by the Trustees.
12. At least 28 days notice of each General Meeting shall be given by post to the local organiser of each Recognised Local Group and in the case of an Extraordinary General Meeting by one advertisement in the Guardian newspaper. Accidental omission to give notice to a local organiser shall not invalidate the summoning of a General Meeting.
13. All members of the Charity shall be entitled to attend and speak at General Meetings of the Charity and each member present shall have one vote on a poll.
14. All resolutions for discussion at a General Meeting must be submitted to the National Organiser at least 72 hours prior to the meeting.
15. The quorum at a General Meeting shall be any number of members being some members of at least one tenth in number of the total number of Recognised Local Groups for the time being together with such number of members of the National Group as for the time being constitute a quorum thereof.
16. All resolutions at General Meetings must be approved by a majority being no fewer than three fourths of the number of members present and voting.
17. If there shall be no Trustee present at any General Meeting who wishes to take the chair it shall be taken by the Chairman of the National Group. If the Chairman be unable or unwilling to do so the National Group shall appoint a substitute Chairman.
18. Amendments to these rules may be proposed at any time, but the full text of any such amendments must be given to the National Organiser at least eight weeks before the date of a General Meeting if the amendment is to be considered at that Meeting. The National Organiser shall include the text of such of the proposed amendments as have been approved by the Trustees in the notice convening the General Meeting next to be held after receipt thereof and the proposals shall be considered at that Meeting.

IN WITNESS whereof the Original Trustees have hereunto set their hands and seals the day and year first before written
SIGNED SEALED and *DELIVERED*)
by the said *BETTY CLAIR JERMAN*)
    EDITH MAUREEN NICOL and
    CHARLOTTE MARY STOTT

Appendix II

Membership Surveys

There has been no lack of questionnaires over the last twenty odd years – 'too many' some members would say. But with no hierarchical system through which views are expressed how else can national officers get some kind of picture of what members want from the organisation unless they ask?

Apart from such opinion-seeking researches there were the Surveys. The first was conducted by members of the Congleton group as part of their WEA course on 'Sociology', winter 1966/7. NHR paid the postage; NO Lesley Taylor held the purse-strings at the time.

Jane Watt, NO, made a Survey in 1970 and got a mixed reception. Out of 400 forms sent out only 275 were returned. A distillation of Jane's Survey follows, with Congleton's answers where appropriate in brackets. Replies to the questionnaire.

Total number of groups responding: 275 (160)
Number of members listed in above groups: 7,250 (3,257)

Size of Groups:
Groups with fewer than 10 members – 2%
Groups comprising 10–15 members 12%
                  15–20 members 14%
                  20–25 members 24%
                  25–30 members 15%
                  30–35 members 9%
                  35–40 members 6%
                  40–45 members 5%
                  45–50 members 6%
                  more than 50 – 7%

Frequency of meetings:
Weekly 8% (7.5%)
Fortnightly 49% (nearly 50%)
Three-weekly 6%
Monthly 34% (33%)
No regular arrangement 2%

Place of meetings
Homes only 94% (92%). Homes and halls 5% (8%). Other, e.g. hotel – 1%.

Appendix II

Times of meetings
Mornings 6% (7%). Afternoons 2½% (3%). Evenings 83½% (71%).

Structure.
Informal organisation – usually local organisers only 86% (85%). More formal organisation – usually with committee 14% (15%).

Recruitment of members
Members joining through the National Organiser   9½%
               through personal introduction   47%
               through local advertising   35%
   After belonging to NHR groups elsewhere   8%

Age of members
A question which provoked some surprising reactions, not the least being a group showing reluctance from some to admitting to being under thirty! Members aged 29 or under 26% (29%)
        30–39   62% (63%)
        40 plus   12% (8%)

Age of members' children
Children under 5 only 36%
       over 5 only   27%
       both   37%
Congleton reported that only 23% had no children under school age.

Isolation from families
Members with no relation living in the same town or country area 70% (77%).

Length of stay in the area.
Members who had always lived in the area 10% (10%). 0–1 years 13%. 1–3 years 26%. 3–5 years 22%. 5 years plus 29%. Jane was surprised at that result since 'most queries which reach the NO come from newcomers to an area'.

Working members
Members working full-time 5½% (3½%)
                part-time 24% (15½%)
Jane Watt found that '29% have returned to work compared with 19% three years ago. Of those working full-time 76% are doing the same type of work as before marriage. Of those working part-time 58% are doing the same type of work.'

Membership of other organisations
Members belonging to other women's organisations   42%
Members belonging 'to "ginger" groups'   17%
Members doing voluntary work and work for charities   41%
'This result' Jane commented 'looks most suspect adding up to 100% as it does. It was based on 3,254 members who answered this section and not on the total number responding to the questionnaire'.

Value of the Register
158 groups answered this section comprising 3,254 members. Members who could easily manage without the Register 41% (22%). Members who

would find being without it a real loss—62% (75%). Members who have made close personal friendships through the NHR 48%. Members who thought of it mainly as a bridge when new to an area: 42%. Members who thought of it mainly as providing stimulating contacts: 88%.

Of the Congleton sample 94% said that the greatest value was in personal friendships formed through the group. Jane found that the question 'seemed ambiguous to some people and too extreme to others'.

Area travelled to meetings

At one extreme no one travelled more than half a mile to meetings, at the other some travelled 25 miles. Meetings within a mile: 11%, 1–3 miles: 24%, 3–5 miles: 29%, 5–10 miles: 31%, 10–15 miles: 5%.

Growth and Organisation

2,704 members were gained June 1969–70. 1,557 members had not seen a leaflet describing NHR. 29% of groups operated a baby-sitting rota. 57% were advertising locally. 82% had seen the local organiser's name in the town hall or Citizen's Advice Bureau.

Husbands' Occupations

This optional question roused a furore. 'We want to be recognised for ourselves', 'a list of husbands' occupations would throw little light on the membership of NHR' were the kind of thing. Jane reported: 'Just over 1,800 members listed husbands' occupations, and of those, the largest single grouping was of engineers—269 of them. There were 119 unclassified, and the remainder were made of 40 different types of engineer. The next biggest grouping was of school-teachers—193 of them. The other groupings were: Education (other than school teachers), educational administration, medicine, vets, agriculture, law, tradesmen, skilled workers, social work, civil service/local government, service industries, industry (selling), industry (office and managerial), research, market research, scientists, mathematicians/statisticians, finance/insurance/banking, draughtsmen/architects/town planners, general office work.'

Jane explained that she did not ask what members' occupations were before marriage because she did not think it was relevant to the particular survey, 'the object of which was to make the NOs job easier. While agreeing with the resentment expressed it is still very difficult for many people not to be tagged to their husband's jobs and surely the growth of a classless NHR is one way of doing something about it. Incidentally Congleton asked the question about wives' occupations and the results were: 19.4% were graduates; 49.5% were professionally trained (mainly teachers, nurses, secretaries) and presumably 31.1% were untrained.'

Membership Survey, spring 1980

This was arranged by the first National Group and the questions were much the same as Jane's. The findings were processed by a computer.

The figures are based on a sample of over one third of groups. Not all the groups in the sample answered all the questions but the response to most questions was very nearly 100 per cent. In some questions the sum of the percentages in categories is greater than 100%, e.g. Question 13.

Appendix II

1. In which year was the group formed? See attached graph.
2. Where do you hold your meetings?
   In members' houses 97.9%
   halls   1.3%
   elsewhere   0.9%
3. Do you have a sole organiser/secretary or a team (committee) to run the group? Sole 46.8%. Team 53.2%.
4. (a) For what periods of time do you plan your meetings? (The question was considered somewhat ambiguous by the analysts but the conclusion was that most people must have understood and answered correctly)
   Monthly   6.7%
   2-monthly 0.3%
   3-monthly 31.0%
   4-monthly 3.1%
   6-monthly 47.3%
   annually   11.6%
   (b) Do you have an open meeting to plan your programme or is the programme planned by the organiser/team? Meeting 70%. Organiser/team 30%.
5. (a) How many people are on your membership list?
   Numbers on membership list range from 4 to 115. Most common group sizes are 20 and 30 (nearly 8% of groups have a size of 20 and nearly 8% have a size of 30). Half the groups are of size 25 or less.
   (b) How many of them are paid-up members?
   Numbers of paid up members range from 0 to 115. Most common number of paid up members is 20. Half the groups have a paid-up membership of 21 or less.
   (c) What is the average attendance at meetings?
   Average attendance at meetings ranges from 3 to 30. Most common attendance is 12 (20% of answers) with 15 and 10 the next most common (12% and 11% of answers respectively).
6. How many of your members heard of NHR in each of the following ways?
   By personal contact –   52.9%
   by personal recommendation –   25.7%
   from national advertising – press   5.7%
                               t.v.   0.2%
                               radio   1.9%
   from local advertising – posters   10.3%
                            radio   0.5%
                            press   2.8%
7. How many of your members are:
   under 29 years: 23%

---

*Author's note: 'advertising' should be interpreted as promotion through the media's interest in the topic not through paid insertions.

30–39 years 64.2%
40 plus years 12.8%
8. How many of your members have lived in the area:
Less than 2 years 17.0%
2–5 years 36.4%
6–20 years 35.3%
more than 20 years 5.7%
born locally 5.6%
9. How many of your members have:
no formal training 20.8%
professional training 57.7%
university qualifications 21.5%
10. How many members have paid employment?
Full-time 7.6%
part-time 29.6%
11. (a) How many children do your members have?
0   2.9%
1   16.9%
2   59.0%
3   17.4%
4   3.2%
5 or more 0.6%.
(b) Into what age groups do they fall?
under 5 years 37.5%
5–11 years 40.8%
12–16 years 12.1%
over 16 9.6%
12. (a) How many of your members belong to other organisations? 57.1%
(b) To which other organisations do your members belong?
Sports 23.9%
Religious 14.6%
Political 12.6%
Professional 9.9%
Women's 15.4%
Pressure Groups 12.9%
Children's 25.8%
Any others 14.7%
13. How many of your members have ever felt housebound?
(a) physically 23.8%
(b) mentally 31.8%
(c) because of moving 22.4%
(d) because of the birth of a child 33.8%
14. Which of the following activities does your group arrange?

Appendix II

Discussions (98.2%), speakers (97.2%), visits (77.8%), social with husbands (87.6%), social without husbands (68.5%), coffee meetings (60.2%), baby sitting (22.0%), book discussions (80.9%), lecture courses (3.9%), sports (14.0%), dining (29.7%), bridge (4.9%), fund raising for charity (25.1%), for group (23.8%), children's parties/picnics (48.3%), creche/play group (8.0%), any other (17.6%).

15. Do your members take part in charity work?
    As a group   6.8%
    as individuals   31.8%
16. How many members are taking part in Further Education courses?
    19.9%.
17. Without NHR how many members would –
    find it difficult to manage   3.2%
    feel at a loss   12.4%
    feel able to cope   36.7%
    be able to cope easily   41.9%
18. How many of your members have belonged to other NHR groups?
    19.6%

The Survey contained two more questions asking for views on the national newsletter and asking for the name of the group completing the questionnaire.

In conclusion

Very little seems to have changed since the last survey. Obviously, the overall size of NHR has increased. Twice as many groups were established in 1980 as in 1970 and the total membership has grown to over 22,000. But where comparisons are possible with the 1970 figures, very little difference is noted: except with regard to organisation at a local level. Here it is noticeable that groups are adopting the committee method, rather than having a sole organiser: over fifty per cent of groups have a committee as opposed to fourteen per cent in 1970. Possibly, this reflects a more democratic tone in local groups, especially when coupled with the fact that two thirds of groups plan their meetings by open evenings rather than the programme coming solely from the LOs.

The size of groups has remained relatively stable: this is due to the fact that groups are splitting once they exceed what they consider an 'optimum' number. One surprising thing, considering the amount of publicity recently, is that nearly eighty per cent of members joined from personal contact or recommendation. Possibly, this is because the advertising works at a subliminal level – it is necessary for the knowledge of the name to be reinforced by personal contact.

One other increase is the doubling of members who've been in other NHR groups – obviously with more groups establishing, it's getting easier to find one when you move.

To sum up, NHR overall doesn't appear to have changed fundamentally; it is simply reaching more people, which can only be a good thing.

One thing definitely hasn't changed – the members still don't like feeling categorised – as the lack of identifiable attributes to produce 'the typical NHR member' is still felt to be one of the most important facets of NHR – along with its basic informality.

Select Bibliography

Pamela Anderson, et al, *Simple Steps to Public Life*, Virago 1980
Betty Friedan, *The Feminine Mystique*, Gollancz (1971) & Penguin
Hannah Gavron, *The Captive Wife*, Routledge and Kegan Paul, (1966) and Penguin (1970)
Penelope Leach, *Who Cares?*, Penguin Special 1979
Suzanne Lowry, *The Guilt Cage*, Elm Tree Books 1980
John MacFarlane Mogey, *Family and Neighbourhood*, Greenwood Press 1956
Michael Young and Peter Wilmot, *Family and Kinship in East London*, Routledge (1957) Penguin (1969)

Julie Davidson, 'Registering a Protest', *Scotsman* 1973
Betty Jerman, 'Squeezed in like sardines in Suburbia, *Guardian*, 19 February 1960
Betty Jerman, 'The Sultanas of Suburbia', *Guardian*, 16 February 1966
Betty Jerman, 'Second-chance wives leave husbands behind', *Observer*, January 1976
Moira Keenan, 'Housewives Register', *Sunday Times*, 12 March 1967
Anne Simpson, 'Think tank for women in the suburbs', *Yorkshire Post*, 1969
Mary Stott, 'Women Talking', *Guardian*, 22 April 1963 and 5 January 1972

BALANCE SHEET

NHR Income and Expenditure Account for the Year Ended 30 June 1980

1979				1980	
		INCOME			
18,566		Subscriptions		21,209.07	
223		Donations		886.72	
342		Building Society and Bank Interest		1,387.38	
	19,131				23,483.17
		EXPENSES			
5,331		Newsletter Printing	5,897.39		
1,091		Newsletter Postages	1,696.97		
				7,594.36	
—		Net Cost of National Conference		631.94	
388		Printing and Stationery		829.14	
695		Postages		1,309.57	
351		Telephone		992.75	
638		Publicity Expenses		533.97	
124		General Expenses		56.10	
—		Legal Expenses		839.47	
175		Accountancy		195.00	
—		Insurance		292.50	
3,600		Honorarium Payments to National Officers		4,075.00	
396		Travelling Expenses for National Organiser		412.94	
802		Clerical Assistance		1,577.57	
143	13,734	National Group Members Expenses		1,778.36	21,168.67
	£5,397	SURPLUS FOR YEAR			£2,314.50

Index

Compiled by Hazel Bell

Note: place names include reference to NHR groups in those areas.

Abergavenny 34
abortion 15
Abortion Law Reform Association 63, 155
Abu Dhabi 189
accounts: *1963–4* 58; *1966* 63; *1970* 97; *1980* 230–1; in constitution 208, 213; in *1980* Rules 216–17
Adam, Ann 154
advertising 47, 61, 225, 227
age of members 45–6, 74–7, 195; in surveys 223, 225–6
Alexander, Frances 71, 92, 116
Amos, Mardy 185
Annett, Ednie 159
Annual General Meetings: in constitution 207, 209–10, 211, 212, 213–14; in *1980* Rules 216, 219, 220, 221
archives 65, 176, 178
Ashdown, Sylvia 106–7
Association for Improvements in the Maternity Services 152
Australia 185–6

Bahrain 190
Bakewell 61
Balfour, Audrey 52, 188
Barker, Sue 189
Bawtry 57, 61
Beattie, Judith 61
Belgium 183, 184, 191
Bell, Hazel 35, 127; *1975* circular 125; on National Group 129, 130, 131, 136, 137; *Newsletter* editor 68–9, 74, 170, 174; since 197, 198
Billericay 72, 92
Bingley 106
Birkenhead 11, 199
Birmingham 46, 121; *1972* conference 88, 90, 99–100; University 199, 200
Blackpool, march 31
Bolingbroke, Jeannine 120, 127, 132
Bolton 35
Bonney, Beryl 136, 176, 177
book discussions 35, 111, 145

Boston 49
Bradford 104–10; *1980* conference 88–9, 90, 93, 100, 138, 140
Bradley, Yvonne 123, 129, 135
Brae 110–12
Bristol, *1976* conference 90, 122, 128, 129, 130
British Federation of University Women 78
Brocklesby, Anita 84, 85, 94–5; National Organiser 94, 96–101, 103, 116, 117; since 200; *photo*
Bromborough and Eastham (Maureen Nicol's first group) 10, 27, 30, 35, 52, 115
Bromsgrove, National Group meeting at 130–1
Brown, Rosemary 120
Brown, Sheila 89
Buckhurst Hill 6–7
Burnham 162, 164
Buxton 62; *1967* conference 62, 88, 89–90

Camberley 78
Cambridge 141
Cameron, Margaret 65, 129, 132
Campaign for Nuclear Disarmament 31, 153
Canada 14, 95, 181, 186–7
Cancer Control Campaign 158–61
Carlisle 120
Carrington, Elizabeth 129, 131, 135
Carshalton 36
Cervenka, Dana 190
'Cestrian Group' 43–4
Chairman, National Group (Co-ordinator) 130, 131, 133, 175; in constitution 207, 210, 212, 214; in *1980* Rules 220, 221
Chaplin, Ann 159
Charitable status 13, 123, 125, 128, 138–40
Charity Deed *1980* 13, 139, 215–21
charity work 223, 227
Cheshire 43–4, 59; *see also* Eastham
Cheshire Forum 62

Index

Chester 27, 69, 136
Chesterfield 62
children, members' 36, 223, 226; during meetings 34, 55; *see also* motherhood
circulars, National Organisers' 65–6, 70–1, 97; Jane Watts' 82; *1970–3* 97, 98–9; *1972* 98–9, 100–1; *1973* 117, 119; *1974* 120; *1975* May 123–5, reactions 125–6; December 127; *1976* 70–1
Citizens' Advice Bureaux 48, 224; working in 31, 199
Civil Service QUANGOS 198
Clarke, Sherry 9–10, 11
class 163
Cleethorpes 35
clerical assistance, paid 101; *1974* 119, 120; *1976* 132, 136; *1976–80* 136–7, 138; paid staff in constitution 206, 210; in *1980* Deed 217
clinics 48
Collins, Deirdre 63, 80, 83, 85
Confederation for the Advancement of State Education 7, 20
Conference Liasion 91–2, 176, 178
conferences 88–93; in constitution 209, 213; day- 91–2; delegate 71; International, *1980* 88, 92, 181, 182–4; NATIONAL: *1967* 62, 88, 89–90; *1968* 64, 81–2; *1969* 82, 83, 85, 95; *1971* 88, 90, 99–100; *1974* 90, 122–3; *1976* 90, 122, 128, 129, 130; *1977* 76, 133, 138; *1978* 7, 8, 90–1, 143; *1979* 137, 139; *1980* 88–9, 90, 93, 100, 138, 140; programmes 90
Congleton group, *1966* survey by 51–2, 63, 222–4
constitution 13; *1969* proposal 83, 122; *1974–5* research into 122–7; adopted 13, 128; amended 135; *quoted in full, 1976* 206–10; *1977* 210–15; *1980* Rules for the National group 139, 219–21
Cook, Judith 152–3
Cooper, Rita 187
'Cornelian Society' 72, 102–4
correspondence magazines 141, 143–6
Cossey, Ann 95, 186
County Organisers *see* Regional Organisers
Crabtree, Ann 146
Craddock, Penny 159, 160
Crewe, *1975* conference 87, 88, 115, 125–7
Croydon 37

Daily Express 28, 166
Daily Mirror 28
Darlington, *1974* conference 90, 122–3

Davis, Moira 160
Debate magazine 154
disabled members 72
discussion topics 30, 35–6
Dubai 14, 190

Eardley, Vivienne 177
Eastham 5, 9, 26; /Bromborough group (Maureen Nicol's first) 10, 27, 30, 35, 52, 115
Edinburgh 113; *1977* conference 76, 133, 138; 'Cornelian Society' 72, 102–4
education, women's 15, 20, 21, 201, 204
educational broadcasts 31
Equal Opportunities Commission 181
Evening Post (Swansea) 142
Extraordinary General Meetings, in constitution 209–10, 214; in *1980* Rules 221

'Fact Finders', *1974–5* 123
Ferraro, Antoinette 91, 137
finance 168–9; *1960–1* 30–1; *1963–4* 58–9; *1970* 197–9; *1975* 122, 125, 128; *1976* 132–5; *1979* 174; in constitution 208–9, 213; in *1980* Rules 216–19; *see also* accounts; honoraria; subscriptions
Fitzgibbon, Clare 159
Formentin, Helen 183–4, 185
Forum magazine (*New Forum*) 42, 150–4
Franklin, Judith 129, 130, 131, 133, 135
Friedan, Betty, *The Feminine Mystique* 11, 203
'Friends Inc.' 186

Gavron, Hannah, *The Captive Wife* 19–21, 202, 203
Gawne, Irene 190
Gibbins, Angela 110
Glasgow 35, 62; conference, *1972* 114; husbands 164–5
Golder, Mel 184, 191–2
Good Housekeeping magazine 150
Goodwin, Jane: on National Group 129, 130, 135; Overseas Co-ordinator 137, 170, 175–6, 181–2, 191, since 197
Goodwin, Malcolm 170
Gorleston-on-Sea 96
Grande, Elaine 20
Grant, Anne 78
Grimley, Eve 184, 188, 189
Grimsby 35
groups, local: *defined* 206, 210–11, 215, 219; activities 35–6, 226–7; new 47–9, 118; organisation and structure 223, 225, 227; size, 53–4, 222, 225, 227

Index

Guardian, The 6, 49, 61, 113, 141, 151, 153, 154; in constitution 209, 214; in *1980* Rules 221; 'Squeezed in like sardines...' (B. Jerman) 1–4, reaction to 6, 25; 'The sultanas of suburbia' (B. Jerman) 203–4; women's letters 18–19; M. Nicol's letters (26.2.60) 5, 25, (7.3.60) 26, (third) 27

Haigh, Barbara 105
Harborne, Joan 129, 131, 132, 135
Harris, Donald 159
Harris, Janet, death of 158
Harrison, Jacky 187
Harrogate 83, 93, 95, 158–9; *1969* conference 82, 83, 85, 95; Women's National Cancer Control Campaign 158–61
Harrow 150, 151, 152, 154
Hartmann, Ivy 188
Healey, Frances 123, 127, 129, 135; and NHR name 73
Health Visitors 23, 48, 49
Help Organise Local Schemes 155–8
Hereford 75
Herne Bay, carnival, *photo*
Hertford/Lea Valley, *1972* Talk-in 92
Hertfordshire 59, 155
Hicklenton, Pat 75–6, 127
High Wycombe 92, 116
Hill, Gillian 147–9
holiday clubs 155–8
holiday house exchange 146–9
Holland 184, 190–1
Hong Kong 184
honoraria: proposed 100–1, 124; opposed 104; in constitution 209, 214; *1973* 71, 101, 117; *1974* 120; *1975* 127; *1976* 132–3; *1978–80* 136–7
house swaps 146–9
'Housebound Wives Register' 19, 28, 72, 142
'housewife', term 73, 202
housewives, surveys of: *1960–1* 19–21; *1980* 202–3
housework 17, 19–20
housing, post-war 1–2, 17
Howell, Shirley 84, 159
husbands 52, 162–71, 174, 204; occupations 224
Hutchinson, Enid 31

informality 21, 52–3, 122, 127
Inland Revenue 139
International Conference, *1980* 88, 92, 181, 182–4; *photo*
international groups 13–14, 181–92

International Women's Register 183
Ipswich, Suffolk 187
Irlam, R., letter from 6

Jaffray, Josephine 101, 113–15; National Organiser 86–7, 114–15, 117–21, 122–3, 125–8; farewell 13; since 198–9; *photo*
Jerman, Betty 6–7; NHR trustee 13, 140, 179, 215, 221; 'Squeezed in like sardines...' 1–4, reactions to 6, 25; 'The sultanas of suburbia' 203–4
Jones, Sue 137

Karplanis, Betty 123
Keenan, Moira 10, 27, 62, 81
Kent 40
Kerr, Pat: Conference Liason 91, 136, 176; National Group Chairman 177, 179; New Groups Adviser 194
Kinnear, Ruth 110–11, 112
Kirby, Elsie 123
Knapp, Betsy 189
Kuwait, 184

Leach, Penelope, *Who Cares?* 21
Leeds 35
Leicester 35
Lepper, Angela 101, 115–16; National Secretary 117–20, 123, 191; since 200; *photo*
libraries 49, 191, 200
Little, Jean 42, 150–4
Liverpool 27
Lloyd, Patricia 129, 135
local groups *see* groups, local
Local Organisers 49, 50, 51, 52, 65; in constitution 206, 207, 211, 212; in *1980* Rules 219, 220; meetings of 68, 174, 194
logos 47, 83, 163
London, *1968* conference 64, 81–2
Lothian 76
Lowry, Suzanne, *The Guilt Cage* 202–3
Lucas, Barbara 185–6
Luxembourg 184, 191–2
Lytham-St. Anne 27

McCalls magazine 189
magazines, women's 150, 151; *see also titles of magazines*
Magee, Liz 189
Manchester 27, 59; *1978* conference 7, 8, 90–1, 143, 167; Radio 28, 166
Marlow, Doddy 159
Marsden, Sue 184
Martin, Pauline 106

Marylebone 152
Mastectomy Association 158
meetings, NHR group 33–4, 54–5; surveys of 222–5; attendance 225; frequency 222; location 53, 165, 168, 222, 225; planning 225, 227; times 223; topics 30, 35–6
membership: age of, *see* age; in constitution 206, 210–11; in *1980* Rules 219; *1980* 224–7; qualifications 45–6, 56, 57, 81–2; recruiting 46–9, 223, 224, 225; surveys of *see* surveys
Menhennet, Audrey, letter from 6
minutes *see* secretary, National Group
Moffat, Betty 102
Moffat, Dumfries 113–14, 115
Morden, Surrey 156
Moreland, Lesley 35, 94, 95–6; Local Organiser 34, 49; Jane Watt and 80, 85–6; National Organiser 94, 95–101, 116–17; *Newsletter* editor 12, 67, 119; since 118, 198; *photo*
Moreland, Vic 96
Moriel, Pat 110
Mormons 34
Mossbank 111–12
motherhood 39, 202, 203–5; boredom in 16–17, 18–19, 21; and work 15, 17–18, 21–1, 69–70
Munday, Diane 63, 155

name, NHR 28, 72–4, 183; groups' other 46; in constitution 206, 210; in Deed 215
National Administrator, proposed 127, 131
National Association of Women's Clubs 43, 46
National Council of Women 78
National Group, the 44, 50; in constitution 206–8, 211–13; *1980* Rules for 219–21; expenses 131, 135, 210, 214–15; and home life 167–8; officers *see* titles of officers
National Group, elections for 11–12; *1976* 128, 129; *1978* 135; *1980* 45, 137–8, 162, 172, 177, 194; in constitution 207–8, 211–13; in *1980* Rules 219–20
National Group, the first 129–40, 193, 196–7; at Sale Workshop 68, 168, 172–6; since office 196–8; *photo*
National Group of *1980* 177–80, 194; 1st meeting 178–9; 2nd 194–5; *photo*
National Housewives Register: concept 5–6; origins 5, 25–32; aims, defined 47, 125, 126, 206, 210, 215; activities 35–6, 226–7; code, unwritten 10, 13, 47–8; organisation and structure 50–3, 66, 78, 83–5, 123–8; surveys of; *see surveys*; tributes 21–3; future 193–6, 201–2, 204–5
National Organiser: function of 60, 83–4, 124–5, 126, 127, 178, 193; *1980* job description 172–4; in constitution 207–8, 209, 210, 212; in *1980* Rules 219, 220; appointment of 11–12, 83, 85, 128, 140, 179; qualities required, *1980* 177; after office 198–201; *see also* honoraria; *names of NOs*
National Women's Register 187
New Forum magazine (*Forum*) 42, 150–4
new groups 47–9, 118; abroad 181
New Groups Adviser 175, 177–8
Newcastle 86–7
Newmark, Jose 41, 57, 59, 60, 66
Newsletter 44–5, 57–8, 66–78; *1960–2* 66; *1962* 32, 40, 41, 66; *1964–5* 57–8, 59–60, 67; *1966* 70, 164; *1967* 62, 115; *1968* 82; *1969* 49, 67, 82–4; *1970–1* 67, 84, 85, 97–8; *1974* 69; *1975* 67, 68 143; *1979* 70; *1980* 54–5; distribution 66, 68, 195; index 68; name 74; questionnaires re, (*1964*) 57–8, (*1975*) 67 (*1980*) 227
Newsletter editor 68–9, 174, 177, 195; in constitution 206, 210; in *1980* Rules 220
Newson, Elizabeth and John 44
Nicol, Brian 24, 25, 26, 165–7
Nicol, Maureen 7–11, 24–32, 35, 72, 77, 165–7, 203; letters to *Guardian* (26.2.60) 5, 25, (7.3.60) 26, (third) 27, reactions 8–11, 25–7; hands over NHR 7, 32, 37; since 7–8, 11, 46–7, 126, 199; at *1978* conference 7, 8, 143, 167; NHR trustee 13, 140, 215, 221; *photo*
Nicol, Simon 26, 166
Nova magazine 150
NOW! magazine 10

Observer, The 90; 'Miserable Married Women' 18, 20; letter from M. Nicol 27; *1965* letter 61; 'Second-chance wives . . .' 163
occupations 224
O'Connor, Pammy 188
office, envisaged for NHR 12, 100, 117, 125, 195
office equipment 39, 117, 173, 177
Oliver, Marina 150, 154–5
Oslo 184
Ousey, Pamela 43
Over 21 magazine 150
Overseas Co-ordinator 175–6, 178

Index

overseas, NHR 13–14, 181–92
Oxford 24

Partington, Shiela 59–60, 61
Pizzey, Erin 202
Popper, Matilda 141–6
Porthcawl 190
posters 60, 81
Potters Bar 49, 95, 96
Pre-School Playgroups Association 28, 42, 151–2
pre-school education 70
pressure group: NHR as 10–11, 31, 56, 62, 70–2, 103–4; members in 223, 226
Preston 27, 35; 'Delta' group 40
Price, Marie 33, 34, 129; National Organiser 131, 133–6; since 184, 200; *photo*
Pritchard, Rosemary 82
programmes: conference 90; of meetings, planning 225, 227; *see also* meetings
Prys Jones, Brenda, National Organiser 19, 37–42, 56, 57, 66; since 199; letter to *Guardian* 19; *photo*
Public Relations Officer 118–19, 131–2, 173, 177; in constitution 212; in *1980 Rules* 220
publicity 45–6; first 27; *1962* 40, 47, 48, 56; *1964–5* 61; advertising 47, 61, 225, 227
Purden, Laurie 150

Quito, Ecuador 184

Rayner, Claire 153
Read, Christine 186
Reading, *1979* conference 137, 139, *photo*
Regional (County) Organisers: *1960* 29; *1962* 38, 40; *1964* 43–4, 59; considered 100, 124, 195
Register for Qualified Married Women 154
'Register Worldwide' 181, 182, 183
Rhodesia 14, 188–9
Rickmansworth 116
Rifkin, Adrienne 187
Roberts, Nick, *photo*
Roberts, Pat 66
Roberts, Pauline 101
Rome 184
rules: unwritten 10, 13, 47–8; *1970* 85; *1980*, for National Group 139, 219–21

Sale, National Group Workshop at 68, 168, 172–7
sales 136, 176, 178, 195

Salthouse, Elizabeth 129, 167; Treasurer 12, 131, 132–3, 134, 174; since 196, 197–8
Salthouse, Ron 168
Sanderson, Margeret 184
Sargent, Carole 188–9
Saudi Arabia 135, 184
Scotsman, The 102, 103
Scott, Anne 102
secretary, National Group; minutes 177, 178; in constitution 207, 208, 212, 213; in *1980* Rules 220, 221
Shanahan, Lesley and Patrick 170–1
She magazine 67, 150
Sheffield 62
Shetlands 110–12
Shingler, Alison 137, 179, 196; National Organiser 88, 100, 194; *photo*
Shingler, Brian 168
Slaughter, Audrey 150
Smith, Angela 111–12
Smith, Margaret 28
South Africa 14, 182, 184, 187–8
Southport, *1971* conference 90
Spare Rib magazine 150
speakers 34, 91, 182
splitting groups 53–4
Stacy, Daphne 75–6
staff, paid *see* clerical assistance
Stead, Carole 159, 161
Steadman, Olive 104–10
Steadman, Ralph 168
Steering Group, proposed 124, 126
Stevens, Carol 111
Stewart, Thelma 105–6, 107
Stirk, Jean 123, 127, 129–30; on National Group 131, 135, 136, 175, 178; New Groups Adviser 47, 136, 175; articles by 75–6, 77; since 197, 198
Stockport 69
Stone, Mary 190
Stoneleigh, Surrey 156–7, 158
Stott, Mary: *Guardian* 6, 18, 19, 61; writes in *Newsletter* 77; NHR trustee 13, 140, 215, 221
Stourbridge 52, 95, 99
Strickley, Julia 181
subscriptions 50; *1960* 30; *1962* 39; *1964* 58; *1969* 85; *1971* 98–9; *1976* 122; *1977* 133–4; *1980* 100; in constitution 206, 211; in *1980* Rules 219
suburban life 1–4, 6–7, 203–4
Sunday Times, The 10, 27, 151; re 1st NHR National conference 62, 81
surveys of NHR: *1964* 57–8; *1966* 51–2, 63, 222–4; Jane Watt's 51, 80, 222–4; *1980* 224–7

Sutton Coldfield 27
Swansea 142–3
Switzerland 184

Talbot, Lesley 43–4
Taylor, Lesley (later Lesley Shooter): National Organiser 56–64, 65, 66, 67, 70; since 199–200; obituary of Jane Watt 79; *photo*
technology, the new 201
Thomson, Dorothy 110–11
Thomson, Pat 123
Thornton-Vincent, Marianne 138
Times, The 20, 154
topics for discussion 30, 35–6
Townswomen's Guilds, National Union of 78, 95, 113
Toy Libraries Association 80, 195, 198
train travel 197
treasurer 174, 177; in constitution 207, 208, 212, 213; in *1980* Rules 216; *see also* accounts; finance; Salthouse, Elizabeth
tributes to NHR 22–3
trustees 13, 206, 208–9, 210, 213, 221; in Charitable Deed 215–19
T-shirts 46; *photo*
Tutaev, Belle 28, 42, 151–2

Uganda 199
United States of America 189

Valentine, Christine 189
Value Added Tax 128, 132–3
van der Linde, Pat 187
Vine, Edward 135
Vine, Gill 123, 127, 130; Public Relations Officer 131–2, 136, 173; National Organiser 12, 21, 77, 80, 135, 136–40, 167–8, 173–4, 179; since 197, 198; *photo*
'Voice of Women' group 152–3
voting: delegate conferences 71; for National Group 11–12, 83, 194; *see also* National Group, elections for

Wakeman, Isobel 43
Walsall 117
Warren, Sheila 100–1
Waterhouse, Susan 146–7
Watt, Jane 63; National Organiser 45, 72, 80–7, 95, 96–7, 122; and successors 85–7, 119; survey of NHR 51, 80, 222–4; death 64, 79; *photo*
Watts, Anne 123, 127
Webster, Pauline 127, 130, 131, 135
Weir, Beth 185
Welch, Hilary 184
Wender, Angela 120
Westgate, Betty 158, 159
White, Adrienne 72
Whitehead, Wendy 15, 155–8
Williams, Pat 101, 115, 116–17; National Organiser 70–1, 86–7, 117–21, 122–8, 169–70; *Newsletter* editor 67, 119, farewell 13; since 131, 200; 'Apathy' speech 90; *photo*
Williams, Robin 169–70
Williams, Val 136, 172, 176, 177
Willington, Sonia 152
Wilson, Judith 159
Wilson, Lorna 130, 131, 135
Wirral, *1975* 'Talk-in' 92
Wolverhampton 24, 185
'Woman's Hour' 111, 136; Maureen Nicol on 28, 166
'Women in Touch' 185–6
women: education 15, 20, 21, 201, 204; position 15–21, 201–5; in suburbs 15, 6–7, 203–4; working *see* working women; *see also* motherhood
Women's Institutes 21, 71, 78
women's movement 202–3
Women's National Cancer Control Campaign 158–61
women's organisations, other 21, 46, 71, 77–8, 223, 226
Workers' Educational Association 46, 198, 199; Congleton survey 51–2, 63, 222–4
working women 15–21; and motherhood 15, 17–18, 20–1, 69–70; NHR members 223; NHR officers 196; Register for Qualified Married Women 154; talk-ins on 92; and unemployment 201–2
Worthing 51, 74
Wyatt, Suzanne 183, 191

Yatton 98
Yorkshire Post, The 80–1
Young & Wilmot, *Family and Kinship in East London* 16

Zimbabwe 188–9

Logo on jacket designed by NHR member Sandra Bancroft

Cover photograph taken at a joint meeting of the West Kirby/Grange and the West Kirby/Caldy groups